FORBIDDEN
Rider
JESSICA AMES

Copyright © 2019 by Jessica Ames

www.jessicaamesauthor.com

Forbidden Rider is a work of fiction. Names, places, characters and incidents are a product of the author's imagination and are fictitious. Any resemblance to actual persons, living or dead, events or establishments is solely coincidental.

Editing by Charisse Sayers

Proofreading by Gem's Precise Proofreads

Cover design by Desire Premade Covers by Jessica Ames

Cover image copyright © 2019

Please note this book contains material aimed at an adult audience, including sex, violence and bad language.

This book is licensed for your personal enjoyment. It may not be re-sold or given away to other people. If you would like to share this book with another person, please purchase an additional copy for each recipient. If you are reading this book and did not purchase it, or if it was not purchased for use only, then you should return it to the seller and please purchase your own copy.

All rights reserved. Except as permitted under Copyright Act 1911 and the Copyright Act 1988, no part of this publication may be reproduced, distributed or transmitted in any form or by any means, or stored in a database or retrieval system, without the prior express, written consent of the author.

This book is covered under the United Kingdom's Copyright Laws. For more information visit: www.gov.uk/copyright/overview.

To Lyndsay and Mark, who show strength at every turn. You both inspire me.

CHAPTER ONE

JEM

I WAKE WITH A POUNDING HEAD, a dry mouth and the urgent need to piss. Throwing my legs out of bed, I stagger to the bathroom, still half asleep and a little drunk. I hit the bottle heavy last night, trying to lose myself in booze to crush the kick of rejection she'd left me with. I sound like a whiny bitch, but I can't help it. Piper's under my skin. She's burrowed so deep, I don't know that I can ever get her out. What she did yesterday hurts and I don't think it's the kind of hurt I can just get over either.

She fucked us both over, and I didn't see it coming. I thought we were on the same page. I thought we were both heading in the same direction. I know she's worried about stuff, her brother mainly, but when I left Manchester on Wednesday, she seemed level, good. I spoke to her Friday night and she seemed fine. For her not to come to the wedding yesterday was a kick in the teeth, and not because I give a shit about her being here to support my brother and Beth. That's not the real reason I wanted her here.

We're supposed to be going public about us after the wedding.

The fact she didn't show, tells me everything I need to know.

She doesn't see an 'us'.

I'm not going to lie, that shit tears a hole in my guts a mile wide. Piper's the only woman I've ever felt a thing for. I've slept with more than my share of people over the years, but I can count on one hand the number I've considered making a life with.

Tripping on an empty JD bottle, I storm up a curse as pain flares in my foot. Fuck, I'll feel that later.

When I stumble inside the small en suite, I can't help but wince against the brightness as I flick the light on. Christ almighty, my brain feels like it's trying to burrow out of my eyes. No more alcohol for at least forty-eight hours.

Blinking, I try to get the spots to vanish from my vision, so I can see enough to relieve myself. Once I've done that, I get in the shower. I smell like a distillery, although I'm not sure I can eradicate the smell with just one round of washing.

I drank far too much last night, at least six pints more than I should have. I could blame it easily on celebrating my brother finally making an honest woman out of Beth. It only took the stupid bastard a decade to do it. I could say I was just doing what I always do—partying hard and living in the moment—but it would be a lie.

I was drinking to numb my pain.

I didn't think it was possible for a woman to hurt me—me, Jeremy Frank Harlow. I didn't think I would ever let a woman have power over me, but Piper Ellis-Wade-Hollander—whatever the fuck her bloody name is—crushed me yesterday.

If I was thinking rationally, I'd get on my Harley, ride to

Manchester and demand answers, but right now, I'm sure I'd throttle her.

So, I opt to stand under the spray until the water starts to cool and I'm forced to step out from under it.

Towel cinched around my waist, I wipe the steam from the mirror above the sink and stare at my reflection.

Was it me Pip rejected yesterday, or was it the fear of coming clean to her brother?

Honestly, I don't know.

Piper's never had family, not really. I love Wade like he's blood, but the brother did her dirty walking away from her like he did. Her stepfather's a piece of shit who, if I ever meet him, I'm going to beat him senseless, and her mum sounds like a complete lunatic. Add to that a sociopathic bio-dad whose only saving grace is he has no idea she exists...

Yeah, Piper lost the family lottery, so I understand why she's desperate to cling to her brother, but Wade's going to have to deal with the fact I love his sister.

And I do love her.

I'm in love with Piper.

Fuck.

I lean against the basin and take a deep breath. What I feel for her scares me, but it feels right, good. I'm getting tired of her pushing me away, though. Patience isn't exactly my strongest suit, and I'm reaching the end of mine. I want her, but I'm done hiding what we have. Coming clean after the wedding wasn't going to be easy, not by a long shot. Wade's not going to be happy we've been lying, but it was necessary.

The fact she didn't show pisses me off.

Is she that scared of putting us out there?

Does she think our relationship isn't worth fighting for?

I'll throw down against Wade for us, I'll do it. I'll stand against my Club, my brothers, my president—if it comes to that. But she couldn't even get on a train and show up.

That cuts deep.

I towel off and pull on my jeans, a clean tee, shirt, boots and lastly my kutte. The leather is old, worn and fits like it was moulded to my body. It has been through years of wearing it. I feel complete with it on my back. I'm Lost Saxons and will be until the day I draw my last breath—something I'm not sure if Piper completely understands. This isn't a choice for me. It's my life. It's family. It's everything, which makes what I've done to Wade a huge deal.

But what did I expect? She's never really been a fan of my way of life. When Piper first came to Kingsley, she wasn't exactly receptive to the Club—although most of that was because of Wade and their past. She's come around a lot since, but maybe not as much as I thought. Maybe she's got cold feet about the whole thing. If she can't accept me, the Club, all of it, then we really don't have a future together.

Heading back into the bedroom, a cloud of steam following me, I snag my wallet, keys and phone off the bedside table. Then I make my way down to the clubhouse's dining room.

I expect it to be empty, given it's not even midday, but it's filled with brothers and old ladies—both my Club brothers but some of the out-of-towners who stayed last night for the wedding.

The smell of fried bacon and eggs is heavy in the air, and through the serving hatch to the kitchen I can see my mother, Dorothy, and Sammy's gran, Jeanne, at the stove.

I give chin lifts as I pass a couple of people, and pat the

shoulder of Foz, one of the Devil's Dogs—another MC we're allied with.

The Manchester Devils have their clubhouse not too far from where Piper lives—but they have bases all across the UK. We've known the guys for years and stop by their clubhouse any time we're in their patch. I've been remiss in my visiting, since I've been to Manchester more times than I can count over the past few months, but no one except Piper and her roommate, Cami, know about my stays.

"You have a good time last night, Fozzie?" I ask.

Their Road Captain smirks as he runs a hand over his bearded chin, full dimples coming out.

Foz is a good bloke, although he's a fucking crazy bastard. Don't be fooled by the smiles. He's lethal. His red curly hair looks wild this morning and I wonder if he bothered to run a comb through it before coming down for breakfast. Feral fucker.

"Yeah, bro. You boys certainly know how to put on a party, and your mum makes a fucking good cooked breakfast."

Mum is an amazing cook, so I can't argue with him on that. He points at his half-devoured plate of sausage, beans, hash browns, toast, bacon, black pudding and tomatoes. I groan, a hand going to my stomach. I can't stand food right now.

"Feeling delicate, flower?" Weed asks from his seat a few places down the table as he stuffs a piece of toast into his mouth.

He's sandwiched between Axel, another of the Devils (who is sitting with his old lady Harper), and Adam. They're all tucking into their own food.

"Not too delicate to punch that smug look off your face, fuck nuts," I smirk back at him, pulling a chair up to the table and sinking into it. I don't really feel like bantering, but I put my game face on. I don't want these nosey fuckers prying into my business.

"Always so aggressive. You should really talk to someone about your anger issues, Jeremy."

I snag a coffee mug off the table and reach for the coffee pot. While I don't want food, I do need caffeine, lots of it. My hangover is making itself known painfully in every cell of my body.

"Call me Jeremy again, *Noah*, and I'll bury you in the woods."

He wrinkles his brow at me using his birth name. I don't blame him. I hate my real name almost as much as he hates his, although he has darker reasons.

Foz arches a brow. "It's like being in a fucking playground."

"You have no idea," Adam mutters.

Normally, I would scruff my little brother's hair for that slight, but I'm not in the mood for messing around this morning. I check my phone instead. No missed calls. No messages. My jaw clenches.

As soon as I'm steady enough to ride, I'll be on my bike. Enough of the pity party. I need to know what is going on with my woman.

"Any sign of the bride and groom this morning?" Weed asks.

I suck back a glug of coffee, and regret it immediately. I expected it to be cool, but it's scalding. No matter. I need caffeine to wipe out the effects of the booze, so I can ride.

"Nope," Wade chirps up from further down the table.

My back stiffens of its own volition.

He's sitting with Paige, the bulky brother's arm around her shoulder as he sips on his own mug of caffeine. He's demolished a plate of food already by the looks of things, while she's made her way through a smaller helping. Not for the first time, I wonder what reasoning Piper gave him as to why she's not here.

I also wonder if he's pissed at her.

I want to ask, but me asking would seem odd, so I hold my tongue. I don't want to do anything that could make things difficult for Piper, in case there is a genuine reason she isn't here.

And I'm seriously hoping she has a good reason.

As I watch Wade, I find myself wondering what he'll do to me when he discovers I've been shagging his little sister for months behind his back. Worse still, that as soon as I can figure out what is going on in her head and get her back on track, that I'm going to claim her at the table as my old lady.

The sick part of my brain that enjoys winding people up almost relishes telling him, just to see his reaction. Yeah, I'm warped, I know.

I take another sip of coffee, this time welcoming the burn. It reminds me I'm alive, which may not be the case when Wade finds out the truth.

Despite their history, and despite the fact he's only been back in Piper's life for a short time, the brother is overly protective of his kid sister. I get it; I have sisters myself—sisters I'd kill to protect. But given Wade walked away from Piper, I'm surprised by this possessive streak he's developed over her. It means me going toe to toe with a brother to have her. I'm willing to do that, and she's not here.

Fuck, Pip, where are you?

I want to be mad at her, but I can't. She's scared, and I get it, I do. She's never had anyone. Even her parents are the worst humans on the planet. Suddenly, she has a chance with her brother and she's worried me and her being together could unhinge that. I understand, even if I don't like it. And I certainly don't like that when things get tough, she runs. I want her to talk to me.

A holler suddenly goes up and I twist in time to see my brother and Beth entering the room looking a little worse for wear. I join the fracas, even though my head feels like it's going to split in two. I'm happy for them both. They had a hell of a journey to get here, and they deserve this.

Logan's hand rests on Beth's neck as he presses a kiss to her hair. They look so in love. I want that. I don't care if it makes me sound like some pansy-assed bitch. I want it. I thought I had it with Piper, but I don't know if the woman is capable of giving me it. All I know is my world feels right with her in it. We're good together.

Beth settles at the table with the girls, who start gossiping like a gaggle of fucking geese, and Lo goes to get them something to eat from the kitchen while the noise resumes. I fire off another text to Piper, even though I'm sure I'm entering crazy territory right now. I don't give a fuck.

I zone in and out of the conversation, my attention mostly on my phone. This is my fault. I should have refused to play along. We should have told Wade about our relationship months ago. Hell, the moment I kissed her, I should have come clean.

At first, she was so against the Club, it was hard to break through that wall. I managed, though. I managed to show her the Lost Saxons is about family first and foremost. We're not choirboys, not by any stretch, but we're not demons either. Everything we do is to protect what's ours. We'll defend our own to the death.

Then she was worried about Wade's reaction to her dating a brother, and for good reason. Wade laid down the law like this was the sixteen-hundreds and his sister's virtue was in need of protecting. I should have nipped that in the bud fast. Fuck what Wade thinks. Piper's his sister, but he doesn't own her. He can take a swing at me, rant, rave—whatever he needs to do—but she's mine and she's going to be mine no matter what he says. I should have claimed her weeks ago. Months ago.

The doors at the end of the dining room suddenly kick open. I twist, instinct pushing aside my fuzzy head, and forcing me into action.

King is in the doorway, his expression focused, but I can see the panic beneath the prospect's tight-set mouth.

"What's wrong?" Logan demands, already on his feet.

It might be the morning after his wedding, but he's still the Club's Sergeant-at-Arms and he's never off the clock.

"There's a woman at the gate. Bleeding, hysterical. She nearly fucking ploughed right through them."

"You left her there?" Slade growls, moving towards him.

My instincts flare, and I nearly mirror his movement. It takes everything in me to keep my head.

I don't trust this fucker, not anymore, not after what he did with that whole Tap situation. The brothers want to move on, put it to bed and leave that shit in the past. What's done is done, but I think Slade's dangerous. His behaviour, even if I understand his anger, was uncontrolled.

So, I brace, ready to act if he decides to do something crazy. The fact Clara is with him might keep him level, but I don't know. The unpredictability of the man makes me on edge. I glance at the small blonde woman at Slade's side, wondering not for the first time, what her life is like behind closed doors. If he's hurting her, I don't give a shit what the others say, I'll bury him myself. Clara's a sweet woman and she's good to our Club.

King doesn't move, but I see his legs snap straight as if he wants to. I don't blame him Slade isn't exactly level lately. Not that King knows what the crazy fucker did to Tap, but the prospect isn't stupid. He knows something happened and that Slade was involved. If he knows the VP murdered and torched a patched member he might rethink signing up.

"We pulled her out of the vehicle, secured her outside. Charlie and Ghost are with her."

"Who is she?" Logan pushes, ignoring Slade.

We all do our best to ignore that crazy bastard.

"I don't know." His gaze slides towards me. "But she's asking for you."

Every eye in the room swivels in my direction.

I'm used to being gawked at. Being in an MC garners a lot of attention, and looking how I look, I get noticed. I'm six-foot-three, with stupid floppy blond hair and I know how to work the charm to my advantage. I know how to get attention. This is a different kind of noticing, though, and it's not one I'm wholly comfortable with.

I blink. "Me?"

What the fuck?

"You piss off some piece of skirt, Jem?" Weed asks, amusement in his voice.

Not lately. I haven't been with anyone but Piper for months. I can't say that, though, not with Wade standing two feet from me.

And it can't be Piper. King knows her, as does Ghost. In fact, the entire Club knows her. She was here for eight weeks looking after Wade, and she's been here multiple times since for various visits, including last week for Beth's hen do.

Mind racing, I shove the chair out of my way and push through the crowd of people.

Mum comes to the kitchen door as I pass. I see hints of Sofia and Adam in her face, but she's most like Mackenzie in the shape of her jaw and slope of her nose. Her colouring is all me and Adam, though, and her personality is all Lo.

"Jem, honey, what's going on?"

"Stay here," I order.

"What's happening?"

"Stay here," I repeat. I don't want her getting caught up in whatever this is.

She looks as if she's going to launch into a lecture about my tone, but I'm out of the doors before she can say shit. I love my mother, but fuck, can she lecture.

Unease swirls in my guts as I hit the front doors, aware of my brothers at my back—both Club and blood. I hope they had the common sense to tell their old ladies to stay inside. I have no idea what I'm dealing with here and I don't want any of them caught up in the crossfire.

I follow King who is leading the way like the Pied fucking Piper, and as soon as we step outside onto the loading bay, my heart drops to my feet.

Sitting on one of the picnic tables, Ghost standing one side of her, Charlie the other like a pair of sentinels is Camille Neville.

She's hard to recognise beneath the blood and bruises. If it wasn't for her mass of red hair and the pendant she always wears around her neck, I don't think I would be able to. Her left eye is swollen nearly shut, the other starting to close, and her jaw is a mass of mottled purple and black. Her top is torn at the shoulder, revealing a hint of lacy black bra beneath and her jeans are intact but bloodied, too, ripped at the knees. I don't even want to think about the injuries hidden beneath her clothes, but she's beat to hell.

I let my eyes slide towards the gate, seeing the abandoned car in the entrance of it, the driver's door still flung open. Christ. How did she drive like this?

Cami raises her head and as soon as she sees me, lets out a sob that cuts through me.

When she comes off the bench, Ghost moves to stop her, but I shake my head, and the huge brother lets his hands drop to his side as she throws herself bodily into my arms. I go back on a foot with the force of her, but manage to wrap my arms around her tiny frame. Cami sobs uncontrollably and I have no idea what she's saying, but my fear is mounting.

What the fuck is Piper's best friend doing here, looking like this?

And where the fuck is my woman?

I've never seen Cami look anything but perfectly put together. This is throwing me completely.

I manage to disentangle from her after a moment, and when I do, I feel rage roar in my gut. She's a mess.

I try to calm myself. I don't want to scare her, but I'm sure my nostrils are flaring as my breath saws out of me.

"Who did this to you?" I'm impressed by how level I keep my tone, considering the fear and rage racing through me.

Cami is a small woman, maybe five-five, and from the looks of things whoever attacked her got most of the hits in.

"I tried to stop them." Her voice wobbles.

"Stop who?"

"There were too many, but I tried."

I don't like where this is going. My stomach twists.

"Cami, what happened?"

She grabs my biceps and squeezes with bruising force. It's a surprisingly strong grip for someone as small as her and as hurt as she is.

"They have her..." she whispers through cracked, cut lips.

Three words. Three words that make fear drill into my soul.

They have her.

"Who? Who has her?" The words taste bad on my tongue, but I spit them out anyway. I need to know. I need the answers she has. Impatience has me wanting to shake them free from her, but I resist. I don't want to hurt her more than she already is, but I need her to give me more than this, faster. I need to know where Piper is, now.

"Men. They took Piper. I tried to stop them, but there were so many of them."

She sobs, clinging to me like she'll fall down if she doesn't. I'm aware of the crowd around us, but I don't care. All I care about is the woman in front of me and what she's saying, the answers she has.

"Somebody took my sister?" Wade's voice cuts through the air. I watch as he mentally throws aside all the questions battering his brain right now, and focuses on the bigger issue at hand.

Cami pulls back from me, releasing her iron-clad grip. I stagger, my heart racing so fast I feel light-headed. A hand steadies me. Logan, I realise. Eyes that mirror mine narrow, no doubt reaching the right conclusion about how Piper's best friend knows me. My big brother is astute. If it wasn't for the fact he's been so caught up in Beth and keeping the Club safe, he would have realised before now what I've been up to and where I've been disappearing to for weeks, and he probably would have smacked some sense into me.

But I don't have time or the inclination to deal with Logan right now. My only focus is Piper, because I can't wrap my mind around what Cami is telling me.

Someone took Piper.

Someone took my woman.

And from the look of her best friend, they didn't take her nicely.

I'm going to kill whoever touched her, and I'm going to hurt them for touching Cami, too.

I was sitting here, sulking, crying over my wounded heart while Piper was in trouble.

I'm a fucking idiot.

I'm worse than that.

I'm a selfish cunt.

Of course she didn't run.

Of course she didn't back out.

Piper is many things, but she's not a coward, not really.

She might have been scared, but she would have talked to me. If my head was screwed on right and if I wasn't acting like a baby, I would have realised that.

"Who fucking took her, Cam?" I demand, tugging her back from Wade.

I need answers and I need them now. I need to be on my bike, looking for her, but I need a thread first and Cami looks about ready to collapse.

I push her back onto the bench and crouch in front of her.

"Who?" I repeat.

"I don't know." She sucks in a breath before running the tip of her tongue over the cut on her lip. It's opened again and blood is bubbling from it. She needs to be looked at by a doctor, and soon, but not before she tells me what I need to know. "They're mixed up with Grant somehow. That's all I know." She folds her shaking hands together on her lap and closes her less swollen eye over.

"Her stepfather?" I question, and I can feel Wade's eyes boring into my back. These are things I shouldn't know, not really.

"Yeah. They were waiting in the loft when we got home. I tried to stop them." Her gaze meets mine and I see tears forming at the edge of the puffy lids. "I fought so hard, Jem, you have to believe me."

I grab her hand and squeeze it. "I can see how hard you fought, sweetheart. Do you remember anything about them?"

"They were definitely local, judging from their accents."

"Were they wearing colours?" Logan asks.

"Colours?"

She sounds confused by his question, and why wouldn't she? Camille Neville isn't from our world. She's a rich girl who doesn't have affiliations with gangs or motorcycle clubs. Piper brought this into her life.

"Kuttes or gang colours," Lo clarifies.

"No. Just jeans and leather jackets. Nothing distinguishing, but I wouldn't know. I don't associate with gangs." It's not said nastily, just as a matter of fact.

"What about tattoos?" I twist to look at Foz as his rumbling voice sounds behind me. I didn't realise the Devil's Dogs had followed us out. "Anything that looks like a reaper? Or an eagle or an inverted cross?"

She shakes her head at the red headed man, but I see a hint of trepidation in her face before she manages to lock it down. I don't blame her. There's a lot of scary looking bastards surrounding her right now, and given she was just attacked by a group of men, she's right to be wary. I suspect her trust in me to keep her safe is the only thing stopping her from freaking out.

"No. I don't know. It happened so fast. We barely got the key in the door before we were attacked. After that, everything was a whirlwind. I was more focused on trying to keep them from taking Piper. I didn't really notice anything else. One of the men..." She chews her bottom lip and winces. "He's been..."

"What?" I push when she breaks off.

She jiggles her leg a little. "He's been following Piper. She blew it off, thought it was Grant trying to scare her. He said he was done protecting her, whatever the heck that means."

Anger rolls through me at her words. Why in the fuck was her stepfather trying to scare her? And why is this the first I'm hearing of it?

"Protecting her from what?" Wade asks the question sitting on my tongue, but I'm seeing red. Asking it isn't in my ability right now.

"I don't know. He's caught up in something... something dangerous. We thought he was talking shit to get P to toe the line. He and Farrah—Piper's mum—are more than a little controlling. They'll do or say anything to get her to do what they want."

I hear Wade growl a curse behind me, but I keep my eyes locked on Cami. I already knew her parents are both shit heads.

Cami slides her eyes from the brother back to me. "I don't know what trouble he got in this time. He didn't say and P didn't know, but Grant said if she didn't do what he wanted, he wouldn't protect her from these men who were threatening him. She thought it was bullshit, so she told him to shove off." She swipes at the tear working down her cheek, but it's an angry gesture. "Then she saw this man when we were out having lunch one afternoon, just watching her. She wasn't sure if he was part of this or not, but he creeped her out—creeped us both out."

Lead settles in my stomach. Why in the hell didn't Piper tell me any of this? I could have done more, protected her. I thought all the danger was in Kingsley—Dylan being on the lam, Slade and his antics, the Club in disarray, this fucking P.I. sniffing around... I never thought Piper was in trouble in Manchester. I thought she was safe there, out of the way. I let my guard down. I got complacent, and now she's gone. That's on me.

"I didn't think anything of it," Cami continues. "I just thought he was a guy... until we walked into the loft. He was one of the men who attacked us."

I straighten from my crouch, my mind on autopilot. I'm going to Manchester and I'm getting my fucking woman back.

I don't even make two steps before a hand fists into my kutte.

"Where the fuck are you going?" Logan hisses at me.

I stare at his hand for a moment before raising my eyes to look at my brother. I love him. He raised me to be the man I am after our dad died, but that doesn't mean I won't punch his lights out if he doesn't release me.

"I'd hate to mess your pretty face up for your honeymoon, Lo, but I will if you don't let go of me."

He doesn't, so I shove him. Unsurprisingly, he doesn't move an inch. Heavy-set bastard.

"You're not going anywhere, you daft shit."

Wade stares at me, and I can see the cogs working in his brain. He's not stupid. He's figuring things out. He turns to Cami.

"Why'd you ask to speak to him? Not me? Piper's my sister."

Cami opens and closes her mouth, as realisation that she's fucked up hits her. I'm guessing Piper's told her we're not divulging our secret until after the weekend. Clearly that isn't going to happen since Piper's God knows where.

Whatever, we don't have time to get into this right now. I need to find my girl and I need to do it fast. Every nerve in my body is fired up. I can't stand knowing she's out there, hurt, alone, scared.

"Let me go, Lo." It's both a warning and a plea I give to my brother.

I see Adam move closer in my peripheral vision. Fine, I'll take them both on.

"No."

I shove him, and this time he does go back on a foot and he releases me.

Wade's not stupid. He's a clever guy, and he's putting the pieces of this puzzle together fast. "Is there something going on with you and Piper?" he demands in a low growl.

Ah, shit. Here we go.

"We don't have time for this," I say, and we don't.

Piper is taller than Cami, standing at around maybe five-eight or five-nine, but she's small-framed despite her height. She's also slender—mainly because she eats like a fucking sparrow (something I think her bitch of a mother instilled in her). She wouldn't have stood a chance against the scum who attacked her. Thinking of her face bruised and bloodied like Cami's makes my entire body lock solid.

"Your sister is in trouble, Wade. I'm going to Manchester to get her back. You can come with me or you can stay here. Up to you, brother."

For a moment, Piper's face floats across my memory.

She inherited her brother's dark hair, which she wears scraped into a top knot when she's feeling more casual, more relaxed. Piper's a beautiful woman, although she'll never believe it, but she isn't a fighter—not physically. I just hope she can mentally survive whatever is happening to her.

I start to move past him, but a meaty hand grabs my bicep, stopping me in my tracks. Shit. I move back out of his grip, and put a little distance between us.

"You didn't answer my question, Jem." Wade's voice is dangerous. "Is something going on with you and Piper?"

The air crackles with tension and I feel Logan shift behind me, preparing for whatever is about to happen. I lick my lips, my mouth feeling a little dry. This is not how I intended to tell Wade I'm with his sister, but fuck it, she's mine and I won't deny it any longer.

"Yeah," I admit and wait for the inevitable fall out.

The brother has made no secret of the fact he doesn't want anyone touching his sister. The fact I've gone there with her isn't going to please him. He's not going to care that I love her, that this isn't a fling for me.

Wade's eye twitches as my words settle into his brain. I steel for his reaction, watching as he squares his jaw.

"How long?" he grinds out.

I don't want to admit it, and it leaves a bad taste as I say, "Months."

I see the punch coming, but I don't move to avoid it. I take it. I deserve it. Wade's fist catches me square in the jaw and I would go down, but Logan catches me, his thick arms wrapping around my back.

I grit my teeth against the pain and shake my head. This is not helping my hangover.

"You done?" I demand, rubbing my burning face.

Shit, that hurt.

Wade glares at me, his chest heaving, his mouth a tight line. "Fuck no, but we don't have time for me to beat you to a pulp, you backstabbing cunt. Piper's in trouble." He turns to the Manchester Devils. "This went down in your patch. You think you can help us?"

Axel and Foz exchange looks. "Let us talk to Dax, but yeah, bro, whatever you need."

Dax is their president, and was here for the wedding last night. He's also a friend of the Club. I can't see him having an issue, but I don't give a shit if he does. I'm going to Manchester and I'll scorch through his territory to get Piper back with or without his blessing. Hell, I'm going with or without Derek's blessing as well. From the fire Wade's spitting, he might just feel the same.

Cami comes off the bench and fists her hands in my kutte. "You bring her home, Jem."

"I'm going to," I promise her.

"I mean it, you bring her home. She's my best friend, and she needs to be okay. So you bring her home." She bats her hands against my chest before she seizes my shirt again.

I prise Cami's fingers off me. I'm not sure if she's trembling or I am. I've been through a lot of crap in my life, but I've never felt dread like this before. Knowing Piper is in danger terrifies me.

I cup the side of Cami's neck, the only part of her head that isn't bruised, and say gently, "Sweetheart, you don't have to worry. I'm not coming back here without her."

And I mean that. There is no scenario that ends without Piper coming back here with me. I'll die before that happens.

God, she better be okay.

Ice settles in my gut and claws dig into my heart. Bike. I

need to be on my bike. I need to get to Manchester and find Piper now. She has to be okay because if she's not, I'm going to tear the city apart.

Whoever took her is going to die slowly and painfully. For every bruise they inflicted on Cami and Piper, I'm going to do ten times worse to them before I eviscerate them. There will be no mercy for these fuckers. They took my woman forcefully from a place she should have always felt safe. They took Lost Saxons property. They're going to die. Horrifically.

I give Wade a look as I pass him. "I'm sorry, brother. I never meant to lie to you, but I love your sister, and I'm going to fucking get her back. You want to come with me, then by all means, come. You want to beat the shit out of me for lying to you, fine. But you wait until Piper's back here and she's safe to do it. I need to be focused on her and nothing else."

Wade stares at me a beat and I can see the conflict playing across his face for a split second before he nods.

"Let's go get her."

CHAPTER TWO

PIPER

FIVE MONTHS EARLIER...

'*Welcome to Kingsley...*'

The sign at the edge of the road mocks me as the car rushes past it in a blur of motion. Nothing about this trip is welcome. I can think of a thousand places I would rather be.

I try to focus on the landscape beyond the windscreen, but my eyes lock on the wipers as they frantically swipe back and forth over the glass, trying to clear the stream of rain battering the vehicle. Since we left Manchester, it's been a nonstop deluge that hasn't let up at all—a fortuitous omen perhaps, one that suggests I should have stayed home. It's too late to turn back now, even if I could. I'm miles from home in a car with a man I met just over an hour ago, a man who could very well slit my throat and dump me in the nearest ditch where even the most vigilant police officer would not find me. I doubt the local bobbies in Kingsley are crack detectives, capable of solving major crimes, however. If they were, they wouldn't have a motorcycle gang operating on their doorstep.

And that is who picked me up almost an hour and a half ago—a member of a motorcycle gang.

Not just any gang, but the Lost Saxons Motorcycle Club—a Club that just under three years ago took my half-brother from me and brainwashed him into joining their little biker cult. From the sounds of it, I'm about to lose him again because of them. This time perhaps permanently. I have no idea what's happened to him, only that he's in the hospital and that it's serious—life and death serious.

The thought sends a chill racing up my spine. Josh and I haven't been close for a long time. We've never really been close, in fact, but knowing he could die is the only reason I'm sitting in this car right now with a total stranger, driving a fifty mile trip to the back-end of Yorkshire to see a brother I haven't spoken to in years—a brother who ditched me for Harleys and drug running and God knows what else.

Cautiously, and without drawing attention, I slide my eyes to the side and sneak a peek at my chauffeur. Charlie—that's the name he gave me when he turned up on my doorstep. He hasn't done anything dangerous or concerning since I got in the car with him. He's been perfectly gracious, if not a little annoying, but I don't doubt he's capable of violence, even though he's just sitting there, his hand lazily resting against the steering wheel, the other on the gear stick. I probably should have thought through my decision to get into his car, not that I had much choice. I was more or less bullied into being picked up.

At the time, I was too muddled by the call to argue and Cami, my best friend since birth (and my roommate), didn't think anything was wrong with me jumping into a vehicle with a near-perfect stranger—one who probably maims drug dealers and steals from grannies in his spare time.

I should have put my foot down.

I should have refused to go anywhere with Charlie, who turned up on my doorstep wearing jeans, a pair of battered boots, and a T-shirt saying 'Motorcycles are not all I ride'.

He's not exactly hard on the eyes, but looks are not the pertinent issue here. He's a criminal, and I've never been in trouble in my entire life. Even at school, I was a straight-A student. This man looks like he teaches mayhem, and I say 'man' in the loosest sense of the word. He looks barely old enough to be behind the wheel.

I'm not an expert on ages, but I guess he's younger than me by at least five or six years, which puts him barely out of his teens at twenty—twenty-one at a push. He has sandy, shaggy-hair that falls into his eyes, and light blue eyes that have been appraising me the entire journey, although he's barely said two words to me. If it wasn't for the ink covering his skin, I'd find him attractive, but I'm not into the punk-rock look—or whatever the heck this is he's projecting. I like my men suited and booted, and less... well, grungy. I'm certainly not a fan of the dirty leather vest he's wearing, proclaiming him a 'Prospect', and I'm not keen on his ties to the Lost Saxons Motorcycle Club either—a club that all but stole my brother from me.

This thought has my jaw clenching, and I turn my attention back out of the side window, watching the high-rises form as the car navigates through the busy town. Kingsley is nothing like Manchester. My hometown is a bustling metropolitan, filled with eclectic architecture and brimming with culture. Where the old and the new meets it gives the city an interesting vibe that is sadly lacking here. Kingsley is washed out, a graveyard filled with throwbacks to the nineteen-seventies and hints of its once industrious history as a colliery town. Even without the rain, it would be a bleak place.

"I didn't know Wade had a sister," Charlie says, finally breaking through the silence. I jolt at his voice and twist in my seat, taking a moment to collect myself.

"I don't imagine he talks about me much."

I doubt he talks about me at all. We haven't set eyes on each other in close to three years, and we didn't exactly part on the best terms.

Charlie brushes a hand through his hair. He could pass for a boy band member, if he wasn't dripping with tattoos and chains.

"Wade doesn't talk much full stop." His lips kick up at the corners. "I'm sensing that's a family trait."

I want to roll my eyes at him, but a healthy dose of self-preservation keeps me from doing so. I still don't know this man and what he's capable of. I also don't know enough about my brother to contradict or agree with what he's saying.

When I first met Josh, when he was in jail, he was surly, angry—not at me, but at his situation, at his father, *our* father. He had no problem talking to me, though. Not that I recall anyway. He'd said plenty to me, not all of it positive.

"You call him Wade," I say quietly. Wade is our father's surname. "I noticed your friend, Weed, did that on the telephone, too."

I don't add how stupid I think *his* name is.

Weed.

He's the man who called me out of the blue to tell me my half-brother is in the hospital and that I needed to come to Kingsley immediately. He told me Josh might not make it and that the prognosis didn't look good, although he didn't say it exactly like that. He used many more F-bombs. What did I expect from a man called 'Weed'? What kind of name is that anyway for an adult man? I was surprised when

Charlie didn't introduce himself as Grenade or Tank, or something equally ridiculous.

"I've only been with the Club four months or so, but he's been Wade for as long as I've been here. I've never heard anyone but you, and now the doctors, call him by his first name before."

This reminder of his situation makes a lump gather in my throat and I have to swallow hard.

"Do you know what happened? Weed didn't really say much."

Charlie's fingers tighten on the steering wheel, but he says, "Above my pay grade, Piper. They don't tell prospects anything other than what they want us to know."

"Right." I rub my hands together, trying to ward off some of the chill suddenly seeping into my bones as I imagine all kinds of scenarios that could have led to my brother getting shot. A question flits across my mind, a question I'm not sure I want to know the answer to, but it escapes my mouth before I can stop it. "Do you know if Josh is alive?"

He shifts in the seat, his hand rubbing at his neck. "As far as I know, he is."

How vague.

"He was shot, right? Weed told me that much."

"In the abdomen. Sorry, darlin'. That's as much as I know."

And he does sound sincere.

Shot in the abdomen.

How does that happen in Yorkshire? It doesn't. Not to normal people anyway. Joe public doesn't get shot in the bloody gut and need lifesaving surgery. Nobody does outside of the police or the army.

Unless you're in a motorcycle gang…

I push that thought down. The last thing I need to do is lose my head with one of its members, even if he's just a novice. The anger I've buried for all these years that the Lost Saxons took my brother from me isn't as deeply buried as I believed and one wrong word has the potential to reignite the embers, so I bite my tongue and remember the manners instilled in me by my mother and stepfather, Grant.

"Why didn't they call me as soon as it happened?"

He lets out a long breath, and I sigh.

"Let me guess... above your pay grade?" I'm unable to keep the bite of sarcasm out of my tone.

He snorts. "Something like that." After a moment, he says, "There was some shit going down. They didn't want to put you in the middle of that, I expect, and then they couldn't find your number to get you here."

I don't even want to know what 'shit' was going down. I close my eyes and take a steadying breath. I should be annoyed they waited to bring me here, but how can I be? Charlie didn't even know Josh had a sister. I'm lucky any of Josh's friends knew I existed, even more so that they managed to find a contact number for me. How can I be pissed off for a situation I caused?

Besides, what could I have done if I'd been here when it first occurred? Weed told me on the phone Josh was in surgery for hours and the drugs he's on have kept him unconscious since.

I tamp down my irritability to ask, "How far to the hospital now?"

"About another ten minutes. I'm sorry I can't tell you more about Wade."

Since there is no point getting annoyed at this guy, I

force a smile and say, "I'm sure the doctors will be able to update me when we arrive."

I doubt this. As his sister, I may be able to get information from the medical staff about his condition, but I've been out of Josh's life for a long time now. I don't know if he has a partner who takes precedent.

"Is... is Josh married?"

Charlie shakes his head. "No."

"Dating?"

"Single, as far as I know." Charlie's smile is a little wry as he splits his gaze between me and the road. "The brothers don't exactly put out bulletins every time they hook up."

I don't even want to consider how promiscuous these men are. I can imagine the debauchery that happens at their little clubhouse. I've seen the television shows and read enough books to be aware of what goes on behind closed doors in these clubs. I have no doubt the Lost Saxons is no different.

"Right."

Silence falls over the car again, and I pull my phone out of my handbag, just for something to occupy myself; I'm not sure talking to Charlie is helping my mental wellbeing.

A text message is waiting for me. It's from Cami, who I am seriously considering killing when I get back home to our very beautiful and safe loft apartment.

CAMI: Are you okay?
ME: I'm surviving.
CAMI: Oh, thank God you replied. I was getting worried they might have dumped your body in the Atlantic.

I half-smile at her message. It's dramatic, but not exactly outside the realm of possibility, given who these men are.

ME: I doubt I'd be responding to you from the depths of the ocean, Cam. And considering you practically shoved me out the door with the strange biker who showed up, I hold you responsible for whatever happens to me.

CAMI: I'm not responsible for anything, not even myself. Are you all right, though?

ME: We just drove into Kingsley, so I'll let you know once I've seen Josh.

CAMI: Whatever happens, I'm here for you, P. I should have come with you.

ME: I can handle myself.

CAMI: I know you can. You can handle anything.

This is not remotely true, but I love her unshakable faith in me. There are plenty of things I can't handle.

CAMI: I still should have tagged along.

ME: You'd be bored to tears. I suspect there's going to be a lot of waiting around. The biker who picked me up said Josh was still being treated.

CAMI: Keep me posted, darling. If you need me, call. I'll be with you in a flash.

I tuck my phone away and resume my vigil out the window. I want to ask Charlie more questions about my brother, about what he's like now, if he resembles the man I knew when he left jail, but the words stick in my throat, and by the time my courage appears he's guiding the car into what is clearly the hospital complex.

Kingsley General looks like any hospital grounds in any town I've ever seen. It's a squat series of buildings spanning across a large area with parking sections around the main building. It appears to have been constructed at least fifty years ago and could do with modernising.

Charlie drives around a couple of times until he finds a space near the main entrance.

"I'll grab a parking ticket," he says and disappears before I can offer any money towards the payment.

When he returns, I ask if he wants cash towards it, but he waves this off, looking almost affronted, and tells me to follow him.

I leave my bags in the boot of the car, taking only my handbag. I packed clothes for a few days, enough in case I need to stay to sort out my brother's affairs, should the worst happen. I'm surprised by the cold detachment I have thinking this, but I shouldn't be. I hardly know him and it's not like we're close. In all honesty, I don't think I would be here right now if it wasn't for Cami giving me a shove out the door. She said that if things are as serious as Weed suggested on the phone and if Josh does die, I would regret not saying goodbye. So, I'm here for my own selfish reasons. I'm here for my own peace of mind, nothing more.

Truthfully, I'm not sure why I'm here at all. We haven't spoken in years. I don't owe him anything.

But he's hurt and he could die...

I tamp that thought down before it grows legs and decides to walk around my brain further.

Charlie leads me into the hospital, which is nowhere near as dingy inside as it is out. It's clean, fresher and actually fairly pleasant—although it's obvious it needed updating a decade ago. It's a contrast to the modern hospitals in Manchester. Not that I'm an expert on these. I've only ever been inside one last year when Cami fell off her Louis Vuitton shoes and twisted her ankle. She didn't have to sit in Accident and Emergency, though. Private health care meant she got X-rayed in twenty minutes at a high-class medical facility, so I'm not sure my experience of hospitals is exactly normal.

I keep close to Charlie as we navigate the hospital corridors, noticing the looks that come his way. People stare at his leather vest with a mix of trepidation and wonder. Some are wholly disinterested, which makes me think the Lost Saxons must be a regular sight around town.

He leads us over to the lift and pushes the button, stepping back to wait for it to come. My heart feels like it's dancing in my chest as we make the trip to the third floor—the Intensive Care Unit. I have no idea what reception I will get from my brother when he wakes up, if he wakes up. I'm terrified of meeting his club members and I'm starting to think coming was a colossal mistake.

When the lift doors open on the correct floor and I'm greeted with two hulking leather vested men waiting in the corridor, the option to run is taken out of my hands.

All eyes come to me and Charlie.

I swallow hard, resisting the urge to step back. Not that there is anywhere to go. The lift carriage is barely six-foot squared. Charlie steps out first, his movement one of confidence, and I fixate on the word Prospect arced across his back. His vest is different from the men he walks towards. They have the words 'Lost Saxons' and 'Kingsley' arced on the top and bottom of their vests, and a grotesque insignia between the text. It takes me a moment to absorb the two crossed swords dripping blood onto a skull wearing a helmet. It has a T-cross piece over the skeletal nose and the eye sockets are red, burning coals. The MC badge sits in the middle of the two, to the right of the insignia, and the one percent logo.

I should let the doors shut, hit the button for the ground floor, and call Cami to collect me. I should not have allowed a criminal to drive me nearly fifty miles up the country to visit my ex-convict half-brother.

It's only fear of offending these men that pushes my feet to move.

I try not to grimace as I trail after Charlie. I also try not to cling to the back of his vest. I'm a grown woman, not a child. I don't need protecting.

Although, as we get closer to the men, I rethink this stance. They are huge. I'm tall. I stand at five-foot-nine without heels on, and I'm wearing a four-inch heel on my calf-length boots. That puts me near to the same height as the men, yet I still feel small next to them.

I want to step back, but I hold my ground as one of the men steps towards me. He's nearly the same height as me, although he would be taller than me if I was barefoot.

"Piper."

It's not a question. I'm assuming I'm the only person Charlie was sent to pick up today, but I answer anyway. "Yes."

"I'm Weed. This is Slade. We spoke on the phone."

He looks nothing like I imagined a man named Weed would look. He has short hair, spiked slightly at the tips in a way that suggests he's put a little hair gel in it to make it stay that way. The five o'clock shadow covering his jaw is more there out of a lack of desire to shave than by design and gives him a rugged look. He doesn't strike me as a man who usually wears a beard, considering his hairstyle. Like Charlie, he is tattooed, but Weed could easily pass for a male model—if he took the worn leather vest off.

As his eyes rove over my face, a hint of unrestrained lust in them, I resist the urge to squirm under his scrutiny. He likes what he sees, and I'm not sure what I think of this. I don't want him to like me. I don't want him to like me at all, even if the man is attractive—they all are, even Slade, if you're into older men.

I'm about to open my mouth and ask Weed what the heck he's staring at when he says, rather oddly, "You look like him."

I draw my brow together at this bizarre statement. "Like who?"

"Wade."

For some reason, this kicks me in the gut, and I don't know why. It shouldn't. Of course I look like Josh—or Wade, as they all call him. We share half a gene pool. It would be weird if we didn't have at least some shared attributes, but hearing Weed say this shreds what control of my emotions I have left. It reminds me of what I left behind, of the fact that Josh and I are not close, of the time we've missed. So when I speak, my words are biting.

"It's not unusual for siblings to look alike."

If I expect my tone to upset him, I'm clearly on the wrong track.

Weed grins stupidly at me. "The acorn doesn't fall far from the tree, eh?"

I have no idea what he's talking about. "Meaning?"

"You're just alike. Peas in a fucking pod."

I deflate a little at his words. We're alike. Josh and I are alike. Strange that we would be, given we hardly know each other, but for some reason it comforts me that we are.

"How is he doing?"

This sobers him, and Weed scrubs a hand down his face. "They repaired his spleen and fixed up the damage to his front and his back. The docs did some other shit in surgery that went right over my head." His mouth pulls tight into a line and I can see the worry in his face. He cares about Josh, that much is clear.

"Is he awake?"

"No. He's been out of it since the surgery. The docs said it's the mix of the meds and the trauma. I don't know. Seems like a long time to be out of it to me, but what do I know?"

It does to me, too. From what Weed told me on the telephone earlier, he's already been unconscious for hours.

I rub absently at my arms, needing a second to collect myself.

Taking a steadying breath, I try to calm my thrumming heart. I have no idea why I'm so worried. It's not like I'm close to my half-brother, but my body feels electrified with tension and disorder. No matter our past, I don't wish bad things for Josh. I still, deep down, love my brother. Regret that we never sorted our problems weighs heavily on my shoulders and I hate that neither of us managed to be the grown up. I want this to change. If he pulls through, it has to change. I'm all the family he has... well, blood family. Clearly, he has Club family now.

He's all the family I have, too. My mother doesn't care about me. She's more interested in keeping my stepfather happy. The only person I have in my life is Cami. If it wasn't for her, I would have gone crazy over the years.

"Is he going to pull through?" I find myself asking Weed. "And please don't lie to me." My voice is a hint accusatory, and I'm not sure why. It's not as if it's this man's fault.

Except, it is. It's his and his entire leather-wearing

brigade of criminal idiots' fault that my brother is lying in Intensive Care with a hole in his abdomen and back. If Josh wasn't in a stupid motorcycle club, he would not be close to death.

Weed shrugs helplessly, and I see the ripple of anxiety roll through him. "I don't know. The docs here won't tell us shit."

"You give me five minutes and I'll get the information we need," the salt and pepper haired man—Slade—growls.

I don't like him already. He has a permanently etched grimace on his face that makes him seem mean. My eyes slide to the word 'Vice President' on the breast of his leather vest and I wonder who put him in charge of anything.

"Yeah, you going to start threatening nurses, Slade?" Weed's voice is light, but there's a bite of irritation in his words. I get the impression Slade might be something of a problem in their ranks.

"And have Clara on my arse later?" He blows out a huff.

"You're not scared of Clar, are you?"

Now, he just sounds amused.

"You'd be smart to be. She knows all the pain points in the body. And she can kill you without leaving any evidence."

This statement makes my eyes flare.

Kill without leaving evidence...

These people are insane. Their stupid banter is also grating on my nerves. I don't need or want to hear this. I just want to know if their idiotic bike club has killed my brother.

"As thrilling as this is," I interrupt, "can someone please tell me if my brother is going to die?" My voice is small, but steeled. I may as well have dropped a nuclear bomb in the middle of the corridor. The silence that follows is deafening. Weed rubs the back of his neck, wincing.

Slade glares at me.

Sorry for ruining your happy glow, Mr Grumpy Pants.

"Darlin', we're not making light of the situation," Weed says, finally breaking through the tension. "Wade's a brother. We're worried, too, but—"

"Crying into our tea isn't really our style, princess," Slade interrupts, then he addresses Weed. "I'm going back to the waiting room. Clara might be able to speak to one of these prick doctors again, get some answers. I'm getting fed up of professional courtesy not counting up here."

I feel tears hot behind my eyes at the fire in his words. Not that I don't deserve them; I wasn't exactly polite.

Weed watches him go before he turns back to me and gives me a smile.

"Ignore him. He's like that with everyone."

His attempt at making me feel better does break through some of my hardness, and my voice is less abrasive when I ask, "Professional courtesy?"

"Clara, his old lady, works in the Accident and Emergency department downstairs. Usually, that's a help when we're in the hospital. These ICU docs aren't telling her squat, though."

I fiddle absently with the strap of my handbag as I consider him, trying to order my thoughts. Maybe I need to dial back the bitch in public, at least with these men. I'm not sure if I'm safe. Weed seems okay, but Slade... I'm not so certain he wouldn't dump my body in the nearest woodland if I annoy him. I have to remember they are not friendly; they're criminal outlaws, and I am an outsider. Being obnoxious and throwing my weight around is a good way to end up in trouble.

I try to bury all my anger and put forward my best front —the one I reserve for galas and photo shoots when I'm with my stepfather. I've spent my life faking it and being nice to people I despise. This situation is no different.

And if I want to see my brother, I'll need to show these people I'm not a threat to him, which I'm not, but dissing their way of life is not likely to make them warm to me.

"Is Josh going to be all right?"

"I don't know," Weed admits, and while I admire his honesty, I almost wish he'd lied. "I hope so. Luckily, he was shot in the hospital grounds, so he got help fast."

He considers this to be luck?

I close my eyes. As soon as Josh wakes up, I'm making it my mission to get him away from this bloody Club, even if it's the last thing I do. These people are completely certifiable.

Weed mistakes my gesture for concern.

"Hey, you don't have to worry about anything, okay? We'll take care of him, and we'll take care of you, too, Piper. There's a waiting room full of brothers and old ladies who'll do whatever you need—no matter what it is. Just ask, okay?"

I open my eyes, trying to keep my anger from boiling over at his sympathy for me. If they'd taken care of him in the first place, he wouldn't be lying in a hospital bed right now, his insides stitched together, would he?

"I'll go and see if I can rouse a doctor," I murmur, plastering a fake smile in place. "Find out how he's doing."

I turn on my heel and walk away from him before I say something I regret, but in the back of my mind, the resentment is simmering. They did this to him. This stupid club. And if he ever wakes up, I'm going to make Josh see just how dangerous they are.

Honestly, I can't believe he walked away from me for this bunch of cavemen. If he hadn't, he wouldn't be lying in a hospital bed with a hole in him, fighting for his life.

I'm so focused on my seething anger that I don't notice the looming body step out from the door—a small single bathroom, I realise belatedly—ahead of me until he collides with me. I go back a step, nearly losing my balance and I'm only stopped from falling by strong hands gripping me.

"Easy, sweetheart."

I jolt at the deeply masculine voice, my head shifting back to meet the gaze of the man it belongs to, the man currently gripping my elbows with a steady hold. His hands are warm, slightly rough against my skin, and his fingers almost caress as they touch me.

A shiver runs through me, not a wholly unpleasant one, and my breath seems to lodge in my throat as I try and fail to draw air.

I've never had such a visceral reaction to touching someone before, but it's like a jolt of energy just got pushed into my body and is firing around all my synapses.

I swallow hard as I take him in. He has a jaw that seems to be chiselled from granite and his dark brown eyes are easy to get lost in. They hide behind a curtain of dark blond hair. He fixes me with a grin that makes me squirm and heat rush between my legs.

"Sorry," I blurt, trying to step back, but he doesn't let me go immediately.

When he does release me, there's a reluctance on both our parts to step away—at least until my eyes lock on the worn leather vest sitting on his back.

He's a Lost Saxons member, and according to the label on his breast, he's their Treasurer, whatever this entails.

He has tattoos peeking out from under the neckline of the short-sleeved shirt he's wearing beneath the cut-off vest. They snake down his arms, stopping just shy of his wrists, which are adorned with leather bands and there's a silver chain around his neck. He looks like he's stepped out of time, should have an axe, a horned helmet and be called Björn or Ragnar. He's a stunning looking man, and I can't deny my entire body sits up and takes notice.

But seeing that vest on his back, I force those feelings back down. He's one of them.

My jaw tightens of its own volition, even as his mouth tips up into a cheeky smile.

"No need to apologise, angel," he says, and even though I want to be immune to his gruff, deep voice, my body reacts. It resonates through me from my toes upwards, settling in my belly.

I shouldn't be affected by this grinning biker who looks like he stepped out of Valhalla, but I am.

"I'm more than happy to catch you anytime you're falling."

I narrow my eyes at him, even as I swallow hard, trying to regain my equilibrium. I'm not sure why I'm off kilter, but I feel off balance with him. I have to keep in mind, no matter how attractive he is, he's the reason Josh is here. It's this thought that makes my next words less than charming.

"Does that line usually work?"

He fixes me with a beaming smile. It's disarming. "I don't know, you're the first woman I've tried it on." When he leans closer to peer at me, my heart stutters. "Did it?"

"No." I swallow again, and this time I struggle to get past the lump in my throat. I need to regain control here. I'm not a hormonal teenager; I'm a twenty-five-year-old woman with a usually iron-clad restraint.

"You know," he says, his eyes twinkling, "people usually exchange names when they run into each other, say sorry, have a little conversation, words. It's polite."

The arrogance...

Is he serious?

It's this that finally breaks through the fog of lusty feelings.

"Well, I'm not polite."

"I'm getting that." He doesn't seem deterred by my blatant disregard or rudeness. "I'll do the introductions then. I'm Jem. I'm thirty-one, a Libra, I don't like long walks in the rain, or Piña coladas, but I do love pizza and craft beer."

I wish I could ignore him, but he's determined, I'll give him that. I consider telling him to shove his introductions where the sun doesn't shine, but since I'm stranded in Kingsley and surrounded by him and his leather-clad friends, I decide this is one occasion I should probably be cautious.

I let out a huff and say, "I have no idea why you told me any of that, but I'm Piper."

His grin fades. "Wade's sister. Shit." His hand goes to the back of his neck, and I watch the muscles in his forearms when he rubs at his nape, the thick veins contracting among the ink work. "I didn't realise. You are Wade's sister, right? Luck hasn't had me run into another Piper."

"I am Josh's sister. And you are in a hospital. It's probably not the best place to try to pick up random women anyway." He looks a little sheepish. "If you don't mind, I'd like to go and find out how my brother is getting on."

I scoot around him and stop at the nurses' station, leaning on the desk. I'm acutely aware of Jem's presence at my back, although I have no idea why he followed me. The nurse's eyes come to me before flicking to the hulking man at my back.

"I'm looking for an update on Joshua Wade."

The nurse lets out an irritated breath. "As I've already told your friends, I can't give out any information."

"I'm his sister." I leave off the 'half' part. I surmise I'm likely to get information faster without explaining mine and Josh's difficult relationship.

"You can prove that, can you?" is her snippy reply. "He seems to have a lot of sisters and brothers and uncles."

"Yes, I can. Would you like a DNA sample?" I snap. "Or I can piss in a cup, if you'd prefer."

Jem snorts at my back, but I ignore him.

She flushes. "I don't think that will be necessary, do you?"

"Well, I don't know. I'm not really sure how these things work. I've never had to give DNA before."

The nurse peers at me for a moment, maybe noticing the similarities in mine and Josh's appearance for the first time. Weed said we looked alike. If this nurse has been around Josh, maybe she's noticing this, too.

"You're really his sister?"

"Yes. Josh is my brother. I'll happily prove it to you." I have no idea how, considering Curtis isn't named as my father on my birth certificate.

She sighs. "I'm done trying to work out who is related to who, and who is feeding me a line of crap to get information."

I glare at Jem. What the heck have they been saying?

Her answer frustrates me. I need to know now if Josh is still breathing. "Can you at least tell me if my brother is still alive?"

For a moment, I think she's not going to tell me anything and I prepare for an argument. Then she says, "Joshua's in a serious condition. He came out of the surgery as well as could be expected, but the damage inflicted was extensive. It's going to be a difficult recovery."

"But he's alive?"

"He's alive," she confirms. "The nursing team is monitoring him in the ICU now."

I don't expect to be so affected by hearing anything about Josh—after all, it's been a while since he and I were in each other's lives—but the relief is overwhelming.

"Thank you," I breathe out the word in a rush of air.

When I start to move away from the desk, my legs suddenly turn to jelly and threaten to give out.

A strong hand steadies me, as my knees buckle. All the stress and strain of the past few hours catch up to me and my stomach roils. It's stupid to feel this way, but I can't stop the flood of emotion.

"Easy, sweetheart," Jem's fingers tighten on my biceps, keeping me on my feet. "Do you need to sit?"

I cling to him, shaking my head, even though I'm trembling.

"He's alive..." I murmur, my voice cracking.

"Yeah, he's alive," Jem repeats and he squeezes my shoulder. "And he's going to stay that way, you hear?"

I glance at him and see the belief in his dark eyes. "You can't know that."

"I know Wade. I know he's a stubborn prick and it'll take more than a bullet to stop him. I know having you here is going to mean a shit ton to him when he wakes up."

He's wrong about that. I'm the last person Josh is going to want to see when he comes around—*if* he comes around. I should leave, but I can't. I need to know he's all right. I stare at the tiled floor and try to calm my racing heart.

"He was in surgery for hours. He's got a hole in his front

and his back. Does that sound like someone who is going to be okay?" I ramble.

"The doctors know what they're doing, Piper. They'll fix him up."

This statement hits a chord with me.

"Really? If they knew what they were doing he'd be in a hospital bed awake right now, not unconscious still."

"Just let them do their thing, okay? Trust them to do what they need to do."

I let go of him and step back, my anger flaring. "I told him this *club* would kill him one day, but I didn't think I would be right."

His dark eyes narrow at my words and I see the hurt they cause. That hurt quickly morphs into something else, something more sinister. I should have kept my mouth closed. Me and my temper. This is why I usually take that moment to think through my words before I speak. If I don't, I engage my mouth before my brain, and things are said that can't be taken back. I'm not on safe ground here and I have to be careful. These men are not friends or family. They have the ability to hurt me, and Jem isn't a kitten; he's a lion with claws. I start to walk away from him, my heart starting to race, a staccato beat building beneath my ribs. I should apologise, cram the words back into my mouth, but they stick in my throat.

Instead, I do what I always do. I run.

Unlike everyone else in my life, he doesn't let me. He seizes my arm, stopping my retreat. While his grip isn't painful, it's certainly enough to stop me pulling away, and it's more than enough to shock me into letting out a squeak. For all the turbulence I've experienced with my mother—and stepfather, Grant—over the years, she's never laid a finger on me. She's never needed to. The threat of her words has always been enough to motivate me into action.

Jem's grip is an iron band around my forearm and it's one that makes it clear I'm not moving until he's had his say.

Just as well. I'm so stunned, I can't move anyway.

"You've had a hell of a shock and that's enough to make anyone lash out." He takes a long breath and his grip on my arm loosens slightly. "I'm an easy-going kind of guy. I don't like to get worked up. It puts me in a funk I can't shake. Your situation gets you a free pass with me this once, but you spout that vitriol at any other brother and they're not going to be as forgiving as I am. Slade especially isn't as cuddly as me."

Despite his easy stance, his words snap with a warning that sends a chill racing through me. I'm far from home, alone, and with a bunch of men who consider crime all in a day's work.

He dips his head close to me and says, "The Club didn't get your brother hurt, Piper. Wade stepped between a psychopath and woman I consider to be a sister to protect her. He got shot as a result. But even if he did get hurt because of the Club, that's the way this world works. It's what he signed up for, and your brother isn't going to appreciate waking up to world war three kicking off between his sister and his brothers because you're spitting poison about it. So, take a breath, wind your neck in, and get fucking control. If you can't do that, you should leave."

I stare at him, my throat working as panic grows in my stomach. Throwing down the gauntlet at these men is not the best plan. I need to calm myself, but I'm running on emotions, and calm isn't coming, no matter how much I count back from ten.

Who does he think he is talking to me like this?

I'm not part of his idiotic club. I don't have to adhere to his rules.

I wrench my arm free from him, and I suspect I am only able to do so because he allows it.

"I need some fresh air," I mutter.

Wrapping my arms around my middle, I turn and walk away from him and the other men in the club. I can't stand to even look at them right now.

If Josh dies because of the Lost Saxons, I'm not sure what I'll do.

CHAPTER THREE

I DON'T KNOW what I expect to feel seeing Josh again, but it's not the kick to the gut I get.

My half-brother is a big man. He was huge the last time I saw him, easily standing six-foot-five, and broad, too. In the hospital bed, he looks enormous still. His legs are curled up slightly, so they don't hang over the end and his shoulders fill the trolley completely, but there's a vulnerability about him lying there helpless that I don't expect. It hits me like a sucker punch.

His bare chest is littered with tattoos that are hidden beneath gauze and wires, and a blanket is pulled up to his hips. The long hair I recall from our last meeting is ratty, having pulled loose of its tie, and I want to brush it, to tidy it. I don't know why, but that's the only thought I have as I take in the two days' worth of scruff covering his jaw and the mass of tubing and medical paraphernalia keeping him breathing.

Frozen, I stare at the bed, unsure what to do. I don't belong here. I'm not his family, not really. The waiting room outside, filled with leather-vested men and women associated with the Lost Saxons—they're his family. Jem made that clear to me when I first arrived after our run-in at the nurses' station, and nothing I've seen since I've been here has changed my opinion of this. I feel like an outsider, desperately clinging to the need to be in the inner circle. It's pure stubborn determination that has kept me here. Josh is my blood, not theirs, and I have every right to be here. That, and the need to protect him from them. Josh may not see the poison this motorcycle club brings to his life, but I need to show him, somehow—before they kill him.

But I may have lost that chance already. Josh is walking a tightrope between life and death, and I have no idea which way he will fall. The doctors give nothing away, but his Club family remains optimistic he will pull through.

I don't see how anyone can look this bad and live.

Standing at the foot of his bed, I can hardly believe the man lying there is my brother. His skin is so washed out, so grey it's nearly translucent. Everything in this room is so clinical, so unreal. Even the lighting is wrong. The lamp over the bed casts an eerie, orange glow over his face that makes him look even more sallow and sickly. There is an unnatural stillness, too. Josh hasn't moved at all in the time I've been watching him. The only sounds have come from the beeping of the machines, my own ragged breathing, and his steady mechanical ones.

Ungluing my feet from the floor, I walk slowly to him. Pausing at the bed rail, I take a moment to let my gaze wander over him. He looks different, but exactly as I remember him. He still has the scar beneath his lip, the wonky nose. Regret floods me for the time we wasted, for the angry words we exchanged that we can't take back, and may never be able to, if he doesn't pull through.

I reach out and brush his hair back from his face, hoping his eyes will flicker open. They don't.

"Hey, Josh," I say quietly. "It would be really great if you would wake up and stop worrying everyone. Mainly me. I'm not very good under stress. It really messes up my gut flora."

He doesn't stir. No surprise. He's a Wade and stubbornness is inbuilt in our DNA.

A tear escapes my eye and rolls down my left cheek, taking me by surprise. I swipe angrily at it. I swore I wouldn't get upset. I swore I would keep my emotions in check, but I can't help it. All I see is the brother I first met at eighteen, when he was in jail—a brother who was as hurt as I was. A brother I should have helped find his way.

A brother I failed.

My big brother.

He's lost to me now, and has been for a long time. The Lost Saxons own him. They have him in ways I can never have him: hook, line, and sinker. They give him things I can never give him. They give him purpose, belonging, meaning. I could never compete with that.

Sometimes, I wonder what life would have been like if Josh and I had been raised by normal parents, if Curtis hadn't been abusive. If my mother wasn't... well, my mother. If Josh hadn't joined a motorcycle club and had been a regular big brother.

What if, what if, what if...

These questions drive me crazy, circling my brain.

Josh wouldn't be lying in a hospital bed with a hole in his abdomen and back, that much I do know.

Pushing off the bed rail, I head over to the chair in the corner of the room and sink into it.

Steepling my fingers together, for the next thirty minutes, I sit there, watching, waiting.

Josh doesn't move or stir or do anything beyond the basic functions of living, although I beg the universe to bring him back to me, to give me the chance to make things right.

It doesn't.

Eventually, a nurse comes in and I'm told to go to the family waiting area, so they can take care of his medical needs.

This is a new kind of hell. The waiting room is filled with Club members and women associated with the Lost Saxons. I sit in the corner and try to block them out, try to block out everything, but it's impossible. They go out of their way to be nice to me. They bring me coffee, and not machine bought stuff from the hospital, but from a coffee shop somewhere in town. It's divine and the manners instilled in me from birth force me to show some appreciation. I can't function without a decent cup of caffeine.

At one point, one of the women brings me some magazines to pass the time and another woman brings me a phone charger, in case I need to replenish my battery. Everyone is so pleasant, it's difficult to maintain my angry front, but I still manage to keep my distance. Beneath the smiles and the charms, these people are still criminals or linked to criminals, and I need to remember that.

God, if Grant and my mother could see where I am now, they would have an apoplexy. I can imagine the fit my stepfather would throw over the damage this would do to his campaign.

Local councillors do not associate with biker gangs. Local councillors' stepdaughters do not reconcile with their criminal half-brothers either, but here I am.

Hopefully, I can get through this without alerting my stepfather and mother. I do not need the hassle. It should be easy enough; neither of them are involved in my life unless I'm needed for a 'happy family' photo shoot opportunity.

I want nothing more than to bundle my brother up and take him away from these people, to protect him from men who got him shot, but fear stops me from throwing my weight around. I don't have any power here, and I'm more than aware of the fact.

They station two men in vests outside Josh's room at all times for his protection—whatever that means. I don't know if they're protecting him from whoever shot him in the first place or from me, but fear they might stop me from seeing him (and hurt me) keeps my mouth shut. I doubt the nursing staff could stop these men from seeing my brother if I requested it. In fact, knowing Clara works in the building makes me wary of even asking it. She may not hold sway up here with the doctors, but that doesn't mean she doesn't know people in this department. Living in Grant's world has taught me valuable lessons in politicking. I know how to play the game, and I know I'm in the middle of a dangerous one right now—that I don't have any power in.

It kills me to do it, but I have to let some of his friends visit with Josh while I sit in the crappy plastic chairs in the waiting area. I may be his sister, but they have more right to him than I do. I'm the stranger here, not them. They could stop me seeing him. In fact, I'm lucky they let me in at all. I have to play things carefully if I'm going to protect him.

I feel so helpless, and this is something I'm not used to.

After a few hours, I'm unable to stomach sitting any longer. I push to my feet.

"Are you all right?" one of the women asks, concern marring her face.

"I'm just nipping to the ladies' room," I lie.

"Do you need me to come with you?"

She's so nice, and I hate that she is. It would be easier if these people were horrid.

"I'll be fine, thank you."

I head off without giving her time to argue or push, and when I'm in the corridor away from all the eyes of the Lost Saxons, I'm finally able to breathe for the first time.

Despite what I told her, I don't head for the bathroom, but I take myself down to the foyer and out into the grounds of the hospital. I need the fresh air; I need a moment alone to recalibrate and plan what to do.

I call Cami and update her on the situation—not that I have much to tell her. There's nothing happening.

"I don't know what to do, Cam," I tell her, feeling completely alone and wishing my best friend came with me. This would be easier to stomach with an ally.

"What do you want to do?" she asks as I find a bench outside the hospital main entrance and sink onto it.

"Get my brother on the first plane out of crazy town," I admit.

She snorts down the line. *"First of all, that's not logical, Piper. Your brother is an adult and whether you agree with his choices or not, this is his choice."*

I let out an irritated noise. "He's not in his sound mind. He can't be. This lifestyle—it's insane, Cami."

"You can't make him fit the mould you want him to fit."

Having experienced this with my parents, I know she's right. "I don't want him to fit my mould. I just don't want him to get shot again." I close my eyes and let out a breath. "It's not safe."

"No, Piper, it's not, but you can't live his life for him either. Just make sure he's okay and come home."

"That's the plan."

I end the call, but remain sitting on the bench, letting the world pass me by for a while, my thoughts running riot before finally slowing down.

It's late afternoon and although it's cloudy, it's fairly mild, and the warm air is a soothing change from the stifling heat inside the hospital.

I don't know why I'm here anyway. It's not like Josh cares about me or will be bothered about seeing me again. We didn't part on the best of terms, so I can't imagine him throwing out the red carpet when he wakes and sees me. I'm here for one reason only: my own peace of mind. As Cami said, all I need to do is make sure he's okay and come home.

"Jesus fucking Christ," a voice snaps to the side of me, drawing me out of my reverie.

I twist to see Jem striding towards me, his wallet chain jangling against the denim of his thick thigh. He looks every inch the biker in his leather vest, a red plaid shirt beneath, heavy motorcycle boots on his feet and ink decorating the skin I can see. His blond hair curtains his face and is offset with a scruff of beard that shouldn't look good, but does—if you like that gruff, rough look. But it's not his appearance that I'm focused on. It's his expression. His lips are drawn into a tight line, his eyes narrowed, his brow knitted together. He pulls out his phone from his jeans pocket and puts it to his ear. After a moment, he snaps into the handset, "Yeah, I've got her."

He's got me?

What the hell?

"What's going on?" I demand, my back straightening as he nears.

He looms over me, his hands dropping to his hips. I

want to stand from the bench to put us on a level playing field, but I don't dare move because the look on his face is more than a little terrifying.

"Everyone's looking for you."

They are?

"Why?"

"You went to the bathroom a half hour ago, Piper, and didn't come back," he says, his tone sharp.

I glance down at my watch and see he's right. Then I frown. "Okay, and that's a problem because...?"

I watch with fascination as his jaw clenches so tight I think he might shatter his teeth.

"You don't think it's a problem that you just disappeared after going to the bathroom?"

"I didn't disappear. I came outside for some fresh air. I didn't realise I had to give a status report every time I leave the building." My tone is more than a little sarcastic, and this might be a mistake, judging from the way his expression goes hard.

Jem's eyes go to the sky as his hands drop to his hips. Then he pins me with a piercing stare that makes my heart freeze in my chest.

"Do I need to remind you that your brother was shot in the grounds of this very hospital? That Beth was—" He breaks off, his jaw tightening further. "We brought you here, Piper. It's up to us to keep you safe *while* you're here."

I have no idea what Beth 'was', but I have heard mention of her through snippets of conversations in the waiting room, so I know she's also in the hospital with another man, Dean, and that they were hurt at the same time as Josh. No one is saying exactly what happened, but I've gleaned it had something to do with a crazy ex-husband. I haven't probed much further than that, since it's none of my business, and truthfully, I'm a little scared to know the details of what went down.

I'm also not his problem, and I don't want to be. I don't need keeping safe.

"I'm not a child. I don't need protecting or looking after by you or your Club."

I resist the urge to tell him Josh and I would be perfectly safe if his stupid Club would leave us both alone. Judging from the anger radiating off the man, I don't think it would be well received.

"Yeah, well, you don't get a say. Wade's a brother, you're his family. Until he wakes up, we'll take care of you. That means you don't disappear on a bathroom break without telling anyone where you're going."

I grit my teeth. "Did you bring me here to be a prisoner?"

The look he gives me is positively amused. "Are you insane?"

"No, but clearly you are. I can't even sit outside without giving someone an update of my movements. I haven't had to tell people where I'm going since I was fifteen, Jem."

"It's not exactly hard to just mention to someone where you're going, is it? It's a two second, 'Hey, I'm going to 'X' place. I'll be back in ten'."

It's not hard, but that's not the point. I don't need a keeper.

"Seriously? You want me to tell you every time I have to go to the bathroom or for food or for a walk?"

"Absolutely."

I stare at him. Oh my word. He's not joking. He's serious.

"You actually want me to do this?"

"Yes."

"Really?"

"Yes, Piper."

"Do you know how insane this is?" I hiss at him.

"Keeping you safe is insane?"

"Demanding a grown woman tells you her whereabouts is insane," I correct.

"Only while you're here. Once you leave town, I couldn't give a shit what you do."

This, for some reason, stings. I don't even want to think about why, because it's as crazy as what he's demanding, and what he's demanding is crazy enough. Checking in with his stupid leather-wearing bike gang is ridiculous. I can't even believe he's asking it, but talking to him is making me a little dizzied, so for the sake of my own sanity, I throw my hands in the air and say, "If it stops you from lecturing me, fine."

"I don't lecture. I helpfully point out when you're being a pain in the arse."

Affronted, but not sure I should lash out at the man who is radiating danger beneath the sexy, easy smile, I mutter, "I just wanted some fresh air."

"All you had to do was tell someone, so we don't think you've been abducted or hurt."

I stare at him. "Someone goes AWOL for thirty minutes and your first thought is abduction?" I shake my head. *What realm of existence do these people live in?* "You don't consider maybe they went for a walk or took a call? Your mind jumps first to that?"

His gaze is weighted as he studies me and I have to look away from the intensity of it.

"I get it. Our life is different from what you're used to. Hell, if I wasn't in it, if I hadn't grown up surrounded by these crazy bastards, I'd be just like you, questioning everything. But you're looking at us like we're scum for wanting to keep what's ours safe, and we're not. And if you think that about us, then you must think that about your brother."

His words hit me like a wrecking ball. Shame fills me. I don't believe Josh is a bad person, not inherently, but he has done bad things. He did go to prison, after all, and I know for a fact he wasn't innocent of the crimes he was sent down for. I know Josh's life growing up wasn't easy, but it doesn't excuse what he did. I didn't have the easiest upbringing either, and I realise how insane that sounds, given the privilege I grew up with, but it's true all the same. I didn't choose to go off the rails and break the law. I didn't get myself locked up.

I also didn't have a grown man beating me senseless every day of my life...

No, but I did have my mother to contend with—and Grant.

"I don't have to explain myself to you."

"No, you don't." Jem stares out at the car park, his expression annoyingly blank. "But you do have to explain yourself to your brother, and if that's how little you think of him, of his life, then I really don't understand why you're here. He doesn't deserve your judgement." He stands and gazes down at me. "We should get back inside. He could wake up at any time."

And without giving me time to explain myself, Jem heads towards the door.

CHAPTER FOUR

"Piper?"

The voice breaks through my haze and I open my eyes to see a mass of blonde hair in my line of sight. Clara Thomas.

The woman has been both a godsend and an irritation. As a nurse, she's been invaluable helping me with Josh's care, but she's also made it her personal mission to take care of me. It's grating on my nerves because I don't want to like these people. They're not my friends, but the way they're treating me is making my walls come down more than I would like.

I blink the last remnants of my sleep away and try to focus on her before my gaze slides to the bed. Josh is lying still, numerous wires and machines hooked up to him. He's been in the ICU for two days, but he's still not awake yet.

"Sorry, I must have nodded off." I shift in the chair. "What time is it?" The smell of antiseptic tickles my nose and I rub at it before I sneeze.

She steps back from the chair, giving me space to stretch and unfurl my legs, which are tucked up underneath me.

I'm stiff, my neck aching, and my back spasms as I move my bunched muscles for the first time in a while.

"A little after eleven o'clock. Why don't you come back to the clubhouse? I can have one of the boys find somewhere for you to sleep. You need to rest in a proper bed—not in a chair."

Go back to their clubhouse, their criminal headquarters?

Absolutely not.

I shake my head. "I want to be here when he wakes up."

Clara glances back at the bed before returning her gaze to me. "That could be a while yet."

"I don't want him to be alone when he comes around."

I have no intention of setting foot in their den of iniquity.

"He won't be alone, Piper, I promise. One of us will stay with him."

There's always someone here, so I believe her when she says this. There has been a steady stream of visitors since I've been here. I've done my best to stay out of the way of the men in vests under the guise of giving them time with my brother, but in truth, they scare me half to death.

It's bizarre that Josh has so many people who care for him while I'm alone. You'd think it would be the other way around, considering he's living in a biker cult, and I was born into privilege, but my life is far from perfect, despite how it looks on the surface. I might have the gorgeous loft apartment in the swankiest part of Manchester, a fabulous education, attend amazing events, but my life is mostly hell.

My relationship with my parents is, at best, strained; at worst, dead. I'm a commodity to them. I'm not even sure if my mum loves me. I don't know if she's even capable of love. I know this sounds dramatic, but it's true. I'm a burden to her. I always have been, and she's not afraid to tell me either, and Grant sees me as a product to pull out whenever he needs a family photograph for his campaign trail. As a local councillor, he needs to look good for the electorate. This means me and Mum need to put on our best smiles a few times a year and get our photographs taken by the media, acting as the picture-perfect family.

I push down my jealousy. I shouldn't begrudge Josh this. He grew up in hell with his father—our father, I correct. He deserves good people around him. Although, I'm not sure a motorcycle club qualifies, but at least they're here. Curtis, I notice, is not. I did wonder if he would be, but I suppose it's just as well he's not. I'm not sure our first ever meeting should be in a hospital room while his firstborn is dying.

"I'm fine here," I tell her, keeping my resolve.

Hell will freeze over before I go back to their clubhouse.

"But thank you," I add. I don't want to seem impolite.

Clara considers me for a moment. "Your brother is well liked in the Club."

"I can see that," I say, not sure where she's going with this.

"He's got a lot of people who love him." Clara moves over to the side of his bed and glances down at him. "And part of us loving him means taking care of the people who matter to him. That means we want to take care of you, too."

Internally, I flinch at her words. I don't think I do matter to him.

"I know you're scared to leave Wade's side, but you're no good to him if you're dead on your feet. You need to be rested, Piper, so that when he does wake, you're strong enough to help him. Wade's going to have a long and difficult road ahead."

I swallow hard. She's wrong about everything, about me, about what I am to him.

"I'm not leaving," I repeat.

She stares at me, then scowls. "I didn't think they could make anyone more stubborn than Wade. I was wrong. You're even worse."

"Then you probably should stop arguing. You're not going to win."

"At least get something to eat."

"I'm not hungry."

"Piper, you haven't eaten in hours. We can't have you wasting away to nothing."

I haven't. I can't even remember the last meal I ate.

"I'm fine." My stomach grumbles, betraying me, and her brow arches. "If someone could get me something, so I can stay with Josh..."

It's rude, I know, but I don't want to leave his side.

She gives me a patient look before she shakes her head. "You've been sitting in that chair for nearly twenty-five-hours. You need a break. I'm sorry. For your own sake, you're leaving the room, even if I have to ask one of the lads to put you over their shoulder and carry you out."

I give her a look. "You wouldn't dare."

"Wouldn't I?"

"This isn't the nineteen-fifties. I'm capable of looking after myself."

"I know you are, but you're not." She sighs. "If you won't go somewhere to sleep, you can at least take half an hour out to grab something to eat."

I'm sure the look I fire at her is laced with daggers. She doesn't seem affected by it, though. "You're incredibly bossy, do you know that?"

"You'll get over it. Come on."

I think about arguing more, but I'm not sure she won't carry out her threat, so I relent. The thought of one of those big men carrying me out of the room is enough to get me moving.

"Fine."

I snag my jacket off the back of the chair and slip my feet into my shoes, giving my brother a final glance. I don't want to leave him, but Clara's right. I need to eat, and I need to move. My neck is a giant knot.

"Will someone stay with him?"

"Yeah, I'll wait with him." When I don't immediately move, she says, "He'll be fine for half an hour, Piper. You need to look after you, too."

I do. I don't know why I'm being so intense. Guilt, I suppose. I walked away, and now he could die. I might never get to tell him how sorry I am for what happened between us. Fear keeps me locked to his bedside, which is ridiculous and irrational, but I can't stop it.

I let her push me out of the room. With no choice, I wander down to the lift and take it to the ground floor. I don't head to the cafeteria, as I told Clara I would, but instead head outside and find an empty bench overlooking the hospital grounds.

I call Cami.

"It's good to hear your voice," she says immediately. *"I was starting to get worried. How are things?"*

"Josh is still out of it, but he came out of the surgery all right. It's just a case of wait and see now."

"Bloody hell, that's vague. Do you want me to see if I can sort some private medical care for him?"

Camille Neville, ever the do-gooder.

"He's getting good treatment here, I think."

"Well, if you want private care just let me know, darling. It can be arranged."

"Thanks."

"How's things with the leather-clad posse?"

I snort at her choice of words. "Fine. They're friendly enough. A little too friendly really. I'm trying not to get embroiled. They seem to want to mother me because I'm Josh's family."

"That's a good thing, isn't it? At least they're not trying to smother you, right?"

This makes me laugh. "I guess."

Cami sighs down the line. *"Just stick around long enough to do what you have to for closure with Josh. No one's saying you have to swear into their little society."*

A loud rumbling sound catches my attention and I twist on the bench in time to see a motorcycle pull into the hospital car park. I can't help but watch as it moves. There is a certain beauty in the fluidity of it as it turns into the bike park area.

"Yes, that's all I'm here for—my brother. I have no intention of making friends with these people," I murmur into the phone, watching as the bike comes to a stop and the engine cuts.

I've not yet come to recognise the men of the Club, but I'm sure from the stature the rider is Jem. When the helmet is removed, I'm proved right, and I don't even want to know how I knew this—especially considering I've seen the man all of twice, and every interaction I've had with him has been negative. Our last one in particular.

I don't approve of Josh's life, this is true, but I don't think my brother is a horrible person—despite what Jem clearly believes.

I shift on the bench, feeling twitchy suddenly. I wonder

if I can run inside before he sees me. The last thing I want to do is get into another argument with the man.

He kicks down the stand on the bike and attaches his helmet to the back, before running his fingers through his hair in a movement that would be attractive on someone less annoying.

"Are you still there, darling? Did I lose you?"

I start at the voice in my ear. "Sorry, what?"

"Oh, I thought I'd lost the signal," Cami says.

"Possibly. I am in the back of beyond."

She grunts into the phone. *"You're in Yorkshire. Hardly the arse end of nowhere, Piper."*

"It may as well be," I mutter as I watch Jem straighten his vest and start up the path toward the hospital entrance, towards me. He glances back at his motorcycle once, before continuing—right towards me. Bugger. "Uh, Cam, I've got to go. I'll call you later, okay? If my parents drop by—"

"I'll tell them you're at a yoga retreat," she interrupts.

I don't bother to tell her how ridiculous that lie is. I'm not a fan of exercise, which my parents both know. My mother has tried, numerous times, to get me to do it. She comments often on my weight.

I don't get a chance, though. Cami hangs up before I can say anything.

I barely manage to stuff my phone back into my bag before a shadow is looming over me. When I glance up, Jem is standing over me.

"You really do have a hard time paying attention, don't you?" The growl in his voice reverberates through me.

"Not at all," I tell him, keeping my tone pleasant. "I'm actually fairly good at doing as I'm told."

"Then what the fuck are you doing out here?"

I glance around the flower pots and benches lining the small garden area I'm sitting in.

"Well, I was enjoying some peace and quiet," I fire back at him.

"Alone?"

"I wasn't aware I needed a bodyguard every time I step foot outside."

"Did we not go over the shooting thing?" He sounds annoyed. I can't really blame him for that. I did ignore him when he said this, but I don't want to be followed around. I don't even have this with Grant, and he's in local government, which does make him a target of threats at times.

"It wasn't me who got shot at, Jem. I'm not the one in danger."

He stares at me as if I have two heads. "No, but you've been seen with the Club."

My brows arch into my hairline at his words. "So, my coming here put a target on my back? That's phenomenal."

"I didn't say that."

"Actually," I push up from the bench, snatching my bag and jacket before I start towards the entrance, "that's exactly what you said. I knew it was a mistake to come here."

He lets me take two paces before he snags my arm and stops me in my tracks. His touch is like fire radiating through my entire body, and I feel him everywhere.

"Jesus Christ, I didn't say someone was going to take pot-shots at you from the fucking shrubberies, Piper, but things aren't exactly level around here still. The last thing I want is for the first thing Wade hears when he wakes up is that his sister's in a bed next to him."

His words send a chill racing through me.

I tear my arm free from Jem, and scorch him with a

look. My chest is heaving, and not entirely from fear. The man is huge, and he is scary, but he's also annoyingly attractive. I'm not immune to the fact that he looks like he stepped off the pages of a sexy bad boy calendar, but right now, my fury overtakes the tingles working through my pelvis.

"I'd appreciate it if you'd stop trying to handle me every time we have a conversation."

"And I'd really appreciate it if you'd stop acting like such a bitch when all I'm trying to do is keep you safe! This isn't a joke, Piper. This shit's dangerous. People nearly died —your brother among them."

His words annoy me. I roll to my toes, getting into his face, which might not be the smartest thing to do, but God, he's an arse!

"I don't need you to keep me safe. I don't want you to keep me safe either. I don't want anything from you or your Club. All I want is to see my brother, make sure he's well and get back to my life."

He dips his head closer to mine. "Believe me, princess, I'd like nothing more than for you to get back to your life, too."

I open my mouth to respond, bitter words sitting on my tongue, ready to spit out, when a male voice interrupts us.

"Is this man bothering you, Miss?"

I snap my head to the side in the direction it comes from, ignoring the muttered curse from under Jem's breath. A chill runs through me as I take in the man standing next to us, watching our argument take place.

He's around Jem's age and wearing a black suit that is without a doubt tailored to fit him and not off the rack. I suspect this is to do with his size, rather than out of any desire or status because his shoes are not new nor expensive.

His hair is a messy brown thatch that isn't wild, but it certainly doesn't look like he's styled it to look this way.

He also carries himself with an air of authority that suggests he's a man used to being complied with.

I don't know why, but something tells me to tread carefully here. This is compounded when Jem stiffens, and the air goes heavy with tension as the man takes me in with one glance. It's not salacious, merely curious. It's a look that sees too much in one sweep, that makes me feel undressed, although not sexually. I feel as if this man unveils all my secrets with a glance. It's unnerving.

Particularly since I have no idea who he is.

Without meaning to, I move closer to Jem. Seeking comfort, assurance, protection—I'm not sure which—but considering his earlier words, I can't help but sidle nearer in case this stranger means me harm. Jem obliges, tucking me behind him, and the man's shrewd eyes narrow as he takes this in.

"Don't you have things to do, Morgan?" Jem demands, sounding irritated. I'm not sure if it's a good thing that Jem knows him or not. "I'm sure there are grannies out there that need help crossing the road, babies that have candy to be found..."

The man—Morgan—ignores him, his eyes gliding towards me.

"Is he bothering you?" he asks me again.

I say asks in the loosest sense of the word. It's a demand, one that I've heard before from the mouths of big business men—CEOs and heads of government departments.

Who is this guy?

I tip my head up to look at Jem, who meets my gaze but doesn't say anything. He keeps his face impassive, waiting to see what I'll do, what I'll say. This is a test of sorts, although I'm not sure what I'm being tested on. All I know is better the devil you know, right?

"No," I say finally. "He's not."

My answer doesn't seem to please Morgan, but Jem beams.

"There you have it," Jem says. "You've done your civic duty, protected yet another damsel. You can be on your merry way now." I resent being referred to as a damsel, but I surmise it's better to keep this to myself, particularly when Jem bends at the waist and leans towards Morgan, retorting, "In other words, fuck off."

Morgan sniffs, his lip curling at Jem. "I'm here to talk to Mr Wade about what happened in the parking garage."

At these words, my own spine snaps straight. I have no idea where it comes from, but the urge to protect my brother rises in me like a tidal wave.

"Absolutely not," I tell him.

His eyes cut to me. "And you are?"

"His sister." I bristle at his tone.

"I wasn't aware he had one. Your name?"

His tone rubs me the wrong way. Who is this obnoxious arse?

"And who are you? Why do you need or want to speak to him?"

"Detective Chief Inspector Alexander Morgan. Kingsley Police."

He flips out an identification badge, as if this is supposed to impress me. It doesn't, although it does send a slight tendril of anxiety through me. I've never been in trouble before, so having a police officer in my space is a little concerning.

Jem doesn't seem to have this same problem.

"You don't have to tell this fucker anything," Jem says to

me, his hand on my arm gently squeezing—reassuring me or warning me to guard my words, I'm not sure which.

Morgan narrows his eyes.

"Why wouldn't you want to talk to me about what happened? You want to catch who shot Mr Wade, right?"

"I make it a habit not to talk to the police," Jem responds, sounding bored. "You never know what may be used against you in a court of law."

Morgan shakes his head. "There's been a run of bad luck going around your club in the past few weeks, Mr Harlow. People seem to be getting shot or beaten all over the place."

"It certainly does seem that way, doesn't it?" Jem's words are clipped, his smile practised, although forced. "Shouldn't you be out there catching the bad guys, rather than talking shit at me? I'm surprised you haven't caught who did it yet, given it happened in a public place. Did it need to happen in the middle of the police station? Would that have helped?"

My eyes flare at his words before flicking back to Morgan. He doesn't seem remotely perturbed, but he doesn't back down either from Jem.

"It's funny how all this shit swirling around my town seems to be centred around you and your club."

"*Our* town," Jem corrects. "Kingsley's not your town, Morgan. That's your first mistake. This is Saxons territory and it'll always be Saxons territory."

"Not for much longer." The threat in his words lingers in the air.

Jem just shrugs. "Bigger pricks than you have tried and failed to take us down. Come at us if you want. We'll enjoy the ride."

"Don't worry, I fully intend to come at you and unlike my predecessors, I have no intention of missing my target."

I have the distinct impression I've stepped into the middle of something bigger than I understand, but I do know one thing. This man wants to bring harm to the Club, and my brother is in that Club—at least for now. Until I can untangle him from there, I'll do what I have to in order to protect him, even if that means keeping him safe from the police.

"Your brother, Miss Wade, will need to give a statement."

I don't correct him on the fact I'm not a Wade, but an Ellis. It's probably not a good idea to have my name out there, given it could get back to Grant.

"You're not talking to him," I tell him. "Not like this. He's been through enough without you treating him badly."

"You don't have a choice. This is an active investigation. I need to know what he knows."

"Well, unless you can communicate with him while he's unconscious, you'll have a hard job. You can speak to him when his doctors say he's fit and able and not a second before. And when you do finally talk to him, DCI Morgan, you might want to keep in mind that my brother is the victim here and treat him accordingly, do you understand?"

He stares at me for a long moment, taking me in, then says, "You're not local."

Unease ripples through me. I should abort this conversation immediately. The last thing I need is for it to get back to Grant that I'm here, but DCI Morgan isn't going to be easily deterred.

"No, I'm not."

"Where're you from?"

"None of your business. Just do your job. I'd hate to

have to seek legal counsel for harassment." I don't have a legal team, but I'll call Cami and sort one if need be; I'm sure she knows solicitors. I won't be bullied. I turn to Jem. "Come on, let's go back inside."

Jem grins at Morgan. "Catch you later, DCI Dickhead."

I snag his arm and tug him away, worried we might get arrested if he continues being obnoxious.

Once we're out of earshot, Jem says, "Legal counsel?"

I wince, biting my lip. "He pissed me off. I just said the first thing that came into my head."

His brow arches. "Do you have a legal team?"

"No, but I'll get one."

He looks at me, and for the first time since I met him, his eyes go soft. "You don't need to worry about legal shit, Piper. The Club's got that stuff covered, but it was good seeing you stick up for your brother."

Of course they have legal stuff covered. They probably have a whole legal team on retainer for all the law breaking they do.

"Obviously I stuck up for Josh," I say quietly. "Despite what you think, I care about him."

"Yeah, I'm starting to see that." He pushes his hair out of his face. "You handled DCI Dickhead like a pro. I'm guessing that wasn't your first run in with the police."

Offended, I say, "That absolutely was my first run in with police. Unlike you, I'm not a delinquent."

"Really?" His brows climb up his forehead. "Okay, I'm surprised, and maybe a little turned on—"

I turn fully to him. "Do not finish that sentence!"

He grins. "It was a little hot."

"It was not." I glance at my hands, which are trembling. "That man is horrible."

"Yeah, he doesn't like us much."

"Well, if he's dealt with you, I can understand why."

Jem folds his arms over his chest. "You really know how to strike a cutting blow."

I roll my eyes. "You'll survive."

"Barely. You might need to kiss my wounds better."

My nose wrinkles. "I can't think of anything I'd like to do less." This is a lie. Jem is easy on the eyes and kissing him wouldn't be a chore, as long as he didn't speak. "I don't care about your pissing contest with the police, Jem. That's not why I did it. I'm just looking out for Josh, that's all."

He stares at me and then says, "That's all we're doing—taking care of Wade. You open your eyes, Piper, you'll see that."

CHAPTER FIVE

It's around the fifty-three-hour mark when Josh shows the first sign of waking. In fact, he scares me half to death. He opens his eyes for about a few seconds, staring at me from across the room before he goes back out. I nearly bolt out of my chair.

For the next few hours, he fights the drugs, but doesn't manage to come-to fully or coherently. Clara and Sofia urge me to go to the hotel and sleep, but I refuse. I doze in the chair at the side of his hospital bed instead. I want to be here when he wakes properly. It'll be soon, I know it.

The nursing staff try to get me to leave. I refuse them as well, and the Club comes in useful. They don't let them kick me out. I don't know what the heck Ghost says to them or the security staff who are sent to remove me, but I'm left in peace.

"Piper..."

I jolt at the sound of my name, and expect to see Clara or one of the guys. The room's empty.

My gaze snaps to the bed. Josh's eyes are open and

they're locked on me. He's awake, and he looks more alert than he has any other time.

I scramble off the chair, nearly tripping over my own feet in my haste, my heart pounding.

"Josh? Oh my God, you're awake. How do you feel?"

He grimaces, and that small act looks as if it costs him his last reserves of energy.

"Sore."

I can see the question in his eyes, the question he's dying to ask: why am I here? I want to explain, to tell him I'm sorry for how we left things, but now isn't the time for that. He needs a doctor and he needs to be taken care of.

I reach for the call button over the head of the bed.

"What're you doing?" he questions, and I don't miss the way his voice cracks.

"Calling for the doctor. You just woke up from major surgery. You need to be looked at."

He ignores this, or maybe he doesn't want to hear it yet, and instead asks, "How long was I out?"

I consider lying to him. I don't want to stress him out when he's just come around, but I don't think it's a good idea to start our first meeting on a lie.

"About sixty hours, give or take. You've woken up a few times since you came back from theatre, but you haven't been particularly coherent until now."

I see the ripple of shock cross his face, and I wish I'd withheld the truth. A number of other emotions play across his face that I can't read, that maybe I would be able to read if I knew him better. The fact is I don't. He's as much a stranger to me as the men outside the room are.

The doctor breezes in and I step back to give him space to work, watching as he examines Josh, checking his vitals and that the pain relief is working. Josh seems with it, although tired, asking him questions about his condition, about his long-term prognosis.

His eyes flicker in my direction now and again as he talks to the doctor and I wonder what is going through his mind. I wonder if this is the end of the road for us. Am I about to be asked to leave?

I knew there was a possibility Josh might demand I go the moment he clapped eyes on me. I'm not surprised this could be on the cards.

Disappointed? Yes, but certainly it wouldn't be unexpected.

I came and did what I intended to do, which was make sure he was okay. Would I like to rebuild bridges? Sure. But his loyalty will always be first and foremost to the Club, and while that is the case, I don't see how we can rebuild anything. I can never be involved with that lifestyle.

"What about riding?" I hear him demand. "When can I ride again?"

I can't help it. I scoff at this remark. He's lying in a hospital bed after being unconscious for nigh on sixty hours and all he can think about is his stupid motorcycle club?

"Mr Wade, there was a lot of internal damage you're not going to bounce right back from." The doctor sounds irritated as he says this, and I don't blame him. Him and his team spent hours upon hours saving Josh's life just for him to be this obtuse.

"But I will bounce back, right?" Josh pushes.

My stubborn idiotic brother...

"I can't say for sure, Mr Wade."

"But you can guess."

"I—"

"I just need to know what to expect."

The doctor glances down as his hands go into the pockets of his lab coat. "This is highly unethical."

Not to mention ludicrous. This doctor has more patience than me. I want to wring my brother's neck right now. What does riding matter? What does his Club matter? He nearly died.

"Then be unethical."

His mouth turns down. "Providing things continue as they are and you rest up the required amount of time needed to heal successfully, then I don't see why not. Additional surgery will complicate matters, but we'll cross that bridge when we get to it."

Josh drops his head back against the pillows and closes his eyes. The relief in the gesture and his next words hits me squarely in the chest. "Thank fuck."

I knew the Club meant a lot to him, but hearing him say it like that makes my guts twist unpleasantly. It's the realisation that I can never compete with that level of commitment. I'll never mean that much to him. I knew that anyway, I knew it by the way he left me behind years ago, but seeing his reaction right now is painful.

I wait for the doctor to finish up, ignoring their conversation as my thoughts turn dark.

Coming here was a mistake.

Watching the doctor leave the room, I consider following him, but my irritation gets the better of me. The good old Wade temper flares. I wait for the door to close before I turn to the bed.

"You're lying in a hospital bed with a hole in your abdomen and your back, and all you care about is that bloody motorcycle?"

"I can't be in the Club if I can't ride." His response annoys the hell out of me, and a bitchy remark sits on the tip of my tongue, until I see how heavy his eyes are. He's struggling to stay awake. Even if he wasn't, what would be the point of blasting him? The Lost Saxons have always meant more to him than his own flesh and blood. I've never mattered to him. No amount of screaming and shouting will change that.

All the fight leaves me.

"What're you doing here, Piper?"

His tone pisses me off and I scowl, crossing my arms over my chest.

"It's good to see you too, you bloody arsehole."

His expression softens a little and I see the regret at his words.

Good. You should feel bad, you bastard. I dropped everything to sit at your bedside for the past few days.

"You didn't need to come all this way."

I didn't. I still don't know why I did.

"You're lying in a hospital bed in intensive care. Of course I had to come." I don't mention the fact it's my own guilt that drove me to be here, that I'm here for partly my own selfish reasons.

He stares at me a beat, and I wonder what he's thinking. He gives nothing away, his face as blank as a slab of granite. Even in the short time I did get to know Josh, I could never read him. I think he got so used to hiding every emotion from Curtis growing up that he's never outwardly shown anything. Now is no different. Even under the pull of the drugs they're pumping into him he's a closed book.

I can understand this; I'm no different. My mother taught me that emotions are a weakness. They can be exploited.

"Are any brothers waiting out there?" His words roll

into each other, the drugs affecting his speech as they take hold of him once more.

"If by 'brothers' you mean the Neanderthals wearing leather vests, then yes. They've been hanging around since I got here."

This probably isn't the politest thing to say, and considering how nice most of them have been to me, I feel bad, but I'm also angry that he's treating me like little more than shit on his shoe to be scraped off. I know we didn't part on the best of terms, but I'm here now, making an effort. That should count for something, right?

The tension in Josh's face eases. "Good. I need to talk to one of them."

Is he serious? I haven't seen him in nearly three years. This is the first meeting we've had, and he wants to see one of his friends?

Disappointment floods me, mixed with anger. I shouldn't be either. I have no right to either emotion. Did I really expect my brother to just open his arms to me, to welcome me back into his life like nothing has changed?

I suppose, naïvely, I did.

What a fool I am.

"What you need to do, Joshua, is rest. You've been out of it for days, you have a hole in your gut, and you are currently being held together with stitches. Your little pow-wow with your friends can wait."

The look he shoots me makes me recoil. For someone who just woke up fully from life-saving surgery, it's a look that promises more anger than he has any right to deliver. I shouldn't be surprised. I've come into his life and turned my nose up at it. I'd be defensive if he'd done the same to mine. If he was rude to Cami, I'd outright slap his face. Still, that doesn't mean I'm going to back down. It's not in me to roll over and play nice.

"You can be pissed off at me, Piper, but you don't disrespect the Club, you hear me?"

"It's bad enough that you joined them, but don't expect me to roll over and play nice. They're your friends, not mine."

He closes his eyes for a moment, seeking patience maybe. I've seen Grant do the same thing many times over the years, before he says, "Piper, I mean it. You don't disrespect them—or me in front of them."

He's serious. Old feelings resurface and for a brief moment, I consider telling him to get screwed, but I keep my tongue in check—barely.

"Fine. I'll behave." I don't say the 'for now' but it certainly hangs silently in the air between us.

I watch as he tugs on the blanket pooled around his hips. For such a large man to appear so weak is concerning. This knocks the anger out of me. He nearly died, and I need to remember this fact. I could have lost this chance to talk to him again. My emotions are all over the place. I'm conflicted and confused, but I'm glad he's awake and alive, even if I feel a little flash of irritation towards him.

I don't know if he'll welcome the help or tell me to leave him alone, but I can't watch him struggle any longer. I move towards him and help him settle the blankets up his bandaged chest.

"Thanks," he mumbles before he slides his heavy gaze towards me. "How did you know I was here? In the hospital, I mean."

"One of your friends—Weed—called me. What kind of name is that, Josh? Weed? Jesus," I mutter, unable to help myself. "Anyway, he called and said you were in the hospital and that it was serious. What was I going to do? Say thank you very much and go about my business? He was kind of pushy about having me picked up, though. Insistent, really, even though I said I could drive myself."

"I wouldn't have blamed you if you'd said fuck it, given how things have been between us."

Shame and guilt wash through me. I had thought this. It was only Cami's insistence that put my bum in Charlie's car. Without her, I don't think I would have come, and I would have regretted it.

But it means Josh shouldn't be looking at me like I made some huge gesture. I didn't. It was only sitting at his bedside, watching him sleep, wondering if he would wake up, that gave me the time to think. Now that I am here, I want to try to fix things.

Maybe candour is the key. Maybe I should just be honest.

"Yes, well, I shouldn't have stayed away so long. That call... it about knocked ten years off my life. I realised we wasted a lot of time together. I know we can't fix everything between us, but maybe we can try to repair some of the cracks."

I hate how small my voice sounds. How much it trembles when I speak. Will he want that? Does he want me here?

He surprises me by reaching over the bed rail and seizing my hand. I freeze, momentarily stunned, swallowing hard. I feel a weight lift off my shoulders as I realise he's not pissed off I'm here. He's actually glad to see me.

Relief floods me and chokes me.

"I'd like that," he tells me, and I can see the sincerity in his words, in his face.

Don't cry, don't cry.

I sniff, my head lowering to stare at our joined hands as a shaky breath rips out of me. "I'm glad you're okay, Josh."

"I'm glad I'm okay, too." He lets out a low breath. "I hate to cut this short, Piper, but I don't know how long I'm going to stay awake. I need to talk to one of the brothers before I crash back out. Can you get one for me?"

Is he serious? No, he must be joking. We're having a moment, a fairly big moment and he's just taken a giant dump all over it.

I stare at him. "But you just woke up."

He doesn't waver, even though his eyes are still drug-heavy.

"Yeah."

"Don't you think you should rest?"

"I will. After I talk to a brother." He juts his chin to the door. "Now, Piper."

I sigh dramatically, because if I don't I'm going to break down into tears or I'm going to unleash a tirade of anger on him. Since he just woke up from being shot, I'm not sure either responses are appropriate.

"Fine."

I head for the door, disbelief swirling around my brain, as I step into the corridor. Ghost is sitting in a chair opposite the door. To my dismay, Jem is leaning against the wall next to him. Doesn't he have things to do? Crimes to commit? Places to be that are far from me?

His eyes, which were locked on the ceiling, lower to me as I exit. The way they rove over me does funny things to my belly. Why do I feel as if he's undressing me with his eyes?

"He wants to speak to one of you." I address Ghost, though my gaze darts to Jem as I speak.

And, yes, he's still staring at me.

"He's awake?" Ghost asks, his gruff voice intimidating.

I nod. "And happy as a clam about it."

Jem pats Ghost's chest. "Why don't you go and see how our brother is doing? I'll take Piper down to the canteen while you're busy."

Uh... what? Spending time with Jem is not high on my to-do list. The man induces a headache.

"Why don't you go and talk to Josh instead?" I demand.

Not that I have any desire to spend time with Ghost. Frankly, the man scares me half to death, but any time with Jem is likely to result in jail time.

Jem shrugs. "Wade just woke up. Let's not torture him with me just yet."

That we can both agree on. Jem is torture.

Even so...

"I don't need an escort, Jem."

"Good thing I'm not providing one."

"But you're coming with me?"

He shrugs. "I'm hungry."

"Fucking hell," Ghost mutters, his patience clearly reaching the end of his non-existent tether. "You two are irritating as fuck."

He pushes into the room, taking the choice away. I stare at the door for a long moment, willing him to return.

He doesn't.

I glare at Jem, who is grinning stupidly at me.

"I'm capable of being on my own for ten minutes while I eat, but if you want to tag along, I can't stop you."

"Well, thanks for making a guy feel welcome."

"You're not welcome."

"I got that message loud and clear."

"Good."

I head for the lifts, trying to ignore him.

"You really don't like me much, do you?" he says.

"I met you just over two days ago. I don't even know you."

Stabbing the lift call button, I don't look at him as he stands next to me.

"I'm a lot of fun."

"I doubt that."

"I really am. You'd like me if you got to know me."

I blow out a breath and step into the lift when the doors slide open. He follows me inside and steps closer as a few other people get in, too. I try not to think about his proximity to me, but this is not easy. I can feel the heat coming off him and I can smell his aftershave from here. I must smell half dead. I've alternated between Josh's room and the family waiting area. My eyes are like sandpaper and my back has knots that no chiropractor is ever going to fix. I've been using the small bathroom at the end of the hall to wash in, but I could use a proper shower.

Jem places a hand on the small of my back, and steers me out of the lift when the doors open on the ground floor. His touch is warm and inviting, and I don't want to think about how much I like it on me, or how much I miss its loss when he removes it.

When he leads me into the hospital canteen, he grabs a tray from the stack and says, "Get whatever you want."

I don't really know what I feel like eating, but I pick up a sandwich and a few other things, placing them on the tray he's holding. People stare at Jem, which makes me incredibly uncomfortable, like a fish in a bowl, but he doesn't seem to notice or care. He's like a child, picking things up and examining them before putting them back down. He can't seem to help but touch everything. I want to tell him to stop, but I barely know him and he's more than a little intimidating, so I hold my tongue.

He also flashes smiles at every single woman we cross paths with, as if he can't stop the flirting. It's like a reflex action. It's annoying. In fact, nearly everything about this man gets under my skin.

When we come to pay for the food, he refuses to allow me to part with any money. I would argue about being independent, but I'm too exhausted.

When he leads me over to a table and orders me to sit, he offloads all my food in front of me. I realise at this moment, all Jem bought for himself is a bottle of water.

"Aren't you eating?"

"I'm not hungry."

"You said you were," I accuse.

"I changed my mind."

My brow arches. "You changed your mind?"

"Yep." He pops the 'P' loudly.

"Between here and upstairs, you changed your mind?"

"Yep."

I let out a frustrated growl. "So, are you just going to watch me eat?"

"I wasn't planning on it." His eyes narrow. "Why? Do you want me to?"

"No. That would be weird."

"I thought you might have a strange food fetish." My gaze snaps to his face, and he holds up his hands defensively. "It's not for me to judge how others live. Different strokes for different folks and all that. Food isn't my thing, though—not with sex. Far too messy."

I'm certain I'm blushing tomato red, and he gives me a lazy grin.

"I've embarrassed you."

This seems to amuse him.

"I don't think it's appropriate to talk about this stuff when my brother is lying upstairs hooked up to God knows how many machines, do you?"

He sobers a little. "No, probably not, but humour in the face of adversity is the best medicine."

This is kind of poignant, and I doubt it's something he thought up himself.

"Says who?"

"Me. And probably someone smart. Besides, your brother is awake now and that means he'll be back to his usual grumpy self in no time. Order will restore itself to the universe and you can go back to your high-flyer life and forget you slummed it for a time."

Ouch.

His words sting, even though he says them with a smile.

I fiddle with my food, trying to think how best to combat this.

Finally, I settle for being honest. "I don't think I'm slumming it, Jem."

"No?"

"No."

His eyes are piercing as he takes me in and I want to shift under his scrutiny. Behind the smiles, this man sees too much and knows more than he says.

"But you refuse to stay at the clubhouse, refuse the hospitality offered by the women of the Club, treat them like shit when they're trying to help you."

Heat infuses my cheeks. I did refuse to stay at the clubhouse, and for good reason. I have no intention of getting caught up in drug-fuelled orgies. Besides, if the media finds out I'm running around with a biker gang, it will ruin

Grant's reputation, and my stepfather will murder me—right after my mother kills me.

Even so, I bristle at his accusation, even if he's mostly right. "I haven't treated anyone like shit, Jem. I don't know any of you well enough to treat any of you badly."

I have purposely avoided talking to anyone long enough to get to know them, though, which is probably worse.

He leans forward on the table and says, "Precisely. I'd love to untangle those knickers of yours, angel. They're twisted into one big fucking sad knot." His words make the apex between my thighs dampen, and I have no idea why. Maybe it was the talk of my underwear or the use of 'angel', but when he sits back again and considers me, his arm draping lazily over the back of the seats, my heart rate kicks up a notch. "You don't laugh a lot, do you?"

"I don't really have much reason to laugh right now. Brother... in the ICU... at death's door. You do remember that, right?"

"I don't have a memory problem, sweetheart. I haven't forgotten, but in case you have, let me remind you of the details. Wade's one of my best friends. He's like blood to me, Piper, but crying over him isn't going to change things. It isn't magically going to heal him or bring him back to health. All we can do is carry on and hope he pulls through. I'm not going to spend however long that takes dragging my fucking jaw around on the floor like some sad depressed bastard."

In a weird way, I almost understand where he's coming from, but for God's sake it's only been a few days. Can I not have a little time to feel sorry about the situation?

I huff out a breath. "Are you always like this?"

"Like what?"

"Joking around? Insensitive. A first-class wanker."

A highly attractive first-class wanker. I shut that thought down.

He shrugs. "Life's too short to take it seriously. And for the record, I'm plenty sensitive."

I pick up my sandwich and start to eat it. Arguing with him is fruitless, given his level of delusion. The man is infuriating.

After a moment of feeling like an animal being watched from behind a glass wall, I scowl at him.

"If you would like to know, my reasons for not staying at the clubhouse are not what you think."

"Oh?" He brushes his blond hair back from his face.

"My stepfather is a local councillor, Jem. If the media even get wind I'm here it would ruin his precious reputation and he will drown me in the River Trent. I can probably damage control a hospital visit, but staying at the clubhouse... there's no way to control that. The headlines will be savage."

This is mostly a lie. I don't want to stay there because I don't like his stupid little Club, but I'm also aware my brother said I need to show respect to these people, and Jem is looking at me like a wounded puppy. A little embellishment of the truth won't hurt if it removes that expression.

Besides, it isn't entirely a lie. I don't doubt Grant would remove me from the equation if I was harming his election campaign. I'm certain I mean less to him than his position in government—despite the fact he's been in my life since I was six-years-old.

"Fair enough, but that offer stands anytime you need it. The clubhouse is always there for you."

I force a smile. "Thank you."

"You don't have to say thank you, Piper. Wade's Club. That makes you family."

Great. Just what I need—to be in an outlaw Club's inner circle.

"You don't have to sit with me. I'm more than capable of eating a sandwich on my own."

He doesn't make a move to leave the table. He sinks lazily back against the chair.

"I'm sure you are."

"Yet you're still sitting here like a guard dog, watching my every move."

"Unfortunately, no matter what my thoughts are on the matter, your brother might consider you precious cargo. Until Wade says otherwise, the Club's going to do everything in its power to keep you safe—whether or not we should."

"What does that mean?"

"Nothing."

This response infuriates me. I place my sandwich back on the tray and give him my full attention.

"If you have something to say, then say it."

"I'm just not sure what your play is here, sweetheart. You clearly don't like the Club or your brother's lifestyle. You haven't been in his life for a long time after turning your back on him, yet you're here, playing the doting sister. I don't get it. I want to know if you're here meaning him harm. I want to know if I need to protect my brother."

My heart freezes in my chest at his words. I have no idea what Josh has told these people about me, but clearly, they seem to think I'm the bad guy here. I got the impression when I first arrived that Josh had said very little about me, but obviously conclusions have been made.

I clasp my hands together on the table. "Wow, okay then. You seem to have made a lot of assumptions there."

"I don't think I've assumed anything. You do hate the Club."

"Yeah, I hate the Club," I agree and watch as his jaw tightens and his body snaps straight. "For good reason, Jem. You took my brother from me."

"We didn't take anyone. Wade came to us."

"You see me as the bad guy," I tell him, "but despite what you seem to think, Josh isn't exactly innocent in all this. I wasn't the only one who let things get this bad between us."

"I never said he was."

"You all act as if it was me who did the dirty on him, as if it was me who left him." I lean over the table. "He's not the one who was left alone, Jem. He's not the one who was left behind. It was me. I was drowning. I needed my big brother to step up for me, and he was more interested in running off and joining a biker club."

Heat rises in my neck, settling in my cheeks. I clamp my mouth shut, realising I've said more than I should. The past is the past, and I'm not about to drudge it up with a near-perfect stranger, but Jem is looking at me with shrewd eyes that suggest he's not about to let this go.

"What do you mean?"

Bugger.

"It really doesn't matter, Jem. What matters is we both messed up, and all we can do now is rebuild what we destroyed."

"Piper, why did you need your brother?" he presses, and I have to admit the look he's directing my way is a little intense.

"Look, just trust me when I tell you I'm not here to cause problems for Josh. I just want to know my brother."

"The Club comes with him."

"Yeah, I'm getting that."

"Then you have to accept that part of his life if you want to be in it."

"He told me as much when he woke up. You don't need to worry about me and Josh. No doubt we'll go our separate ways again as soon as he's back on his feet."

Jem's brows draw together, but before he can counter my words or start poking around more, I say, "Come on, I've eaten enough. Let's head back upstairs."

CHAPTER SIX

When I first arrived in Kingsley a few weeks ago, wild horses couldn't have dragged me into the Lost Saxons clubhouse. Now, I find myself almost itching with curiosity to see the inside of the building.

I follow Beth, one of the old ladies, inside. Although why they call her an old lady, I have no idea because she's about thirty and gorgeous—even with signs of the beating she took at the hands of the same man who shot my brother still evident.

She has dark brown hair that is pulled into a ponytail, the ends curly, exposing her neck, which is encircled with bruises, the black fading to a mottled purple now. There are other marks across her face, and her clothes hide more injuries, I'm sure. The police still haven't found the man who inflicted them, although that horrible DCI Morgan chap who harangued me outside the hospital that day with Jem has been by the hospital several times over the past few weeks. I tried to intervene, to keep him away, but Josh told me—ordered me, really—to stay out of it. He said the Club would handle it... whatever that means.

I like Beth, but I can tell she's clearly haunted by what she experienced. Behind the smiles and bravado, there's a hint of fear in her eyes, ghosts that I'm sure did not exist before.

She also happens to be engaged to Logan, Jem's big brother. Luckily, the two men share few similarities beyond being huge, scary looking behemoths, so being around him isn't too traumatic.

Logan is dark haired, where Jem is blond, and Logan seems much more stern, quiet, while his younger brother takes nothing seriously. They do both have those dark brown chocolate eyes, though. I see why Beth falls into them when he looks at her, because I get lost in Jem's sometimes, even though I know I shouldn't. Jem shares more traits with their younger brother, Adam.

If I'm being honest, I've found myself latching onto Beth for no other reason than she reminds me a little of Cami, and I miss my best friend. Beth's been good to Josh, too. She's been at the hospital almost as much as I have, annoying my brother, but I think he needs it. Josh has become increasingly morose in the past week. I think the speed of his recovery is getting him down, especially now Beth and Dean are both home and getting back on their feet.

Considering the extent of his injuries, I'm not sure what Josh expects, but if it's to bounce back to full health so quickly, he's going to be disappointed. The doctors have been hinting rather loudly that his recovery could take months, depending upon the physiotherapy he needs to rebuild the muscles in his back and chest. Josh isn't listening, though. He wants to be back to himself instantly.

My eyes rove the walls as Beth leads us through the maze of corridors. I guessed the building was big from the outside, but I'm already turned around, even though I'm attempting to take in everything. I've never had a particularly great sense of direction, but all the twists and turns and doors off each hallway have my mind spinning. I would need a map to find my way around this place.

If I'm being honest, it's not what I expect. Where's the caches of guns and knives lining the corridors? The stacks of drugs? The mass orgies? The debauchery?

So far, I've seen two prospects painting the picnic tables out the front and some old bloke supervising them while swigging a beer like it's juice. It is barely lunchtime, but I've been known to imbibe the odd glass of wine before eleven, so who am I to judge?

It's quiet as we make our way down the narrow hallway lined with photo frames. I don't get a chance to stop and look at them, but I can see they are members of the Club with various women. I catch flickers of people I recognise: Beth, Logan, Jem, other members. My eyes try to linger on the blond giant as we pass and seem to magnetise to other photographs of him as we move up the corridor. Jem's clearly an exhibitionist: he's in nearly all these pictures.

What a bloody show off.

The décor is pleasant, plain, no skulls and crossbones, no half-naked women. Just plain. There are lots of Lost Saxons emblems emblazoned at different locations around the place, and there's even a wall of mug shots.

Tasteful...

"So, your brother kicked you out of the hospital?" Beth says over her shoulder at me, not slowing her pace.

I slide my gaze to her. "Apparently he's sick of looking at my face and I need to do something other than staring at his hospital walls." He used far more colourful language, but that was the gist of what he said.

Beth grins. "Sounds like Wade. Tactful as usual."

A few weeks back, this statement would have hurt—the fact she knows Josh better than me. Now, it rolls off my back. I'm coming to terms with things, and I'm getting to know my brother better with every passing day. We're not exactly a happy family yet, but I think we're making progress. I feel like we're making strides anyway.

"He cut his hair," I say.

"I heard."

"Jem came in with clippers. He was getting sick of trying to keep it clean, so it made sense to do it, but he's been grumpier than usual since he did. Do you know why?"

I'm hoping she will offer some insight into why my brother has been like a bear with a sore head over this. It's just hair and he was the one who suggested cutting it in the first place.

Beth stops walking and turns back to me.

"I shouldn't say. This breaks all kinds of bro codes, but Logan did tell me. He said cutting his hair was a big thing to Wade. He's had it long since he's been with the Club—since before that."

I think back to when I first met him prison. "He wore it long when I first met him, too."

"Lo said it was something to do with sticking it to Curtis. Does that mean anything to you?"

"Curtis is mine and Josh's father, but I've never had anything to do with him. He doesn't even know I exist, so I have no idea why he would care about his hair."

It's yet another puzzle piece to my brother I don't understand.

"It's probably not a good idea to ask either."

"No." Josh and our father did not have a good relationship.

Beth smiles at me. "Well, I'm glad you decided to come and have a drink with us—even if it was by force. Your brother is right to make you do it. It's not good for you spending all your time at the hospital or shut up in Wade's flat."

She's not wrong, although it is slightly humiliating being forced to have 'fun' like some socially inept pariah.

"I must admit, I am starting to go a little stir crazy. Not that Josh's place is terrible, but he doesn't even have any streaming services. I had to buy a couple to keep myself sane."

I've been staying at Josh's flat. He insisted after he found out I was staying at a hotel and not bedding down at the clubhouse or with one of the girls. It was a blessing when he gave me the keys. My bank account was not thanking me for spending so much on room fees.

Beth steps through the doors into the common room. The bar runs the length of one wall and looks well-stocked with a range of beer and spirits. There's a mix of old and new furniture that doesn't match, but seems to work in a strange sort of way. The dark wood floor looks newish, but is nicked in places. I imagine these boys like to party and party hard. There's a few empty pint glasses and bottles littered around the room, but other than that, it seems clean enough.

I notice a few brothers are hanging around playing pool, some drinking at the small tables while a few have gathered around a large flat screen television watching a football match.

Jem, I notice, is not here, thankfully.

Not that I'm looking...

The girls are sitting together in a huddle around two tables on the far side of the room and wave at us as we enter.

"Let's get a drink before we join them," Beth says, waving back to them.

Since I figure I'm going to need some Dutch courage, I nod and follow her to the bar.

King, one of the prospects, gets us drinks while we wait. There's an older man sitting at the far end, nursing a pint. His shoulders are hunched over, as if he's trying to get as close to the glass as he can.

Beth sighs when she notices him.

"How long has Tap been sitting there?" she asks King when he returns with our drinks.

"Most of the day."

She lets out a frustrated breath. "Does Derek know?"

King's expression softens. "Yeah, he knows. Don't worry; I'm keeping an eye on him."

"If he needs a lift home let me know, okay? I'll call Logan."

The prospect nods and wanders back down the bar. I want to ask more about Tap, but I don't, sensing it's a topic that I shouldn't push.

Beth, a little more subdued, grabs her gin glass off the bar, and we both head over to the table where I'm greeted like a long-lost sister.

After three gin and tonics, I'm starting to relax and actually enjoy myself. These girls are fun. Josh was right to make me unwind. I needed this. Weeks of nonstop bedside vigils have taken a toll. It's nice to just relax.

"I hear you're heading back to London tomorrow," Sofia says to Beth.

Jem's little sister looks like him. She definitely got all the good Harlow genes, because she's stunningly beautiful with all that dark hair that falls around her shoulders. So is Mackenzie, her older sister, although her colouring is a lighter brown. In fact, the entire family is too good looking for its own good.

Beth snorts. "Yeah, somehow it's turned into a road trip with your brothers."

Mackenzie's hands flash back and forth, and I watch them, not understanding what she's communicating, but enjoying the motion, nevertheless. She's unable to speak, so uses sign language to talk, but she can hear.

"Alistair pretty much said if I don't pick up my stuff, he'll have it sent to charity." Beth rolls her eyes and rubs at her neck, over the bruising. She winces as she does this and everyone seems to notice. "I'm not sure he's entirely happy about our breakup."

"Well, screw him," Sofia mutters. "I'm ecstatic you broke his heart. It means you're coming home. Although you and Logan need to keep the PDA to a minimum. All that tonsil tennis is gross."

Beth chuckles. "Get used to it. I can't keep my hands off him."

Mackenzie's nose wrinkles before her hands flash.

"Kenz says try to keep it PG-rated," Sofia translates her signing, "and I agree."

It's Jamie, the little red head with the short hair and filthy mouth, who interrupts this time.

"Screw that. You girls are crazy. Your brothers are hot. Please ask Lo to parade through the clubhouse topless as often as he can manage, girl. If you can get Jem and Adam to do the same, I will forever be in your debt."

Sofia smacks her bicep.

"Stop it!"

"Oh, come on, Piper, you're the new girl. You're an unbiased opinion: back me up here. Those boys are hot, right?"

I blink at Jamie's question.

"What?"

"The Harlow wonder triplets." She points at me using her glass, sloshing the liquid over her hand in the process. She either doesn't notice this or doesn't care.

"Uh... I..." I stare between the four girls, my face heating. "I've never really thought about it."

Liar.

Jamie's brow arches. "You've never thought about Jem Harlow. Naked. Not even once since you got here?"

"I'm not sure this is an appropriate conversation with his sisters sitting right here." Because I've thought about it more than once.

She grins at me. "You totally have."

"Why would I think about a man who is utterly irritating to the point of infuriation?" I turn to Sofia and Mackenzie, wincing. "No offence."

"None taken." Sofia waves this off. "Jem drives us all nuts." She turns to Jamie. "I am with Piper, however. This conversation is not appropriate—and it's gross. Leave your dirty bedroom fantasies about my brothers locked away in your filthy brain, please."

"I need to use the little girls' room," I exclaim suddenly. I don't need to think about Jem Harlow or how hot he is or his abs, or bedroom fantasies.

Jamie grins at me. "Are you drunk?"

"Drunk on three G and T's?" I scoff. "Please. I could drink the bottle and still be sober."

This is not a boast. Years of imbibing at black tie events means I have a fairly high tolerance level to alcohol.

Mackenzie's hands flash back and forth, even as her mouth kicks up into a grin.

"Kenzie says that sounds like a challenge," Sofia translates Mackenzie's signing for me. I need to learn BSL. It's mesmerising, watching her hands move the way they do. "Kenz, do you really want to face Wade after we get his sister blind drunk?"

The elder Harlow sister shrugs, her expression mischievous. Clearly, she is not afraid of my big brother.

"Okay, no one is getting blind drunk," Beth interjects. "Logan will hit the roof if he has to take anyone home and they vomit in his car. He's not going to be happy about having to cart anyone around either."

The thought of her enormous behemoth fiancé carting me around does not give me happy thoughts anyway, so I have no intention of getting that drunk.

"I'd need a vat of it," I admit. "I have a titanium stomach when it comes to alcohol. I do not when it comes to the actual process of putting it into my body, though, so I do really need to pee."

"Do you remember where the bathroom is?" Beth sounds amused.

"I'm sure I can find it."

This assertion might have been a little overstated. The moment I step out into the corridor, I realise I have no idea which way to go. Pride prevents me from returning to ask, so I pick a direction and start walking in it. I consider backtracking, but the laws of probability suggest I'll hit one sooner or later. The building is huge, but it's not infinite.

I come to the end of the corridor and round the corner, but I don't see anything that looks remotely like it could be a bathroom. Then again, it's not like any of these doors are labelled. They really should think about handy little signs. I don't want to try any of the doors in case I bust in on a sex room or drug store.

I'm about to turn around and head back the way I came

when the sound of a door opening ahead of me catches my attention.

Glancing up, I see movement and a figure step inside from what looks like an external door, if the change of light is anything to go by. It's one of the brother's—Dylan, I think. He's been by the hospital a few times, but Josh doesn't seem overly fond of him, none of the boys do.

He gives me the creeps.

Instinctively, I turn and start to walk in the opposite direction. I'm not sure why, but intuition tells me it's a bad idea to get caught alone with him.

"Hey!"

Too late. Bugger.

I stop and slowly turn to him. He saunters towards me, his mouth tugged into a grin. It's not like Jem's, which is usually playful, whimsical. I've only spoken to Dylan a handful of times, but I always feel like there is something more sinister with him. I have no idea why I think this because he's done nothing to me and has been nothing but polite when we've met, but he still puts me on edge. It's crazy to feel this way, but I keep my wits about me when he approaches, even though he doesn't move into my space either.

Dylan, like all the men in this Club, is easy on the eyes. He's got dark hair, a clean jaw, and an accent that is not northern. He's also heavily tattooed, and wearing an assortment of jewellery on his fingers and wrists. His vest, which I've learnt over the past few weeks is called a kutte, is not nearly as worn, and his patches are not dirtied—unlike most of the other brothers' kuttes, which are scuffed up, implying his is newer.

"What're you doing down here?" he asks with a smile, although there is a hint of suspicion in his tone.

Right. Of course. I'm the one skulking around.

"I'm looking for the bathroom. I got horribly lost."

He rubs at the back of his neck, a grin playing at his lips. "Yeah, I'll say. It's right back that way." He points down the corridor I came up before.

I groan.

"I thought it might be. Everything looks the same. You guys need to invest in some signage."

He snorts. "Yeah, they don't really do signs for motorcycle clubs."

I wonder what kind of signs they would need...

"What are you doing here anyway?"

"I'm having a drink with the girls. They're probably ready to send out a search party by now," I joke. "I've been gone for a while."

He ignores this, and asks, "How's Wade doing?"

"About the same. He's hoping he can come home soon."

I don't think that is likely, but I keep that to myself. His injuries are extensive and taking time to recover from.

"We're all hoping that, sweetheart." His eyes rove over me in a way that is not entirely comforting and definitely salacious.

Yuck.

"We haven't really had much of a chance to talk since you got into town." He says this innocently, but there is something more in his words, something I can't quite put my finger on.

I stare at him a beat. Is he... is he *flirting?*

"I'm not sure now is the best time to get acquainted, Dylan."

He doesn't seem deterred by my sarcasm because he asks, "Are you staying in town long?"

"I'm not sure. I really should get back to the girls."

I try to move past him, but his big body stands in my way. He's not stopping me getting around him, but he's not moving to let me get by him either.

"What do you do, Wade's sister? For a living?"

"I work at a children's education centre."

Would it be rude to bodily shove him out of my way? Could I bodily shove him out of my way? He's not exactly small.

His brows arch.

"Are you sure you're related to Wade?"

This makes the hairs rise on the back of my neck. What exactly is he implying? Does he think I'm lying...?

Why would he think this?

Josh is awake and isn't exactly denying I'm his blood.

My voice is steel when I say, "Why?"

"Well, it's just Wade's Wade." Whatever this means... "And you're so smart and beautiful."

"Yeah, and fucking very much off limits," a voice growls from behind him, a voice I recognise immediately.

Jem.

And for once, I am so glad to see him, that I forget how annoying I find him.

"We were just talking, Jem. No law against talking now, is there?" Dylan's acidic words snap out.

"Yeah? Just talking? About what?" Jem's voice bites just as hard.

Clearly, he's just as unimpressed by Dylan's attempts at flirting as I am. At least, I think that's what he was doing. Poorly, I might add. He might look like these men, but he certainly doesn't have a way with the women like them.

The air between them grows heavy and I have no idea what is going on, but after a moment, Dylan mutters,

"Whatever, *brother*. If you want to grab a coffee at any point while you're in town, Piper—"

"She doesn't," Jem snarls at him.

Dylan glares. "She yours?"

Am I his? Am I his *what*? I know the girls talk about being 'claimed' by their men. It's some archaic ritual that means they're essentially married or something. Is that what Dylan is asking? I'm absolutely not Jem's. I barely know him for a start, and what I do know of him I can hardly stand.

"I'm not his," I say, but neither men are listening.

Jem steps up to Dylan, his face contorting. "She's Wade's sister, fuck nuts."

"So?"

"So you keep your dirty nasty paws to your fucking self. That means you don't ask her for fucking coffee, you dumb shit."

Dylan's lips tip up into a smirk. "She's his sister, not his wife. She's a free agent."

He's not wrong, but clearly Jem does not agree with this sentiment, because he mutters, "Fuck me..."

Dylan darts back from Jem before he can grab him—presumably to throttle him—and heads up the corridor. He tosses a glare over his shoulder before he disappears around the corner, leaving me and Jem alone.

I'm mulling over Dylan's words when Jem spins back to me and I'm faced with a six-foot-three irate blond man.

He's not wearing his jeans and kutte, but he's in shorts and a black singlet that is moulded to his pectorals like a second skin. There's also a towel slung around his neck and his hair is damp, as if he's just showered. The man might irritate me, but he looks phenomenal. He has well-defined legs that are tattooed just up one calf. The ink continues up his arms and around his neck, a canvas of colour that I want to explore further.

"What're you talking to that motor-mouthed fuck for?" Jem demands, not too pleasantly, I might add. It breaks me out of my voyeurism.

Okay then.

I glare at him. "Am I not supposed to talk to him?"

"Fuck no. He's a dick. Stay away from him. Wade will lose his mind if you go anywhere near that shit head."

This surprises me. Josh made a huge song and dance about respecting the Club and the brothers, yet Jem is disrespecting one of their own.

I shouldn't ask. I should head back to the girls, and forget any of this happened, but curiosity gets the better of me.

"I have no intention of 'going anywhere near' him, but he's one of your brothers, isn't he?"

"Only on paper," is his bizarre response.

"Dylan was right about one thing, Jem. Josh isn't my keeper. I'm a big girl. I can make my own decisions."

"Yeah, I'm sure you can, but not on this. Stay away from him, okay?"

"Jem—"

"Piper, stay away from him."

There's something in his tone that tells me I shouldn't push him, and I have no interest in Dylan anyway, so I relent. "Fine."

He casts an eye over me and his anger drains, his shoulders relaxing as he takes me in. "Has hell frozen over?"

I blink at the sudden change in direction.

"What?"

"I figured that was the only time you'd step foot inside

the clubhouse." He peers at me. "Have you been kidnapped?"

The absurdity of this statement makes me smile, but I don't want him to see I'm amused, so I direct it at my feet. "Sort of."

This is not entirely a lie. I am here under duress; Josh bullied me into coming.

Jem suddenly grabs my shoulder, pulling so he can see behind me. My eyes flare even as heat scorches my skin where he touches me.

"What are you doing?" I squeal, reaching for the back of my skirt to make sure it's pulled down with one hand while simultaneously trying to snag his fingers latched onto my collarbone with the other. Not that my skirt has any chance of riding up. It's tightly fitted to my backside and my hips. I should focus on his touch, which is searing into my flesh like a brand. Electric currents dance across my skin.

"I'm checking for ropes in case you actually were hogtied and brought here," he says. "The last thing the Club needs is the Old Bill knocking on the bloody door."

I roll my eyes at him as I finally manage to find my senses and push him off me. "I was joking, Jem."

Mostly, anyway. An hour ago, I would have preferred to be at home, alone, watching a crap movie with a glass of wine, but now that I'm here, I'm surprisingly having a good time. Maybe Josh was right to push the issue—not that I would *ever* tell my brother this.

When I first came here, I wanted to hate these people, hate their lives. They're making it increasingly difficult—even Mr Obnoxious in front of me.

"I didn't think you knew how to tell a joke."

"Well, I don't need to, do I? You do enough larking around for both of us."

"Good thing, too," he says, then leans towards me to stage-whisper, "You're not very good at it."

Affronted, I mutter, "And you are? All your humour seems to consist of is jokes that are bad taste or groan worthy."

"My repertoire is so much more than that." He glances up the corridor, which is empty aside from us. "So, if hell hasn't frozen over and you haven't been abducted... what are you doing here?"

"I was ordered to be here."

"Ordered by who?"

"Josh."

This statement confuses him. "Your brother ordered you hang out with Dilhole Dylan?"

"Don't be a wanker. Of course not."

His eyes dance with mischief. Maybe I shouldn't have mentioned *that* act in front of him. I blush at the heated look he's directing at me.

"Only if you ask nicely."

"Are you always so crass?"

"Are you always so uptight?"

I fold my arms over my chest, which draws his eyes to my breasts. Not a good idea. I unfold them and drop my arms to my side.

"Not wanting to hear you talking about your little Jem makes me uptight?"

"My little Jem?" He guffaws. "Woman, you're fucking hilarious, and I can assure you, no one has ever called it 'little' before."

"I'm not trying to be funny. I'm actually disgusted by you."

This is a lie, and I can't stop the upturn of my lips as I say it.

He leans back against the wall, pulling the ends of the towel around his neck as he does. The gesture is small, but it does funny things to me. I will admit, I'm not completely immune to his charms. The man is exceptionally good looking. My body recognises this, even if my mind refuses to acknowledge it. I will never tell him this, though. Arrogant bastard.

"You should probably say it without the grin then."

"I can't. You're so full of yourself, it's hilarious. I'm here with the girls because Josh said I needed to have fun."

He tilts his head to the side. "And are you?" He sounds amused by the very concept.

"Yes, actually." The gin is certainly helping me unwind.

"Consider me surprised."

"I am capable of enjoying myself, Jem. In fact, believe it or not, but before I set foot in your little kingdom of Kingsley I regularly had fun. I was known for it, in fact."

He doesn't get close to me, but he doesn't need to. My heart is already racing just having him in my immediate proximity.

My eyes rove over his damp hair, which hangs loosely around his face in a natural wave, and for some ungodly reason, I have the urge to run my fingers through it, which is ludicrous.

I must be staring because he says, "You see something you like?"

I snap my gaze to his eyes. "What?"

"You're gawking." He smiles at me like the cat that got the cream.

"I am not."

Buggering hell. I was.

"Angel, it's okay to look. I'm an attractive man, after all."

My mouth slackens. "Modest, too."

"You're a beautiful woman yourself and I'll never make apologies for staring at you."

I narrow my eyes, sure he's joking, but there's no sign he is in his face. I know I'm not beautiful. Don't get me wrong, I don't think I'm ghastly, but I'm average. My mother has told me often enough that I'm lacking. My nose is not straight enough, my jaw is too large—I got my father's wide chin. My shoulders are too broad, too manly. I'm not slim enough, despite dieting my entire life. My faults are endless.

My stomach twists.

"Don't make fun of me, Jem."

There's a moment of silence that seems to stretch between us. "You can't even take a compliment, can you?"

"It depends if you really do mean it as a compliment, because you haven't exactly been Mr Complimentary before now."

"Well, you haven't given much reason for me to be." He leans into me and says, "I don't know if you've noticed, but you have been somewhat hostile, angel, since you got here."

"I have a name, Jem. And it's not angel. It's Piper. Use it."

"See what I mean, and I've been nothing but friendly." He places a hand over his heart, as if he's mortally wounded by my words. "You cut me deep when you act like this."

"I don't need friends," I tell him, and I don't. I certainly don't need friends that look like walking sex gods.

"Everyone needs friends." He stares at me, his dancing eyes seeing more than they should. "You're not one of those loners, are you? I mean, you are Wade's sister, so it would make sense. Wade's a freak." It's said with a grin, which softens the words, but I take affront at the slight.

"Josh isn't a freak."

"He'd be thrilled to know you're sticking up for him."

His relaxed pose is at odds with my stiff, uptight stance. I'm so tightly coiled I might fire across the corridor like an elastic band.

"Of course I'm sticking up for him—he's my brother."

"Yeah, but in our world, blood doesn't always count for shit."

That statement hits me in the stomach like a rock. It's no secret to anyone that Josh and I have a difficult relationship.

It also surprises me that Jem would say this. His brothers and sisters are lovely people.

"I'm not sure you're talking from experience. I've met your family."

He shifts the towel around his neck. "My family is fine, but a lot of the guys in the Club don't have that. The old ladies too." I watch as his head tilts to one side. "What about you, Pip? What's your family like? I don't mean Wade. I already know he's a pain in the arse. I mean your family back in Manchester. You haven't mentioned them much."

And for good reason. There isn't really a good way to start a conversation with my parents are complete crazy narcissists...

"Oh, you know. Like most families, I suppose," I hedge.

I'm not touching this with a ten-foot barge pole.

His eyes twinkle. "You don't give much away, do you?"

"There's not much to give away. I'm really rather boring."

"I doubt you could be boring if you tried, Piper."

"You'd be surprised."

"I'll be the judge of that."

My words die in my throat as he pushes off the wall and

steps into my space. He's a big man, both height and width wise and while I'm tall, I feel tiny next to him.

I tip my head up and swallow. This earns a lift of his lips as he notices my reaction, but I lose his face as he dips closer, his mouth moving to my ear. His breath is warm against the shell and I can hardly breathe as all I'm aware of is him—his bulk, his warmth, the smell of whatever shower gel he's washed with and a scent that is uniquely Jem. This may be the most intensely sexual moment of my life and he hasn't even touched me yet.

"You're not boring, angel," he says into my ear. "I know boring. You're not it. You're obstinate, ornery, but kind, compassionate, scared of being hurt. You're an enigma, Piper Ellis, and I will figure you out."

My heart rate kicks up a notch as his hot breath fans against the side of my face.

"And for the record, Piper, no lies, no jokes, you are an intensely beautiful woman."

He pushes back from me and I stand, dumbfounded as he starts up the corridor without another word. My heart is hammering in my chest, my breath ripping out of my mouth in heavy pants as I watch him go and the apex between my legs is throbbing as dampness seeps into my underwear.

What the bloody hell just happened?

CHAPTER SEVEN

"Do I need to think about shipping your things over to Kingsley?" Cami demands down the line in a half-joking, half-serious voice a few days later.

I cringe, readjusting my phone against my ear and juggle the bags of groceries I'm trying not to drop as I make my way down the road towards Josh's flat.

Bugger. Three weeks. It's a long time to be gone, considering I was only supposed to be staying a couple of days at most to check on a brother I hadn't seen in years. Now, I'm living in his flat, hanging out with his friends—friends I swore I would not get close to—and I'm fairly certain I'm having some less than platonic feelings for one of his brothers after Jem told me he thought I was beautiful.

Yes, he said I was beautiful and I'm fairly certain he meant it. Since then, I haven't been able to stop thinking about why he said it and what it means. Why would he say it?

"Of course not. I'm coming back." I should have come home weeks ago, but I can't bring myself to leave just yet. I don't know why either. I should go home and build a relationship with my brother from Manchester, but right now, I have a captive audience with him. It sounds terrible, but I'm taking full advantage of the fact that he's stuck in the hospital and has no choice but to deal with me.

"Are you sure?" she teases. *"I'm getting worried I might need to change my address to Kingsley, Yorkshire."*

I snort, pausing on the pavement and trying to catch my breath. I should have taken a taxi back from the supermarket, but I thought I would attempt to be healthy, given my bum has been stuck in a hospital chair for weeks. I should have been lazy. I'm so tired and this walk is destroying me. I'm physically and mentally burnt out.

"No chance of that. Josh and I are sorting things out, but I don't think I'm that welcome here."

At least not welcome enough for the invitation to be extended long term.

She pauses. *"No love from the big brother yet?"*

"We're getting there, but he's focused on recovering—as he should be. I don't think this is something we can stick a plaster over and kiss better. It's going to take time."

"Probably not. I don't think bikers wear plasters anyway. Is work okay about you being off this long?"

"They've been fairly understanding under the circumstances. I've been keeping up with my cases remotely while I've been up here, but Brian is handling my workload on the ground. I think Karl wants to hand over completely to him if I'm going to be off for much longer, though. The kids need consistency, and they need someone doing it face-to-face."

I know I'm only getting such leeway from my boss, Karl, because of who I am, because of my connection to my stepfather, Grant. Usually, I would balk at that, but right now, I'll take it. I need to be here, and I don't want to risk my job.

"Shit, P. How much vacation time can you take if you do stay there?"

"I haven't taken any time off this year yet, so I still have twenty-one days."

"For the love of... Please tell me you're not staying at the biker commune for another month nearly. Will the centre even sign off on that?"

I fall silent. I have no idea what my plans are beyond the fact I'm not ready to leave yet, and I don't understand why that is.

"Piper?" Her voice cracks with warning. *"Are you being held there against your will? Smash your palm against the screen if you are."*

This makes me laugh. "No, I'm not. I don't know what I'm still doing here, though. I just... can't bring myself to leave yet. Not while we're making progress."

"Darling, you can make progress on the weekends. You don't have to put your life on hold."

She's right, of course, but walking away from Josh when we haven't sorted anything doesn't feel good. But I don't want to lose my job, which could be a possibility if I keep this up. Work has been so understanding, probably because Grant funds the education charity I work at through his council work. I know it's wrong to abuse my status as his stepdaughter, and while I haven't said anything, I know Karl is only being so understanding because of this.

"No, you're right. He's doing better. He's alert and he has lots of people here to take care of him. I can always come back on the weekends. Besides, I'm sure my parents will notice sooner rather than later that I'm missing."

The last thing I need is to explain why I'm running around Kingsley with an outlaw motorcycle club.

Cami makes a noise in the back of her throat. *"Well,*

they haven't noticed so far. They haven't dropped by or called... nothing."

I'd like to say I'm surprised by this, but I'm not, although a stab of hurt does lance my chest. My parents don't give a toss about me. I see them on special occasions—Christmas, birthdays, election campaigns. It's not unusual to go weeks without seeing them, sometimes not even hearing from them. I'm a prized trophy to get out of the cabinet whenever they need to show me off.

"Are you coming home then?"

I consider this for a moment, then say, "Yes, I suppose it's time. I'll visit with Josh today, wrap up things here over the next few days and think about heading back."

I shift the bags in my hands and almost sigh with relief as the front door of the flat comes into view. I can't wait to sit down. Next time I want to be healthy, I'll go for a walk around the block, sans groceries.

"All right, darling. If you need anything let me know."

As I hang up and move towards the flat, I notice something doesn't seem quite right. The way the door is sitting on the frame looks... odd. As I get closer, my heart starts to race. The door is open just ever so slightly.

Is someone inside?

Fear grips me.

I can't go in, but I can't stay out here either.

Glancing around the street, I can't see anything untoward, but Jem's words rattle around my brain about being a target because of being seen with the Club. Not to mention the man who shot Josh still hasn't been apprehended by the police. Could he have come here to finish off what he started with Josh?

I bite my bottom lip as ice settles in my stomach. Maybe I just forgot to lock it. I'm so exhausted from all the back and forth between here and the hospital. I barely sleep. It wouldn't be the first time I haven't locked the door, although I've never forgotten to shut it before.

Do I really want to call the police and cause a huge scene over nothing? Besides, calling the police could put me on the radar of a certain councillor. I would have to file a report, give my name and Grant's team could find out. That would be bad. So far, my stay here has flown under the radar. I'd like to keep it that way.

Placing the grocery bags on the ground, I pull my phone back out of my bag and I scroll through my phone book. I'm grateful Weed insisted I store all these numbers—and a few of the other brothers'—in my phone for emergencies.

I call Weed first, but it rings out with no answer. Crap. I scroll through, looking for an alternative contact. My finger hovers over Logan's name in my phone book. I've met him a few times through Beth, so I don't feel weird about calling him. Yet, I don't hit dial. Instead, I find myself scrolling up and pressing connect on his brother's name.

What the bloody hell am I doing?

I wince as I lift the handset to my ear.

Jem answers on the third ring.

"Hell really must have frozen over, angel, if you're calling me. To what do I owe this pleasure?"

"Didn't we talk about the angel thing?" I chastise, my eyes locked on the door.

"You talked, I ignored."

"Yes, I'm getting that you're not really that good at listening."

"I listen. I just chose to ignore you on this one. Although you've got more claws than an angel." He pauses, then says, *"As much as I love hearing your voice, I'm sure you didn't call for a chat, Piper. You don't like me that much."*

"I don't like you at all," I mutter without any heat in my words. It's also a lie. Strangely, I do like him, and I like him more than I probably should. I find him irritating, but weirdly comforting.

"There's the Pip, I know and adore." He sounds amused, but his words make flutters take off in my belly. He adores me? I guess he's being flippant, but even so, I can't help but feel a little tingle of pleasure at his words. *"Do you want to tell me why you're calling?"*

"I... uh... I have a situation."

"What kind of situation?"

"I'm probably overreacting. It's fine. Forget I called."

"Piper, what's going on?"

"When I got home, the flat door was open. I probably forgot to lock it, but—"

"Are you safe?" All signs of joking are gone from his voice now.

"I'm outside."

"There's a shop across the street, right? Go there. I'll be with you in five."

I'm not used to business Jem. I'm used to stupid, joking around Jem. This side of him alarms me a little.

"Jem, I don't think—"

I realise I'm talking to the dial tone.

Bugger.

With nothing else to do, I put my phone away and grab my groceries. Then I haul my bum over to the shop to wait inside for him, as he demanded.

As I wait, the shop owner keeps shooting me suspicious looks, and why wouldn't he? I'm hanging out in his store, looking shifty.

I keep my eyes locked on the flat door in case anyone tries to enter or exit, but no one does.

After what feels like an eternity, I hear the rumble of a bike and I see Jem pull up at the kerb opposite. I come out to meet him, clutching my bags with whitened knuckles.

"You said the door's open?" He's off the bike by the time I reach him, his head also free from him helmet.

"Yeah. I probably left it open, Jem." I try to reassure him as I place the bags on the ground by my feet, but he doesn't look comforted by my words.

"Just wait here," he orders.

I reach for his arm as panic stirs in my guts. "You can't go in there alone."

I assumed he'd bring backup, one of his brothers maybe. I didn't expect him to come here like the Lone Ranger.

"I'll be fine. Wait here."

"Jem…"

He gives me a smile. "Don't worry about me, Pip. I'm tougher than I look."

He looks fierce, and the set of his jaw, the tightness of his mouth tells me he's also pissed off.

His eyes soften slightly as he takes me in. "Are you all right?"

I meet his gaze before lowering my eyes, cringing. "I feel stupid calling you."

"Hey, the last thing you should feel is stupid. I'm glad you called. You should always call any time you think something is wrong, do you hear?"

When I don't answer right away, he places two fingers under my chin and lifts it, forcing me to look at him.

"Do you hear?" he repeats, his expression so serious, I nod.

"I'm sure it's nothing, Jem."

"Well, it's better to be safe." He glances over his

shoulder towards the flat before bringing his attention back to me. "Let me go and check it out. Wait here."

I can't stop from reaching out and gripping his arms as fingers claw around my heart.

"Please be careful."

"Always."

I watch him approach the flat cautiously. Then he pushes the door that leads into the flat with his foot. He pauses for a moment before he disappears inside. My heart rate goes through the roof as the minutes drag by. My feet itch with the need to move, to follow him, but I stay rooted to the pavement.

After what feels like eternity, he finally re-emerges and my pulse begins to return to a normal beat when I see he looks unharmed.

"Well?" I ask as he approaches me, brushing his hair back from his face.

"Nothing looks disturbed. There's no sign anyone tried to break in. Come and see if anything's been taken."

I reach for the grocery bags, but he grabs them. "I can manage it, Jem."

"I know."

"But you're going to carry them anyway," I surmise.

"Yeah. Go on inside."

He lifts the bags I struggled with like they weigh nothing, his other hand coming to the small of my back to steer me towards the flat. I pause in the doorway and he gives me a nudge.

"It's safe, Piper. I checked it."

I swallow, and step inside. The flat is quiet, still, but nothing looks out of place considering the door was open and has been open at least the entire time I've been out shopping.

Sliding my handbag onto the kitchen counter, I rest my palms on the top and let out a breath. My face burns as I tip my head away from him. I want to crawl into a hole and hide.

"I'm so sorry calling you out like this."

"Don't be daft," he says, placing the bags next to me. "You're scared about anything, Piper, you call. I don't care what time of night or day it is, you fucking call, you hear?"

"I mustn't have pulled the door properly closed when I left for the supermarket." My fingers go into my hair, my voice sounding ragged. "I'm just so tired. I can't think straight."

"You need to sleep."

"I can't."

"This running backward and forward between here and the hospital nonstop, it's no good. Look, we all see what you're doing and how much you clearly love your brother, but you're running yourself into the ground."

I make an indelicate snuffling sound in the back of my throat. "You thought I hated Josh when I first came here." I give Jem a wry, tired smile. If I wasn't so exhausted, I might have guarded my words, but my filters are broken.

"I never thought you hated Wade, angel. I thought you hated the Club."

Pushing off the counter, I toe my boots off and barefoot, I move into the kitchen and grab the kettle. I need caffeine if I'm going to stay awake.

"I did. I told you, you took my brother from me."

Jem leans a hip against the breakfast bar. "And do you still think that?"

"I think wild horses couldn't make my brother do anything he doesn't want to do. If there is one thing I've learnt in the time I've been here, it's that Joshua Wade is the most stubborn man on the planet. If he's here, it's because he wants to be."

"I told you as much when you arrived."

I reach for two mugs from the cupboard. The least I can do is caffeinate Jem after dragging him down here, but one of the cups slips and in slow motion hits the counter, obliterating into a thousand pieces across the surface and the floor below.

My throat clogs. Oh my God. What is wrong with me?

"Don't move, I'll clean it up." Jem pauses. "Does Wade have shit to clean it up?"

"Under the sink. There's a dustpan and brush."

This entire situation is just going from bad to worse. I really want to cry and I am not a crier, but I'm also exhausted.

"I just wanted to make you coffee."

"I don't give a shit about coffee. Go and sit on the sofa. I'll clean this up, okay?"

I nod, and try to step through the minefield of ceramic pieces. In my bare feet, this is difficult. Jem loses patience quickly and sweeps me into his arms bride-style.

I let out a shriek.

"What are you doing! Put me down."

"I don't want you to cut your feet."

Oh.

This is sweet.

I stop struggling and when he puts me down on the other side of the breakfast bar, my body is tingling and not in an unpleasant way. He stares down at me through his blond curtain of hair and something passes on his face that I can't read, a flash of something—I'm not sure what.

The air between us feels different, charged. I don't know why or what is happening, but I stare up at him, unsure what to do next. He reaches out, as if he's going to touch me, then drops his hand.

"Go and sit, Piper." His voice sounds a little hoarse.

"Okay," I whisper.

Since I've caused him enough problems, I do as I'm told and take a seat. I listen as he cleans up my mess. There's something strange about a huge man wearing leather and denim cleaning my kitchen—well, Josh's kitchen. Weirdly, it doesn't feel wrong to have Jem in my space, but it should.

After a few minutes, he comes into the living area and hands me a mug. It's not coffee, though, it's tea. I raise a brow at him.

"You need sleep. Coffee's not going to help with that."

"No, I need to be alert, so I can get to the hospital. I need caffeine for that. This weak as dishwater tea isn't going to cut it."

"You're not going to the hospital."

"I'm not?"

"Angel, you're so tired you left the front door open and you've just dropped a mug. You're not taking care of yourself. Until you're able to do that, I'm putting my foot down. You're resting."

He's not wrong, but even so, I balk at being treated like a child.

"You can't tell me what to do, Jem."

"You're not leaving this flat until you get some sleep."

I stare at him. "You can't stop me."

"Watch me."

He's actually serious. "Jem—"

"You got off lucky this time, Piper. You noticed the door was open. What if someone was waiting inside and they had the foresight to close the door behind them? What if you came inside not suspecting a thing? Do you know what kind of damage someone could do to you in an hour? Christ, even just ten minutes? The kind of irreparable shit another human can inflict on another? I don't really feel like explaining to your brother that his little sister got raped or killed under Club watch because she forgot to lock her front fucking door because she's so tired, so humour me, okay? Take a nap. Please."

His words hit me in gut, but it's the 'please' that gets me. "Okay."

He sinks onto the sofa next to me. "Drink it all."

"What about Josh? He'll worry if I don't show."

"I'll ask Mum to drop in and visit. She can tell him you're having the night off. Honestly, I think your brother will be glad to see the back of you for a night."

"He got rid of me the other night," I protest. I'm starting to feel like a chore.

"When he forced you to have an evening off with the girls?"

"Yes."

He rubs at the bridge of his nose, and I can see his barely-there patience fraying. "Piper, don't you think maybe that's a problem?"

I sit straighter. "What do you mean?"

"The fact that your brother has to order you to leave his hospital room to unwind."

When I don't say anything, because really, what can I say to that? He adds, "Look, I don't know what happened between you and Wade, but you don't have to drill yourself into the ground to show him how much you care. He can see it. We all can."

I swallow hard, and run my hands around the outside of the mug, letting the heat warm my hands, which suddenly feel chilled.

"I'm not trying to prove something," I say quietly, even though I suppose I am.

"Whatever happened between you and Wade, it's going to take time to fix, but destroying yourself isn't the way to do it."

"I don't know why I'm being like this, why I'm being so intense." I chew at my bottom lip. "I know it's pathetic, worse than pathetic, but I can't help it."

Jem doesn't speak, he just watches me, waiting for me to say more. I shouldn't. I should keep my silence. Jem isn't my confidant; he's my brother's, but for some reason the words come spilling out of me.

"My whole life, I've never been wanted by anyone. My mother, stepfather—I was a hindrance to them. I thought I found my place with Josh. I thought he'd come out of jail and we'd be this happy family, but that was a lie, too. He didn't want that, not really. He didn't want his little sister hanging around his neck. He didn't want the responsibility of a twenty-one-year-old with baggage to deal with. He wanted what your Club offered—freedom without boundaries, without rules. And once again, I was pushed aside. It broke me, realising that I would never be enough for anyone. That I could be so easily discarded by everyone."

I watch as sympathy crosses his handsome face, and I hate seeing it there. I don't want pity, not from him.

"Piper..."

"Don't." I raise a hand. "You don't have to say anything, Jem. I understand. He's your Club brother. I don't expect you to badmouth him. I'm just telling you how it is for me. Losing Josh again will destroy me, Jem. I can't do it."

He doesn't say anything for a moment. He leans forward on the sofa, clasping his hands between his splayed legs. Then he says, "Your brother's an arse."

I blink. "What?"

"Wade's an arse for walking away like that. I get he was going through shit, that he was spiralling after jail, but you don't walk away from family. Not ever. He's an arse."

That's it? He's an arse?

"Jem..."

He sags back against the sofa.

"Drink your tea, angel."

"What are you going to do?"

"I'm going to wait for you to fall asleep."

"Jem, I'm not going to fall asleep here."

"Well, I'm not leaving you alone. Not now."

I stare at him, my eyes feeling suddenly gritty and heavy with the sting of tears. "I didn't tell you that so you'd feel sorry for me."

"I don't feel sorry for you, but I'm still not leaving you."

"You are the most stubborn man."

"Says the woman who hasn't slept a full night in a month." He tugs the blanket off the back of the sofa and drapes it over my legs. "Drink up."

I stare at him, trying to fathom him out. I want to ask why he's looking after me, but I'm not sure I want to know the answer.

Jem grabs the remote and switches the television on, and my courage flees. He puts some action film on and settles back against the cushions. When I'm done with my tea, he takes the mug from me and places it on the coffee table.

Absently, I watch the movie with him, my eyes drifting as he gently strokes a hand up my arm. I shift closer to his shoulder until I'm completely tucked against his side. It doesn't take me long to succumb to the pull of sleep.

CHAPTER EIGHT

Two days later, a bang on the flat's front door draws my attention. I pull my head out of the sink, my toothbrush half hanging out of my mouth. I'm not expecting anyone yet. My taxi to the hospital isn't due for another twenty minutes, and he usually calls when he's outside.

Spitting toothpaste, I quickly rinse my mouth, and head for the front door.

When I peek through the spy hole, I'm surprised to see Jem standing on the other side—who is steadfastly becoming the object of a few late-night fantasies after seeing him in his workout gear the other day and after falling asleep on him. I can't believe how sweet he was to me. I didn't think he was capable of it.

Since I got into town, he's either been a completely sarcastic arse or total joker. I thought he might make fun of me for calling him over nothing with the door situation, but he didn't. He forced me to get some rest. I slept for seven and a half hours, during which time he didn't leave my side. When I woke, he ordered us takeout. He fed me and then he left. The whole situation was surreal.

I haven't seen him since that day, though, so seeing him now has a tendril of fear rushing through me. What if something is wrong with Josh?

I tug the door open a little more forcefully than necessary.

"Is Josh okay?"

He smiles at me, and I can't deny I'm not affected by his silly grin, because I am. In fact, I'm starting to become affected by almost everything he does, and I don't want to read too much into why that is.

"Not quite the greeting I was looking for."

Irritation flares in me. "Jem, is he okay?"

"Wade's fine. Are you just going to leave me standing out here?"

I peer at him through the open door.

"Why are you here?"

"We really need to work on your hospitality, Pip."

He pushes past me without waiting for me to extend an invitation inside, clearly realising I'm not going to give him one, and makes a beeline for the kitchen. I watch him, bemused, as he starts to boil the kettle, reaching for the cups to make us both a brew.

I continue to stare at him, hoping this will make him talk. It does not.

I may have to take the initiative here...

"I think it's the other way around." I fold my arms over my chest. "Your manners are atrocious. Who just comes into someone's home uninvited?"

He glances over his shoulder at me. "Friends, that's who."

"I didn't realise we were friends."

"You drooled all over me for more than seven hours," he says as he reaches for the sugar. "I think we've extended our relationship into the friendzone, Piper."

Mortified, I hiss, "I did *not* drool on you."

This seems to amuse him more. "I have the shirt and the stain to prove it."

"You do not."

"In your defence," he says, "it was the most adorable drooling I've ever seen."

"I don't drool—adorably or otherwise," I snap, but my voice is less heated than I would like. Mostly, because I can't stop watching him moving around the kitchen in his perfectly fitted jeans that hug his stupidly, amazingly pert arse. Nor can I stop ogling the outline of his thick biceps in his ridiculously well-fitted shirt either. His kutte is annoying me; it's in the way of the view.

This has to be one of the most surreal things I've ever witnessed—a huge six-foot-plus biker with far too much hair and a scruff of blond beard, looking like he stepped off the pages of Beowulf, making coffee for me.

"Do you feel better for catching up on your sleep?" he asks.

It breaks me out of my gawking.

Heat infuses my cheeks and I'm glad he's focused on making the drinks, and not the fact I'm blushing like a teenage girl at having been caught.

"Yeah, actually I do." And because I have manners, I add, "Thank you."

He waves this off. "You need to take better care of yourself."

"I know."

"I mean it, Piper. You're no good to Wade if you're barely functioning."

"I know that, too," I tell him quietly.

I watch as he pours the water over the coffee granules and stirs both contents of the mugs. I'm not sure whether I should be impressed or slightly concerned he knows how I take my coffee. He has bought cups for me from coffee shops in town while I kept vigil at Josh's bedside, so I don't know why it surprises me that he remembers, but it does.

When I take the mug from him, our fingers scrape over each other's and my eyes meet his. There's heat there for just a second before he shuts it down.

Maybe I imagined it. I am still tired, after all.

Weeks of sleep deprivation can't be fixed with one catch up session. I do feel more invigorated, having slept on him the other night, but I suspect my sudden burst of energy in this moment is more to do with the man standing a few feet from me right now. My pulse certainly seems to be moving a little faster than it was before I opened the door.

Jem confuses everything. I shouldn't be feeling anything for him, but he's a hard man not to like. He's funny and although he would probably hate being labelled it, he's sweet.

As much as I've tried to keep my distance from the Club, I've struggled. I wanted to hate them all, hate the people I saw as destroying my life, but the time I've spent here has shown they're not who I should be directing my anger towards. These people are not my enemy. They're actually good people, as bizarre as that is. The way they have rallied around my brother and me to help has been astounding. I can't imagine any of my parents' friends reacting this way if they were struck ill.

Mary, Dorothy and Jeanne, three of the older ladies associated with the Club, visit Josh often. They do laundry for him, bring him magazines to read, books, sweets, treats. They look after his bills, other affairs, too. They've tried to take care of me, as well, although I was not receptive at first. It was only fear Josh would make me leave that kept me holding my tongue, but now, it's a mutual respect.

These people may be criminals, but I don't think they are any worse than the people I deal with back in my own life. In fact, I think those in Grant's circles are worse. At least Josh's friends are upfront about who they are.

"Clearly, you missed your calling as a barista," I tell him.

"I make a mean cheese and bacon bagel, too."

I don't point out that there's no 'making' this. It's just prep work. I don't want to hurt his feelings.

I point to his 'Treasurer' patch on the front of his kutte. "You'd have to give up the day job to do it."

He, and a few of the others, have similar patches with different roles. Logan's says 'Sergeant-at-Arms', Adam is 'Road Captain', Slade—the mean man who I met with Weed when I first arrived—has 'Vice President'. Weed does not have a patch, however.

Jem seems amused by my statement. "I guess so."

"Do you enjoy being Treasurer?"

"It's not about enjoying it, angel. It's about what the Club needs."

"It sounds fairly important. You must be skilled to do it."

He shrugs. "I'm good at making money appear and disappear. I'm not sure if that's a skill or not."

"Trust me, it's a skill. Businesses pay people lots of money to do precisely that. It would certainly pay a lot more than the coffee making if you did it in the corporate world."

I have no idea what the criminal underbelly pays, and I'm not about to ask.

"That I don't doubt, but I'm not much for suits—or

customer service. There's a reason they don't let me do any customer-facing jobs in the Club." He wiggles his brows at me. "I lack diplomacy skills."

"I can believe it." I sigh. "While I appreciate the coffee, I'm not going to have time to drink it. I have to leave shortly."

"To go to the hospital," Jem correctly surmises. It's not a leap. I spend all my time there.

"Exactly, so you need to go."

His jean-clad legs cross at the ankles as he leans back against the counter, clutching his mug tighter. "Why're you taking taxis?"

His question seems to come out of left field. "Excuse me?"

"There's plenty of brothers and old ladies who can run you back and forth. Why in the hell are you putting money in some taxi driver's back pocket?"

"Because... the hospital is five minutes up the road and a cab is easier."

He shakes his head. "Wrong answer."

"Jem, you're being a little ridiculous."

"No, what's ridiculous is you forking over money for rides to the hospital every day when we've got prospects who can do that shit for free. Christ, I'll run you around myself. Just ask, angel."

I sigh at him. "You're not a taxi service, Jem. You have things to do. And didn't we talk about the 'angel' thing?"

"Didn't I explain about the ignoring thing?"

I throw my hands up in the air, my frustration mounting. "Did you just come here this morning to lecture me?"

"I came here to give you a ride to the hospital."

"I don't need a ride. I have a taxi booked."

"No, you don't."

The flippant way he says this puts me on alert.

"Yes, I do."

"I cancelled it."

I stare at him. "You didn't."

"Yeah, I did."

I can't work out if he's being serious or not, but he hasn't blinked or made any indication he's joking, so I press on. "How did you cancel a booking I made?"

He shrugs. "It wasn't difficult. There're only two taxi firms in this town. I called them both, figured out which one you're using, told them not to take bookings from you anymore. I told the other one the same as well, in case you're considering using them instead."

What the absolute bloody hell?

I think my head might be about to explode.

"Why would you do that?" I demand, my voice tight.

"I told you why."

He is certifiable. Who does this? Who controls people's lives like this? I take it back... I take back everything nice I've said or thought about Jem bloody buggering Harlow. He's a monster. He's got screws loose in his head. He needs professional help.

Slamming my mug down on the counter, I snap, "You are an absolute lunatic."

"Possibly." His tone is light, lofty, and supremely annoying.

"Jem! You can't control where I go, or with whom."

"No, but I also don't like the idea of you moving around town with total strangers either," he says, serious now. "I can't protect you if I don't know where you are."

What is he talking about?

"I don't need protecting."

"I sincerely hope that's the case."

Is he for real? I want to throttle him. The urge to wrap my fingers around his stupid, thick neck is so overwhelming I have to clench my fingers into fists for fear I might follow through with it.

Instead, I give him the dirtiest glare I can conjure up. "You are completely and utterly deranged."

"I don't think so, but if it makes you feel better about the situation to think that, then by all means…"

"Jem! I need to use taxis to get around town. I don't have a car here."

"You have the Club. That's your taxi firm, Pip."

Is he really this obtuse? Does he really not understand this situation and how insane he is being? For a man who is obviously intelligent, he acts like a dolt at times.

"I don't want to rely on the Club."

He folds his arms over his chest and leans back against the counter. "Because you think we're all crooks?"

"Well, aren't you?"

His lips tug into a grin. "Only sometimes."

This answer infuriates me. "Are you worried about the man who shot Josh coming back? Because the police are still looking for him."

Jem shakes his head. "I'm one hundred percent not even remotely concerned about him."

The way he says this makes the hair on the back of my neck stand up. His answer seems a little too definite for my liking.

"Why not?"

He shrugs. "I don't waste my time worrying about psychopaths like Simon Wilson. And neither should you."

"Is he still a danger to Josh? To me?"

"Nothing is a danger to you, as long as you let the Club do what it needs to in order to protect you."

I roll my eyes. "And forgoing a taxi is going to help with that?"

"Absolutely."

His hedging is driving me insane, and so is his calm demeanour. He has yet to show a single emotion outside of level-headed, while I'm one step from raging banshee. What is wrong with this man?

"You're infuriating," is my less than stellar comeback.

"No more so than you are, angel."

He steps into my space, and I move back, my spine hitting the counter. With nowhere to go, I'm trapped. My breath quickens as I glance up at him and try to regain my equilibrium.

"A lot of bad things have happened lately to a lot of people in our family," he tells me softly. "I couldn't bear it if something happened to you, too."

His words slice through me—not only at the implication that he considers me family, but that he doesn't want anything bad to happen to me. Considering my brother is still in the hospital recovering and the Club is still patching itself up from the aftermath of that, I gentle my voice. I'm not completely unfeeling, after all.

"Jem, nothing is going to happen to me. Certainly not from getting a taxi in the middle of the day."

His eyes scan over my face and I feel heated under his gaze. Something is changing between us, but I don't know what or why.

"Yeah, well, you're not always getting them in the middle of the day. I know you come back late some times."

This is true. Visiting hours don't end until gone nine o'clock in the evening.

"Jem, it's the summer. It's still light when I get home."

For the first time, a crack appears in his calm. A ripple of irritation wavers across his face.

"Fucking hell, woman, you'd argue with an empty room, wouldn't you?"

Probably, but my lips tip up as I say, "No."

He dips his head down to mine, his mouth inches away. I feel his breath against my skin, warm and heated. Tingles race across my skin. My chest feels tight as the air stops in my throat. I can't draw it further down as he gives me a cheeky grin that melts some of the hardness around my heart.

"There's absolutely no denying you're a Wade."

This makes me laugh a little. "Was there ever any doubt anyway?"

"I did hope," he murmurs, somewhat bizarrely.

I frown at him. "Why would you hope that?"

"Because it would make things easier if you weren't."

I pull back slightly, so I can see his face. "What do you mean?"

He scans my face. "For someone smart, angel, you can be incredibly imperceptive sometimes." It's not said nastily, but with a hint of regret. He pushes back from me. "Come on. Let's get you to the hospital. We don't want you to be late."

CHAPTER NINE

J~~EM IS~~ late to pick me up, which is just as well because I'm not ready for him. I didn't get to bed until gone three o'clock this morning and I'm exhausted, so dragging myself out of bed at nine was always going to be a challenge. Never mind burning the candle at both ends, I'm burning it at all ends. I'm working remotely using one of Josh's old laptops, which seems to be appeasing my bosses. This is now my fourth physical week of absence from work, and so far, they've been great about things, but I fear their patience is not infinite. At some point, they're going to demand I come back, although for now they seem content to let things continue as they are—as long as I'm doing what is needed. I suspect my name and links to a certain councillor Grant Hollander and the funding he provides for the centre is about all that is keeping my neck off the chopping block. That won't last forever, though.

But for now, I'm stuck in this dreamy bubble, where my real-life doesn't exist and I don't have to deal with my mother or Grant. I know it's fake, that my life in Kingsley isn't mine, but I can't help but cling to it. If I'm being honest, I don't want to return to my life in Manchester. Everything is hard there. Here, I have the illusion of easy.

And then there's Jem. I'm warming to him. I shouldn't be, but I can't stop myself. I have no misconceptions about who he is and what he is. Beneath the smiles and jokes, I know he's dangerous, but there's something strangely compelling about his silly antics. I find myself eager to see him in the mornings when he picks me up. Since he blacklisted me with the local cab firms, he's assigned himself as my personal driver. I thought maybe the prospects would run me around, but after visiting ended with Josh, it was Jem waiting in the corridor to drive me home. The next morning, it was Jem who knocked on the door, and it was again Jem who took me home.

I try not to read too much into this, but I can't help it.

Is he only doing this because of loyalty to Josh?

Probably.

But it's nice to live in the fantasy for a while.

I'm just considering texting him to see where he is when there's a knock on the door. I still have nothing on my feet, but I rush to the door anyway to let him in.

"I'm late, too," I blurt as I tug it open. "Give me two minutes and I'll be ready."

But he doesn't fire back the expected smart remark. In fact, he looks worried and that sets me on edge.

"What's wrong?" I demand.

He scrubs a hand over his bearded jaw. "Wade's in ICU. They think he's got an infection or some shit from the second surgery. I don't understand the medical crap, but—"

My legs go wobbly even before he finishes speaking. Josh had to go back under the knife earlier this week to further repair some of the damage caused by the shooting. This wasn't unexpected, the doctors told us this could be a possibility. The surgery went well, though. He was recovering fine. They were talking about discharging him in a few days' time. This is not good news.

Then again... I think back to yesterday during my visit. He seemed lethargic, a little out of it. He's been a little out of it since the surgery, if I'm being honest. I thought it was just part and parcel of the process. What if he's been worsening again and I didn't realise?

My knees threaten to fold and Jem reaches out, grabbing my elbows, keeping me upright.

"Whoa, easy, angel."

I cling to him, my nails digging into his biceps. I can't lose Josh. Not like this. Not before we've truly fixed things.

"Oh my God." Cold fills my belly. "Is he... is he going to—"

I can't say the word, but it sits on the tip of my tongue and fills the air. Is my brother going to die?

Jem cuts me off with a finger to my lips. "No. Don't think it."

I stare up into his dark brown eyes, begging him to tell me things are going to be okay. "I can't lose him, Jem."

"You're not going to. It's just an infection."

I feel suddenly cold and I shiver. Infections kill people all the time.

"You can't know that." I sound on the edge of hysteria.

"No, I can't know that, but I do know Wade. He's a tough bastard." He rubs my arms and the warmth of his hands infuses my skin. I take comfort from the gesture. "He's going to be okay. Believe that."

"He's in the ICU." I sound shrill.

"It's a precaution given the other shit he's been through, that's all." His voice is soft, reassuring, and I feel reassured by it.

He keeps hold of me with one hand, the other cupping my face. The air between us changes, feels suddenly charged with electricity. I should pull back, move away, but I can't. Instead, I stare into his eyes, eyes that are watching me intently. This is more than just offering comfort, but I don't know what he is offering.

My tears, which have been brimming, break through the moment by spilling over. Jem watches them fall for a beat before his thumb swipes over the apple of my cheek, wiping them away. Then he pulls me against him. I stiffen for a beat and then I cling to him, taking the comfort he offers. His chest is hard, and I can smell the leather of his vest, his aftershave and a scent that is just him. I don't want to think about how good and how right it feels to be in his arms, to have him wrapped around me. I can't.

"It'll be okay, Piper. I promise. I'll take you to him, so you can see for yourself, okay?"

"Okay."

He lets me go, but I sense his reluctance and when I stumble, he reaches out to steady me again. "You need help?"

Yes.

But I shake my head. Having Jem in my space makes my head foggy and I need to think clearly right now. Time is of the essence.

Before he can say anything, I stagger into the bedroom and scrabble around for my boots. Hugging Jem Harlow is not what I should be doing after learning my brother is ill again, but I can't beat myself up either for taking a little comfort when it's offered. I'm alone here in Kingsley, and while I'm used to being on my own, I don't go through life without support. I have Cami. Okay, latching onto Jem while having a mental breakdown is not the best plan, but I can't be held responsible for my actions when learning bad news, right?

Shucking into my jacket, I make my way down the hallway to Jem, who is leaning against the kitchen counter when I step back into the living area. He glances up when I re-enter, his face still unreadable before he does a full body scan of me.

"You'll do."

My brow knits together. "I'll do?"

"I didn't have time to get a cage, Piper."

A cage is a car in biker vernacular.

"Okay..." I have no idea why he's telling me this.

"I'm on the bike," he explains. "You need to be wearing suitable clothes, so you're protected on the back. You'll do."

There's a lot to unpack there, but I start with the first thing. "You're on the bike?"

"Yeah, Piper. As soon as I heard the news, I got on my bike and came right here. I knew you'd need to get there."

He came straight to me.

He knew I would need to get to Josh.

This statement warms me in a way I don't expect. It surprises me that he cared about what I would need.

Why *does* he care so much?

I know we've been getting on a little better lately, but this implies something more, something deeper.

The man is an enigma. First, he told me he thought I was beautiful, then he let me sleep on him, now this...

I can't figure him out.

"Babe, come on, we need to go."

This statement breaks through my reverie, and brings me back to my current predicament: transportation.

"Hold on." I hold up a hand. "Are you expecting me to get on the back of your bike?"

"Well, unless you plan on holding onto the handle bars..."

I ignore his sarcasm. "I'm not getting on that death-trap."

He stares at me a beat, then shrugs. "Fine. Make your own way there then. I'll see you at the hospital."

Bugger. I don't have time for this. If anything happens to Josh while I'm arguing about road safety, I'll never forgive myself.

I grab his hand. It's warm, rough beneath my palm, and reassuring. I don't want to let him go, but reluctantly, I release him.

"Wait..." I swallow hard, staring up at him.

He stares at me through the blond curtain of his hair.

"I won't let anything happen to you, Pip. You're safe on my bike, I promise. Trust me, yeah?"

I ignore the fact he calls me 'Pip'. I also ignore the fact I find this name, like angel, makes my belly flutter when it spills from his mouth. It no longer annoys me, as it did previously. And I ignore what this means.

"Fine, I'll trust you, but if we crash, I will kick your arse."

The smile he gives me is worth risking my own sanity. It's so radiant, so beautiful.

"I haven't crashed my bike since I was a wet behind the ears prospect. I'm not about to do it with precious cargo on the back."

He called me precious cargo before, when I first arrived in Kingsley, but then it had been a slight. Now, I don't think he means it as an insult, not if I'm reading the soft look on his face right. My heart gives a quick lub-dub.

Why is he looking at me like that?

He juts his chin at me. "Grab your stuff. We need to get going."

Right. Stuff.

I shrug my bag over my shoulder and snag the house keys off the table near the door.

He follows me out of the flat and waits for me to lock up. His hand goes to the small of my back, steering me out towards the exit of the building. The urge to step away from his touch is intense, but I don't want to cause a scene. Besides, part of me likes the feel of his touch on me.

When we get outside, he leads me over to his bike and my heart starts to pound in my chest. I cannot ride that thing. Don't misunderstand me, I can appreciate it is a beautiful piece of machinery, but they are not safe.

I give Jem a concerned look before bringing my attention back to the bike. It's sleek and a light red, almost blood red. He hands me a helmet. It's not a fully enclosed thing with a visor, it's open at the front.

"You need to put that on," he instructs, "and this."

Jem hands me a piece of material with a bold blue skull on it. When I stare blankly at it, he says, "It's for your face. Unless you like eating flies."

He's far too amused by this entire process. I resist the urge to punch him in the gut.

I make a disgusted sound while wrinkling my nose, then I turn the cloth in my hand, trying to fathom how best to put it on.

"How do I...?"

Placing his helmet back on the bike to free his hands, he demands, "Didn't they teach you this shit at private school?"

His tone pisses me off. I am well educated, but just because I wasn't running around learning 'Bikers for

Dummies' doesn't make me stupid. I hate that he's talking down to me. Jerk.

This makes my next words terse. "They taught us maths, English, science... you know, the things we needed to learn for everyday life?"

His lips tip slightly as he snatches the cloth from me and shakes it out a little. "So, you did go to some fancy as fuck school."

I'm not sure why he sees this revelation as a victory, but he does. I actually went to a very prestigious school, but I keep this to myself. No need to keep handing him ammunition—especially since I have no idea what he's keeping it for.

"I went to a school, Jem. What does it matter what kind it was?"

"It doesn't."

I stare at him. "I know you revel in giving me a hard time, and usually I wouldn't care, but right now, I don't have the strength to come back with a witty retort. Please, just help me get on the bike so I can see my brother and make sure he's okay."

His entire face softens in a way I've never seen before.

"Fuck, angel... I'm just messing with you. I'm sorry. I can't help it. I'm a wanker; it's a reflex action." One of his hands cups my cheek. "Wade's going to be fine. He will. It's just part of the process. The doctors said infection was a risk of the second surgery, didn't they?"

They said a whole bunch of stuff. I was more focused on getting my brother conscious and talking to me than listening to potential outcomes.

My eyes fill with tears. "I just want him to be okay, Jem."

"And he will be."

He surprises me by leaning forward and kissing my forehead. It's a gesture that wouldn't be out of place if my own brother did it, but it doesn't feel familial. It feels like more than that. It holds the promise of so much more. It tells me he cares, and that he wants me to know. It feels protective.

I raise my eyes to his when he pulls back and ties the face covering around my nape. Despite my outburst a moment ago, my heart starts to quicken as his fingers brush over the sensitive skin there and I have to swallow hard to control myself. He keeps his eyes locked on mine as he gently pulls it up over my mouth and nose. My breath is warm behind it.

"There you go," he says quietly.

"Thank you." My voice sounds muffled behind the material, which makes him smile a little.

"Helmet now. We have to protect that clever brain of yours."

He reaches for one of the helmets on the back of the bike and helps secure it onto my head. It's an intimate gesture, buckling it under my chin and even with the worry for Josh, I can't help but squirm under his gaze. I'm glad when he finally gets it locked into place and turns to pull his own on.

Finally, he secures my bag in the locker on the back.

I raise my eyes to Jem.

"How do I get on?"

He runs through the process and I wait for him to throw his leg over and climb on before I attempt to follow the instructions he gave me. It's simple enough. I have to use his shoulders to steady myself, but I manage to get on the back and seated without issue. I scoot back so there is a little distance between us.

"What do I hold on to?" I ask him.

He doesn't respond. He grabs my hands and pulls them around his waist, which drags my pussy closer to his back.

Tension ripples between us.

Maybe this was not a good idea.

He glances over his shoulder at me and heat stirs in his eyes. I have no idea what is happening, but I get lost in his eyes for a moment.

"Jem..." I murmur behind the bandana.

"Fuck," he mutters.

Then shakes himself.

Jem turns forward and I let out the breath I've been holding. He pulls a pair of sunglasses out and puts them on. Then he starts the motorcycle up. It roars to life, and the vibration of it beneath me is intense.

"Hold on," he yells back at me.

Revving the engine again, he gives it a hit of gas and the bike takes off. I squeal and grab him tightly around the middle, holding on for dear life. This was a bad idea. I should have got a taxi...

I close my eyes, burying my face against his back, and I feel him vibrate. It takes me a moment to realise he's laughing at me, and despite the gravity of the situation, despite knowing we're riding to the hospital where Josh might be in a bad way, I'm so glad he is, because it makes me laugh, too.

And my only thought as he weaves the bike through Kingsley's mid-morning traffic, curled against the back of a giant of a man who looks like a modern-day Viking, a man who drives me insane, is Cami would be so bloody jealous if she could see me right now.

CHAPTER TEN

"Will you stop staring at me?"

Josh doesn't open his eyes as he says this, so I have no idea how he knows I'm watching him, other than the fact I have not moved from his bedside for the past twelve plus hours other than to pee. His infection is severe, but he's doing well, all things considered. My heart has been in my throat from the moment Jem brought me here this morning. The doctors spouted a load of medical jargon at me, but the upshot is they're pumping industrial grade antibiotics into him with the hope it will clear it fast. His immune system is already working at less than optimum levels because of his recovery. My watching him like a hawk is seemingly not appreciated, however. Not if the impatient timbre of his voice is anything to go by anyway.

I can't help it, though. He looks small in the bed, a shadow of the man he was four and a half weeks ago when I first arrived in town. He's lost weight, a side effect of being bed bound for so long, and probably the hospital food. If they're serving the same stuff to the patients as they are the visitors in the canteen it's no wonder he's shifting the pounds. I'm certain I've lost a little off my hips myself.

Joking aside, Josh is going to need serious building up when he gets out of here. I told Cami I was going to return home, but that's not looking likely now. Even if the infection clears up, it's obvious Josh is going to need help when he's discharged. He's weak—not that I would ever utter those words to him—but he can barely take care of himself. I'm sure his strength will return before they toss him out of the hospital, but he's going to need support, and while the Club have been good taking care of him, I can't see him allowing anyone else but me to stay with him.

And that's what he needs. He needs someone in the flat with him until he's back on his feet fully.

"I'm not staring at you," I mutter, lowering my gaze to the magazine I've been pretending to flick through for the past hour.

"I can feel you watching me."

"You've got your eyes closed, so how would you know?"

His voice is softer when he says, "I'm not going anywhere, Piper."

Bugger.

I swallow past the lump in my throat. He's not allowed to do that, go from gruff to soft. I don't know how to handle when he does. He's always so guarded with me. I thought my trust issues were bad, but Josh is another level. He's doing his best to let me in, I can tell, but he's wary. Curtis really did a number on him. I don't think Josh has ever been loved a day in his life. I wish I knew where our father was. I'd like to smack him, hard.

This time around, I can see the damage done to my brother, but I've got my own issues, too. I was too wrapped up in my own issues, my own pain, to recognise how screwed up Josh was back then. If I hadn't been, I might have been more forgiving of his behaviour. I might not have ignored him for as long as I did. He's as much a victim of his circumstances as I am.

Freud would love us. We're practically a case study on how parents can screw up their children beyond all recognition. Neither one of us has healthy relationships—although at least I know this. I don't know if Josh is aware.

It makes me quietly cautious of getting close to Josh because of our own history, because of the shit my parents have done to me over the years, but also determined this time not to let him push me away again. Why? Because I'm desperate for a connection with him, and I think he needs this as much as I do. Josh has never had anyone, and I know he has the Club, but it's not the same as having blood family.

This means I fear any little action I do might push him away again. It's a terrible tightrope I'm balancing with him, terrified I might fall at any moment. Maybe coming here, trying to rekindle something with him, was a stupid mistake, but Josh is all I have to cling to. Don't get me wrong, if he wasn't trying, I would be long gone, but Josh is giving back in his own way, and it's that which keeps me here. He wants to be a big brother. He just doesn't know how yet. Maybe, just maybe, I can teach him this time.

"I know you're not," I respond quietly to his statement.

"Piper, I'm not going anywhere, period."

And I don't think he's talking about his health anymore. I shift on the chair, unsure how to answer. Is he giving me an assurance he won't walk away this time? I don't know that I can take that from him or believe it, as much as I want to. I don't think he can promise something that he isn't sure he can deliver himself yet.

Even so, I answer, "I know you're not." I say it because I think he needs to believe I believe it.

Seemingly satisfied, he pulls his eyes from me to the ceiling and scratches at the edge of the gauze taped to his side from the surgery he had earlier in the week, the surgery that led to the infection that landed him back in the ICU for a brief spell before he was moved a few hours ago to a high dependency unit.

I resist the urge to smack his hand away.

"The doctor told you not to mess with your stitches." I ignore how wobbly I sound. God, do not have a breakdown in front of him. That is a sure-fire way to have him push back.

"I'm not messing with them," he grouses.

"You're worse than a child," I chastise, grateful to be onto another topic.

My phone vibrates on the small table next to me. Bugger. I should have turned it off. The nurses are strict about the no-phone policy up here. I'm just about to hit the power button when I notice it's a text from Grant.

Great.

I quickly open it and read the message. It's a list of engagements he needs me to attend over the next couple of months for the start of his election campaign trail.

Crap. I forgot how insane he gets during an election year. I knew about the photo shoot, but there's about six different events listed on this message—two black tie events, a magazine spread about our family and a couple of other interviews.

Is he crazy?

I'm not doing all this. I have my own life—one that does not revolve around him getting re-elected, which I'm sure he can manage without painting a picture-perfect family, which we absolutely do not have. My parents haven't even noticed I haven't been in town for nearly five weeks. Even if we were close, I wouldn't partake this closely in my stepfather's career. I'm twenty-five, for God's sake, not a child, and I'm busy. Okay, currently I'm running around Yorkshire with an outlaw motorcycle club, but that's not the point.

"Bad news?"

I raise my head and see Josh is looking right at me. Of course *now* his eyes are open.

"No, everything's fine."

I shut down my phone and stuff it back in my bag, feeling a weight in my stomach as I force a smile.

"You don't seem fine."

"You're the one with paint-stripping antibiotics being pumped into your body and you're asking if I'm okay?"

He stares at me, unperturbed by my attempt to brush him off. "Piper?"

"Honestly, Josh, I'm fine. I'm just tired."

"Yeah, I can see you're tired. You're tired because you're always here. I appreciate it, kid, but you need to ease off."

My stomach clenches unpleasantly. "You don't want me here?"

"I didn't say that. I just don't want you here at the expense of your own wellbeing. The docs are going to keep pumping this shit into me," he nods his head up at the IV antibiotics. "I'm going to get some shut-eye. You should do the same."

I want to argue with him, but I'm exhausted and frankly, the thought of getting into bed sounds divine.

"Okay."

He arches a brow. "No argument?"

Rubbing at my neck, I shake my head. "I'm dead on my feet, Josh. Even I know when to admit defeat."

"Ask one of the lads to take you home. They won't mind."

"I know they won't."

I'm more than certain they won't since Jem put a ban on me using taxis while I'm in town. Only Club approved rides are allowed. I have no idea if Jem's still here, but since he's blacklisted me from both taxi firms in town, he can drag his backside here and take me home if he's not.

"Will you send a nurse in on the way out?" Josh asks as I start to gather my things together.

"Are you in pain?"

He gives me a smile that is tight. "I'm fine. Just send one in, yeah?"

I frown at him, but come to the edge of the bed. Grabbing his hand, I give it a squeeze.

"I'm glad you're okay," I tell him. "You gave me a fright today."

He squeezes back. "I'm good, Piper."

"I think good might be overstating it, but you're doing better than I was expecting."

"Get yourself home, yeah?"

After saying my goodbyes, I head out of his room and I'm surprised to find Jem sitting in one of the chairs in the corridor. He glances up when I step out.

"I didn't realise you were still here," I say, moving towards him.

"It didn't feel right leaving you here alone." He juts his chin towards the room. "How's he doing?"

"He's surprisingly chipper. I thought he would be a lot more out of it. He's tired, though, I can tell the infection is taking a toll on him."

"He sent you packing?" he guesses as he pushes to his feet, straightening his kutte as he does.

He looms over me as he comes to his full height and I have to tip my head back to meet his gaze.

"That obvious?"

"Well, you look like you're about to fall down yourself, which I'm guessing Wade could see. You want to go home?"

"Actually, I thought we could hit a bar, get tanked up."

He blinks at me. Then I watch, slightly mesmerised by the way his mouth moves into a grin. "Angel, did you just make a joke?"

"I'm actually quite funny, you know when I'm not hanging out in hospitals."

Jem dips his head forward. "I think we'll have to hang out a lot more for me to judge that."

My stomach somersaults at this statement. He wants to hang out? "Please, you can barely stand to be around me most of the time."

"Not true. I actually find your company refreshing, Pip. It's a change from the usual empty-headed bimbos Weed and the others bring around the clubhouse."

I meet his gaze. "That's not very nice, Jem."

"I know, but it's true all the same. I like a woman with a little something about her."

We start to walk towards the lifts.

"Maybe you should stop expecting Weed to find you dates."

"I don't need anyone's help to find me a woman."

Hearing him talking about being with someone strikes through me like fire. It shouldn't. I have no claim to him, but it does.

I give my focus to hitting the call button for the lift as I say, "No, I don't imagine you do."

"Piper?"

"What?"

"Jealousy is a good look on you."

I jolt and twist to him. "I'm not jealous."

"It's okay that you are, angel. I mean, I understand it. I'd be jealous, too."

The lift doors open and I step inside. "You *are* crazy."

"Babe, I'm a catch. Why wouldn't you be insanely put out about the idea of me with other women?"

I lean against the back of the lift and try to ignore him as he props himself next to me. Considering there is only us and one other couple in the carriage, I don't know why he has to stand so close to me when he's being so irritating.

"I don't know how any woman puts up with you for more than five seconds," I hiss at him under my breath.

He grins. "I have many talents that make my bad points worth putting up with."

I flush at the look he's directing my way, and my eyes skitter past him to the couple in the lift with us. They are murmuring to each other, seemingly not paying attention to us—thank God.

I elbow him in the ribs. "Stop it."

He leans towards me. "I can't. You bring this out in me."

"I bring out the fifteen-year-old dirty teenage boy in you?"

"You bring out many things in me, Piper, but it's not a teenage boy."

The molten look in his eyes has me swallowing hard. His tone has shifted from playful banter to something different. He's not playing any longer. The game between us has changed, only I no longer know what the rules are. Truthfully, the game has been shifting for a while now.

The lift stops and the other couple disembark, leaving

just Jem and me in the lift alone. I stand awkwardly, unsure if I should say something. As soon as the doors slide shut, he surprises the hell out of me by moving into my space. His hand goes to the back wall of the lift, just above my head, the other near to my hip and he leans into me, his chest nearly flush to mine. Our bodies are inches from each other, his mouth dipping close, so close I only need to roll slightly to my toes to capture it.

I raise my gaze to meet his, unsure what he's doing, my heart stuttering in my chest as I try to fathom what his next move will be. Right now, he looks like he's considering devouring me whole, and this makes wetness pool between my legs and tingles rush to my pussy.

He doesn't touch me, but his fingers reach out, as if he wants to.

"I shouldn't even be thinking about you like this," he murmurs as his eyes rove over my mouth, as if he's contemplating taking it. He moves closer, so close his breath clouds against my chin. "Do you know the trouble I can get in just by having these thoughts?"

My heart is hammering now.

"Jem..."

"Shit, Wade'll gut me if I touch you, but I want you so much. Just a little taste..."

He dips his head closer and his mouth moves nearer to mine.

I hold my breath. He's going to kiss me.

Jem Harlow is going to kiss me... in a hospital lift... It's not the most romantic place, but who cares? This sex god man is about to lay a hot, wet kiss on me.

His lips feather across mine and my heart stops before it beats a staccato rhythm. I grip his forearms, grounding myself as my legs go wobbly and—

The lift pings and the doors slide open.

Reality crashes down around me.

What the hell am I doing?

How can I let him kiss me?

Jem Harlow—a criminal biker, who makes money disappear, who runs rings around the police for fun, who makes my traitorous body take notice just by breathing in my space.

A man who is also as close to my brother as blood and should, therefore, not even be on my radar. Especially given the strides I'm making with Josh and the tenuous ground those steps are being taken on.

Panicked, I shove him back. I think surprise more than anything else has him go back on a foot as a handful of people step inside the lift from the lobby. Did they see us about to make out like teenagers? I quickly duck around them, lowering my head as my face heats and I make like a torpedo for the entrance. I'm not the girl who kisses men in hospital elevators. Especially men who are dressed like chaos.

"Piper, wait!"

I don't. I keep walking. What is he doing trying to kiss me? Is he completely insane? He can't kiss me. He's my brother's friend. He's also a biker whose life is completely and irrevocably incompatible with mine.

And I'm worried if I kiss him back, I'm going to want him, too.

Fear drives my feet into a run. I make it to the hospital doors before I glance back and see he's still stuck navigating the busy stream of people all leaving the grounds. I'm surprisingly fast when I need to be, and I don't think he expected this. I've done my share of running away over the years, though. I'm an expert at fleeing scenes. Head down, I manage to double back on myself and lose him in the crowd of visitors.

Knowing I can't get a cab home, no thanks to Jem's antics, I walk the fifteen-minute car ride, which takes me three times longer on foot, my head a minefield of colliding thoughts—first and foremost, what on earth do I do about Jem Harlow trying to kiss me?

More importantly, what do I do about the fact that I'm disappointed he didn't succeed?

CHAPTER ELEVEN

When I approach the flat, I know I'm in trouble. There's a Harley parked outside the kerb underneath the streetlight, the kickstand down, the headlight off, but even under the fluorescent lamp, I know it's Jem's. Even if I didn't recognise the motorcycle, there is no mistaking the hulking man leaning against it, and he looks a tad annoyed.

Bugger.

During my trek home from the hospital—or my cowardly fleeing from the scene of the 'incident'—Jem tried to call me repeatedly. I had no idea what to say to him. Mostly because I was a mix of boiling mad and completely confused.

Did I lead him on somehow?

Did I make this situation happen?

Did I want this situation to happen?

Yes... I absolutely wanted it. When he leaned in and I felt his mouth against mine, for the briefest moment, I was elated. My heart soared, my head sang, my stomach flipped.

How could that ever be wrong?

But then reality hit me the moment the lift doors opened.

Kissing Jem would never be right. If Josh knew, it would upset him.

It's an unwritten rule—you do not go there with your siblings' friends. Ever. Would I be angry if I caught Josh and Cami kissing? Well, in truth Cami could steal the moon and I would forgive her, but Josh is not like me. He seems to have fairly traditional ideas about things, and our relationship is already so complicated without adding in another level of complication in the form of a six-foot-three giant called Jem Harlow.

I know I shouldn't have, but after I fled from the hospital, I turned my phone off. I couldn't face speaking to Jem. What could I say? I'm sorry you didn't get to kiss me, but I wish you had even though it would have been completely wrong?

Now, I'm regretting that decision. I should have spoken to him and told him to leave me alone—at least until I've had a chance to work through my thoughts on the matter. Him sitting on my doorstep looking for all intents and purposes like a furious behemoth is not welcome. I don't have the energy to deal with him tonight, nor the head space. I need to work through what I'm feeling, and I don't think he's going to give me that time.

What did I expect, though? Jem to just slink off quietly to lick his wounds after I rejected him? It's not really his style.

What I should do is get the hell out of the blast zone. He's about to explode. If his eyes were not locked onto mine, I would.

But I don't want to run again. I'm exhausted, and the stubborn part of my brain refuses to back down. I didn't do anything wrong. It wasn't me trying to kiss him in a hospital elevator. It wasn't me pushing boundaries. He's the one in the wrong here, not me. He's the one who needs to apologise, not me.

Even so, I feel like a fifteen-year-old coming home late to face my parents' wrath.

But I'm not fifteen. I'm an adult and I don't have to answer to Jem.

Steeling myself, I hoist my bag up my shoulder and head towards him.

"What are you doing here?"

"Inside," he snaps.

Oh yeah, he's angry.

"What?"

"Unless you want to do this in the middle of the street."

I absolutely do not, although I'm not keen on having a pissed off Jem in the flat either.

When I hesitate, he takes the decision out of my hands by moving towards the front door of the flat.

I watch him for a moment before trailing after him.

I guess we're doing this now.

I do owe him an explanation, and possibly an apology of sorts although I'm not sure what I need to apologise for—running, ignoring him or rebuffing him.

Without a word, I dig my keys out of my bag and with fumbling fingers, I unlock the door. He doesn't speak either and the tension between us is horrendous. I want to say something, anything, but I don't know what. I realise my behaviour, in hindsight, was childish, but I don't know how to broach it with him either when he's clearly so steaming mad at me.

He doesn't speak a word as we get inside the flat. Nor does he say anything as I shrug out of my jacket, hanging it on the hook near the door. By the time I've divested myself of my handbag and shoes, I'm out of things to do and feeling stripped bare to him.

Standing near the front door, I stare at him as he waits in the middle of the living room, his back to me. What he's waiting for, I don't know, but I can hardly draw air as I wait for him to do something.

Finally, he tips his head towards the ceiling and lets out a long-suffering breath.

"After you ran off into the dark and didn't answer a single one of my calls or texts to tell me you were okay, I spent nearly half an hour riding around town looking for you, sure that you'd been abducted or hurt." I wince at the quiet rage in his tone. "When I calmed down enough to think rationally, I figured you'd eventually have to come home, so I came here to wait for you. And lo and behold—" He holds his arms out at his side. "Here you are."

I swallow down the guilt gnawing at my throat. I didn't mean to make him worry, but logically, why wouldn't he? It's dark now, the dusk that had been in place when I ran from the hospital completely obliterated by the shadow of night. He had no idea where I was, just that I was out there.

"Jem—"

He holds up a hand, and I clamp my mouth shut.

"Are you completely insane?"

"I don't think so—"

"Why didn't you answer any of my calls or messages? I was about a cunt's hair away from calling the entire Club to go looking for you. Where the fuck have you been? It's been over forty-five fucking minutes since you disappeared?"

He paces the space in front of the sofa, twisting on his booted heel when he gets to the end of it, his hand tearing through his hair as he rants.

I'm not sure if silence or explanations are my best course of action here, but he doesn't give much opportunity to respond anyway. He's too busy berating me, and I'm not entirely sure I don't deserve it, given how worried he clearly is. I was feeling like the aggrieved party, but now, I'm feeling like the worst kind of brat.

"I walked back..." I say when he pauses, clearly expecting a response.

I should have kept my mouth shut because his head looks like it might explode.

"You walked back from the hospital? It's nearly eleven o'clock, Piper. Are you fucking deranged? The route back from the hospital takes you right past the fucking park—a park I know for a fact is used by people who are not so fucking nice."

The number of F-bombs he drops tells me how stressed he is. He turns from me, giving me his back and the full view of his kutte. I stare at the Lost Saxons insignia, getting lost for a moment in the macabre burning ember eyes in the skull as his hands drop to his hips.

"What the fuck were you thinking?"

I bristle. "I could have got a taxi, but you blacklisted me, remember? I didn't have a choice but to walk."

This is not the best thing to say because his head snaps back to me. "Don't even go there. You did have a choice. I would have taken you home. You didn't have to run after I tried to kiss you. Jesus fucking Christ, Piper. All you had to say was no. I'm not a scumbag. I don't force women to do shit they don't want to, but you running off like that was dangerous. You scared the shit out of me. I don't know if this bears repeating, but when people go missing around here, it doesn't usually herald good things."

I feel terrible.

"I wasn't missing," I assure him.

He crosses the room and I find all six-foot-three of him in my space suddenly. I let out a small gasp as I'm backed up against the wall near the door, his hand going to the wall next to my head as his face moves inches from mine. The seriousness of his expression frightens me a little, as does the tone of his voice.

"You don't ever do that again, Piper. I don't give a fuck what happens. You don't run off like that and you don't ignore calls. I've been losing my mind over here thinking something happened to you."

My body relaxes at his words. "You were worried."

"Yeah, Piper, I was worried. Of course I was fucking worried. You took off and I couldn't get in touch with you."

More ugliness creeps in as I realise how selfish my actions were.

"I'm sorry. I know it was stupid. I just... I panicked."

He rubs his forehead. "Jesus. I've never tried to kiss a woman and their response be to panic. You're not doing much for my self-esteem, angel."

I relax. He's calling me angel again. This means he's no longer angry with me, right?

"Well, you could probably do with it knocking down a notch or two."

He lifts a lofty eyebrow at me. "And you're the one to do that, are you?"

"I don't want to knock anything out of you, Jem."

He roves an eye over me and his voice gets soft when he says, "Too late. You've already knocked me for six."

I feel heat rising in my cheeks. Is he serious? I study his face, seeing no hint of humour in it. He's not joking. I've knocked him for six? We barely know each other.

How can I have affected him at all?

"Jem—"

He cuts me off before I can speak. "Why did you run?"

"I told you."

"Yeah, you panicked, but Piper, I'm not an idiot. I like to think I can read people pretty well. And you're not a mystery. I can read you like an open book. You were into that kiss. You wanted it. I wouldn't have continued with it if you didn't. Like I said, I'm not into unwilling participants. You wanted to kiss me back. You can't deny you like me."

I can't deny it. I don't want to deny it. My chest heaves as I stare up at him and his head moves closer to mine. His body is nearly flush to mine, our chests practically touching. Electricity zings through my every synapse. What is he doing? This close, I can't think straight. My brain is fog, my thoughts consumed by one thing and one thing only... him.

"You wanted it, right?" Jem questions quietly.

I lock onto his lips, the mix of dark and blond hair surrounding his mouth suddenly mesmerising. I should tell him no. I should do a billion things that all start and end with the word no, but I can't and don't because I do want him. Wanting him is not the problem.

"Yes, Jem, I wanted it," I tell him, my voice breathy, "but that's not the point."

He grins as if he's just won a crowning victory. "Then I'm sorry, angel."

His words confuse me.

"For... for what?"

"Because I am going to kiss you, and this time you're going to let me."

At his words, my world stops.

He's going to kiss me, and I'm going to let him...

Then, his mouth crashes down on mine. His fingers

thread through my hair and his hands come to rest at the nape of my neck as he pulls me closer.

I stiffen at first, taken completely by surprise. I should push him away, but I don't. I can't. My legs wobble beneath me, and I suspect if he wasn't holding me, I would be a puddle of goo on the floor. Even so, I cling to his biceps, needing the support as he presses against me, ravaging my tongue as he seeks deeper inside my mouth. In my entire life, I've never been kissed like this. It's the kiss of a man, who has proven his worth. It's the kiss of a man who has conquered in the bedroom. Jem Harlow looks like a sex god because clearly he is.

His fingers move to my hip, steadying me before sliding up to my breast. I let out a moan as he cups it, then slides both hands under my sweater. In the back of my head somewhere, a voice is urging me to stop, that what we're doing is a bad idea, but I shut it down. I can no more stop what is happening here than I can prevent the sun rising in the morning.

I rub my thighs together to create friction to alleviate the tension growing down there, wishing his hands were also down there.

I'm dizzied and my underwear is uncomfortably damp already. My chest feels tight as air sits trapped while he plunders my mouth. There is no other word for what he is doing. He is plundering me. I try to rub against him, needing more, but he doesn't give it.

Instead, he recoils as if I've burnt him, sucking back his own breaths. His pupils, I notice, are blown black. His hands rake through his hair, as I'm left panting against the wall, barely able to focus on anything but dragging oxygen into my heaving lungs.

I watch as his eyes squeeze shut and I can see him struggling to gain control. I don't blame him. I'm struggling myself. I tug my top back into place as he tries to ground himself, unsure what is running through his head.

After a moment, he stops tearing at his hair and turns his gaze to me, and for a moment I see beneath the wall, beneath the bravado as he says, "Fuck, angel. You're killing me."

He sounds ravaged, but he's not the only one. My brain is whirling at a thousand miles a minute. Jem just kissed me, and he really kissed me. It wasn't just a peck or a normal kiss. He kissed me like I was his lifeline. But kissing him, as good as it was—and it was good—is not something that can happen again.

"I can't get you out of my fucking head. And now that I've tasted you..." He closes his eyes, as if he's remembering it. "Kissing you was everything I thought it would be."

My breath catches as my own memory stirs. I raise my fingers to my lips, which feel bruised, puffy from his assault of them. I can still taste him on my tongue. My body tightens in recognition, in remembrance, begging, wanting, needing, demanding him.

He wants me, I can see it in his eyes, but Jem doesn't strike me as a guy who sticks around after he gets what he wants. Even if I've misjudged him, and he will be the perfect partner, we can never be. We exist in different worlds. Our lives will never mesh. His Club is dangerous, his life is dangerous. I don't even want to be a part of it for my brother, but I have to. I won't be like Beth or Liv or any of these women. I won't be an old lady to an outlaw biker.

So, I push aside anything I feel for Jem, bury it.

He can't be mine, even if I want him. He's the ultimate forbidden fruit, and I don't dare take another bite because he's so tempting I won't be able to resist more.

Regret floods me as I whisper, "We can't do that again."

His mouth pulls into a tight line even as his eyes go distant. Then he mutters a "Fuck" before blowing past me and out of the flat, leaving me wondering what the hell happens next.

CHAPTER TWELVE

The last Saturday in July is the Lost Saxons' monthly 'family day'. The entire Club comes together to hang out, catch up and have a rip-roaring good time. It spans through the day and then into the evening, with the common room bar open until the early hours. Only family is invited—no outsiders. At least this is what I'm told when Sofia extends the invitation to me. I'm both touched and slightly perturbed by this. I've been told repeatedly I'm part of the family because of my ties to Josh, but getting asked directly to join a day specifically aimed at family unsettles me in how much I'm not unsettled by it. Five weeks ago, I would have freaked out and run for the hills screaming. I didn't want to be embroiled in a criminal gang. Now, I'm becoming friends with half the women in the Club and I'm falling for a member—and I am falling for him, as much as I try to deny it. Jem is in my thoughts more than he should be, more than he has any right to be. Since he kissed me a week ago, I haven't been able to get him out of my head, and why would I? That kiss is emblazoned in my memory like a brand. I can still feel it now, a week after the fact, on my lips.

It's lucky my memory is so good.

I haven't seen the man himself since he took off that night after kissing me senseless. At first, I counted it as a blessing when Weed showed up the following morning to take me to the hospital, rather than Jem. I was grateful I didn't have to address the humongous elephant in the room. What could I say to Jem anyway? Thanks for the leg-shaking, mind-blowing, pussy-quivering, tongue-melting kiss? Let's never repeat it, even though I would happily sell my soul for round two. If that was the preview, I can only imagine what the full show would be like. However, imagining sex with Jem is a bad idea, but unfortunately, he has been the starring role in a number of my fantasies over the past week.

But when Charlie was waiting to take me home after visiting hours ended, I felt irritation gnawing at my guts. I realise people in glasshouses should not throw stones, given I ran out of the hospital like my feet were on fire, but his avoidance of me is maddening.

We're both adults. We should handle this like adults, right?

Apparently not.

When he didn't show the following day, my anger turned to something else. Rejection burnt a path through me as the days continued to pass and Jem stayed away. Logically, I know we can't go there together, but ignoring me as if I did something wrong hurts.

As angry as I am, I'm nervous the morning of the family day party. He'll be there undoubtedly. Everyone will be there—apart from Josh who is still in the hospital. I have no idea if I should give Jem a piece of my mind or just ignore him, as he has been content to do with me.

This decision is taken out of my hands after I get out of the shower. I'm sitting on the edge of the bed, a towel wrapped around me, when my phone beeps. Reaching for it, I groan when I see it's a message from my mother.

MUM: Come to the house for two o'clock.

I stare at the text and grit my teeth. This is typically my mother. No question of whether or not I'm busy, no asking if I want to come, just be there. As much as I'm not over the moon about seeing Jem today, part of me is looking forward to this party. I like the girls, and spending time with them is preferable to my mother.

ME: I'm busy today. Can we reschedule?

My leg jiggles, my fingers tugging at my lip as I wait for a response. I know what the answer will be before it comes. My mother only contacts me when she needs something. If she wants to see me it's not because she's missed me—although it has been a while since we last met up. I've been in Kingsley five weeks already, and it was at least three weeks before that since I saw Mum. I wonder what the problem is now.

The handset vibrates in my hand and the message icon flashes across the screen.

MUM: Darling, are you honestly too busy for your own mother?

I groan as I read it. She's a travel agent for guilt trips. I tip my head back to stare at the ceiling.

Bugger.

ME: Of course not, but I need a little more notice than a couple of hours. I have things to do today.
MUM: If you can't come to the house, I'll drop in to see you.

My heart flips as I read the only words guaranteed to get me to the house without argument. She cannot come to the loft—mainly because I'm not there.

ME: I'm not there.
MUM: Well, where are you?

Bugger...

ME: I told you. I'm busy.
MUM: Well, this won't take a moment, Piper, and it really is important we talk. I'll be at your place this afternoon.

And she will. She'll camp out there until I turn up. I don't want to put Cami in a position where she has to fend her off, so I text back my response.

ME: I'll come to your house.
MUM: I knew you'd see sense. I'll see you later, darling.

"I guess I'm going back to bloody Manchester then," I mutter.

I fire off a text to Sofia to tell her I'm not going to make it to the party today, that I've had to go home to deal with a family issue. As I expect, she asks if I need help, which makes me feel even worse about missing today.

I tell her I'm fine, then I drop a message to Cami to let her know the situation and get packed up.

Thankfully, it's not a long journey between Kingsley and Manchester by train, so I manage to get back to the city centre with plenty of time to spare. This means I head home first. As I leave the train station, I can't help but notice the Devil's Dogs clubhouse. It's funny. I've walked past it a hundred times on my way to work, but I've never paid it much heed, other than in angry thoughts about how much I hate motorcycle clubs for taking my brother from me. This time, I slow my walk, taking a moment to appreciate the bikes lining the street outside the building and the large banner over the front door. Weirdly, I find myself missing Kingsley, yearning already to be back there. The fast pace of Manchester holds none of the appeal it used to. I find myself missing the rundown high street in Kingsley, the few small bespoke shops that cater to everyone but no one. It's a strange, sad place, but comforting in its uniqueness.

Even so, I have missed my best friend, and as I near home, my feet move at a faster pace. Cami and I live in an old converted cotton mill in the Northern Quarter. I don't know much about architecture, but I adore our loft apartment. It's fabulous. It's got huge windows that look out over the city centre and let in a ton of light. It's one of the things that really drew us to the building in the first place. The red brick stands out against the modern architecture surrounding it, and the wrought iron railings around the perimeter gives the illusion of security. In reality, it's not a deterrent. Cami's shimmied over that fence more times than I can count when she's lost her keys and come through the back entrance.

It sits on the sixth floor and towards the back of the building with a view to the canal—at least the slither visible between the squeeze of concrete surrounding us. It also costs an arm and a leg, and was paid for outright by Cami with money from her Trust Fund, which she gained access to the moment she turned eighteen—although her parents tried everything to stop that from happening. They didn't think their rebellious daughter could be trusted to manage her own finances; a Judge thought differently. That was more or less the beginning of the end for their relationship.

I barely manage to get the key into the front door before I'm accosted by my best friend. She may only be five-foot-five, but she's strong, and when she throws her weight at me, I go back on a foot. Somehow, I manage to keep hold of her and not go down as I hug her close.

"Oh my God, I'm so glad you're back!"

"I missed you, too, Cam," I tell her through a smile.

She drags me inside, and I barely manage to kick the front door shut behind us. I can't help but take in everything as we move into the loft. It looks the same but different at the same time. The open space is as I remember. The dark wooden floors, the open plan kitchen with black cupboards and oak tops, the large sectional sofa that me and Cami love to curl up on to watch horror movies on the weekends, the open metal staircase that goes to the bedrooms and the cast iron supports that run through the building, giving it that industrial feel. There's exposed brickwork on the walls and everything feels urban and raw. I love it. So did Cami. It's why she bought the place when we saw it.

"Tell me everything. Your phone calls don't give me enough gossip," she says, heading straight for the kitchen and the coffee machine.

Good God, I've missed proper coffee.

"There really isn't anything to tell."

Other than my brother's friend tried to kiss my face off last week and is now avoiding me...

I keep this to myself, however. I'm not ready to divulge this with anyone yet, even her.

"Seriously?" She flicks her auburn braid over her shoulder and fixes me with a sceptical glare. "You've been with the biker cult for five weeks and you have nothing to tell?"

"They're not a cult." I wrinkle my nose at her, watching as she fills the coffee pot.

"Have you been acclimatised then? You're one of them now?" she jokes.

"No, but they're not bad people, Cam. They're just like you and me. Well, more like you really."

Her lips tip up. "Oh, it's been a while since I got into trouble. Maybe I should come and visit."

"I don't think Kingsley is ready for your brand of mayhem," I mutter, leaning my hip against the counter.

I'm not entirely lying either. Cami takes rebellion to a whole other level. She's been practising for years. At first, it was to annoy her father. Now, I'm not sure why she's doing it.

"Things with you and your brother are going well?"

I nod. "Yeah, I think so. He's struggling with how to fit me into his life still, but we're both struggling with that."

She studies me and I feel like she's pulling all my secrets out of my head. "You don't need his approval, P."

"Good thing I'm not looking for it."

She gives me a sceptical glare. "Darling, you may be able to fool everyone else, but you can't fool me."

No, I've never been able to fool Cami.

"I don't know why I care," I admit finally.

"Because he's your big brother."

"That shouldn't matter after what he did."

"You've always had a big heart." She hands me a mug of freshly brewed coffee.

I take it, holding it under my nose and sniffing it. It smells divine. "I missed percolated coffee."

"You're going back, I take it. After you've seen Mumzilla."

I wince. "Yeah, I'm going back. Josh is still unwell. He's got an infection—"

"And about a dozen people who can take care of him," she interrupts.

This is true, but...

"I'm his sister, and I'm the only one he's got."

"You were also his sister when he walked away from you, Piper."

She's not telling me anything I don't know. "People deserve a second chance. He's trying, really trying, to make things right. Curtis—our father—he screwed him up, Cam. Josh doesn't know how to let people in. I have to take that into account."

"That didn't give him carte blanche to treat you like shit."

"He's trying," I say quietly, clutching the mug like a security blanket. "And I want to try, too. We were both dealt a shitty hand in life. His worse than mine. That doesn't get him carte blanche, no, but it does get him a do over. I need him, probably more than he needs me. I only have you in my life, and you're amazing. You have got me through so many things that I would never have survived otherwise, but—"

"But he's your brother," she cuts me off with a sigh. "I get it, darling, I do. He's family. I just might have to kill him if he hurts you again."

If he finds out about my less than platonic feelings for Jem, she may not have to worry. Josh may not be a problem in my life, period.

"Is it a big deal about siblings dating sibling's friends?" I ask.

She arches a brow. "Do you have a confession to make?"

"No. Just one of the girls in the Club is dating her brother's best friend. It came out and things got a little messy," I lie. "I thought it was a bit ridiculous."

Cami tugs on the end of her braid, her other hand clutching her own coffee mug. "Personally, I couldn't care less, but these men sound a little bit on the traditional side."

"They are."

"Sisters are probably off limits, meaning the best friend committed a grievous faux-pas going there. Was there a punch up?"

I wouldn't have thought of Josh as being particularly traditional, but he has quite traditional views on taking care of the women in his life. Actually, all the men in the Club do. They look after the girls surprisingly well.

"Piper!"

"Hmm?"

"You said it got messy."

Caught in my lie, I shrug, "Oh, it didn't get that far."

"That's too bad. I'll just have to imagine hot leather-clad bikers wrestling each other instead."

I frown at her. "You need to get laid."

"I have been. I'm back with Spense."

Spense being Spencer, her on-again, off-again boyfriend who seems to be more of a friend with long-term benefits.

"I can see that ending well."

She shrugs. "For now, it suits us both. Whether it will in a week or two is another matter. Anyway, don't you have an appointment with your mother?"

I shake my wrist to turn my watch and groan. "Yes. I better leave if I'm going to make it to the house on time. She'll throw a wobbler if I'm late."

Once I've finished my coffee—because I'm not that much of a heathen that I can leave a full mug of the stuff—I borrow Cami's car and take the twenty-minute drive out of Manchester city centre, north. I can drive, but I don't have my own vehicle. There's little need living in the centre of town and Cami lets me use her car whenever I need to, since she rarely drives it herself either.

My parents have a large detached property in a small village near to the canal. Ironically, it's part of the same canal system that runs through the city centre and behind my apartment.

It's a lot more rural out here, though. Where my home is surrounded by industry and urban sprawl, theirs sits among fields and farmsteads. It's a quieter pace of life, and one fitting to a local councillor and his wife.

I pull the car up outside the double garage and cut the engine, staring up at the house that is ostentatious in its size and appearance. Considering there are only the two of them living here, they really do not need a five-bedroom property, but what do I know?

With a sigh, I snag my bag off the passenger seat and climb out. I don't bother to knock on the front door, instead heading for the conservatory, which overlooks the garden and has views over the fields beyond. It's a beautiful location, but it would drive me crazy being this far away from everything.

When I step inside the house, it's quiet. My boots are loud on the tiled floor, even though they barely make a sound. I glance around the perfectly laid out furnishings. Everything has its place. It's like a show home, rather than a lived in house. I hated growing up here. I was never allowed to breathe, to be a kid. No toys out, no mess. It sounds ridiculous to complain about, but I was constantly on edge, worrying about every little speck of dust. As an adult, I can't stand disorder myself. It makes me twitchy. Everything has to be just right. I know that's my mother's doing, a side effect of her neurosis. I should have rebelled, gone the other way and become a total slob, but mess terrifies me. Cami has dampened down some of my worst fears on that front. I'm not as bad as I once was, but it's still there, that need to keep order. It came back in full force when I first moved into Josh's place. It took me a week to get it organised enough to settle.

"Mum?" I call out, wondering where on earth she is.

Usually, she'd be in the conservatory or the little snug room off it. She's not in either.

I get no response, so I move further into the house, finding myself in their huge kitchen. Still no sign of Mum—or Grant for that matter, but that's less unusual since my stepfather is a workaholic and rarely here. I'm about to call her name again when I hear raised voices coming from the main living room. I'm about to make myself known, but something stops me. I pause in the kitchen doorway as a voice says, "...that naïve, are you, Farrah?"

It's the venom in my stepfather's voice that makes me take notice. I've never heard him speak to her like that before and honestly, it makes the hair on the back of my neck stand up.

"I don't know what else to suggest," she bites back, but I notice there isn't the usual heat in her words I would expect if anyone else spoke to her in that manner.

I want her to lay into him, to give him a dressing down. I have a difficult relationship with both my mother and stepfather, but I do love them both. Hearing Grant disrespect my mother this way doesn't sit well with me.

"Well, of course you don't," he says with derision in his voice. "Why would you? This isn't a bloody bake sale. You can't knit it better or make a flower arrangement. We're fucked. Completely and utterly fucked."

I've never heard my stepfather swear before. He's usually Mr Pristine, so his language shocks me, but not nearly as much as my mother.

"Grant! Honestly, there's no need for such vulgarity."

"If this little twerp manages to carry out his threats, then I'm fucked."

"Well, if you hadn't felt the need to push him in the first place, it wouldn't be an issue, would it?"

There's a moment of loaded silence. *What on earth has Grant been up to?* My cleaner than clean stepfather wouldn't know trouble if it hit him around the head. He's the councillor who managed to reduce homelessness in Manchester by ten percent over the last five years since he's been in office, he's the councillor who improved education outcomes for disadvantaged children in the foster care system, he's the councillor who opened fifty-seven more care beds for the elderly. He even funds the learning support centre I work at.

"Everything I've done has been to keep you and Piper in the lifestyle you have now."

I blink. I never asked for any of this. I never wanted it either.

"This is insanity, going up against someone like him and his organisation!" Mum hisses. "Then again, you've always believed you were cleverer than you are, but you're just a silly, little man trying to play with the big boys—"

Crack.

I hear the smash of flesh meeting flesh. I move before I realise I'm doing it, and I'm in the room. I take the scene in with a flick of my eyes and my blood boils. They're both standing near the sofas. Grant's holding Mum's arm, as if he's grabbed her and her head is down. I can't see her face, but it's clear they're in the middle of an altercation by the tenseness of their stance.

"Let go of her," I grind out, bringing both their gazes to me.

When Mum's head comes up, I see the red mark on her cheek.

A handprint.

I grind my teeth together, and cross the room, putting myself between them. Grant is taller than me, although not by much. He's much bigger than my mother, though, who is closer to Cami's height.

"Take your hand off her, Grant. Now."

For the first time ever, I see a flicker in the veneer my stepfather puts on, a veneer I didn't even realise he put on. It's there, though, and I glimpse the darkness beneath for a split second. The urge to step back is overwhelming and if I wasn't protecting my mother, I would.

He releases her and moves back, running a hand over his dark, salted hair. He's wearing his suit still, along with a tie and a shirt. He's every inch the gentleman, and the complete opposite to the denim and leather-wearing bikers I've been surrounded by for weeks, but I've never worried one of those men, as big as they are, as brawn as they are, would raise a hand to me or any of the women around them. I thought suits and money bought class and status. I was wrong.

I glare at him. "You ever touch her again and I'll ruin you and your fucking career," I growl at him.

Again, the veneer slips, and this time I don't glimpse the monster, I get a full eye of it. He jolts towards me and snags my arm.

"You want to threaten me?"

The shock of being grabbed renders me almost paralysed. Violence may have been something my brother lived with growing up; I'm considering if it's something my mother has also dealt with, but it's not something that has been in my world.

Emotionally, I've been abused, yes, but physically, never. So, Grant putting his hands on me shakes me to my core, and his touch isn't gentle. His hold is bruising and the clamping of his jaw is so tight I feel real fear.

"Grant, let her go," Mum pleads in the background. Her words fall on deaf ears.

I don't back down, although I should.

"If you raise a hand to my mother again, I'll do more than threaten you, I'll end you," I somehow manage to grind out the words, even though my fear levels are through the roof.

He snarls at me and releases me with a shove. Mum catches me, and I watch as Grant storms from the room.

When I hear the front door slam shut, I turn to her, adrenaline flooding my body and leaving me trembling slightly.

"Are you all right?"

I watch as her face pulls into a mask of indifference. "You shouldn't speak to him like that."

What the hell?

She pats at her hair, making sure it's still in place, still perfectly coiffed, the chignon tidy. I stare at her in disbelief, waiting for the joke to end. It doesn't. She's serious.

"Are you insane? He just hit you."

Mum's throat works before she manages to regain control. She's not as unaffected by what just happened as she wants me to believe. "Grant's a very passionate man."

She moves over to the sofa, straightening up the cushions unnecessarily. I watch her, mesmerised by her behaviour.

"Passionate? Is that what we're calling domestic abuse now?"

Mum rounds on me, anger lining her face. "Don't you dare say that to me. I'm not some helpless victim and your stepfather isn't a violent man. He's a good person."

I splutter. "Good men don't hit their wives."

"You're naïve to the ways of the real world, Piper. You've never seen hardship. Grant is facing a lot of stress—stress that you're making all the more difficult, by the way." She sinks onto the sofa. Her elbow rests on the arm of the chair, while her fingers massage her forehead.

No doubt she has a migraine brewing after that sideshow. I have one myself.

I try not to focus on the increasingly growing red mark on her cheek.

"How am I making things more difficult? I haven't even seen either of you in weeks."

I don't sit. I can't bring myself to. My body is wired for action, fight mode still activated.

"You didn't reply to Grant's message about the engagements he needs you to attend. It's just another stress on top of everything else he's dealing with. You know how he gets during election term."

"I couldn't care less if he was running for Prime Minister. It doesn't give him the right to hurt you, Mum. Look, if you're scared of leaving him, I'll help you. You can come and stay with me in the loft."

She scoffs at me. "I'm not scared of the man, and I'm not leaving him either. Good lord, what would people say?"

I stare at her. She's either completely insane or in total denial. "I really don't think what people say matters."

"Of course it matters. Grant will lose the election if this gets out."

"Rightly so, Mum."

Her eyes go to the ceiling. "Oh, you really are a silly girl, aren't you? How would that benefit anyone?"

I can't believe what I'm hearing. "Mum, he hit you."

"Yes, he hit me, not you, and I'm fine, so can we please just drop it?"

It's like I've stepped into an alternative dimension. How is she okay about this? My arm, where he grabbed me, is already starting to hurt, so her face must be on fire.

But this is the story of the Hollanders right here. We can't possibly let the world see the truth of what goes on behind closed doors. Everything must seem perfect, even when it's not. My whole life has been a nonstop production. I went to the right schools, had the right friends, did the right activities. Everything is a carefully choreographed dance. We're marionettes on a stage, and Grant controls us all.

I got out, in a way. Cami helped me to escape, but I still have to get back on that stage and let them pull the strings now and again. It's galling. I'm tired of being in their sideshow.

"It's all about keeping up appearances, right? That's all that matters."

She shoots me a look, and for a moment I see a flash of something beneath the hardness—hurt, maybe. She's not as unaffected by this as she's making out. Maybe I need to tread more cautiously.

"If you'd just responded to Grant's messages," she fluffs her hair again, trying to regain her composure, "none of this would have happened." I gawk at her. Is she really blaming me for his actions? "He isn't good under stress, and needs to know, darling, so he can organise what he's doing PR wise."

I was busy nursing my brother back to health and falling for a biker—both secrets I will take to the grave. If Mum got a slap for... whatever that was... I can only imagine what I'll get if they find out what I've been up to.

When they discovered I'd been seeing Josh the first time, that had caused a hurricane force argument, one that had taken a long time to recover from. "What were you even fighting about?"

"Anyway, none of that matters now. Just ensure, in future, you let him know these things. It's polite to respond, darling."

I couldn't care less about being polite right now. I want to kill Grant.

"Mum, is Grant in trouble?"

"Don't you worry about him."

"I don't give a crap about him. He can rot for all I care, but I'm worried whatever he's doing is going to roll back onto you."

"I can look after myself, Piper."

This I don't doubt. My mother is a survivalist. I want to push it, tell her I'm not going to do the photo shoots, the dinners, but honestly, I'm a little worried about her and this situation. Those events are the only real links I have into their lives outside of special occasions. As much as I hate to do them, I can't lose those connections, not if Mum's in trouble. She drives me nuts, but she is my mother, and now I'm starting to question everything. Have I missed tell-tale signs over the years? Has Grant been hurting her and I just haven't noticed? Does she put up with it because she doesn't want to lose her standing in society? Position is everything to Farrah Hollander-Ellis. She would put up with being abused if it meant keeping the big house and the fancy lifestyle, but I won't let my mum be a punching bag for my stepfather.

"Tell Grant I'll be there at the events he sent me." I'll be there if it keeps her safe, and if it keeps me on the inside.

Mum smiles. "Of course, darling. He'll be pleased to hear that."

"I'm sure he will." My voice is tight, but if she notices, she doesn't say.

"Now," she rubs her hands together, "can I get you a cup of tea?"

And just like that, normality resumes—apart from the blooming red mark on her face. "No, I'm fine. I can't stay long."

CHAPTER THIRTEEN

By the time I get back to Kingsley, my head is pounding and my thoughts are a jumbled mess. I don't know what to do to help Mum, not that she seems to want my help. Clearly, she thinks there is nothing wrong with my stepfather taking his hand to her. I feel like I've stepped into an alternative dimension. The Farrah Hollander-Ellis I know and grew up with would never allow anyone to touch her like that, yet she barely blinked at Grant hitting her. She took it like it was nothing. I'm angry on her behalf, but I'm angry that she's not angry.

When I returned to the loft and told Cami what happened, she wasn't surprised. In fact, she said more or less what I accused Mum of—anything to keep up appearances. I swear, though, if Grant touches her again, I'll break his fingers. I don't care if Mum thinks it's normal and fine. I don't. I don't tell Cami that Grant grabbed me. Mainly because she would end up in a jail cell for punching his lights out, but my arm hurts. It's definitely going to bruise.

I hate saying goodbye to my best friend, but it should only be for a short time now. As soon as Josh has cleared this infection, I'm coming home. I need to get back to my real life. I can't continue to live in this fantasy bubble I've created in Kingsley. Ironically, the criminal biker club bubble is the one I'd rather stay in than my actual life.

I get back to Kingsley early enough that I could head to the clubhouse and drop in on the party, but I'm so tired and drained that I just head straight for the sofa. I order in pizza, eat a quarter and leave the rest boxed up in the kitchen. Then I take myself to bed.

I've been lying there less than twenty minutes, unable to quiet my brain when a repeated booming breaks through the silence of the flat, splinting through my thoughts.

What the—

The front door, I realise belatedly.

I glance at the clock, it's just after midnight. Panic squeezes my belly. Who would be knocking on my door at this time of the night? Tossing back the covers, I slip out of bed and reach for my dressing gown as another bang sounds on the door—this one more frantic.

Moving out of the bedroom while raking my fingers through my hair in an attempt to tame it, I pad silently but quickly through the darkened flat to the front door, clutching my phone in my hand, the light from the screen illuminating my path. I should call someone, but my go-to is Jem and he's currently ignoring me.

Maybe it's just a random drunk, nothing sinister.

Carefully, I leave my phone on the side table near the door, pointing up so I have some light and creep to the peep hole. As stealthily as I can, I put an eye to it, and in the hazy darkness on the other side, I catch a glimpse of messy blond hair.

Jem.

What the bloody hell is he doing here?

I quickly tug it open as he raises his fist, presumably to hammer again on the door.

"Are you trying to wake up half the block?" I sound terser than I intended, but him pounding on the front door like an irate caveman is ridiculous.

He lowers his hand as his gaze moves from my sleep shorts to my camisole, both of which are clearly visible beneath my dressing gown. I quickly pull the two halves of the robe together, tying the belt securely at my waist as my neck gets hot.

His expression shifts from heated to annoyed. "You didn't show at the party," Jem grinds out.

I blink at him. This is why he's banging on the door at gone midnight?

"Hello to you, too."

He pushes inside the flat without asking, kicking the door shut with one of his heavy motorcycle boots. I have to step back to avoid his large frame. I don't even bother to examine how good he looks. Of course not... Although I do note he's wearing his kutte, his thick leather jacket on underneath that he uses to ride in, and a pair of blue worn jeans that hang loose around his hips, unfortunately hiding those legs of his—legs I know look amazing.

He also looks tired, his hair unruly, as if he's been pushing his fingers through it all night. Did I cause this?

An unpleasant feeling settles around me. I don't want to be the cause of this expression on his face. He seems... lost—well, beneath the mind-bending ire.

"Why didn't you show?" he demands.

This tone, the bossy, arrogant, 'give me answers' one, riles me up, and given the day I've had, I'm fresh out of patience to tread lightly with him. I don't care if he's a biker who could, quite possibly, make me disappear without breaking a sweat. I can't hold my tongue with him.

"I'm not entirely sure why that's any of your business, Jem."

"Seriously? I thought you were over your little spat with the Club. Then you don't show to family day. What gives?"

Oh. So, this isn't about me ignoring him. This is about me ignoring his precious Club.

"Not that I owe you any explanation, given you've blanked me since you kissed me, but I told your sister I had to go home for the day. I had a family crisis I had to attend to."

His brow pulls together. "Which sister?"

"Sofia."

"Fuck, she never mentioned it."

"Well, why would she, Jem? Why would she think you'd be interested in me at all? It's not like we're friends."

Judging from the way his brow gets heavy, he doesn't like this statement. He chooses to ignore this last barb.

"What family crisis? You okay?"

Internally, I freeze. Oh bugger. I shouldn't have mentioned it was a crisis. He's staring at me now as if he needs to solve this problem.

"It's nothing." I wave it off.

"It was obviously something if you needed to go home."

"Just my mother being my mother."

"Are you all right?" he asks, his voice dropping low, soft, and it's filled with concern. It makes my stomach dip.

"Do you even care?"

He recoils as if I've slapped him. "Of course I fucking care, Piper. What kind of question is that?"

"Well, you've completely erased me from your existence

since you kissed me. I can only assume the memory of it was so awful you had no choice but to avoid me."

I suddenly fear for my wellbeing. His left eye is twitching slightly and his jaw is working as words try and fail to form in his mouth, which is also moving, but making no sounds. Usually, I would find this amusing. I've done what I've been trying to achieve since the first moment he opened his mouth—rendered Jem Harlow speechless—but the darkness clouding his face is a little scary.

After what seems like an insurmountable amount of time, he manages to grind out a strangled, "What?"

I should let sleeping dogs lie, but since I started this, I'm going to finish it.

"I'm sorry if kissing me was so terrible, Jem, that you had to completely erase my entire existence from your memory. You can leave now. As you can see, I'm fine. You've done your duty to my brother. I'm safe, whole. I'd like to go to bed."

I start to push off the wall, but I'm suddenly surrounded by Jem, who crowds me. His hands come to my shoulders, pinning me, stopping my attempt to flee.

"What the fuck are you talking about?"

"Let go of me," I whisper.

His hands on me are too much. They ignite embers that I doused after the kiss, embers that should not reignite. He doesn't. He presses my back against the plaster, and I tip my face forward, not wanting to see him.

"Piper, look at me."

I don't. Instead, I tell him in a small voice, "I want you to leave."

"I'm not going anywhere until we talk."

I shove his chest, but he doesn't move. The man is like a

brick wall of muscle. "The time to talk was a week ago!" I yell at him.

He lets out a breath and I watch in fascination as his dark brown eyes become tortured. "Fuck... I'm sorry, angel. I messed up."

He's... apologising?

I keep my eyes locked on his, unsure what to say, unsure what to do.

"I didn't mean to completely avoid you, although you did tell me to."

"I told you we couldn't kiss again. I didn't tell you to blank me like a pariah."

"I know, but avoiding you seemed easier than facing the truth."

Drawing air, something I've done every day of my life, suddenly feels like an arduous task.

"What truth is that, Jem?" I ask.

"That I want you, and having you puts me in a difficult position." He closes his eyes and breathes in through his nose. Then he snorts a laugh. "If you were anyone else's sister, it wouldn't be a problem..." He moves closer, his palms going to the wall next to me, his face dipping into my neck. My respiratory system goes into overdrive as his nose nudges up my throat. "It's not unheard of for inter-Club dating. Look at Logan and Beth, my parents, but Wade's on this whole overprotective big brother ride."

This surprises me. "He is?"

"Angel, he's had 'the talk' with all of us at least ten times since he first clapped eyes on you."

A lump is forming in my throat, a lump I can't swallow around. I had no idea Josh cared that much. I know we've been working on rebuilding our relationship, but this action says so much more than any words over the past five weeks could. Tears burn behind my eyes, and I have to blink them back.

Jem cups the side of my face. "He made you forbidden fruit the moment you entered our world, Piper."

"Is that why you want me?" I ask, resisting the urge to lean into his touch. "Because I'm off limits? Is that all I am to you? A challenge?"

He doesn't hesitate to answer. "No, angel. Wade doesn't control what I do or who I'm with. I want you because I want you. I want you because when I'm with you my world feels a little less frantic."

It scares me that he sees me as a grounding force for him. Mainly, because I feel the same, and I didn't even realise it until this moment. Having him in my space, my head, which had been spinning a mile a minute when I returned home, is emptied, relaxed, for the first time in hours. I try not to read too much into that, or consider why that is. I try not to think about why this giant of a man with all his stupid jokes and irritating behaviour stops my brain in its tracks.

"But wanting you is going to put me against your brother. He's fairly adamant about no one touching you. He's going to kill me for even contemplating the things I'm thinking about you."

"I can't have you and Josh fighting."

"You don't need to worry about me. I can take care of myself, but I do need to know that you feel this, Piper, that I'm not imagining this thing between us before I go to bat for us."

His words are a plea, a demand.

I should deny my feelings; it would be the easiest course of action. Josh clearly does not want me with any of his brothers. He's warned them all to leave me alone, but my heart thumps rapidly beneath my sternum as I think about Jem being gone from my life. This past week without him has been horrible. Forget the kiss, even without his presence. I've got used to him being around. As my unofficial taxi driver, he's usually there at the start of my day and at the end, unless he has Club business to attend to. As much as he irritates me, I also enjoy his stupid banter. My week without him felt void.

It's selfish, but I don't think about my brother, about what this will do to our relationship. My only thought is of the man standing in front of me and what it will do to me if I let him go.

I dig my teeth into my bottom lip. "I don't want you to walk away."

Relief floods him as he leans his forehead against mine. "Thank fuck."

Then he attacks my mouth with a ferocity that takes me by surprise. There's no hesitation, no wavering in this kiss. He takes what he wants and he wants me. He's not coy, even if I am. His hands wander, dipping inside my dressing gown, finding their way beneath my camisole. I'm not wearing a bra, so he finds my nipple easily. He rubs it, drawing an embarrassingly needy moan from me. It's been a while since I was last touched and Jem has magic hands. I'm a panting mess. I rub my thighs together to create friction to alleviate the tension growing down there, wishing his hands were also between the apex of my thighs.

I shiver and let out a shaky breath as I feel his hand slip down my belly, the muscles quivering as he slides past the waist band of my shorts and inside to cup my pussy. I barely breathe.

My brain is no longer calling the shots, my body is and

it doesn't care about propriety because his other hand is undoing the tie of my robe.

"Such a wet cunt. You're wet for me, angel?" he murmurs into my ear, his breath warm against the shell.

I nod, my eyes going to the ceiling as his filthy words send a jolt of pleasure to my pussy.

"Words, Piper."

"Yes," I gasp as he tugs my shorts down my legs, leaving me exposed.

He slides a finger through my folds, even as his other hand keeps tweaking at my nipple, and my breath rips out in ragged pants. I should stop him. He's Josh's friend. He's also a criminal. A biker. Our worlds exist on different planetary orbits, spinning on different axes, but as he strokes across my clit, a shiver rolls through my pelvis, and I know there is no force that could make me stop what is happening here and now. I'm too far gone.

Dark brown eyes lock onto mine as he slips a finger into my slick pussy and stretches it out before quickly adding the second then he moves them back and forth, hard. I grip his shoulders, widening my legs to give him better access. I feel full with him and when he adds a third finger, I dig my nails into his skin, my head tipping back as the pressure builds. I barely draw air as he keeps his pace and I topple over the edge, planting face-first into his chest.

"I need to be inside you right now."

My pussy throbs with his words, my stomach somersaults. I want him in me, too. I want him in every way I can have him. He lifts me, his hands coming under my bum, and instinctively I wrap my arms and legs around his neck and hips.

Kissing me, he walks us into the bedroom and slowly lowers me onto the bed. As my body hits the mattress, he lifts off and removes his kutte and his jacket. In my daze, I didn't even realise he's still fully dressed.

I come up onto my elbows to watch as he strips for me. Then, getting impatient, I move off the bed, reaching for the hem of his plaid shirt and pull it up, so I can undo his belt. He lets me work on the buckle while he unbuttons his shirt and shrugs it off his shoulders. The undershirt he's wearing is tugged over his head a moment later.

I have only a brief moment to admire his physique. He's buff—I knew that from seeing him in his workout gear—but now, I'm getting the full show. He's all hard edges and sculpted muscles beneath the ink work scattered over his body, and he is a work of art. I wish I had time to study the tattoos covering him, but there will be time for that later, maybe. He toes his boots off while I get his jeans pushed down his thighs far enough to release his cock.

It's thick, veiny, beautiful, and already hard. I reach out and run my fingers over the shaft, ignoring the slight tremble in them. He makes a noise of appreciation in the back of his throat that goes straight between my legs.

That's hot.

Softly, he pries my fingers away and I watch as he pulls a condom from his jeans pocket. I'm transfixed as he rolls it down his cock and into place before he meets my gaze.

"Are you ready, angel?"

Are we really going to do this?

Am I really going to sleep with my brother's friend while my brother is in the hospital?

I pause and then I lick my lips. I'm weak because I want Jem, and from the moment I kissed him, I was done for.

I nod.

"I'll take it from here."

He pushes me back onto the bed, thumbing my nipple

as he does, then lines his dick up with my pussy, running the tip through my folds. Lifting one of my legs higher around his hip so he can get a better angle to drive his cock deep, his fingers bruise my hips as he pushes inside me.

I gasp as he fills me completely from root to stem in one hit, my fingers grappling for his forearms as I try to ground myself. The intrusion burns for a second before my pussy relaxes. He doesn't take his eyes off me the entire time as he stays seated inside, letting me adjust to him.

"Are you all right?" he asks, brushing my hair off my face as he looms over me. The gesture is so tender, I feel a lump in my throat.

How can this big man be this caring?

My breathing is laboured as I say, "Yes."

He leans down and kisses me. Then he pulls back and pushes back into me. My legs wrap tighter around his hips and all that gentleness dissipates, replaced by a burning passion. This isn't making love. It's raw passion. It's fucking —plain and simple. And he fucks me hard.

He slams into me over and over with just enough bite to sit on the edge of pain, but to elicit that pleasure that is driving me wild. I've never had it so good.

I dig my nails into his back, dragging him closer to me, trying to force his thrusts deeper still, urging him harder. We're animals, nothing more. There's no sweetness here, nothing more than desire and need.

And afterwards, I'm certain there will be regret—regret for breaking the code of brotherhood, for sleeping with a man like Jem, for crossing lines that should not be crossed, but for now all I care about is the man giving me the best sex of my life.

CHAPTER FOURTEEN

I WAKE with a dry mouth and a dull headache. I blink until Josh's guest room comes into focus and the last remnants of sleep are chased away. It's then I become aware of the body at my back, and I remember what I did last night—or rather *who* I did last night.

Buggering hell.

I hear movement behind me. Jem. Oh my God.

We had sex last night.

We had *sex*...

Multiple times.

I am the world's worst sister.

I lie still for a moment and realise he's moving around the room—perhaps getting dressed? Does he already regret what happened? Do I regret it? I don't think I do. I had the best sex of my life, and I truly mean that. Jem was amazing. I doubt he felt the same way about me, but from my perspective, I have no complaints.

He fucked me again for hours until my body felt bruised and spent. I expected him to leave afterwards, but he didn't. He pulled the covers over us both, kissed my head and fell asleep. I thought it was strange that he did that, given we probably won't repeat this again, but maybe he didn't want to be an arse. It was nice. I liked falling asleep with him. I liked it too much. It felt good. Right. Perfect.

In the stark light of the morning, it's almost cruel to remember how good it was. It promises so much that can't be delivered. It would be better if I didn't remember any of it.

The sound of his belt buckle jingling makes me stiffen. He's getting dressed, meaning he's readying to leave. I close my eyes quickly, wondering if he will go without a word. Do I want him to leave without saying goodbye? Do I want to do the awkward morning after dance? Not really, especially not when I'm feeling a little attached. I should have known it would never just be sex, not for me. I'm not a girl who does one-night stands. In fact, this is my first one, and it's not my finest moment. I should have listened to the sensible part of my brain, the part that said this would be a disaster. Not only is Jem in a motorcycle club, but he's also Josh's friend. My brother is going to hit the roof when he finds out.

If he finds out.

Let's hope that never happens.

"Angel?"

A feather light touch on my arm sends a shiver through my body and I can't stop my eyes opening in response. When I do, I'm greeted with Jem's brown eyes. He's crouched at the side of the bed in front of me. I expect to see displeasure, censure in his face for what we did last night, for the fact we crossed the unspoken line, but all I see is warmth.

This surprises me.

I thought he might blame me for last night, be angry, ignore me again.

"Hey," he smiles. "I'm sorry. I hate to wake you, sweetheart."

He shocks me further by leaning in and brushing his mouth over mine. I respond more out of instinct than anything else, but when his fingers move into my hair, my body takes over and I kiss him back like a love-starved woman. I need him. God, how did I get to this place where I need this irritating, but handsome man?

When he pulls back, he leaves me panting, and a little shaky.

"I have to go and sort shit out this morning. I really wish I didn't have to. I would love to stay in bed with you."

As he speaks, he caresses his fingers up my arm and I shiver at the gesture.

"It's okay..." I say slowly, not sure what to make of his words, surprised he's being nice. I thought he would be gone in record time.

"I'll be a few hours at most. Beth and Lo got engaged last night," he says.

I blink. "Oh! That's amazing." I suddenly feel terrible for not being at the party, and for dragging him away. "I'm sorry you had to leave last night."

"Don't be. They disappeared halfway through the evening anyway, which I really do not want to think about why, but I need to be at Mum's this morning for some family breakfast thing. Will you wait here for me until I'm done?"

I want to, I really do, but I have my own commitments. Besides, I don't think it's a good idea to wait here for him. This implies carrying on... this. Whatever the heck this is.

"Visiting is in a few hours. I'll need to get to the hospital."

"I'll message one of the brothers, ask them to tell Wade that I'm giving you a day of R and R."

I arch my brow. "Is that what we're calling what we did?"

He smirks. "We can go with the truth instead. I'm sure 'I'm fucking your sister's brains out' will go down a treat."

I flush. "Don't be so crass."

"I can use nicer words, but I don't think you're ready to hear them, Pip." He's right about that. "I don't care if Wade knows we slept together."

I sit up in the bed, my legs sliding over the edge, careful to make sure I keep the sheet with me. I don't know why, given he saw every inch of me last night, but in the cold light of day, I'm feeling a little exposed. Especially as he's fully dressed in jeans, his plaid shirt (which I adore on him) and his kutte. He looks good, too. Too good. My mouth waters. He shouldn't get me this hot and bothered; he's not even my type. I like my men clean, shaven, groomed. Jem is the opposite of all these things. He's wild, with unruly hair and two-day growth on his chin that isn't by design, but because he hasn't shaved. His tattoos span up his arms, under his clothes and he's so masculine, even standing there with a lopsided grin on his face.

"You should care. We both should."

"Okay, maybe I phrased that wrong. I care, I really do, but I'm not going to apologise either for what we did."

I close my eyes briefly. "He's going to hit the roof."

"You think he's going to be pissed off that I deflowered his little sister?"

"Deflowered me?" I snort. "Hardly. I didn't go to bed with you a virgin, Jem, so you can knock that fantasy out of your head."

"Angel, I really don't want to know about you with

other men," he growls under his breath. "Especially not after I just spent the night inside you."

"Sorry."

He pushes his hair back from his face. "Look, it's as simple as this: Wade's a brother and a friend, but he's not my keeper—nor yours—and he can keep his fucking nose out of my business."

"It's really not that simple."

"Yeah, angel, it is. I took my colours because I wanted to live a life without rules and boundaries. And the only person I take orders from is my president, and that's hit and miss. Your brother doesn't get to lay down rules about who I sleep with and spend my time with. I respect Wade, and I hate that he's going to feel put out by this, but it's too bad. We both had a good time last night and that's all I give a shit about." He cocks his brow. "You did have a good time, right? I mean, I don't want to toot my own horn, but I know I'm not exactly shit on that front."

Jesus.

"You're perfectly fine on that front."

More than fine, in fact, but I'm not giving him the satisfaction of knowing he's a sex god in the bedroom.

"I don't honestly know, Jem. Mine and Josh's relationship is... complicated. I hardly know him myself. I don't know what he'll do if he finds out we slept together, but I don't want to do anything that might jeopardise what we're building."

"He might be annoyed, but not at you, angel. It'll be me he'll be mad at." He kisses me. "Don't overthink it."

"How can I not overthink it? We slept together."

"So?"

His blasé attitude annoys me.

"Well, I don't want to lie to him."

"So, you want to come clean?"

"Absolutely not."

"Then you do want to lie?"

I open then close my mouth. "I don't know," I say finally. "He's still unwell. I don't want to make him worse."

And this undoubtedly will make him worse. I don't think he's going to like knowing I've slept with his friend.

Jem stares at me a moment before he lets out a long breath that is filled with unveiled frustration.

"He's a big boy, Piper. Us sleeping together isn't going to push him into a stroke."

I blink at him. Sleeping together? As in continuing? Does he think this is more than a one-time thing? Do I want it to be more than a one-time thing? I have no idea. I didn't think he would consider it more than a fling, so I'm not sure how to deal with this sudden roadblock. Even without the issue of Josh, I can't date a biker.

"Jem... this can't happen again. You know that, right?"

"Why not?"

"Well, because it can't. Once was bad enough."

His eyes widen. "Wow, way to kick a guy in the balls. 'Once was bad enough?'"

I cringe. "I don't mean it like that. It wasn't bad. Not at all. Actually, it was completely fabulous." I shake myself when he grins at me. "That's not really the point, though."

"It was fabulous, huh?"

"Focus, Jem. Your prowess in the bedroom isn't in question here."

"Then what is?"

"This." I point at the bed before pointing between us. "Us. We can't continue this."

"Why not?" he repeats, sounding very much like an annoying child. "We just had fabulous mind-blowing sex.

Why can't we continue that? I'm certainly not opposed to the idea. In fact, I'm very much in favour."

"Of course you are, but we're not the only people in this equation."

"As I keep saying—Wade doesn't get to pick who I sleep with."

I frown at him. "Isn't there some unwritten rule about not sleeping with friends' little sisters?"

"Why? Do you want there to be?"

I shift in the bed. "Yes. No." I wince. "I don't know."

He cups my face. "From the moment I met you, I've been trying to ignore this pull between us. We have chemistry that is off the fucking charts. I'm drawn to you, and unless my dick is completely broken, I'd say you feel the same. I'm tired of ignoring it. Life's short. My father dying how he did taught me that. You have to seize the day, live in the now, all that feel-good shit they put on fridge magnets."

He pries my fingers off the sheet, and it falls, exposing my breasts. The grin that crosses his face as he stares unabashed at my naked chest makes me blush. "You have very stunning tits, Pip."

He grabs one and squeezes before latching his mouth around the nipple. I can't help but gasp. My hands slam into the mattress behind me to anchor myself as he swirls his tongue around the hardening bud. I watch as he pulls the sheet down and parts my thighs.

"You also have a very beautiful pussy."

He pushes two fingers into my wetness. I sag back against the mattress, my bum hanging over the edge, my feet flat to the floor, my thighs as wide as I can get them, and let him finger-fuck me. And he doesn't do it gently. He goes hard and fast and deep.

My orgasm hits me embarrassingly fast and when he

pulls his fingers from my body, he sucks my juices from them.

His grin makes me blush. Oh my God, he's so dirty. I raise my hands to cover my face and as I do, I hear his sharp hiss of breath, followed by a 'fuck'. I uncover my face as he moves back to the bed and gently, but firmly, pulls my arm down. I have no idea what he's doing and it takes me a moment to realise he's clocked the nasty bruise that has formed on my arm where Grant grabbed me yesterday—a bruise that, in the morning light, has started to form into three separate bruises... finger marks. I know exactly what they are, but to anyone else it looks like just three contusions.

Maybe I can spin this...

"Fuck, angel." His voice sounds laden with guilt. "You should have told me I was being too heavy-handed with you last night."

Uh, what?

Oh, bugger. He thinks *he* hurt me? And he looks devastated by the prospect. He scrubs his fingers over his mouth as he stares at the darkly mottled contusion. It would be easy to let him believe it. We were rough last night, no bones about it. Between my legs aches deliciously with the evidence of just how rough. Letting him think he caused this would avoid the conversation about my stepfather being a complete bastard and my mother putting up with him hurting her, but I can't let him think he did this. It wouldn't be right.

"You didn't hurt me, Jem," I tell him quietly.

"Piper, I can see the evidence right there." He rakes his hair back from his face, a gesture I notice he does when he's stressed.

"It was there before you came here last night."

His brow draws together. "What?" His face morphs from confused to rage as he pushes back from the bed, from me. "Who did this to you?"

I don't bother to snag the sheet again, this time reaching for a clean tee in the bedside drawer. I tug it over my head.

"No one did this to me, you silly lout. I'm clumsy and tired, and clumsy, tired people are accident-prone."

He stares at me and for a moment, I'm not sure he buys my story. Then he sighs. "You need to start taking care of yourself more."

"I know." Emboldened, I reach out and stroke him through his jeans. "But let me take care of you first."

He glances down at my hand, his face softening. "Are you trying to distract me, angel?"

I smile. "Is it working?"

"Absolutely." I reach for his belt and undo the buckle. He doesn't stop me, so I undo his buttons and drag his jeans down his legs. "Sit."

He surprises me by obeying my order and climbing onto the bed, then I push his shirt and kutte up his stomach out of the way. He's already hard in his boxer briefs and when I run my hand over him through the material, his legs twitch. I glance up his body and watch his darkening eyes as they lock onto me.

I feel elated that I can make him look at me like this. I've never had a man look at me like this in my entire life.

Slipping my fingers under the waistband of his underwear, I slide them down his hips, which he lifts a little off the bed so I can move them, and I reveal his hard cock. It's thick, veiny and looks ready to blow. I start at the tip. The first swipe of my tongue has his legs twitching. Good. I want him writhing, like he had me writhing before. I swirl my tongue back and forth, tasting the precum leaking from the top, loving the little grunts he's making.

Then I move down the shaft. I alternate between licking and kissing, placing my mouth around him completely, and licking up him. I play with his balls as I go, applying more or less pressure, depending upon his reactions. He grunts and groans, moans and whimpers through the whole thing, playing with my hair, my tits when he can reach them, swatting my arse when I'm close enough, stroking me, and biting his bottom lip.

I've never liked giving head before—until now. With Jem, it's different. I want to please him, I want to see his pleasure. And when he finally comes, I feel like I've won the lottery. I would have taken it in my mouth, but he pulls back and sprays it onto his stomach at the last moment, his head thrown back, neck muscles corded tightly.

"Fuck, you really are an angel," he breathes out.

I snort at his words, but guilt rolls through me. I was not nice when I first came to town, I was not nice to him or his friends when they were trying to take care of me. Had I known he had this sweeter side to him, a side he keeps showing me, I might have been less bitchy.

"I'm pretty far from that, Jem." My voice is soft as I head into the bathroom and get some tissue and a cloth to clean him up, so he doesn't get his clothes soiled. It also gives me a moment to collect myself.

When I return to the bedroom, he hasn't moved from where I left him, but he has a sated, dreamy look on his face as he stares at me. I'm not sure I deserve it.

"I should be looking after you," he tells me.

"Who made that rule up?"

"I don't know, but isn't that how it works? Chivalry and all that."

"This is the twenty-first century."

He tosses the cloth onto the bedside table and fixes his clothes. Then he stands and pulls me against him, squeezing my bum, which is exposed under my tee.

"I like you being easily accessible."

"Well, don't get used to it. I meant what I said: this can't happen again." No matter how amazing the sex was, and it was amazing. Our lives are incompatible—not just because of the distance, but because he's who he is and I'm who I am. I'm not looking to take a walk on the wild side. I'm not Cami. I'm too old for teenage rebellions.

"Absolutely not," he agrees. He kisses me again before he rests his forehead against mine. "I better go before I climb back into bed with you and my mum kicks my arse for being late."

"You shouldn't come back here later."

"I know."

"I mean it, Jem. Don't text the boys. I'll visit Josh instead. This can't happen again. We have to stay away from each other."

Saying those words cuts through me, but it's true. Being around him is too tempting, too hard.

"I know." He hasn't moved his forehead from mine, but he grips my bum tighter.

"We can't do this. We're playing with fire."

"You've already burned me, angel."

He kisses me once more and then leaves.

CHAPTER FIFTEEN

JOSH IS FINALLY COMING home from the hospital. I'm so relieved, but I'm also pissed off. Weed is picking him up. He doesn't want me there. I'm to meet him at the clubhouse for some party they're hosting to welcome him back. Weeks, I've been at his bedside, taking care of him, seeing to his every whim and need. It shouldn't bother me that he doesn't want me to walk him out of the hospital and put him in a car just to drive him across town, but it does. It's stupid, it really is, but it feels like another rejection. Leaving the hospital is a milestone I should have been a part of, and I hate that he's not letting me be.

I tamp that down, and tell myself I'm being a fool, but I don't hurry to get ready. In fact, by the time my taxi arrives and gets me to the clubhouse, I'm late—a taxi I only managed to get because Jem lifted my blacklisting ban after I ran out of the hospital. I think he was worried I might get stuck somewhere again without the ability to get a ride, although he warned me I could only use the service in emergencies. Well, tonight, I'm breaking all the rules, and I could not care less.

Childish? Maybe, but I feel slighted.

My brother might just be the biggest arse on the planet, and since I'm a grown woman, I can get a taxi across town without having to ask permission.

Even so, I feel a hint of nerves as I peer through the side window of the cab and notice the clubhouse car park is filled with bikes and cars. This rapidly growing tingling feeling only solidifies when I hear the dull tones of the music coming from within the building. Jem is not going to be happy I didn't get a ride with him (or one of the brothers), but since he also doesn't own me, he can go to hell as well. I'm tired of being bossed around and, when it comes to crunch time, getting shit on.

Things between me and Josh have been tense this week —or rather, Josh has been like a bear with a sore head this week. He's driven me nearly over the edge. At least twice I've considered getting on the train and going home before he was released from the hospital. It's only the fact that I know he's so stressed that's kept me level and calm. None of this is easy for him. The surgeries, the infection and the hospital stay is only the first hurdle. He now has a long recovery ahead. Physiotherapy will commence to strengthen his chest and back muscles where the bullet hit him. The doctor warned him this could take months. Josh wasn't happy hearing this. He wants to be back on his motorcycle sooner rather than later, but he can't ride if he doesn't have the upper body strength to do it. I know he's worried the Club will boot him out if he can't get back on his bike, but honestly, I'm wondering if that would be a bad thing.

Not that I would ever say this to him.

I value my life.

With all this going on, I didn't think it would be a good

idea to drop the bombshell that I slept with Jem on him, too. Cowardly? Definitely, but the mood my brother has been in this week, he's likely to put me on the train to Manchester himself and put Jem six feet underground.

Even so, I should have told Josh straight away. I should have come clean, admitted my misdemeanour, and dealt with the fallout, but every time I try to broach the topic the words stick in my throat. Guilt is a demon that eats at me daily, yet the thought of admitting what I did makes my stomach roil. I talk myself out of it, convincing myself it was a one-off, that it won't happen again, and so far, that has been true. Jem has avoided me and I've avoided him. That's been easy to do.

Until tonight.

There is no chance in hell we can avoid each other tonight. The only saving grace is we're going to be in a room full of people, so that will make it easier to steer clear of him.

I just need to show my face for a few hours and then I can get the heck out of here.

Paying the driver, I climb out of the vehicle, and head for the main gate, smoothing down my skirt, even though it doesn't need fixing. King is already opening the foot entrance gate as I approach. He gives me a chin lift, which I've come to learn is a 'hello' from these men, but he doesn't say anything to me. I've already had a handful of text messages from both Beth and Sofia, asking where I am.

I messaged them both back, telling them I was on my way, so they didn't worry. I don't want to discuss why I'm late, especially because the reason seems so petty. What does it matter who brings Josh to the party? It doesn't...

I have no idea why it matters so much to me either, only that it does.

I hear the gate clang as King shuts it behind me, cutting off my means of escape. Bugger.

I don't want to go inside the clubhouse, and for a moment, I think about calling the taxi back and going home —and by that I mean back to Manchester. I've already stayed longer than I should. Six weeks. My bosses have been fairly relaxed about me having time off, more lenient than I have any right to expect. I know Josh was incredibly ill, but compassion only goes so far. Any other employer would be pitching a fit to rival all fits. I'm sure the only reason I haven't been thrown out on my ear is because of who Grant is. The centre where I work receives hefty local funding from my stepfather's council office. I know they don't want to rock the boat and risk losing it by sacking his stepdaughter, so for now they're sucking it up and letting me work remotely while using my vacation time and every other piece of time owed or sick leave I can stitch together as necessary. Frankly, I don't care what the reason is. I'm just glad they are not kicking up a stink—yet. On this occasion, I'm more than happy to use my affiliations to Grant to keep my job. I really don't like to throw his name around, but I will if I need to, and staying with Josh in Kingsley is currently more important than my pride.

But Josh is better. He doesn't need me now. Today has proved that. Granted, I don't have a vehicle to pick him up in, but I could have been with him. I don't know why he excluded me. Has he had enough of me, too? Have I overstayed?

Of course I have.

Six weeks I've been in his bloody pocket. He's probably sick to death of me.

I should leave, but then he only just left the hospital after two major operations, and an infection. Although he's on the road to recovery, he's still recovering. He still needs help. How can I leave him like this? What kind of sister would I be to just walk away?

I ignore the fact I'm not needed. Not really.

He'll have people around.

Friends.

The Club.

I close this thought down as I push through the main doors and step into the foyer of the clubhouse.

Josh is already here and when I slip into the back of the crowded common room, he's being greeted by his brothers like a long-lost family member. Jem, I notice, is among the men, his patented smile in place, looking his usual glorious self. I try not to ogle him, but it's not easy when I know what it feels like to be with the man.

I swallow hard and leave the crowd behind, heading over to the empty bar—well, almost empty. Tap, one of the older Club brothers, is sitting at one end, a pint glass nursed between his hands. I ignore him and focus on the prospect—Lucas—who is wandering towards me.

He doesn't speak to me, simply gives me a lift of his chin, which I interpret as 'what can I get you?' I wish these men would learn to use their words.

"I'll have a vodka, please."

"Straight up?" he asks.

I nod.

He comes back with a glass of what is absolutely not a bar measure. I sip, not swig. I need a drink, but I don't want to get hammered. Not with Jem loitering around. I need to keep my guard up. The last thing I need is my defences to fall and to start rubbing up against him like a horny dog in front of my brother.

I'm not sure how he's going to receive me being here.

Will he reveal our secret and tell Josh what we did, or will he ignore me completely? I have no idea what to expect and the uncertainty is driving me crazy.

"Are you hiding over here?" Jamie's voice startles me.

I turn to her, sloshing the vodka in the bottom of the glass. Of all the women in the Club, she's the one that I'm least close to—mainly because she's got a mouth like a sailor and frankly, scares me a little. She has a penchant for saying whatever thoughts are in her head without filter. I should find this refreshing, but truthfully, I find it rather disturbing. I never knew people could be so honest.

"No, of course not. I just needed a drink before the bar gets busy."

Her red hair dances around her shoulders as she leans back against the counter, her eyes sparkling with scepticism. She also sees too much.

"Don't think I didn't notice you slipping in late, girly."

"I was stuck in traffic," I lie. "Did Josh notice I was late?"

"It freaks me out when you call Wade Josh."

"It is his name."

"He'll always be Wade to me."

And probably to everyone in this room. I am doomed to be the only person on the planet who calls him Josh. Maybe I should acquiesce and call him Wade, too...

"And I don't think he had a chance to notice you were late." Jamie tilts her head to the side. "So, now Wade's out of the hospital what're your plans, Piper?"

This is the million-pound question. "I suppose I should think about returning to Manchester at some point. I can't keep sleeping in my brother's spare room forever."

"Or, you know, you could just stay."

"In Kingsley?"

She shrugs, glancing over at the crowd as a ruckus laugh erupts over something Derek says, although what, I don't know.

"Why not? Your brother's here, and I know you haven't always seen eye to eye with the Club side of shit, but you're over that now, right?"

I feel my face warm a little at her words. Did I really project that much disdain? Clearly, I need to hide my feelings more.

"I didn't mean any ill will—"

Jamie's hand comes up. "You don't have to explain anything to me. My dad died a few years back. I blamed the Club for it, and I did a few things I'm not really proud of. I wasn't very nice for a period of time, so I get the whole projecting thing."

I freeze at her words and it takes me a moment to reclaim my voice. I had absolutely no idea about her father.

"I'm so sorry, Jamie."

She shrugs, as if she hasn't just dropped that bomb on me. "Don't be. Dad knew it was a risk, but he didn't care. He loved this Club and everyone in it. Always did." She glances into her glass. "Jeff was a foolish idiot, but his death wasn't the Club's fault, and I'm sure whatever happened between you and Wade wasn't the Club's fault either." She smiles as she says it, but there's a hint of sadness in her words.

She's right about that, too. I've had a lot of time to think over the last few weeks and reflect. The Club didn't take my brother from me. Josh would have gone either way. The Lost Saxons was just a convenient escape route at the time.

"You're angry at your father?" I ask, hesitantly.

"For dying? Fuck yeah. If he'd been a normal dad, he'd still be here." She takes another swig of her drink, this one longer and deeper. "But I can't turn back time and I wouldn't want to either. He's gone and I hate that he is, but he gave me this."

She gestures around the room at the motley crew of men and women gathered around my brother. There's a lot of smiling and laughing going on, even Josh seems to be happy for the first time in weeks.

"If you can hack the Club shit that comes with this life, it's worth it," Jamie continues. "Having people who care about you, protection, security, family. Overbearing fuckers who are up in your shit for the rest of your days—yeah, it's worth it. If anything ever happens to you, knowing you and any rug rats you have will be taken care of makes everything else worthwhile. Plus, you get a group of sisters that'll have your back forever. You can't ask for better than that."

I let that settle in my brain for a moment. She makes it sound so good, so appealing. Except she left out the weeks spent in hospital recovering from bullet wounds, potential prison visits and dead fathers. I don't think it's all sunshine and rainbows, but I am starting to like these people more than I should. In the time I've been here they've been nothing but kind to me, as much as I've tried to avoid getting embroiled with them.

"So, will you stay?" she presses.

"As appealing as that all sounds, I can't," I tell her. "I have a job in Manchester, a life there."

Although it's not much of a life. The only thing tying me there really is Cami, which is a huge factor. Here, I have my brother, the start of some crazy but potentially interesting friendships, and Jem...

Good God.

"So, get a job here."

"It's not really that simple."

"Of course it is. Beth's opening her new office soon. If she can start up her own business, I'm sure someone as smart as you can come up with something."

I smile at her, but I don't know how to answer her without saying something she might take the wrong way. Fortunately, I don't need to say anything because my brother is making a beeline for me. He pulls me to his side and kisses the top of my head in a gesture so brotherly, my heart swells.

Would it be so bad staying here?

It also makes me wonder if him asking Weed to pick him up wasn't a slight, after all. It's so easy to read into everything while our relationship is still so uncertain.

"There you are. I couldn't see you in the crowd and I was accosted as soon as I got here."

"You don't have to explain," I tell him. "You looked like you were having fun."

He rolls his eyes. "Yeah, these guys like to do shit to make me squirm." He roves a gaze over me. "You doing okay?"

"Shouldn't I be asking you that?" He looks tired and a little pale.

He huffs. "I'm fine, and getting tired of that question."

"I see they didn't remove his grumpy fucking dickhead gene in the hospital," Logan quips as he comes up beside us, earning him a thwack to the gut from Josh. It would have put me on my back if he hit me that hard, but Logan barely flinches. He does laugh, though, before taking a sip of his pint.

"You're hilarious," Josh mutters.

"He's funnier than you, fuckface," Weed fires back with a grin as he joins us.

Surrounded by these huge men, I should feel afraid.

When I first arrived in Kingsley, I would have done, but now, I don't. I feel a strange sense of belonging.

"How's my favourite Wade?" Weed asks.

I blink.

Oh. Me? Weed's talking about me. I don't point out that I'm not a Wade, and that my surname is in fact Ellis. Grant tried to insist I use Hollander-Ellis after he married Mum, but I rarely use the double-barrelled moniker and haven't done for the past decade.

"I'm fine and dandy," I tell him.

This makes him guffaw. "Fine and fucking dandy. Where do you come up with this shit? I fucking love your sister, Wade. She's a riot."

Josh suddenly stiffens. "What the fuck did I say Weed?"

Weed's hands go up defensively. "Is your blood pressure okay, buddy? You've got this twitch in your eye..."

"You touch her, I'll cut your balls off."

Weed groans. "You had to say that, didn't you?"

Logan nearly chokes on his pint and then moves quickly to fist a hand in my brother's kutte before he can reach out and, I assume, throttle Weed.

"She's off limits, you hear me?" Josh growls in a voice I've never heard him use before, and honestly, it scares me a little. It's a side of him I've never seen before. Weed seems wholly unperturbed by it, however. "No brother touches her. I mean it, Weed, you go near my little sister and I'll cut your fucking dick off and feed it to you."

Impressive imagery.

Terrifying, too, because I'm certain he will follow through with this threat to the letter.

Weed holds his hands up in supplication. "I got it, brother. Sheesh, calm down. Your sister's virtue is safe from me. For now." He wiggles his brows at me.

Oh my God.

Then my heart starts to gallop in my chest and the back of my neck feels warm.

I slept with Jem.

I fucked him in Josh's flat a week ago.

It was the best sex of my life.

Even thinking about it makes between my legs dampen.

I thought Josh would be annoyed I slept with Jem, put out maybe, but judging from that reaction, my brother is going to go nuclear. This could be the end of our rekindling. He's probably going to kill Jem as well. I don't want to be the reason for that. It reaffirms my belief that firstly, he can never know, and secondly, that I need to stay far away from Jem. Like another postcode far. Maybe even another country.

"I will kill you," Josh growls at Weed.

"No one's killing anyone," Logan says, sounding like an irritated father.

I need to calm this situation down. Quickly.

"While I'm grateful for your clumsy attempt to defend my um... virtue," I say to Josh, "I'm not off limits, and I don't need your protection. I can look after myself." I turn to Weed. "You're a very nice chap, but you're not my type. I like my men a little more... grown up."

Although I chose Jem, so...

Logan makes a pained sound.

Weed rubs at his chest and for a moment reminds me of Jem when he says, "Ouch, Piper. I thought we were friends."

"We are, which is why I'm saving your life from my brother."

Weed laughs. "It's sweet that you think I need protection from this fucker."

"Give me a few weeks to get back on my feet," Josh says darkly, "and I'll show you how much fucking protection you need."

Bloody hell. The testosterone in the room is clogging my throat.

I glance across the bar and my gaze catches on Jem, who is standing talking with Beth and his sisters. When his eyes lift to me, my breath locks in my chest. My legs go wobbly and my brain short circuits. I swore I wouldn't care, that I wouldn't be affected by him, but I am. My body reacts without permission. It remembers what he did to me, it remembers just how talented he is and when his tongue dips out to wet his bottom lip, the apex between my thighs tingles.

I knew seeing him would be hard. I didn't think it would be this hard, though. How can I walk away from him when he looks like this? Everything about him makes my body sit up and take notice. He's sinfully good-looking and tonight he looks amazing. Heat pools between my legs as his lips lift in a lazy smirk, one that promises so much. I need to get out of here. Now. Before I run over there and drag him in a side room.

I drain my glass and slide it onto the bar. "I need to use the ladies' room."

I excuse myself and leave the common room. I don't head to the bathroom, however. Instead, I find myself outside the clubhouse. There's a couple of people milling around, but I head to a quiet corner. The cool night air clears my head instantly and I take a deep breath, letting it blow away the cobwebs even further.

No one has ever stood up for me before—at least not outside of Cami, so I adore Josh for defending me, for having my back, but his words hit me square in the gut.

I slept with Jem, and whether I want to believe it, it will change things between us.

Having a big brother who cares is going to take some getting used to. I almost wish he didn't. It would make me feel less of a bitch for what I've done. He clearly doesn't want his brothers near me.

Or maybe it's me he doesn't want near his brothers...

"Should you be out here alone?"

CHAPTER SIXTEEN

I FREEZE at the familiar voice, my eyes closing of their own volition. His gruff, deep timbre shouldn't soothe me, but it does. It's like a balm to my soul.

God, why did he follow me out here? Being with him is dangerous, especially when my defences are low.

"Why shouldn't I be out here alone, Jem? Am I not safe?"

I'm not safe alone with him. He makes me feel things I shouldn't, want things I can't have. He's the ultimate illicit desire. Having him is perfection, but keeping him is treacherous—because of who he is. His links to the Club make him dangerous. Look what happened to my brother. He was pulled into this world and he nearly died as a result. Look at Beth—she wore bruises around her neck for weeks because of her dealings with the Club. Jamie lost her father. Do I want to put myself in a situation where I could risk everything, lose everything because of who I share a bed with?

Logically, my brain says no, but then Jem steps out of the shadows of the loading bay to the side of the doors and into the lights and rational thought goes by the wayside.

He's such an attractive man, and as always, I'm taken aback by his size. He's around six-foot-three, but he seems so much larger. In the dark, illuminated by the spotlights hanging on the external walls of the clubhouse, he looks enormous as he steps towards me—a blond giant.

I want to move away, put distance between us, but I don't want to wound him either. Such an obvious gesture clearly will send a message I don't want to give him.

"You're always safe with the Club, angel, and with me, but it doesn't hurt to be cautious when we're dealing with precious things."

"If we're playing it safe, should you be out here then?" I quip back. I can't resist it, although I shouldn't joke with him. I should get myself back inside and put a room full of people between us. I can't seem to make my feet work, though.

He laughs and I want to hear him laugh more. It sounds amazing.

"I can handle myself, but thanks for that stunning emasculation."

"I didn't mean to emasculate you, although I imagine there's very little that can anyway. You're hardly unsure of yourself on that front."

His eyes take me in, and I feel like he's undressing me with that one look. I meet his heated gaze with one equally as scorching. I need him, I burn for him.

"You'd be surprised."

He steps closer to me, and my mind blanks for a moment. I can smell his aftershave, the leather of his kutte, the booze on his breath and a scent that is uniquely Jem. I can feel the warmth radiating off him as he circles me before he closes in behind me, his hands spanning my hips. Air catches in my throat at the touch and I dip my head to my chest. I should move away from him. Having his fingers graze my sides like this does funny things to my belly.

I've thought all week about how I would handle seeing him. No scenario ended with me leaning back into him, tilting my head to the side and granting him access to my throat, but this is precisely what I do.

He gently scrapes my hair from off my neck and my lids flutter, my lips trembling with anticipation. I need him, and it scares me how much after such a short time. His touch ignites a fire inside me. Maybe it is the forbidden element that fans those flames higher than they would usually flare, but when I sag against him, I can feel his hardness pressing against my bum, so I know it's not just me that is affected.

I want to get lost in him. I want to lose myself in him and forget about my brother, the crap with my parents, about everything.

But reality is cruel. You can't run from it or hide from it. No matter how much you wish you could.

Laughter from nearby brings me crashing back to earth with a bump.

We can't...

Not here. Not with my brother just inside the building. Not with eyes around us. We're in a quiet area, but that doesn't mean we don't risk being seen, and these people, I've learnt in my time here, gossip.

With Herculean effort, I pull free of him and step out of his grasp. This seems to amuse him, but he doesn't call me on it. Instead, he moves to the wall of the clubhouse and leans against it.

I watch him, unsure what he's going to do next or say. Anxiety stalks my heels, nipping at my feet as I wait for him to speak. I don't know if I want him to walk away or stay.

He scrunches his eyes, glancing over the lit car park,

filled with bikes and vehicles, before bringing his gaze back to me.

"I'm sorry I didn't come back after we slept together," he says finally. "I acted like an idiot. It's a rare occurrence, but it has been known to happen from time to time. I should have come back. I shouldn't have listened to you. Fuck the consequences."

His response is not what I expect, so I stare dumbly at him for a moment. I thought he would tell me I was right to walk away, that we should continue to avoid each other. Maybe that we should take what we did to our graves.

"You did the right thing," I finally manage to get out.

He pushes off the wall and paces slightly, dragging his fingers through his hair.

"The fuck I did. Walking out of that flat was the stupidest decision I've ever made. Not coming back, acting like you don't exist all week was the second stupidest. I thought it would get easier with time, but it hasn't."

I don't know why, but hearing him apologise loosens the heaviness that has settled in my chest. Despite my words to him, I didn't want him to leave, and not just because he was the best sex I've had in, well, maybe ever. Jem's become someone I rely on, a friend, even. Dare I say it, but I've missed him.

But it was the right thing to do. We can't have a relationship, particularly not in light of what Josh just threatened to do to Weed.

"You don't have to apologise, Jem. All you did was what I asked."

"Yeah, well, I should have ignored you."

"No, you shouldn't have. What we did was wrong. You have to know that."

He eyes me, his tone a little sharp when he asks, "Are you saying you regret it?"

I should say yes, but I can't lie to him. I won't. "I regret the act because it will hurt Josh, but I don't regret sleeping with you. Not at all."

His lips kick up. "Well, that's reassuring. I can work with that."

I roll my eyes at him. "That doesn't mean you're in with a second chance. Even if Josh wasn't a factor, it's not happening again, understand?"

Even as I say this, I know it's not true. If he touches me again, I'm lost to him.

Jem brushes his hair back from his face and he fixes me with a resolute glare. "No."

"No?"

"No, I don't understand. I don't know about you, but this week has been utter fucking hell for me."

The way he says this makes my heart clench in pain. I don't like hearing he's suffered. In truth, it hasn't been easy for me either. He's been in my thoughts more than I care to admit.

"I tried to respect your wishes, Pip. I really have, but it's been horrible. I thought distance would make it easier, but it hasn't. If anything, it's made it worse. I like you. You like me. Why can't we shag our little brains out until we have our fill?"

I blink at him. I've never met a man with such a lack of filter before. It throws me off balance even as it sends a thrill racing through me. I never know what I'm going to get with him.

"Because I live in Manchester. You live here. I have a completely different life to you—one that doesn't involve motorcycles and denim. My life is made up of galas and black-tie events. And there's not just us in this equation, Jem. What about Josh? I'm just getting to a good place with him. I don't want to ruin that progress."

Jem lets out a low breath. "I get that, but it won't. Josh'll rant and probably throw a tantrum, but he'll come around. You'll see."

He's full of it. I fold my arms over my chest.

"Would you be so understanding if Josh was sleeping with Sofia or Mackenzie?"

I watch as his jaw tightens.

"I thought as much," I say.

"I didn't say anything," he counters.

"You didn't have to. Your face did all the talking, Jem."

"My face didn't do anything."

"You nearly broke your jaw."

"Okay, so I'd be a little upset for half a second, and *then* I'd be fine because Wade is a good bloke and I know he'd look after my sister."

I roll my eyes at him. "You'd beat him senseless."

He huffs out a breath. "I'd beat him senseless, then I'd be fine."

I can't stop the small victorious smirk that plays across my lips. I'm surprised I got him to admit to this.

"Josh was just in the common room threatening to chop Weed's penis off if he touches me. Given how attached you are to your cock, I think you'd be wise to abort this crazy mission, don't you?"

He smiles. "You're worried about me."

"I couldn't care less about you," I lie.

"Angel, you don't have to worry. I can handle your brother."

"Well, I can't. I already lost him once. I can't go through that again."

"He's not going to stop talking to you because of what is going on between us."

He can't promise this. Jem doesn't know what Josh is capable of. He walked away last time without a second thought. I have no doubt he could cut me out of his life again in the same manner. And this time, it would destroy me. I'm getting attached. Despite my intentions to keep my distance, I've failed. I'm in deep with my brother. Taking care of him these past few weeks has forced us together.

"No, because nothing is going on between us."

"Yet," he says.

"Ever, Jem. This can't be. It was fun while it lasted, but face it, we're not meant to be."

He rubs his thumb over his bottom lip, perusing me. "You look amazing."

I blink at the change of direction.

"What?"

"You look amazing. I really love this naughty skirt, angel. Did you wear it to drive me crazy?"

I glance down at my attire. I'm wearing a hounds-tooth mini with a black long sleeve top and a pair of ankle boots I picked up from one of the boutiques in town. It's not biker attire, not by any stretch, but it is me. I'm not sure why he's complimenting my outfit, however.

"Uh... no. I just... this is what I usually wear."

"It's sexy as fuck." He growls low in his throat, his eyes heavy and Lordy, if my pussy doesn't clench at the look he's giving me.

"Really? I don't think I fit the mould," I say, my voice catching as he rounds me, studying me like an artefact in a museum.

"The mould?"

I twist to glance over my shoulder to look at him. I'm not keen about him being behind me at all. I'm edgy, in fact.

"Well, I'm not wearing leather or denim."

He laughs, stepping close to my back and wrapping his arms around my hips. I jolt, stiffening as he nuzzles against my neck and I can't stop the pant that escapes my mouth.

"Who gives a shit about moulds? We're all here because none of us fit."

"You fit. I don't."

"You fit right here in my arms."

This is sweet.

"Jem…"

"Your brother is going to have to get over whatever hang-up he has because now that I've had you, Pip, I'm sorry, but I can't let you go. I thought I could, but I can't."

Jem releases me and grabs my hand, tugging me around the corner of the building. Surprised, I trail after him like a leashed puppy. There are lights illuminating the way, but he finds a shadowy area and pushes me up against the corrugated wall. Then he steps in behind me, turning me away from him so my back is to his chest, my front facing the wall.

My heart starts to race as his hands snake around my waist. What is he doing? His big body shields me and there's no one around this side of the building, but if someone walks down this end we will be seen.

I try to pull away, but he doesn't let me.

"Jem, not here."

"Why not?" His nose goes to the crook of my neck and I forget to breathe.

I hope the shadows keep what he's doing hidden, but I also find I don't care as he peppers kisses down the length of my throat, trying not to groan.

"Someone might see."

"No one's here," he assures me, but I'm not feeling reassured.

"But—"

"Angel, I'll take care of you always. Trust me, okay?"

I want to deny him, but I don't. On some level, I do trust him. I probably trust him more than my brother, which is ludicrous. I relax against him and give a small nod.

One of his arms wraps around my hips like a steel band while the other rubs at my breast through my top. I draw in air through my teeth. I rub my thighs together, trying to gain friction to ease the growing ache.

The arm around my hips slides down and moves over my thighs. He reaches the hem of my skirt and slips under it. All the air in my lungs freezes as his fingers find the edge of my thong.

Is he going to... is he...?

Here...?

He removes all doubt as he pushes the material aside and slips a finger through my wetness and inside me. I gasp. Not at the intrusion, but at the sheer shock of the situation.

Exhibitionism is not something I've ever thought about, but my pulse is through the roof, excitement pushing my orgasm closer before he's even got his second finger inside me. The thought we could get caught is heady, and I can hardly catch my breath.

I press both palms to the wall, trying to keep my balance as he pumps his fingers into me hard, and I know it's not going to be enough. I need him.

But that's a risk too far.

Josh is inside.

His brothers are inside.

So are a dozen women who gossip worse than the average glossy magazine.

We can't get caught.

But the excitement...

I want him.

I shouldn't.

God, I shouldn't.

He's not for me. He's not. But right now, he's mine and all I'm focused on is what he's doing to me. It feels so wrong, so dirty, and this makes my orgasm race faster.

I grit my teeth and squeeze my eyes shut as my climax builds. I can't scream out. It'll bring people, so I have to swallow my moans as I go over the edge. I dig my teeth into my bottom lip to stifle the sounds building in my throat.

Good lord.

Boneless, my legs give out and I sink back against Jem. His strong arms encircle me, holding me tightly as I fight to catch oxygen from the heavy atmosphere.

"You okay?" His breath is hot against the side of my neck.

"No," I murmur.

He chuckles as he nuzzles me. "You need a minute?"

"I need several."

"You don't have several," he says softly in my ear. "I'm going to fuck you now."

No.

It sits on the tip of my tongue. I nearly let it fall from my lips, but I mash my teeth together to stop it. My pussy is pulsing as my orgasm rolls through me, and my legs are shaking, but I need more from him. I want him inside me, and my heart and head are on different pages. His filthy words are reverberating through my brain.

He's going to fuck me, and I'm going to let him.

In the dark, against the wall, my skirt hoisted over my hips, my bum exposed, my thong pulled down my thighs, I'm going to let him take me outside like some back-alley tramp. I should feel disgusted, but my clit throbs with the need to have him touch me. I hate myself for how much I crave him, how much I want him. What is wrong with me? I'm going to let him take me where anyone can see, where my brother could see. This isn't me. At least, this isn't the Piper Ellis of six weeks ago. I have no idea who I am now.

When I make no protestation, I hear the jangle of his belt and the rustle of denim as he frees himself from his clothes. I feel him moving behind me, and shiver as his hand presses against the curve of my bottom. His cock swipes through my folds and without any hesitation he pushes inside me.

I try not to make a sound as I stretch around him, feeling the pinch of pain before it settles to a fullness. I can't stop the groan that leaves my mouth as he pulls back out to the tip and slams back into me.

My palms flatten against the wall, trying to get purchase as my entire body rocks. Oh, God, that feels good. His hands curl around my hips, holding me steady as he repeats the motion, back and forth, dragging his cock in and out of me. I widen my stance as much as I can, my underwear a clamp around my thighs, stopping me from moving too far, but it gives him the space to do what he needs.

I don't need much coaxing either. The mix of the risk of being caught and the angle he has me pushed against the wall at has me coming apart in record timing. I swallow my mewl as I go over the edge, panting through my orgasm, and I feel him judder before he finds his release as well.

Sagging against the wall, my legs jellied, I try to keep

traction while he slowly pulls out of me. I moan at the loss of his dick, and he chuckles at me.

Bastard.

His hand comes to the back of my neck, collaring me, and he kisses the side of my face.

"Let me get rid of the condom, angel, then I'll take care of you."

I have no idea where he's going to put it. I didn't know he'd even put on one, but at least he was thinking about protection. Not that it matters, I'm on the pill, but it doesn't hurt to be careful.

Slowly, I unglue myself from the wall. I'm gross between my legs, slick with my wetness. I need to clean up down there, but unless I want to parade back through the clubhouse half naked, I have no choice but to pull my underwear back on, which I do.

I'm just settling my skirt back in place when Jem reappears out of the darkness, his belt and jeans undone. He quickly fastens them and gazes over me.

"You okay?"

I nod. "Yeah. I need to clean up, though."

"I have a room upstairs."

I give him a look. "That's not a good idea."

"Despite what you think, I can keep my hands to myself. I'm not a rampant sex pest."

I laugh quietly. "I didn't say you were."

"The implication's there, Pip." He steps into me, his big body crowding me, his arms sliding around my back. "You are utterly irresistible, but I'll keep my filthy paws to myself while you clean up, deal?"

Since I feel disgusting, I agree. "Well, if you think you can manage. I'll allow it. We should get back inside and clean up fast, before we're missed."

"In a moment."

He bends at the neck and kisses me gently, so gently I almost forget I just said we should move quickly.

His kiss scorches my lips, branding me his.

Staying away from Jem is no longer an option, no matter what my head tells me. It's no longer calling the shots. My heart is, and the heart wants what it wants.

Right now, it wants Jem, and it doesn't care about big brothers and relationships being ruined. It doesn't care about distances or incompatibility. It doesn't care about dangerous liaisons.

All it cares about is this man who is searing my mouth with the most divine kiss I've ever experienced in my life.

CHAPTER SEVENTEEN

In the two weeks since Josh's welcome home party, I've taken to avoiding Jem like the plague. This has been relatively easy now Josh is no longer in the hospital. I have no reason to run into any of his brothers unless they come to the flat or I go to the clubhouse. Since I'm hardly a frequent visitor to the latter, it's been relatively easy to closet myself away from all things Lost Saxons, and thus keep myself out of the path of temptation.

And this is precisely what Jem is. He's a blond god wrapped in layers of tempting honeyed desire that I cannot resist. Avoiding him is the only way I can keep my sanity.

If I'm being honest, I should have gone back to Manchester weeks ago. I know Josh is still not back to his full strength, but he doesn't need me here, not really. He struggles with certain things, mainly anything that means he has to lift or reach a certain way, but he's managing fine without my help. He spends most of his time at the clubhouse or out with his brothers, leaving me to my own devices—those devices mostly comprise of fantasising about

Jem Harlow and coming up with ways of getting my relationship back on track with my half-brother.

Don't get me wrong, Josh has made time for me. It's not like he's ignored me. In fact, he's made a whopping great effort to get to know me better, which makes my behaviour even worse. We're hanging out and doing things together—bonding, as he calls it—but he's also been weirdly quiet and out of sorts since his welcome home party.

I know he left early, although why, I don't know. When I came out of Jem's room after our... tryst (this is what I'm calling the event where Jem fucked me up against the wall of the clubhouse, since I feel absolutely mortified by it), I tried to find him, but he'd absconded. I wanted to go after him, but I was accosted by the girls, and found myself drinking with Beth for the rest of the evening. She got trashed and had to be practically carried home by Logan—much to his irritation and my amusement. When I got back to the flat, it was quiet, but Josh's door was shut. He's been weird since.

Truthfully, we've both been dancing around each other since the party. I'm also avoiding him because I can barely look him in the eye with my guilt eating at me, and Josh has been like a bear with a sore head, frustrated by his body's inability to do what he needs.

When the doctor finally clears him for work, I'm half-relieved because at least it means he has something to focus on other than moping over his recovery, but I can't help but be concerned as well. I think it's too soon. He's only been out of hospital a fortnight and he's having fairly intensive physiotherapy. I don't think he should be doing anything strenuous at all, considering he nearly died eight weeks ago.

The day he's due to start back at the bar he manages, I decide to bite the bullet and raise my concerns, even though

I'm not sure he's going to appreciate me interfering. It takes me a couple of goes to raise my courage to broach the subject, but I manage to find the words and push them out of my mouth. Fear he could end up back in the hospital forces me to speak. I can't deal with him getting sick again. I can't go through weeks of worry again.

"Maybe you shouldn't go back to work yet, Josh," I say, nibbling on my lip as my belly fills with ice. I mean, what do doctors really know anyway? His physician hasn't seen him struggling with everyday things. He doesn't realise how hard it is for my brother to lift objects or reach for simple things. Going back to work after getting shot, having double surgery and a major infection that only cleared up a few weeks ago seems ludicrous. "Don't you think it's too soon? I mean, are you really sure you're well enough? It has only been two weeks since you got out of the hospital."

We're standing in the kitchen of his flat and while I know it's pointless to try to make him listen, given he's a grown up and he's not really inclined to pay attention to me, I have to try. It's my duty as his sister, right? This is what sisters do—protect their siblings, even if it is from themselves.

Josh's attention, however, is not on me. I'm not sure where it is, but he seems distracted, unfocused.

When he doesn't answer me, I snap out, "Josh! Are you listening to me?"

He finally gives me his attention. "I'm fine, Pipes."

I'm not sure where this nickname came from, but secretly, I love it. He started calling me it over the past few days just out of the blue and it's stuck.

"You keep saying that but you're getting over the second of two fairly major surgeries, Josh." I drop the hand not clutching my coffee to my hip, doing my best mother hen routine, and give him a chastising glare. "If you need more time off then take it. You push it and you'll end up back in the hospital."

"I'm fine, Piper," he repeats, his tone firm.

"Are you fine?" I ask, peering at him, trying to see what is going on behind the shutters he has up. Is he ignoring me because he doesn't care for the little sister pushing him around routine, or is it something else? It's something else... "You've been quiet since you got out of the hospital."

He freezes for a split second, which is how I know I'm on the money. I further know I'm right by the fact he changes the subject completely.

"Are you hanging around here today or heading into town?" he asks.

Nice sidestep, brother.

Since I am also a master at this game, I can't blame him too much for avoiding my question. I keep my walls firmly up and locked in place, too. If I didn't, Josh would know all my secrets, including the fact that my stepfather is a complete arse who I still have no idea how to handle, and I slept with one of his best friends.

The situation with Jem is difficult. Mum is another matter entirely.

I know I should message her, make sure she's okay after Grant hit her, but in truth, I don't know how to handle her. She was more concerned about her reputation if it came out. Who thinks like that? Sod reputation, she should have told everyone who will listen what a scumbag Grant Hollander is. He portrays himself as this saint in the community, helping the elderly, fixing homelessness, securing education places for disadvantaged young people, increasing employment opportunities, but behind closed doors he's someone else, someone darker. I've never seen that side of him before. Sure, I knew both of them were forceful, overbearing, difficult. My life growing up wasn't the easiest. There's a reason I sought out a brother in jail and saw him as a better alternative to a supposed happy home in a middle-class suburban life, but I had no idea Grant was capable of violence. He hit her, and Mum stood by while he hurt me and said nothing. I think that's what upsets me the most. I jumped in front of him to protect her. Hell, I would have taken whatever hits he threw at me to save her, but she only cared about protecting his reputation. I would have said she was scared of him, except she warned me to say nothing that might harm his position.

The sad thing is he did hurt me. He bruised my arm badly. It took over a week for the finger-marks on my skin to fade. But Farrah Ellis-Hollander cares more about keeping up appearances than protecting her own daughter, and that is what it always boils down to—their social standing. Grant's position, his job, matters more than anything else. When I managed to speak to Mum on the phone and tell her this, she told me I was being dramatic and I should grow up. That hurt more than the contusions marring my skin.

Maybe I should have gone to the police and reported it, but Grant is the kind of man who would have talked his way out of it. I doubt Mum would have come down on my side either. She seems to think it's perfectly acceptable what happened. Honestly, Grant's rage scared me. I've never seen him like that before, and I'm not sure what he's mixed up in either, but I don't want to be tangled in it. Maybe I should have told Jem or Josh what happened, but my brother was in the hospital and I have a feeling Jem's retribution would not have been pretty. I don't need to complicate matters more than they already are.

Besides, this is my problem. I'll solve it myself. I don't need my brother wading in to save the day.

For now, staying in Kingsley gives me a buffer from Grant and my mother.

"Actually," I lift my coffee mug to my mouth but don't drink, "I thought I'd head up to your clubhouse."

When he was in the hospital, I wouldn't have bothered asking. I would have just gone. Not that I was a frequent visitor up there, but I feel weird about going over there now that he's out. In truth, I feel like an intruder in his world, like I don't belong. I'm struggling to find my place in this new dynamic we have.

My brother's head snaps in my direction. "Come again?"

"Well," I lower the mug, "Beth and Liv were talking about a shopping trip to look at baby clothes and they asked me to tag along. I didn't want to be rude, since they did so much to help while you were in hospital, so of course I said yes."

On the few occasions I've been pushed into social situations with the women in the Club, I've had a surprisingly good time. I do feel somewhat beholden to them, considering how much they did to help me when Josh was in the hospital, so when they asked me to come on this shopping escapade, I could hardly say no, but I'm also not adverse to getting out for a while either. I'm getting slightly cabin fevered. However, going to the clubhouse is not without risks. It puts me in the path of a certain Harlow brother who I have been trying to avoid, and not without difficulty. He's messaged a few times and while I've responded, I made it clear we should keep things platonic. He seemed to agree, but then he agreed last time—until we were in each other's orbit. Within minutes my skirt was around my hips and he was fucking me against the wall. I don't seem to have any sort of control when it comes to Jem.

I would prefer to avoid the clubhouse altogether, but I feel I owe Beth at least for her help with Josh. So, I'm going to the clubhouse.

"That sounds fun." He says this in a way that suggests it sounds the absolute opposite.

"I don't know if it will be or not, but they seem nice and..."

"Pipes, if you want to go, go. I don't mind."

"You're sure? I don't want to step on your toes or anything."

Josh takes a swig of his own coffee before saying, "Why the fuck would you be stepping on my toes?"

I carefully put the mug onto the counter before giving him my full attention. "Because this is your world, Josh, not mine. I don't belong in it, and let's face it, I haven't exactly been supportive of it. I could understand if you didn't want me trespassing here."

This might be the understatement of the century. When I first arrived, I was a raging bitch. It was Jem who bore the brunt of that anger. Although I'm not sure I can honestly say I remain unsupportive. Not that I can tell Josh this. I can hardly admit that I'm bonking one of his best friends, can I? I'm not sure this was what he meant when he told me I had to respect his brothers.

He stares at me a beat, as if he's trying to fathom what is going on in my head before he lets out a long breath. "Club's family. My family. That makes them your family, too. If you want to hang out with the old ladies, I'm not going to say shit about it."

One big happy family...

I most assuredly do not have familial feelings for Jem.

"All right then."

He empties the last of his coffee then sticks the mug in the sink. He doesn't rinse the cup.

What the hell, Josh? Would it kill you to clean it and put it away?

I want to say something, but I don't. I've learnt the best approach with Josh is not to nag. It's pointless anyway.

"Do you need a lift?" he asks.

"Um, no, but thank you. We're not meeting there for another few hours."

He grabs his kutte off the back of the sofa and shrugs into it. I notice the discomfort on his face as it pulls his back doing it. He's still so stiff, so sore. I wonder if he'll ever be back to how he was before he was shot. Not that I know what that was.

"Will you be okay getting there?" he asks as he settles the leather in place.

This question is sweet, but I roll my eyes, playing the little role that is expected of me. It's a role I'm more comfortable in with him.

"Believe it or not, Josh, I'm quite capable of taking care of myself."

"I was shot eight weeks ago, Piper. Just fucking humour me and say you'll be careful, yeah?"

Oh, shit.

His words are a kick to the gut. It steals the air from my lungs as all the memories, all the worry, all the feelings of doubt and fear race through me. For a second, I struggle to draw air.

"Don't," I choke out, my arms wrapping around my middle.

"Don't what?"

"Remind me!" My eyes dart away before I squeeze

them shut. "It was the worst moment of my life getting that call. I thought you were going to die. I didn't know what to do."

It seems so long ago that call came through. Another lifetime, in fact.

"You did fine," he says, his voice flat.

Something in his tone sets me on edge. What does that mean? I did fine? Is he annoyed at me? Upset with me?

I search his face, looking for answers and finding none. In many ways, Josh is still a stranger to me and the nuances of his behaviour are a mystery to me at times. Case in point, this right here. I have no idea what his problem is. What did I say?

I'm about to ask, press for more information, when he offers the answer himself.

"You're here, you're not here—that's up to you. Doesn't matter to me."

His words are a wrecking ball to the chest.

What. The. Hell?

Tears clog my throat as pain steals my breath. Does he really think that? Well, fuck him! Two months of my life I've given up to be here with him. Two months.

I've risked my job, my security, everything to make amends, and that is his response?

What has he sacrificed?

Nothing.

I rub my chest, trying to dispel the pain lancing through my heart, but it doesn't help. I can feel the tears brimming in my eyes, even as I try to bring my shields back up to protect myself, but they're lowered. I let my guard down too far, and I shouldn't. Never again. What a fool I was to believe he wanted me here, really and truly.

I close my eyes for a split second, trying to ground

myself before I find my centre, then I spit my words at him, finally finding my anger.

"Yeah, well, I only came to make sure you didn't fucking die!" I snatch my handbag off the kitchen counter and give him a glare that I hope tells him how much I hate him for saying that before I rush to the door. I slam through it, shutting it behind me hard enough to rattle the walls.

Fuck him.

Everything I've done for him and that's the gratitude?

I have no idea where I'm going, I just walk blindly away from the flat, away from my brother, until the anger becomes hurt and the hurt becomes exhaustion. I wander aimlessly in the opposite direction, trying to order my thoughts.

I understand on some level why Josh is pushing back. He's scared, just as I am, and when he's scared, he pushes away. God, when he finds out I slept with Jem and kept it quiet...

I wonder then how hard he will push me away.

I'm suddenly yanked back and a horn honks. I fall, hitting the pavement on my bottom hard, pain ricocheting up my spine.

"Lady, are you crazy?" the man who yanked me back yells at me. "You nearly got wiped out by that car!"

I glance up from my seated position and realise he's right. I must have stepped straight out into the road. I didn't even realise. I push up from the pavement, brushing bits of debris off my palms.

"Thank you. I was in a world of my own."

The middle-aged man eyeballs me like I'm crazy. "Yeah, well, pay attention. You don't want to become roadkill."

"I will," I promise.

I brush my hair out of my face and carry on walking.

Eventually, I head over to the clubhouse. The last thing I want to do is be late to meet with Beth and Liv. These people have a penchant for melodrama when it comes to being late.

The two women seem pleased to see me when I arrive.

"I can't wait to buy things for the baby," Beth coos. "Tiny booties and little baby grows."

Liv groans. "You can do the throwing up three times a day thing, too."

"No, you can keep that part."

"Now that you and Logan are engaged, will we be hearing the pitter patter of tiny Harlow feet?" she asks as she leans back in the chair.

We're sitting in the common room waiting for Logan. He's in church, which is a Club meeting. Once he's done there, we're heading into town to shop. Dean's here, but he's at the bar talking with Weed, who seems to enjoy flirting with me more than is healthy.

If Jem catches him—

I cut that thought off dead. He'll what?

Jem isn't mine, and I'm not his. Good God, what am I thinking?

He's playing with fire, though. Between Jem and my brother, Weed is setting himself up to get slugged in the face.

Beth scoffs. "Not for a while. I'm getting my business set up, and I want to enjoy my man for a bit. We've had ten years apart. We need to just... be us, you know?"

Liv nods. "Yeah, I know. This little one wasn't exactly planned." She places a hand on her baby bump. It's only slight, but it's clear she's pregnant now. "I think me and Dean would have waited, given the choice, but I'm happy that we're having our baby."

"Just as well," Beth says, "you're stuck with her."

"Or him."

"Or him."

"What about you, Piper? Do you want kids?" Liv asks.

I blink. "Oh. I haven't really thought about it."

My parents aren't exactly the greatest role models. Children haven't been on my agenda.

"There's no one special in your life?"

My hands suddenly feel clammy. Do they know about Jem? Does everyone know about Jem?

"Not really," I lie.

"Well, take it from me," Beth says, "don't date a biker. Overprotective, overbearing, bossy bastards."

My guts roil. Externally, I maintain my calm, but internally, I'm freaking out. What do they know? Do they know anything? Am I reading too much into this?

Liv smiles. "You love it."

Beth shakes her head. "I can't even drive myself to the clubhouse without Logan needing a status report."

The smile fades from Liv's face. "Given recent events, I can't say I blame him."

"I can. That's over and done with. Life has to go on. I'm tired of being coddled. I didn't die. I'm here, alive, breathing, ready and raring to get on with things. I can't do that with him hanging around my neck all day."

"They just worry about us," Liv says softly.

"They need to let loose on the reins a little. It's ridiculous."

"Can I see your ring?" I ask, wanting to break through the suddenly heavy tension mounting between the two women.

It has the desired effect because Beth holds her hand

out to me, showing an enormous diamond ring. It's gorgeous and it must have cost a fortune.

"Wow, it's magnificent."

"I know. I would have been fine with something a lot cheaper."

"You're a lucky lady. You both are."

A feeling I'm not used to stabs at me. Jealousy. I've never really felt it before. I've lived a charmed life. I've never wanted for anything, besides affection, but no one in my circles got that from the people around them. Seeing love, true love, yeah, I feel jealous.

It's amplified further when Dean saunters over and helps Liv to her feet. His hand skims over her belly with such reverence as he kisses her that I feel that stab of pain again. Could I have this with Jem? Do I want this with Jem?

"Lo just messaged. He's leaving church now. You ready to go?"

"Ready as ever," Beth says.

We pile out into the corridor and Logan joins us as we do, making a beeline for Beth. He tucks her straight into his side, kissing her in a way that makes my stomach dip.

"Just a heads up, Piper," Logan says as we head towards the exit, "your brother may be in a shitty mood when you get home later."

"Why?" I demand, wondering what they've done to him. Nerves run through me. Does he know about me and Jem? Logan wouldn't be grinning if he did, would he?

"He just got made the manager of a new Club business. He's not too happy about it."

I have no idea what he's talking about.

"What Club business?" Dean asks.

"A new strip club called Lace. You'll find out about it tomorrow, I'm sure."

Liv's eyes flare. "Well, that sounds tacky." She winces. "No offence."

"That's nicer than what Wade was thinking, I'm sure." Logan grins.

I tune out their banter as we cross the car park, lagging slightly behind the two couples. They look so normal, so at ease, and I want that. I want it with Jem, and the longer I'm in Kingsley, the harder it becomes to deny it to myself.

But having Jem means potentially losing Josh. I can't have both.

I need to leave town. I can have a relationship with my brother from Manchester, without being involved in the Club side of things, but I can't do that as I am now, so involved with the Lost Saxons. Shopping for baby clothes, being friends with them... fantasising about being an old lady, it's a dangerous path to tread.

I need to get back to my own life, my own world, and I need to forget the name Jem Harlow ever existed.

CHAPTER EIGHTEEN

My decision to leave Kingsley is taken out of my hands. I'm getting ready to go out for breakfast two days later with Josh when my phone rings. A tendril of anxiety goes through me. The screen says 'MUM CALLING'. Shit. This can't be good. We've both been avoiding each other since Grant had his epic meltdown when I visited last. I consider for the briefest moment letting it go to voicemail, but dismiss this almost immediately. What if she's in trouble? What if, despite her bravado, she is really frightened of him? Liv works at a domestic violence shelter. Maybe I could ask her if what my mother is doing is normal behaviour for a victim—not that Mum would ever allow herself to be considered a victim, but Grant did smash his palm right across her face.

Suddenly, I feel guilty as hell for being bratty about this. I spat my dummy out of the pram for her not protecting me, but maybe I should have been more understanding. She has to live in that house day-in, day-out with him.

What if she's terrified?

What if she said what she had to in order to keep herself safe?

What if she did all that and I ran off like a bloody child?

I duck into the bedroom quickly to take the call, not wanting Josh to overhear.

"Mum?" I murmur into the handset as I sink onto the edge of the bed. "Are you all right?"

"Hello, Piper," a male voice that is not Mum says down the line. It's Grant.

My stomach fills with ice.

"What are you doing on Mum's phone?"

"Considering how we left things last time, I didn't think you would answer a call from me."

He would be right about this. "I would have thought you'd at least call to attempt an apology by now," I mutter.

"Believe it or not, I am sorry for what happened. However, mine and your mother's marital affairs are nothing to do with you."

"You hit her," I hiss at him. "And bruised me."

"That was unfortunate."

"Unfortunate? You really are a prick."

"Yes, well, it seems I'm not the only one who is misbehaving in this family." That ice in my stomach turns glacial. *"I heard a funny story this morning. I was calling around some of my campaign supporters, getting a feel for who I can rely on ahead of the local elections. Imagine my surprise when I called Karl Jakobs and he offered me condolences on my family situation."*

My entire body freezes. Karl Jakobs is one of my bosses. He would, of course, offer condolences to my stepfather. He probably thinks Josh is Grant's stepson, too, since he's my brother.

Shit.

"*Would you like to explain what is going on?*"

I really would not.

"Well, that's between me and Karl," is my less than stellar come back.

"*I'm in the middle of a campaign, Piper! Local elections are just five months away! Karl seems to be under the impression you're with your brother, which is bizarre to me, since you don't have one.*"

I swallow bile. "I do have a brother."

He guffaws. "*No, Piper, you don't. The only brother you have is a criminal that I know for a fact you wouldn't be stupid enough to get embroiled with—not after last time.*"

I don't say anything for a moment. "I'm not a child, Grant. I don't have to explain myself to you."

It's the wrong thing to say because he loses what little composure he has left. "*Are you joking? I took you in and raised you as my own, you spoilt bitch! I paid for your education, ensured you never wanted for anything and this is the attitude you give me back? All I've ever asked from you is that you don't do anything that jeopardises my reputation as a councillor, anything that could prevent me from getting re-elected every four fucking years. You running around with an outlaw motorcycle club does exactly that. What are you even doing there? Karl said you've been absent from work for eight bloody weeks!*"

"You jeopardised your reputation when you hit my mother. Beating your wife doesn't really fit with your holier than thou persona, does it?"

"*Are you still harping on about that? Farrah's fine. She's forgotten about it. You should, too. And I hardly beat her. I gave her a slap, that's all. Honestly, you're so dramatic.*"

I grind my teeth. "So, we just brush it under the carpet? Forget it happened?"

"Yes, Piper. Mistakes occur in the grown-up world. Lord knows, we've spent enough time having to fix yours over the years."

His words are a kick to the gut. It always comes back to that. I'm the dirty secret in Mum's life—the kid born outside of marriage. In their world, I might as well be the Scarlet Letter. Mum left town and came back pregnant without a man on her arm. Grant raising me as his own practically makes him a saint among his friends. He took on another man's child without question. What a hero. I can't count the times Grant and Mum have had to paper over the fact that I'm the stepchild, or spin a story a certain way to cover the fact I'm not his by blood.

Being born of a violent sociopath was my first mistake. My transgressions over the years continued to pile up. I was never thin enough, or smart enough, or passionate enough, or funny enough, or pretty enough. I tried hard, I really did, to live up to the unrealistic expectations set firstly by my mother and then by my stepfather when he came on the scene a little later. Camille Neville is the only reason I'm still here, standing tall. She saved my life, both mentally and physically.

I was eighteen the first time I met Josh. Cami helped me set it up. My parents had no idea. When they found out, it was too late. I'd been meeting with him in secret for years by that point and Josh had left me in the dust for the Lost Saxons.

Grant lost his mind. I could have killed his career by fraternising with a man just recently out of prison. I didn't care. My heart was broken at losing my brother.

"I apologise if my existence is an embarrassment to you and Mum."

"Don't be ridiculous."

"Come off it, Grant. That's what you think."

"I think you running around with a known criminal is an embarrassment."

"He's my brother and he was dying. I had to be here."

"I wouldn't have given a damn if he had died and neither should you."

"Grant!" I gasp. "How can you say such a thing!"

"Do you know what this will do to your mother? The hurt this will cause her? She can't even bear to hear that bastard's name without it causing a breakdown. If she knows you've been staying with him for weeks..." He lets out a breath that is laced with anger. *"I can't believe you would disrespect your family like this."*

His words settle in unpleasantly. I know Curtis put her through hell, but he put Josh through worse.

"Josh is my family, too. And he's as much a victim of Curtis Wade as Mum was."

"That boy is nothing to you! He's never been anything to you, Piper. He never wanted to know you. Don't forget how he left you!"

Those words hit a little too close to my own insecurities, but I stomp them down. Josh does want to know. He's trying. We're getting on well, we're rebuilding, becoming closer, trying to become siblings. It's not been easy, but he's making amends—even if he's struggling. I know he pushed me away the other day, but we're bound to have these setbacks. We're both damaged.

Anyway, this time it's not Josh failing. It's me falling short. I'm lying to him by betraying him with Jem.

God...

I close my eyes and swallow back the bile crawling up my throat.

"With the greatest respect, this isn't your business."

He scoffs at me. *"If the media finds this out, it becomes my business. You have one job in this family and that is to uphold the Hollander name."*

Ellis. Wade. Hollander. I'm pulled in three directions.

"My name is Ellis. Not Hollander. Not Ellis-Hollander. Just Ellis. And I do that. I do everything you ask of me and more, but I'm not a child, Grant, you can't control me."

"I think you'll find, Piper, there's a lot of things I can do."

My stomach rolls unpleasantly at the bite in his tone.

"What does that mean?"

"It means you have a lot to lose by staying gone, Piper. Your mother needs you here. I need you here. So does Cami. It would be a shame if something were to happen and you weren't here to stop it, or to help, wouldn't it?"

I don't miss the veiled threat in his words. It's almost laughable to hear it coming from my stepfather's mouth. I know he's a man of means, and I know how important his career is to him, but despite what he did to me and Mum, he's not this kind of person. He's a suit and dinner jacket bloke. He wears sandals and socks together, for Christ's sake, and thinks it's acceptable to drink Irish Coffee only after dinner, not just because.

"What does that mean?" I demand, my voice taking a higher pitch than usual as my fear mounts.

"It means it's time to come home," he orders me.

"If you hurt them—"

"Oh, don't be ridiculous, Piper. Honestly, these silly fantasies of yours... I'm tired of entertaining them."

I can't tell if I'm being paranoid or if he is actually dealing out threats. His clever words are hidden beneath friendly barbs.

"Grant—"

"I'll be at your loft this evening. If you're not home then, I'll be incredibly disappointed."

He hangs up without another word.

For a moment, I sit in stunned disbelief. Did that really just happen? My heart starts to pound fast beneath my ribs.

I should be used to Grant interfering like this. He's always playing in my life, controlling. It's always been this way, but I thought I had stepped out from under his thumb a little by moving into my own place with Cami, putting distance between us. Clearly, not.

I don't know if he could hurt Cami. I have no idea if he has that capability, but I'm not willing to risk it. Cami's in Manchester alone, with no one to protect her.

I nibble on my thumbnail, my brain whirling. Shit. I can't exactly tell Josh what's going on. What would I tell him anyway? I may or may not have just been threatened? I don't even know if that's what Grant did. It was all so vague. Besides, I don't imagine my brother will handle this situation with any sense of subtly. What do motorcycle clubs do to people who threaten 'family'? I suspect it isn't pleasant.

I need to go home. I need to protect Cami and I need to protect my mother—even though she may be less inclined to allow it. She's under whatever spell Grant has over her, but I won't leave her vulnerable either. Oh God, how in the heck do I explain just leaving suddenly to my brother without looking suspect or drawing questions?

On autopilot, I grab my bag and head out of the bedroom. Josh is waiting in the living area.

"You ready?" he asks, his kutte on his back.

He looks almost happy—well, as happy as Joshua Wade can be. I chew the inside of my cheek, my guts burning with acid. I'm not ready. I don't want to leave.

We're just starting to get to know each other, and whatever I tell him as to why I'm suddenly departing he's going to be hurt.

"Josh?"

He meets my gaze. "Yeah?"

I'm leaving...

The words sit on my tongue. Spit them out Piper. Spit them out.

I can't. I can't say them.

"Thank you."

God. It's not what I meant to say at all, but I can't tell him I'm leaving. Cowardly, absolutely, but I can't.

"What for?"

"The last two months. It's meant so much getting to know you again."

He shifts uncomfortably, his hand going to the back of his neck. He's not great at doing the heart-to-heart stuff.

"Fuck, Pipes, for me too. And I'm sorry about the other day. I know I upset you with what I said. Sometimes, I don't engage my big arsehole brain before I speak."

He's apologising? Has hell frozen over?

"It's okay."

"No, it's not. I shouldn't have said it. Look, I don't know how to do this brother shit, but I'm trying, and I'm probably going to fuck it up a lot along the way."

I snort. "Yeah, probably."

He half grins. "You're going to have to cut me slack while I'm getting to grips with things. I just want you to know it means a lot that you've been here while I was recovering. I'll never forget that."

I wonder if he'll remember this when I tell him I'm leaving, and I'll have to tell him and soon because Grant gave me a timed deadline.

I also wonder if he'll remember this if he ever finds out about me and Jem...

Bugger. Jem.

What do I do about him? Nothing, I suppose. It's not like we haven't been avoiding each other since we last hooked up. The distance will make it easier to dance around each other.

Maybe it's just as well I'm leaving. We can never be anyway. Grant hit the roof over me rekindling my relationship with my brother. He would lose his mind if he found out I was hooking up with a biker. He'd probably ship me to Antarctica.

"You okay?" Josh asks, breaking through my thoughts.

"What? Oh, yes. Just hungry."

"Let's get you fed then."

I wait until we're at the cafe to break the news I'm heading back to Manchester. This is deliberate on my part. Firstly, because we're in a public place, and I hope it will curb his response, but also because I wait until the last possible minute I have to tell him. I don't want to ruin our morning. I make up some bullshit about work freaking out about the time I've missed. He seems to buy it, and why wouldn't he? It's a reasonable explanation and I haven't given Josh any reason to doubt my word, but it's another lie, another deception on top of the one I'm already keeping from him. The lies I'm weaving are winding around me tightly, constricting my lungs until I can hardly breathe.

He takes it better than I expect, doesn't question my lies, which makes them stick in my throat like barbed thorns, and promises we can still see each other on weekends. He even suggests he'll visit Manchester. I don't deserve him, I really don't. He's doing his best to be a good brother and I'm treating him like this. Tears clog my throat as he asks if I want to stay tonight and leave in the morning, but I tell him I need to leave immediately. I hate to see the disappointment behind his eyes. It makes my guts twist, but what choice do I have? Grant has become unpredictable, and I have no idea if he will follow through on his threats. I can't risk Cami's safety on a hope that he won't.

I try to hold it together until I get on the train, but I can't. I'm not usually an emotional person, but leaving like this kills me. I sob brokenly. I can tell Josh is lost, that he doesn't have a clue how to handle a crying female, but he does his best to offer comfort. He hugs me tightly to his chest and I cling to him like he's my saviour, all the time wishing he was Jem, and hating myself for thinking it. Josh is my brother and should be the one to offer me comfort, not the man I've shagged a couple of times in secret.

Josh wipes my tear-stained face as the train starts to pull into the station. "No more tears, yeah? You can visit anytime, Pipe. I mean it. You're always welcome here."

This would change if he knew the truth, if he knew the real me. I'm a terrible person.

"You're too good to me," I tell him in a wobbly voice.

"I'm nowhere near as good as I should be." He kisses my forehead. "Thanks, kid, for coming, for taking care of me. You can't know what it means to me that you did."

I give him a watery smile and glance over my shoulder as the train grinds to a halt behind me, the hydraulics making a racket. "Josh, promise me something."

"What?"

"No matter what happens, don't walk away from me again. I don't think I could take it. Not this time."

His brow draws together, the consternation clear on his face. "I know I haven't been the best brother, but I'm not going anywhere."

A whistle sounds down the platform and I snag my suitcase. I need to get on the train if I'm going to make it before it leaves.

Moving towards the open door on the carriage, I say, "No matter what happens, Josh, you promise me that."

I don't know if he senses something in my words, or a change in my tone, but there's a definite shift in his demeanour when he says my name in a questioning tone, "Piper…"

"Say the words," I press, needing to hear it.

"I promise."

Relief floods me and I climb the step and hoist my suitcase onto the train. "I love you, Josh."

I don't care if he says it back. I just need him to know it because I have the feeling things are going to get ugly down the road. I need him to know before that happens that I do care, that I'm not this horrible beast.

He stares at me for a moment, and I don't think he's going to say it back, then he says, "I love you too, kid."

The carriage door slides shut and the train lets out a groan and rumble before it starts to move. I watch my brother through the window of the carriage, standing on the platform in his jeans and kutte, looking every inch the biker he is and my heart feels full and yet empty at the same time.

Leaving is wrong.

I stand in the doorway until Kingsley's urban sprawl gives way to fields and hills. It's been a while since my life last felt like it wasn't mine and I hate that Grant took that control from me. Even more so, I hate that I allowed him to. I should have told him to shove off, but the education centre would die without the funding and the kids need it. I couldn't do that to them.

By the time I'm back in Manchester, I'm bone-tired and

ready to crash. I text Josh when I get off the train to let him know I arrived safely.

I feel drained, defeated, deflated.

I start the walk back to the flat I share with Cami. It's the weekend, so she's probably staying with her on-and-off again boyfriend, Spencer.

I'm looking forward to having a bath and a glass of wine, and offloading my feelings about the weekend with my best friend.

As I step out of the stairwell onto my floor, I stop in my tracks. Grant is waiting outside the front door of the loft. Great. I don't have the energy to deal with him right now.

Why is he waiting here, waiting for me?

Grant doesn't move as I approach, his eyes tracking my movement as I get closer. I stop a few feet away, feeling it's prudent to keep some distance between us. He doesn't speak, merely roves an eye over my suitcase before bringing his attention back to me.

"Why are you here?" I demand finally.

He pushes off the wall, straightening his suit jacket.

As usual, he's impeccably dressed. He grabs the back of my neck and I freeze, my entire body going tight as he leans down to kiss my forehead. It's a paternal kiss, but it's laced with so much danger, my legs shake.

When he pulls back, his eyes are hard as they meet mine.

"No more visits to Yorkshire, Piper. Understand? I would hate for there to be any mishaps."

He releases his grip on my neck and my throat throbs. Then he makes his way up the hallway to the exit, leaving me reeling.

CHAPTER NINETEEN

"Can you turn your head slightly to the left, Piper?"

I jolt out of my daze, my eyes snapping towards the photographer who is smiling at me, his camera poised ready. I must have zoned out again. I can feel everyone's eyes locked on me, waiting for me to respond. Discomfort slithers down my spine. I've never enjoyed being the centre of attention and now is no different.

I shift on the soft cushions, trying to get comfortable, but my dress feels constricting, more like a straight-jacket. My hair is also pinned too tightly, making my scalp tingle, and the lights overhead are too hot, the megawatt bulbs radiating so much heat I feel light-headed.

I shift my gaze towards Mum and Grant who are watching me carefully from the other end of the French-style chaise we've been perched on like circus animals to undergo this latest ritual humiliation. I'm sure they're waiting for me to crack.

Grant looks unhappy, Mum a little embarrassed by my lack of focus. I don't care. I'm done with this day. I feel like a marionette, being positioned this way or that for some stupid pictures I have no interest in.

I have no idea why I'm here, or why I even *need* to be here, but for the past hour I've been subjected to pose after pose of us playing at the perfect family. It's sickening really. We're not even close to perfect. I wonder what this roomful of people would think if they knew the truth behind the fake smiles and suave clothes. I wonder what they would think if they knew the great Grant Hollander is both a handsy bastard and threatens to hurt women in the name of his campaign for power.

"To the left," the photographer instructs again.

He's a forty-something-year-old Boho wannabe from London called Damien or Duncan. He's wearing skinny jeans and has been wandering around all afternoon in bare feet, directing this shoot.

He's also getting on my last nerve. I want to go home, have a glass of wine, a shower and forget today ever happened. Unfortunately, I'm stuck here until Damien or Duncan and his hoard of helpers decide we're done. I don't even know what magazine this shoot is for. Honestly, I don't even care. What does it matter? It's the same shit, rinsed and repeated, no matter whose name is attached to it.

I comply with the devil photographer's command, turning my head to the left, even though I want to tell him to shove off. I wouldn't be here at all if it wasn't for Grant's barely veiled threats to Mum, Cami and me—although my safety matters less than the other two. I feel caged, trapped, and I have no idea how to fix things. Would he really hurt them if I don't do as he asks? Part of me thinks Grant is posturing, that he's not capable of the threats he hinted at, but then he did bruise me and he did hit Mum. She's in that house alone with him. Maybe I can convince her to leave.

I've been trying to get her alone since I got back, but she won't meet with me. I'm going to ask her to come to lunch after the shoot, see if I can convince her to move out. That will remove one piece of leverage Grant has over me.

In all honesty, I want to go back to Kingsley, which is something I never thought I would say. My life there was simpler. I miss my grumpy brother. Josh has been texting me and we've spoken on the phone a few times, keeping up correspondence, as he said he would. I'm worried about doing much more than that in case he realises something is going on with me. I can't have him white-knighting into my mess, so when he asked if he can visit, I made excuses. I feel terrible for doing it, but until I know what danger Grant poses to me and Cami, I can't risk Josh being here.

But not seeing my brother jeopardises the bridges we've been building. I have to find some way to visit him, to get back to Kingsley, which means I have to discover if Grant is just posturing.

I also miss Jem.

Ridiculous, I know, to miss someone I've shagged twice, but I do. We haven't spoken since the night we fucked outside the clubhouse. Then again, this is becoming a ritual with us. We hook up, and then avoid each other until we next run into each other and hook up again. Only this time, I'm breaking the cycle by leaving town. I don't know if he's aware I've gone. It was all so sudden, but it's probably for the best. All the lying, all the sneaking around, it's not good for either of us.

But I can't say I don't yearn for him because I do, and the mind-blowing sex is only one part of why. Jem has been a constant in my life for the past few months. Despite being supremely annoying, I also find him... well, a little endearing and a whole lot of fun.

He also makes things quiet in my head, which is ironic, given the man never shuts up. I wish he was here now. My mind is storming, and I'm struggling to keep my emotions locked behind my walls to maintain my polite front. Really, what I want to do is grab the front of Damien's shirt —I'm fairly certain his name is, in fact, Damien, not Duncan—and toss him and his stupid camera across the studio.

I'm sure Grant would murder me on the spot if I did.

"Okay, and I think that's a wrap," he says, finally.

He's barely finished the words before I'm pushing up and moving away from the lights. I take a bottle of water that is offered to me by one of the assistants, uncapping it and glugging down at least half of it before I feel the pinch of my mother's fingers on my elbows.

Without risking causing a scene, I have no choice but to let her steer me over to a quiet corner of the studio, away from the hustle of people. Grant, I notice, keeps them busy —schmoozing and doing his usual routine of playing cock of the walk.

My mother glances around me, no doubt making sure we are actually alone and not about to be overheard, before she hisses at me.

"What on earth has got into you?"

I stare at her perfectly coiffed hair, her overly done makeup and her no doubt botoxed forehead.

It's all a front.

Everything is a lie.

I thought Josh's life was the falsehood, that he lived a sinister existence behind the kuttes and bikes, but he's not the fabricator. He's upfront about his criminality. It's Grant that is the deceiver. He's violent, and he's not above using threats to get what he wants. I always saw Grant as this holier than thou kind of person. I'm coming to realise this is not the case.

"How are you with him?" I demand in a low voice.

"What?"

"Grant, Mum. How are you with him?"

She stares at me, her forehead not even moving. She could be trying to frown. It's hard to know. "What in the bloody hell are you talking about?"

"He threatened me. He threatened you and Cami, too, if I didn't do what he asked. He's not a good man."

I watch as her hand flutters to her hair, checking it's still in place. It's a nervous tick she has. It also tells me something. She knows he's threatened us.

"Don't be ridiculous. And you should show Grant some respect. That man clothed you and kept a roof over your head from the time you were a little girl."

"So, that gives him the right to push me around? To threaten to hurt me if I don't do what he demands?"

"It does when you're spending your time with bloody criminals," she hisses in my face. "I would have him beat you every day if it kept you away from that man."

Oh, yes, she knows. She knows I was in Kingsley, that I was with Josh, and that my stepfather threatened me with violence if I see him again. And not just me, but my best friend, who isn't even involved in this.

"You think Grant isn't a criminal?"

"He's never been in prison, unlike that scumbag you're visiting." Mum roves an eye over me like I'm shit under her shoe. "Knowing what that family did to me! How could you go there, Piper?"

Curtis Wade hurt her, I know this. It was why she ran from him, why she left town, alone and without anything to her name. I think she was genuinely scared of what he might do to her if she didn't. I don't know the full story of what happened between them, but I can surmise it was not a fairy tale romance. I do know Curtis employed my mother and charmed her into bed. She was young, impressionable, and she thought she'd landed on her feet when her handsome boss was showering her with attention and gifts. Curtis had other ideas. He had his fill of her and then made her life a living hell until she was forced to leave town. Mum discovered she was pregnant with me weeks later. My biological father is one of the few topics that causes my mother genuine pain, so I've never pushed, but I do know it's why she never once told my father I existed.

But Josh isn't Curtis.

He hurt me emotionally in the past, sure, but he'd never lay a hand on me—or any woman—physically. I've never felt threatened by him that way, by any of the Saxons men, in fact.

Except Dylan, but he was more pushy than anything else, and Jem got me out of that situation anyway.

My denim-clad white knight.

"Josh is my brother, whether you like it or not. He's family, and he's been good to me."

Which is more than I can say for her and Grant right now.

"So good he left you a wreck?"

I jolt at her words. "He was a different person back then. Curtis messed him up, Mum, then prison—"

"Don't talk to me about *that* man or his spawn!" she growls at me. We're lucky there is so much noise from the other end of the room to mask the anger in her voice right now. "You stop seeing him, Piper, immediately."

Her tone makes me bristle. I'm not a child, and despite

what she and Grant think, I don't have to dance to their tune.

"No, and you'll tell Grant to stop making threats."

"I won't, and I won't be responsible for what he does if you don't do as you're told."

Bile collects in my throat. She's throwing me to the wolves. My own mother is choosing the side of a man who thinks nothing of hitting her.

"You deserve him," I tell her. "And I'm done helping you. I thought you were a victim of his temper, but you're just as complicit. You would help him hurt me, hurt Cami to protect your reputation, to keep this lifestyle you've built. That means more to you than your own daughter."

"Don't be so dramatic. Of course it doesn't mean more, but Grant and I have worked hard to get here, Piper. Do you expect us to let you undo all that work because you're having a teenage rebellion?"

"I'm twenty-five, Mum. I think the days of teenage rebellions are long over."

I try to push around her, but she grabs my bicep, pulling me close to her. From a distance, I'm sure it can't be seen that she's digging her claws into the soft skin of my arm, but I can sure as hell feel it.

"You end things with that man, Piper. Immediately. I mean it."

I tear out of her grasp and push past her to quickly gather up my things off the table near the door. I don't bother saying goodbye to anyone. I just grab everything and rush for the exit. Grant's eyes catch mine as I step through the door, narrowing, and I see the anger there, but he masks it quickly to resume his conversation with the assistant he's talking to.

Fuck him and my mother.

As soon as I'm out on the street and the Manchester hustle and bustle hits me, reality crashes down around me.

What have I just done?

Have I just put me and Cami in danger?

Is Grant capable of actually hurting us?

I can deal with whatever he does to me, but Cami? If he touches her, I'll kill him. I quickly shrug into my jacket and pull my bag over my shoulder. I need to get home. I need to warn her.

I barely register the journey back across town, taking a cab, rather than the bus. I take the stairs two at a time and practically run up the hallway to the front door, fumbling to get the keys in the lock. By the time I get inside and shut the door behind me, I'm a panting, sweaty mess.

Cami glances up from the sofa and the magazine she's flipping through. Her brows immediately draw together.

"What did they do to you? I knew I shouldn't have let you go." She unfurls her legs, coming to me quickly, her hands latching onto my shoulders. "P, you're shaking."

"I think we're in trouble."

"Why?" She rubs up my arms. "Come and sit, and tell me everything."

I let her lead me over to the sofa and push me on to it. My head drops into my hands as I let my despair over the situation overwhelm me. How do I explain to my best friend that my stepfather and mother are complete monsters?

"Piper, talk to me."

I do. Haltingly, I tell her everything that's been happening with Grant and Mum. She's not too happy I didn't tell her about the threats, and she's even less happy that I'm dancing to Grant's tune to protect her.

"Grant is all talk, P. What can he do? He's a paper-pushing suit."

"I don't know," I say, wrapping my hands tightly around the mug of coffee Cami presented me with during our conversation. I clearly seemed like I needed caffeine. "I didn't want you to get hurt because of me."

She scoffs. "Darling, I'm a big girl. I can take care of myself. Besides, I'm not scared of your stepfather. He's a pushover."

I shake my head. "He's not. When he grabbed me that day, he hurt me. He's more intimidating than he seems."

"Piper, Grant's not stupid. He has to know it's idiotic to threaten me if he wants to make his way to Westminster and a seat in parliament. I don't have any loyalty to him, and I will blab to whoever will listen to me about his less than gentlemanly ways if he tries anything." She smiles at me, trying to reassure me. "He's about avoiding scandals, not creating them."

This is true.

"But—"

"No buts, Piper. He's posturing, and I think your mother is in on it somewhere along the way. Don't get me wrong, I think Grant did hurt her that day, but I don't think she's a hundred percent a victim either. Your parents have been pushing you around for years, controlling you, manipulating you. It has to stop."

I push my hair back from my face.

"I know."

"You want to know your brother?"

"Yes."

"Then know him. Fuck what they say."

"I don't want them to interfere or make things difficult."

"Just because they're your blood, doesn't mean you owe them shit. The old adage, you can't choose your family is true. You can't, but that doesn't mean you have to put up with them. Josh is your brother and if you want to have a relationship with him, you should."

I mull over her words.

"It's a bit more complicated than that."

"Is it? I'm really not seeing how."

"Well, Josh may not want a relationship with me." I let my head fall back against the cushions. "I did a terrible thing while I was in Kingsley," I whisper.

Her eyes slide towards me. "Do we need bail money?"

"Is bail money a real thing?"

She shrugs. "I have no idea, but I can get it if you do."

I huff out a breath. "I went there to see my dying brother, to fix things."

I don't say anything else, not sure how to explain my behaviour. Cami straightens on the sofa, one hand clutching her coffee mug, the other fiddling with the pendant she always wears around her throat.

"That's not a terrible thing, Piper. It's what most sisters would do."

"No, it's not."

"Darling, I'm not keeping up here. You're going to have to help me out. Didn't things go well with Josh? I was under the impression you mended bridges, that you were talking and getting to know one another."

"Things went as well as could be expected—better, really. He's messaged me since I've been back to make sure I'm okay. We're... bonding, I suppose."

"Right... so...?"

"Visiting Josh isn't the terrible thing I did."

I know Cami won't judge me, she never does, but even so, saying this, feels so wrong.

"Girl, just spit it out. You're killing me. Did you sign up to their gang? Are you now a sworn in sister?"

"I have no idea what any of that means."

"What did you do, P?"

I nibble on my lip before I blurt, "I slept with one of Josh's friends."

Her eyes flare and then she grins. And I mean she beams. "Shut the front door!"

I groan. "What am I going to do?"

"Firstly, you're going to explain why you've waited all this time to spill this to me. Then you're going to tell me everything."

"Well, there isn't really a good time to say 'oh, by the way, I'm a huge slut', is there?"

Cami rolls her eyes at me. "You're absolutely not a slut. There's nothing wrong with a healthy sex life."

"No, but there is something wrong with sleeping with your brother's friend while said brother is lying in the hospital on death's door."

"Quit being a drama queen. Who is this guy?"

My mouth tastes of ash as the guilt settles in me. "Jem. His name's Jem."

"Is he hot?" She wiggles her eyebrows suggestively at me.

I take a long sip of my coffee. "That's not the point at all."

"Well, is he?"

I click my fingers in front of her face, bringing her out of her dreamy state. "Cami, focus. What do I do?"

"What do you want to do?"

"I don't know. The guilt is tearing me apart."

"Honey, why do you feel guilty?"

"Because he's Josh's friend and he's off limits. I'm off limits to Josh's friends."

Cami scoffs. "What is this? The nineteen-hundreds?

Off limits? You can date who you want."

"I don't want to date him!" I squeak. "Jesus, he's in a motorcycle club, for Christ's sake." Although I did enjoy being on the back of his bike more than I would like to admit, and I really do like seeing him on the back of his bike.

And I really love his tattoos...

"So, you're just fuck buddies?"

"Yes. No. I don't know. We've only slept together twice."

She stares at me. "Except you left Kingsley without him and now you're pining over him." Her face breaks into a grin. "That's why you've been so fucking glum since you got back. You miss him!"

"I'm not pining over him."

I am, and I do miss him. I'm not ready to let him go, but I can't have him either. Being with him makes things difficult between me and Josh, between Jem and Josh, and the last thing I want to do is destroy their friendship.

"Tell me everything from the start."

I do, leaving nothing out. When I'm done, she narrows her eyes at me.

"Okay, let me get this straight," Cami says, rubbing at her brow. "You and this Jem chap have off the charts sex twice while you're in town, then you just leave without a word and ghost him faster than you can say 'Casper', and you don't think that's a problem?"

I consider her words with a frown.

"Of course it's a problem, but what else can I do?"

She closes her eyes, as if asking the universe for patience. "Continue having off the charts sex? Maybe explore things further with him?"

"And risk my brother disowning me again?"

"Piper, you don't know that will happen. Josh might be happy the two of you are together."

This makes me laugh, but there's no humour behind it. "He practically threatened to castrate Weed if he went near me. He doesn't want me involved with his brothers. I'm not good enough."

Admitting that fear out loud eases some of the heaviness in my chest.

"Bollocks," she snaps. "You're more than good enough. Most likely it's the other way around and he doesn't want his friends to have their grubby paws on you."

"I doubt it."

She lets out a frustrated breath. "Honey, he's just flexing the big brother muscles, that's all. If you like this man you should just tell your brother and stake your claim."

Stake my claim?

"This isn't the wild west, Cami. There's no claiming. It was sex. Nothing more."

And that's all it's ever going to be.

"Darling, I don't think it was 'just sex' for you or for him. From what you're telling me, he's interested in you, and you're certainly interested in him."

I stare at her a beat before I laugh. "You're crazy. The last thing he is, is interested in me. I'm just something to pass the time. We didn't exactly get off to the best start. You do remember me telling you how much he hated me in the beginning?"

"There's a fine line between love and hate."

"Jem and I would never work. I haven't made it secret that I don't like his little gang of leather and denim wearing bikers."

"Are they really that bad?"

I take a sip of my coffee while I consider her question.

"No," I admit. "They've been nothing but gracious, to be frank, although Jem is an enormous man-child."

"So, what's the problem?"

"Apart from the obvious? That my brother doesn't want me dating his friends?"

"Well, he'll get over that."

"I lied to him."

"Yes, you did. You should have been forthcoming, but it's not like anyone died."

She doesn't understand how Josh thinks, and trying to explain it is pointless, so I try a different tact.

"What about the fact Josh got shot and nearly died? The Club isn't exactly safe. That's the kind of life I would have with Jem—wondering if he's going to get hurt, or arrested, or worse. Dead. I don't want it, Cam. I want normal. I want boring. Suburban. That makes him off limits to me, because I'll never have that with a man like Jem—even if we were at that stage, which we're not because all we've done is shag twice."

Although I'm lying to myself. I'm already in deep with him. Cami is right. I am pining for Jem and I have been since I got back to Manchester. That hollow, cold emptiness in my gut that I thought was fear over Grant's antics is actually the loss of Jem.

Yikes, when did I fall this hard? Part of me thinks I might just walk through hell to have him, but I keep this to myself.

"I thought that was because of a domestic abuse thing, not the Club."

"Yeah, it was, but that doesn't mean the Club is safe either."

Although it has softened me somewhat towards these men. They stepped in to help a woman who was clearly in danger, without caring about their own safety. My brother took a bullet to protect Beth. None of this sounds like the behaviour of men who are inherently bad to the bone, but the Club still isn't innocent. No one has said anything outright, but reading between the lines, I get the impression Simon Wilson was made to disappear. Knowing Jem probably had a hand in that makes me feel conflicted.

On the one hand, I know the terrible things that man inflicted on several people I've come to care about—including the years of abuse he put the sweet, kind, caring Liv through. But on the other... vigilante justice isn't the way to deal with things, is it?

"So... what's the problem?" Cami repeats.

"They're still outlaws, Cam. He's still an outlaw. I don't want to spend my life worrying about police and prison visits."

She waves a hand at me, sloshing her coffee in the mug. "Darling, half the people we know are bloody criminals."

"Well, Grant has certainly proved he's not a saint with recent events," I grumble.

I'd be amazed if Grant gives two shits about the people he serves in his local area. Everything Grant Hollander does is for publicity. He'll get down and dirty in the local allotments because it looks good in the papers, he'll help walk the kids to school in the morning because it makes a good news segment, he'll visit the elderly in care homes because the media lap it up. Does he enjoy those things? Doubtful. Grant likes golf, relaxing beach holidays and crosswords. Infants annoy him, he despises children and he thinks old people are a drain on his budgets. He would never say these things, of course—at least not outside the privacy of our family home. His entire life is a show he puts on, and I'm a part of that event.

Cami's expression turns serious. "Grant is full of shit. He's not going to do anything to you or to me."

I don't know if Cami is right, but I'm not sure we should risk it. I've never seen this violent side of him before. Honestly, it's unpredictable and that puts me on edge.

I open my mouth to counter her words, but before I can say anything, a knock on the door has both our heads swinging towards it.

"If that's your mum or Grant..." Cami starts.

I push off the sofa, but Cami jumps up, too, and we both head to the door together. We fight over the peep hole, but she gets to it first.

"Holy shit!"

"What?" I demand.

"Did we order Thor's twin?" When she pulls back her eyes are wide.

What?

I roll to my toes and glance through the peep hole. And my stomach flips. On the other side of the door is Jem.

CHAPTER TWENTY

I CONSIDER NOT OPENING the door, but Cami takes this option out of my hands by reaching for the handle. I stop her, and she gives me a questioning look.

"That's Jem," I whisper.

Her mouth falls open. "That's your hot guy?"

My head bobs and my heart races. "What's he doing here, Cam?"

"Uh, I imagine wanting to see you. Piper, you left town without a word. He probably wants to find out why."

I did leave town really quite abruptly, but considering we were not even dating, it's not like I needed to tell him, right? What on earth can I even say to explain that? She gets a dreamy look on her pale face.

"It's really quite romantic."

"It's not romantic," I snap. "It's ridiculous. He shouldn't be here. And I didn't leave without a good reason. I left because Grant was threatening bodily harm to us both. What choice did I have?"

My best friend considers me carefully, tugging absently at the end of her auburn braid. "I'm not saying you didn't have a good reason, darling, but he doesn't know that. From his perspective you hooked up, had your way with him, and then ran away. Maybe you owe him some explanation."

Her description makes me flush. It sounds so callous. "That isn't what happened."

"I'm not saying you did a bad thing, P, but maybe you do need to give him some closure on the situation, explain why you left."

I shake my head. "No way in hell am I telling him that. He'll blab to Josh and they'll both murder Grant."

Especially if they learn my stepfather put his hands on me.

"Would that be a bad thing?" she mutters darkly.

I smack her arm. "Absolutely it would."

"So, you'd rather look like the bad guy here, than tell the truth?" Her whispered voice does nothing to mask the disappointment in her tone.

"I'd rather my brother and the bloke I'm having casual sex with don't end up in jail."

"Piper, lies are what got you into this mess in the first place."

When did she become all Miss Wisdom?

"Don't become sensible on me. I need you to be Cami, right now. Not the cleaned-up version of her."

Her eyes nearly roll out of her pretty head. "Quit being ridiculous."

Knuckles rap on the door again, and we both freeze like naughty kids before our eyes snap in that direction. Cami starts to move towards the door.

"What are you doing?" I demand, sounding strangled.

"Well, we can't leave him standing out there."

I nod vehemently. Absolutely we can. "No."

She shakes free of my grip and tugs the handle down.

All protests die on my lips the moment I see him. He looks... well, magnificent. I want to run to him, touch him, but I keep my feet still, forcing myself to remain locked to the floor.

He isn't quite so reserved. His eyes move up my body in a way that heats me from head to toe and my lips part as I almost pant. My reaction to him is visceral, a primal response I can no more control than he can. My chest feels heavy, tight, and my heart is moving with the speed of a racing train the moment I lay eyes on him.

"Holy hotness," Cami murmurs.

This breaks me out of my Jem fog and I shake myself. "Uh, what are you doing here, Jem?"

His face becomes hard at my words.

"It's nice to see you too, angel." His voice drips with sarcasm that has me internally wincing.

Maybe I should have been a little less acerbic.

Cami leans around me and holds out a hand. "I'm Cami—the best friend. You hurt her, I'll kill you. I don't care if you're a big tough guy. I'll dump your body in the nearest pig pen and let them devour you. Treat my girl right. She's amazing and she deserves good things." She reaches for her bag near the door. "I'm going to give you crazy kids some space to work out your... 'issues'. I'll be at Spense's if you need me."

I glare at her. "You don't have to leave."

Traitorous mare.

She grins at me. "You'll be fine. Work it out, P." Then under her breath, she says, "He calls you angel. Work it out." A beam crosses her face as she raises her voice to add, "It was nice to meet you, Jem."

"Yeah, you too, sweetheart," he says, but his eyes stay locked on me.

Cami leaves, firing a smile at me that is mostly a wince. I could kill her. Jem steps inside the loft fully, shutting the front door behind her, locking us both inside.

Oddly, this makes the usually airy, open space feel small and claustrophobic. Heart racing, I watch him, waiting for him to move, to act, to say something. My stomach is dancing as the seconds crawl and the silence lingers between us.

Finally, he says, "You left."

"Yes," I say on a breath.

"Without a word."

"Yes," I repeat.

His brow gets heavy. "You didn't think you owed me anything? A goodbye maybe?"

Unease prickles through me, and the desire to explain sits on my tongue, but I push it away. I can't tell him, even though Cami thinks I should. It'll cause a fallout I won't be able to control.

"I'm sorry," is the pathetic response I give him.

He huffs out a breath, his hands dropping to his jean-clad hips. He looks handsome, standing there in his leather riding jacket, his blond hair swept back from his face, clearly as if he's pushed his fingers through it after pulling his helmet off. His entire body seems wired beneath the easy stance he's trying to portray.

"Sorry? Well, all right then. That makes it better."

The sarcasm dripping off his words makes me cringe, but I sally forth with my stance. I've started walking this path, so I'm committed to it. I hate Grant for making me into this person—the one who has clearly hurt Jem. I didn't think it would be possible to hurt a man as big and brawn as him, but I can see it in the tightness of his shoulders and the way his mouth is pinched at the corners. It doesn't sit right with me that I've caused this.

"Jem, it's not like we're dating or together," I say as softly as I can. "I didn't owe you an explanation."

The hardness in his eyes makes my throat clog. "Right. We fucked. That's all I'm good for, yeah? Just a bit of rough and tumble? I'm just a dirty biker, nothing more."

Pain lances through my chest at the look in his face. I don't want him to think he's not good enough. I don't think this at all. If anything, I'm the one who is beneath him. I suffer from many terrible weaknesses of character: pride and cowardice are at the top of the list.

"Don't put words in my mouth."

"That's what you mean, though. I'm good for a lay, and that's all."

"It's not what I mean."

"Oh, come off it, Piper. You came to Kingsley hating the Club, hating everything it stood for. So, what was I? A taste of rough? A walk on the wild side. Something to brag to your friends about?"

His words pierce my chest like ice picks. Does he think I'm that shallow? That I would use him for that kind of purpose?

"Don't be an arse! Of course not. I don't care about bragging rights, and I'm not here for a 'taste of rough'—whatever *that* means." I cock my head slightly. "But I can't deny I didn't hate the Club when I first arrived in Kingsley, I did, but you knew that and still pursued me. If you knew that and it's such a problem then why did you kiss me, why did you sleep with me?"

Why did you make me want you...?

"Because I saw the real you beneath the front."

"Exactly, Jem. When I'm with you, I don't care about

the Club or Josh or Manchester or anything. Everything disappears but you!"

"Then why'd you leave without a word, Piper?"

I sigh.

Because my stepfather threatened to hurt me and my best friend...

The words sit on my tongue. I thrust them down as I wrap my arms around my middle, pulling the second part of my reasoning out of the bag.

"I couldn't exactly ask Josh if we could stop by your place before I left, so I could kiss my secret affair goodbye, could I?"

His lip curls and I'm not sure which part of my statement bothers him. I surmise it's the 'secret affair' part. I doubt Jem is thrilled about being anyone's clandestine bit on the side.

"Why not?"

I give him a dark look. "Why do you think?"

He pushes his fingers through his hair. "I'm getting tired of sneaking around."

"Me too, which is why I left the way I did." I close my eyes. "Don't you see? This can't work between us. We have to stop before someone gets hurt."

"Why?"

"Because it's too hard." My voice sounds ragged.

"Anything worthwhile is hard."

I let out a small scoffing sound. "I'm not worthwhile, Jem, believe me."

"The fact you believe that, and actually believe that, worries me more than you can imagine."

He moves into my orbit, his heat searing against me, and cups my face. I need to move away because letting him touch me is a recipe for disaster. I can already feel my walls coming down, my resolve weakening. When it comes to him, I have no willpower. I can't resist him. He's my only vulnerability, and I don't understand it. He is the antithesis of everything I am. He's part of a criminal gang, he's the consummate bad boy, while I'm a holier-than-thou choirgirl. And he's off limits, forbidden in every way imaginable. Yet, this makes him all the more desirable. Do I want him because of this? I don't think so. Underneath the kutte, the Club, everything else, Jem is just a man, and it's the man I want. He's funny, smart—too smart at times. He ties me in knots with that clever mouth of his and I like that. He challenges me, questions me, pushes me. He makes me question myself.

"Jem..." His name is a plea on my lips—to let go of my face, to pull me closer, I don't know which.

He gazes down, his large frame looming over me. He's so big, so overwhelmingly big. I should be frightened of his bulk, but I'm not. I'm not scared of his size, of his criminality, of my brother finding out. Not in this moment. What I am scared of is what I feel for him. I've never experienced this depth of emotion for anyone before. It's like I can't breathe when I'm with him and then I can't breathe when I'm without him.

Jem gives me a half-lift of his mouth, like he knows he's vaulted over my wall, and has won this battle. One of his hands moves from my cheek to my neck, collaring my nape as he sweeps his lips over mine. I'm so weak because I don't stop him, even though I should. My hands sneak under the waistband of his jacket, and I grip the leather tightly as his tongue slides in past my teeth. It's a fevered exploration, one that shows urgency on both our parts to reconnect. My greedy body presses against his, feeling the hard edges of his body as I melt into him.

"Angel..." He gulps air as he draws back from my mouth, his forehead resting against mine. "What are you doing to me?"

I pant too, my lungs struggling to refill.

"I don't know, but you're doing it to me too," I admit, and I hate myself for giving into my desire to have him.

"I am?" He rubs his hands up my arms.

"Yes. I'm not completely unfeeling, Jem."

"No, you feel too much, which is the problem. You consider everyone but yourself and what you want." He lets out a long, frustrated breath. "I'm pissed as hell you left town without a word."

"If you're so mad, then why are you here?"

He smiles stupidly.

"Because when I'm pissed off I do really daft things, like get on my bike and travel across the country to tell you how mad I am. I'm a spur of the moment kind of guy."

I find myself matching his expression, albeit a little coyly. "I can believe that."

Pulling out of my grip a little, he glances around the loft. "So, this is your place?"

"Yeah, this is mine and Cami's home."

His eyes are everywhere, taking in my things, my life. Interest blazes in his gaze.

"Jesus fucking shit, this is the tidiest place I've ever been in."

I snort. "I'm sure it's not."

"Angel, there's not a speck of dust or an ornament out of place." He doesn't let me go as he turns to run a fingertip along the top of the console table to check.

I am unusually neat, I suppose. Cami isn't, but she's learnt to pick up after herself to keep me from freaking out. "There's nothing wrong with being organised, Jem."

"Personally, I'm a fan of chaos. There's a certain artistry to it."

I roll my eyes as I keep my arms around his waist. "Of course you are."

He smiles down at me. "I like chaos in most aspects of my life, Piper, but not this. Not with us."

Us... such a small word that holds so much weight. Is there an 'us'? Can there ever be an us? Do I want there to be?

"I can't give you what you're asking for." My voice is quiet, but I may as well have shouted it.

"Not yet," he agrees.

"Maybe not ever." The warning is clear, but he doesn't heed it. I can tell by how soft his face is when he brushes my hair back behind my ear.

"You're scared, angel, and it's okay to be scared, but it's not okay to let fear hold you back from living your life."

I stare at him. "Don't go all fortune cookie on me now."

"You bring this out in me. I'm not like this with anyone else."

I dip my chin, trying to get control of my feelings, of myself, and when I raise my head again, I feel strengthened.

"I am scared, you're right. I'm so scared of what happens next." And that's the truth. I'm freaking out. "For you, this is easy. If things go wrong, you lose nothing. You still have your family, your friends. Me? I lose everything. I lose Josh. He's all I have."

His head tilts to the side. "You think the stakes aren't high for me here? This could cause a shit storm in the Club. Wade's made it fucking clear he doesn't want any brothers near you. That makes what I'm doing all kinds of shitty, but I wouldn't have touched you if I wasn't willing to go the distance, Piper. I'm in this for the long haul. I want to see where this goes between us. I've never been with anyone like you before. You woke me up."

I think I understand because he did the same to me. Before, I was going through the motions of life, but when I'm with him, everything feels different.

I let his words settle warmly in my belly, but I try not to focus on what they mean. It gives me hope, and I'm not sure I can allow myself to have hope I can have Jem, my brother and the fairy tale ending where everything works out in the end. Things generally don't go that way for me.

"I think you don't lose a brother if things go sideways."

Jem lets out a gruff snort. "Wade finds out I'm fucking his sister and thinks I'm not doing it with good intentions, do you think that ends well for me?"

I shift my shoulders. "I don't know. I don't know how your Club rules of brotherhood work, but I'm guessing you don't get disowned and sent back to Manchester as if you never existed."

"And neither will you. But you're wrong about Wade going easy on me. You, he'll forgive. Me, he'll string up by my bollocks for even looking at you. For tasting you, for touching you, he's going to do worse."

My vision swims. "He'll hurt you for being with me?"

Jem grins. "He'll try."

"I don't want you to get hurt, and I don't want you to fight with Josh either."

"If he stays out of my business, we won't have a problem," is his flippant response.

"Jem—"

"It'll be fine. Wade'll be pissed off, but he'll get over it. He'll have no choice because honestly, I can't give you up. Not for him, not for anyone. And I don't know if what we have will work, Piper. Despite all my fucking bravado, I'm not an oracle. I can't see the future, but I do know when I'm with you, things feel better. You fill a hole inside me that I didn't know I had."

My belly flutters. All my fears about prisons and hospitals and shootings melt away. In this moment, I don't care. I would walk through hell to be with him. When I'm with him, none of that seems to matter.

"I feel it too, but again, we barely know each other."

He takes my hand and kisses my knuckles and my stomach dips pleasantly.

"So, let's fucking change that. This isn't a fling for me. You're not a one-time thing. I wish to fuck you were. It would make this shit a lot easier if I could just walk away."

His words surprise me, but I don't get a chance to question him as his hand moves to my breast, cupping it. My breath catches as he rubs through my clothes.

"I'm sorry."

"I know you are, but it stops now. No more running. Knowing you left without me, it felt like you took a piece of me with you," he says into my ear.

Crushing shame steals my breath. I hurt him by leaving the way I did. I didn't think about it. We've only been together a few times, I didn't think I mattered that much to him, but clearly, I was wrong.

"No more running," I agree.

"Angel, I think we have something good here, something better than good. I know you're scared. I'm scared too, but forget everyone else. Just focus on you and me, and let's just see where this goes, okay?"

"Keep lying, you mean?"

He moves his hand from my breast to sweep his thumb over the apple of my cheek. "The minute we tell people there is an us, it's going to become about your brother, my family and the Club. We'll get dragged into the drama of it all, babe, we'll get lost in their shit. Let's just see where this goes between us, if it's even going to go anywhere, before we shake the apples loose of the cart. I don't like keeping it from the people who matter to us, but yeah, angel, I think we keep lying."

Since I really have no inclination to come clean to Josh, I say, "Okay."

He studies me for a moment. "I don't know what the fuck to do with you, Piper."

Pushing his hair out of his face, I roll to my toes and kiss him. Then I whisper, "Fuck me."

His lips curve. "Is that all I am to you? You just want me for my body. I feel so used. So cheapened."

"Absolutely. Come to bed with me."

I take his hand and give him a tug. He doesn't resist, so I lead him up the stairs to my room.

"Angel, aren't you at least going to buy me dinner first?" he says from behind me, his hands going to my hips as we traverse the open steps.

Architecturally, they're amazing and one of the things I love about the loft. Right now, I love them because it means Jem's hands are on me, steadying me.

"Stop talking, Jem."

"I love when you're bossy."

I barely get him into the bedroom and the door shut when he pushes me against the wall and attacks my mouth. His hand goes under my top, skimming up the skin of my spine as he works my mouth.

Clearly, despite his words, he prefers to be in control.

Between kisses, we both divest each other of our clothes until I'm left only in my bra and a pair of lacy black knickers, him in his boxers.

Jem makes a sound of appreciation in his throat before his hand roams to my bum cheeks.

"I love these, angel. Very pretty."

He drags the lace down my legs, pulling them off and dropping them to the floor. Then he lays me back on the bed. Instinctively, I widen my thighs as he moves over me, dipping his fingers into my wetness and running them through my slit before pushing one inside, the second following a moment later. I suck in a breath as my body remembers him and yearns for him. I tremble with anticipation as he drops his mouth to my clit and licks over the nub.

I nearly stop breathing.

The man is a genius with his tongue. He swirls and laps and licks, even as he moves his fingers inside me. I cling to his shoulders, digging my nails into his flesh until I'm sure I must be bruising and marking him. He doesn't say anything or try to stop me, though. He just continues his unrelenting pace.

"Jem..." I whimper, trying to regulate my breathing and failing. I'm a ragged, panting mess.

He lashes his tongue over me again, and my thighs quiver as I feel my orgasm starting to build. He alternates between soft and hard, and the dual sensations are heady and push me to the brink only to drop me back down. When I finally go over the edge, I do it biting my lip and trying to swallow my moans.

Jem doesn't allow me any respite, he removes the rest of his clothes and pulls a condom from his jeans, pooled on the floor. I watch as he rolls it down his length and then he's on me. He doesn't fuck me as I asked him to. This is different. This is different from the past two times we've been together as well. There's a deeper connection than before, a blazing passion I haven't felt. I stare into his eyes as he fills me with quick strokes that have my orgasm rebuilding fast.

I'm so close already to that edge, teetering over it. He doesn't let me fall though. He turns me onto my stomach and drags my bum into the air and slams into me from behind, his arm locked around my waist to keep me in place as he pushes impossibly deep into my pussy. I try to stay on all fours for him and rear back to meet him, but I fall onto my elbows, my face going into the covers as I let out little whimpers. I'm no longer in command of my body. All I can do is take what he offers and what he offers is spectacular.

I feel his hand run up my spine as he continues to circle his hips in and out of me. White dots spill in my eyes as my pussy contracts around his thickening cock. I'm so close again to falling over the edge of pleasure as the scrape of pain rushes through his rough actions. He's unrelenting, unforgiving, and I want him harder and deeper.

Just as I'm about to scream my pleasure, he pulls out and I gasp. I'm turned on my back once more and he pinches my nipple hard enough to hurt, but the sting of pain is followed by pleasure, eliciting a groan from me. Then he's inside me again, his hands on my breasts while he fucks me, his eyes locked on mine. The intensity of him both scares and thrills me, and I'm almost relieved when I climax this time and he comes with me.

His hips twitch as he spills inside the condom. He moves in and out of me a few more times, his cock softening until he collapses on top of me, his nose going to my neck. Then he rolls us both to the side and more gently then I thought possible, given what he just did, he kisses me like I'm the most precious thing in his world.

"Did I hurt you?"

I shake my head, even though I feel sore and used. I stroke down his arms. "No. It was good."

His brows quirk. "Just good? Angel, I need to work on my bedroom technique if this is my feedback. Good is not what any man wants to hear after he just pulled out all the stops." He brushes my hair back behind my ear and kisses me again.

"It was better than good."

His lips twitch. "That's getting better, but I was hoping for some more elaborate adjectives."

"It was tremendous?"

"Are you asking or telling?"

I laugh and bury my head against his chest. "You're ridiculous."

"But I give you good sex, right?" He tries to lift my head. When that doesn't work, he tickles my side. I squeal and bat his hands away.

"Yes, Jem! Oh my God! Yes, you give me great sex! Stop tickling me!"

He does, but he doesn't release me. He stares in my eyes and the look he gives me scares me half to death. There's so much feeling there, so much promise.

Then he says, "Don't run from me again, angel."

"I won't."

"Promise me."

I run my fingers through his hair. "I promise."

CHAPTER TWENTY-ONE

A WEEK LATER, I go for a drink after work with my colleagues. I'm trying to rebuild bridges there, get my feet back under the table after such a long absence. I can't prove anything, but I have my suspicions that Grant has my boss, Karl, keeping an eye on me. If I ask for time off again, I'm sure he'll report back to my stepfather like a good little lapdog. It's amazing what the threat of losing funding can do. Not that I blame Karl—or Carrie, my other boss. They built the education centre up from the ground and sunk all their time and effort into making it what it is today. It's years of work that could be undone because of me. If I was them, I would sack me, but I think they're scared to do that in case Grant hits back at them for that as well. They're in the ultimate catch-twenty-two. I would quit, if I thought it would help their situation, but I'm not sure it would.

While I can't make amends with my bosses, I can smooth things over with my colleagues, so Friday night drinks in the Wheatsheaf, a pub about a ten-minute walk from work, seems like a good idea. Brian, who is the junior who replaced me on the ground, has been weird about stepping aside to let me reclaim my job. Clearly, he wasn't keen on the fact he was doing my role temporarily. After a few drinks, he's mellowed a little, but he's been making digs all night about how he has never been handed anything on a silver plate and how his daddy never got him where he is. It's getting on my last nerve, but since I'm trying to make reparations, I hold my tongue.

By the time I make the short walk home, I'm on edge and drained. I understand Brian being upset, but this mess isn't my fault. Okay, it's sort of my fault, but why's he being such a jerk to me? It's not like my life is exactly roses and unicorns.

I'm so deep in my head, I barely notice I'm nearly at the front door of my building. I certainly don't notice, or at least pay any heed, to the hulking figure sitting off to the side of the main entrance until a familiar voice says, "Angel."

I snap my head in the direction it comes from, and I see Jem sitting on the low wall surrounding the building, his arms crossed over his chest, his feet at the ankles. He's wearing his leather riding jacket sans kutte, and his bike is parked up in front of the wall, his helmet on the back of it.

Jem makes my pulse race the moment I lay eyes on him.

"What are you doing here?" I sound husky, my voice tinged with excitement.

I had no idea he was coming. He never said anything when we spoke last night, nor when he last messaged at lunchtime.

"Waiting for you. I knocked on the front door, but no one answered."

"Cami's at Spencer's, and I was having post-work drinks. You should have called. I would have come straight home."

I walk towards him, eager to have my hands on him, but

I'm a little unsure. It's been a week since he showed up unannounced on my doorstep, demanding answers as to why I left Kingsley without a word. A week since I last had my hands on him. Him showing up unannounced is becoming a habit I could get used to, but I'm not sure what I'm supposed to do, where we stand in our newly found relationship status. Should I kiss him... or are we taking things slow here? What's the etiquette for 'seeing how things go'? I want to be in his arms, but I don't want to presume either. Fear of rejection has me waiting for him to take the lead, but I don't need to worry. The moment I'm in front of him, he pushes up off the wall and pulls me against his chest, his arms wrapping around my back. I go willingly, letting him crush me to him, and when he lowers his head, I move to meet him, seeking his mouth like we're both magnets and I'm polarised to him.

"I've missed you." His eyes crawl over my face when he finally releases my lips.

"You did?" I'm a little winded. "You saw me a week ago, and you've spoken to me every day since."

Fingers wander under my top, seeking the bare skin of my back and I shiver with delight at his touch. I've missed him as well, but I'm not telling him that. Treat them mean to keep them keen—isn't that the old adage? And while I'm not going to be mean to him, I do want to keep him keen.

"Yeah, I've missed you." He pulls me tighter into him. "This is the part where you tell me how you've yearned for me."

I drop my head against his chest, clinging to his jacket as I chuckle. "Is that so?"

"I'm getting a little wounded that you're not saying the words, Pip."

"Fine, I missed you too."

"Hmm, I'm not hearing sincerity." He tickles my side with the ghost of a touch.

I lift my head to meet his gaze.

"I sincerely missed you."

He steals a kiss again, this time devouring my mouth with a raw passion that leaves me unable to breathe. I lean into him, feeling his hardness against me as our mouths duel for control.

"Would you like to come inside?" I ask him.

He gives me a lopsided smile. "Unless you want to give your neighbours a show, it might be an idea."

I lead him into the building and we take the lift up to the sixth floor. I expect him to jump on me as soon as we enter the loft but he doesn't. Instead, he shrugs out of his jacket, revealing a dark blue button-up plaid shirt that fits him snug across the chest, accentuating his well-defined pectorals and broad shoulders—it's my favourite shirt.

I'm so busy ogling him, I don't notice for a moment that he tosses his outdoor wear on the end of the sofa.

Without a word, I move behind him, picking up his jacket and hang it on the coat rack standing against the wall.

"You really are a neat freak, aren't you?" he says around a grin.

"No, but what's the point of leaving them there when there's a rack right there?"

He's looking at me like I'm the most adorable thing on the planet right now.

"It's just stuff. What's it matter?"

"Well... It doesn't. I just like things to be in their place and ordered. When it's not, I can't concentrate. It makes everything feel wrong and out of control. So, everything should be in its place."

I chew on my lip. I didn't mean to divulge so much, but

the words started to spill and I couldn't stop them. Now, I sound crazy. Does he think I'm crazy? Thank you, Mum, for creating this completely neurotic version of me. This is her fault. Nothing was ever allowed to be out of place at home growing up. She would lose her mind if it was. And I'm not talking about a little shouting. I've seen my mother absolutely meltdown over me leaving a toy in the living room before. In fact, that is one of my earliest memories. I must have been maybe three or four-years-old. The house always had to be pristine. Ordered, like a show home—it's still like that now. It's one of the few lessons that is emblazoned on my brain, and no matter how hard I've tried over the years, I can't break that habit.

And believe me, I've tried.

In the past, even the hint of mess would cause me to fall apart, because in the back of my mind, I'd be waiting for my mother's wrath. Cami helped me over the worst of that. I can deal with some level of clutter now, but not for long. I need order.

Jem comes to me, rubbing his hands up my arms. "Okay, I'm sorry. No mess."

"I don't mean to be hysterical."

"You're not."

"I am a bit."

"Pip, I don't give a shit. I'll hang my fucking stuff up. No sweat."

He doesn't make a fuss or a big deal about it—not like other boyfriends have in the past. I stare at him, dumbly. I've never experienced this, so I have no idea how to take it. He isn't bothered by my obsessive tidiness. This has been a relationship ender before.

"You okay with me staying tonight?" he asks.

"I can hardly turn you away after you rode all this way, can I?"

He grins. "You could, but I'd be pretty devastated. I'm not sure I'd get over it."

"I think you'd survive."

"I think you overestimate just how strong a person I am, angel. I'm a sensitive soul. I've got serious confidence issues. When you say things like that it cuts me to the bone."

I go to hit his bicep and he snatches my hand before it connects, lifting my knuckles to kiss them.

"Come sit with me."

He leads me over to the sofa and he sinks down first, bringing me down next to him. I nestle into him, my head leaning on his shoulder, my arm snaking around his waist. For the first time in a week, I feel all my tension drain from me.

"How are things in Kingsley?" I ask as he strokes up my arm. I'm anxious for news. "How's Josh? He's been a little quiet this past week or so."

We've messaged back and forth and he's been keeping me updated about his life, mainly the management of the bar he had foisted on him just before I left town—a strip club called Lace. I don't think he was particularly happy about this new venture. From what he told me, he previously managed one of the Club's other bars, Venom—a trendy place in town that serves cocktails and the after-work clientele. I would probably drink there myself if I lived there permanently. But his messages have been fewer and farther between lately. I'm not sure if I've upset him by spurning his attempts to visit me here, but things with Grant are still so up in the air. Then again, with Jem coming here uninvited now, and Cami on alert and seemingly unfazed by Grant's threats, maybe I should just extend the invite.

"The bar's keeping him busy. He had to recruit all new staff."

This statement, for some reason, has him smirking.

"Is he okay? He's been… quiet with me."

"He's fine. He's just swamped with work shit. Lace is in a bad way and he's working around the clock to get it up and running."

"I hope you're not working him too hard. He's still recovering from his injuries."

Jem kisses the side of my head. "Your brother's fine, but it's adorable you worry about his grumpy ass."

"I mean it, Jem. He's still having physio for his gunshot wound. He can't even ride yet. Don't you push him too much. He shouldn't even be back at work."

He smiles down at me. "Babe, Wade's a big boy. The doc signed him off for light duties—"

"Which is not what he's doing from the sound of it. He nearly died, Jem. I sat by his bed for weeks thinking he would."

With a steadying breath, he says, "The doctor cleared him, and he is only doing light duties. He needs anything heavy doing all he needs to do is pick up the phone. He's not out on any Club runs, and we're not pushing him to do anything that will set back his recovery. Angel, Wade's a miserable bastard, but we love that about him and we want him out there with us riding again too. Trust that we're taking care of him, okay?"

"Jem—"

"Piper, I promise."

I huff. "You'd better be right. I can't deal with any more hospital visits."

"We're all heading over to Lace next weekend to help him with decorating."

"He better not be doing any painting."

"Woman, quit worrying."

"I can't help it."

"You should come visit, help with the painting. Then again if you're going to be this much of a spoilsport, maybe not."

I poke him in the side. "I just don't want him to overdo it."

"He's not stupid. He won't. So, can you come?"

"I can't. Cami's already pre-booked me." I wince. "I'm sorry. Are you angry?"

He frowns at me. "Why in the fuck would I be angry? You have a life here too. I'm disappointed I won't see you, but no I'm not angry."

"It's probably a good thing anyway. I don't think I'd be able to keep my hands off you, which wouldn't really help with our flying under the radar."

I run a hand over his abdomen, wishing his shirt wasn't in the way and I could feel the hard planes of his stomach.

"True, but you can't avoid Kingsley forever either, Pip."

This is also true, but I'm not sure I'm quite ready yet to be in his presence and not able to touch him.

We talk for a while about our lives. Jem fills me in about his time at university. I knew he was smart, but I had no idea just how smart. He talks to me about the fun he had. Honestly, he's like two different people. It's hard imagining Jem the student and Jem the MC member. I can hardly imagine him sitting in the library, his nose stuck in a book, learning, but when he talks about numbers, he has a passion that I've never heard from him before.

He also talks a little about his father and his death.

"How old were you?" I ask quietly, caressing a slither of skin I've managed to uncover on his side.

"I'd just turned ten two weeks before. Lo was barely eleven, and just finding his feet in high school. It was weird that day. I just knew something was going to happen when they left."

The thought of him being so young, so vulnerable, and suffering such loss hits me square in the chest. I feel for all his siblings too.

He lets out a breath.

"Anyway, Mum had three kids under six, and me and Lo. Logan had to step up and help out. I was next to useless."

"You were a little kid yourself, Jem. Don't be so hard on yourself."

"So was Logan, but he still did what was needed."

"You're not like your brother. Logan is a man who thrives on leading. Don't try to compare yourself."

He kisses the side of my head. "It's a good job he does. Otherwise, we'd have been fucked. The Club stepped in, though. Helped us out a lot. Derek and Slade especially. They practically paid all our bills until Mum could get things sorted, they ran us kids to school, made sure we were taken care of. Hell, Derek even sat through some fucking Christmas concert shit Kenz was doing in school a few weeks after the accident..."

They rallied in time of need.

Like a family...

I can't recall Mum and Grant ever attending any of those type of things for me when I was a child. There was always some media event or something else that took precedent. Grant was usually trying to get elected or trying to bump up his local presence. I came second to that. For all my looking down my nose at the Club, it's clear they care about the people in it. I'm sure Jem and his sisters never felt unloved. I'm sure my brother has never either.

"I'm sorry you had to go through that, Jem."

"Yeah, me too, but these things happen. There's no point second guessing or dwelling on the whys and what ifs. I wish it didn't happen, that my dad was still here, but I can't change it."

He rubs circles on my arm as he talks.

"That's why I don't like having regrets, Pip. Life is short."

He's not wrong.

"What about you? What's your family like? Other than Wade, I mean."

"Oh, you know... the usual."

I don't have a lot of nice things to say about Grant or my mother, so I tell him stories about me and Cami and our antics—mostly Cami's, since I tend to verge towards the more sensible side of things.

I snuggle deeper against his side, feeling a little sleepy. "Jem?"

"Yeah, angel?"

"Thank you."

"For what?"

"Not judging me earlier."

"It's not my place to judge you."

"Yes, but others would, and have."

"Well, they're clearly not as amazing as I am."

I half lean up so I can look at him. "You are amazing. You hide a lot behind jokes and humour, but that's not all you are. Don't think you fool me for a moment."

I see the crack in his walls for just a second. It's there,

before his veneer comes back up. "I'm not trying to fool you, angel. What you see is what you get with me."

"You say you see me, well, I see you too. Not the jokey Jem, but the real you."

His smile is no longer in place, but there is an unreadable look on his face. "And who exactly do you think the real me is?"

"A good man."

He laughs, but there's no humour in it. "I'm not a good man, Pip. Not at all."

"You are. I can tell." I shift on the sofa and take his face in my hands. "I've learnt that not everyone can be trusted, Jem. I know that people pretend to be who they're not. They put on a mask for the world, let them see the front they want to present, not the real them. You don't wear a mask. You are who you are, unapologetically so."

His eyes scan my face, his brow drawn.

"Who pretended with you?"

"Does it matter?"

"To me, yeah."

"The point is, I know who you are and I trust you."

His hands skim up my back. "You can always trust me."

"I know."

"Angel, whatever happens, I'll always take care of you and protect you."

I kiss him. It's a soft, lingering brush of our mouths, but I push all my warmth, all my emotions down that kiss.

"And I'll always take care of you, too."

CHAPTER TWENTY-TWO

"You're... dating?"

I hold my breath as I wait for his response. There's a crackle down the line as Josh huffs and then a pause before he says, *"Why does everything need a fucking label?"*

I bite my bottom lip to keep from laughing at the ire in his tone. What a grumpy arse! I knew he was seeing this woman—Jem's been keeping me up to date during his visits to Manchester. I can't tell my brother that, of course, but I'm well aware of his blooming relationship with this new lady.

Over the past two weeks, Josh has been distant—Jem has not. I thought he knew about me and Jem, that I did something or slipped up somewhere, and I was getting worried, but Jem told me when they were painting Lace, there was an employee there—Paige—who Josh was a little... well, closer to than was right for a boss to be. He didn't use that exact wording, obviously. He was a lot more crass, but he implied my brother was infatuated with this woman. He also insinuated it was probably the reason our communication was a little on the cooler side.

I tried not to take that to heart, but I did. I'm busy with a new man, but I'm still finding time to send a text message or call. That said, I haven't exactly been a frequent visitor to Kingsley since I left either. I must try harder, too.

"I don't think everything does need a label, Joshua, but is that what you're doing with Paige? Are you dating?"

He hesitates. *"It's complicated."*

"It always is, but what does that mean?"

"I don't know, Pipes, she's an employee. I'm her boss."

"You've already slept with her," I surmise, grinning.

He makes an irritated noise down the phone. *"I didn't say that."*

I laugh. "You have, haven't you?"

"We shagged before she came to work for me," he reluctantly admits. *"The night of my welcome home party, in fact. Then she walked into Lace looking for work. I wanted to kick her arse right out the door, but Paige is a fucking good dancer and I need the staff."*

Hmm. I think back to the night of his welcome home party, and the fact his door was closed when I got home. Was she there when I was? I'm glad I saw nothing. No amount of bleach would clean that from my brain.

It was also the night Jem fucked me against the wall outside the clubhouse...

My neck heats at this, as my memory stirs, recalling what he did.

"You like her?"

"Yeah."

"Then what's the problem."

"Why are we even talking about this shit? I'm not one of your girly mates. I don't need to 'talk it out'."

"No, but you're my brother, and I'm interested in your life."

There's a pause, then, *"Oh."*

I can almost hear the cogs turning in his brain as he digests this thought. I can feel my own guilt splashing like acid through my stomach about the whopping secrets I'm keeping from him. I'm such a hypocrite. Then again, I'm fairly certain my big brother is keeping his own secrets. He seems... out of sorts almost. Edgy. Tired. Wary. I can't quite put my finger on it, but there's something going on with him. He seems almost drained beneath the happy glow of starting something new with this woman. The paradox is troubling, but since I'm keeping my own huge secret, I'm not about to judge him for keeping his.

"Yeah, I like her, but shit's complicated."

Isn't it always? I don't even want to think about how complicated things are when it comes to me and Jem, but there definitely is something there between us. Does it have the potential to be something good, something long-term? I'm not sure yet. He seems to think so, but I'm more cautiously optimistic. In my experience, people don't tend to stick around, so I'm not banking on the fact Jem will either, but we'll see.

Josh lets out a breath, bringing my attention back to the current conversation. *"I want to see you, Pipe, I really do, but things are crazy around here at the moment with Lace and... Club stuff."*

Disappointment swells in me, but I'm also a little relieved. I'm not sure I can hold up the pretence of being around Jem and acting like he means nothing to me in front of people. I know we agreed to play it cool until we know where things are going with us, but sneaking around is not as much fun as it sounds. Josh giving me a free pass to avoid him a little longer is actually a weight off my shoulders.

"It's okay, I get it. Life gets busy. Just let me know when you're free."

"I don't want you to think I don't want to see you."

This warms me and makes my guilt intensify. Yes, I am the worst sister. "I don't think that. Besides, I know what it's like juggling a new relationship. Enjoy it."

He snorts. *"Yeah, well, a relationship might be overstating shit, but we'll see."*

"Just turn all your charm on, Josh, and she won't be able to resist you."

"Charm... right."

He sounds amused by this concept. I'm not surprised. Charm is not something my brother particularly exudes. He's more a brooding type.

"Anyway, enough about me. Are you doing okay?"

"I'm fine." It's not entirely true, but I tell him this anyway. I don't want him to worry, nor do I need him riding down here trying to fix things.

"Fine? That's all you're saying? Kid, you're going to have to give me more than that."

"Spectacular, stupendous, splendiferous."

He makes a strangled sound in the back of his throat. *"Let's go back to fine."*

I laugh a little. "Things are good, Josh. Really."

Apart from my stepfather and mother being insane and the fact I'm carrying on with one of your brothers behind your back.

"Well, I'm glad to hear it." There's a pause and I think the line has gone dead until he says, *"I can't believe I'm even going to fucking ask this, but what about you? You... uh... dating?"*

Shit.

This is an outright question—one I'm going to have to

lie to his face about. I wince as I say, "No, Josh, my love life is still as dead as the proverbial dodo."

I'm going to hell...

"Good," he mutters, *"keep it that way."*

I don't know why, but his response slightly irritates me. It's not like I'm fifteen-years-old. I'm a grown woman—who is currently lying about who she's sleeping with.

"I'm not a nun," I tell him. "There have been men."

Not that many, but there have been some. I didn't go to bed with Jem some sacrificial virgin, despite what he might like to think. I was more than aware of what I was doing in that department.

"Jesus fuck, Piper. Stop. I don't need to hear this."

He sounds disturbed, and it warms me a little. It's such a typically big brother response. I've noticed over the last few weeks he's doing more and more of these things, seemingly without noticing, falling naturally into that brotherly role. I can't say I don't love it, although I do wonder how much of a gasket he's going to blow later down the line when me and Jem finally come clean—if me and Jem actually work out, that is.

"Well," I say, "I didn't realise you were so delicate."

"I'm not," he protests, *"but the last thing I want to hear about is my sister with men."*

"I wasn't planning on telling you about the finer details, Josh."

"Good," he says, *"because you start talking about that shit and I'm going to have to start hurting people."*

"Is that why you warned all your brothers to stay away from me?" I ask quietly. "Or was it because I'm not good enough for them?"

"Fuck? What? Pipe, no. They're not good enough for you. I don't want their grubby fucking hands anywhere near you.

You're far too pure for those dirty bastards. Why? Have any of them tried anything? I'll kill them."

Only Jem, and I very much like what he tried.

"You don't have to protect me, Josh. I'm not a little girl and I don't need you to ride in on your steed and save me. I can take care of myself. I've been doing it a long time."

"Yeah, well, you don't need to now. You've got me."

It's on the tip of my tongue to tell him I had him before, when I was younger, and he walked away then, but I don't. It's in the past, and dredging it up isn't going to change things—not if we're going to move forward. Josh seems like he's trying to make amends and I want for him and me to have a relationship, which isn't going to happen if I can't let go of what happened before.

"I know."

"Hey, kid, I've got to go. You need me, call."

"Yeah, you too. Don't push yourself too hard. You're still recovering."

"You worry too much."

I don't think I worry enough, but I say, "Probably, speak soon."

"Yeah, later."

He hangs up and I try not to let my guilt wash over me again. Everything will come right in the end.

I fire off a message to Jem, just checking in, making sure he's okay and then head up to the shower. He's tied up with Club stuff this weekend, so I can't see him until midweek, which is rotten, but it's one of those things. Considering he's doing all the travelling lately, I'm not going to give him a hard time about it. I did offer to come to him, but he won't hear it, and honestly, I don't want to get caught at his place by someone we know. It would raise too many questions about why I'm there and not staying with my brother. Plus, here, in Manchester, we can be together without risk, and that enables us to relax together.

I've just pulled on some clean skinny jeans and a loose sweater when there's a knock on the door. Since Cami forgets or loses her keys at least once a week, I assume it's her, so I wander across the main living area of the loft bare footed and open the door without much thought. I should have checked the peep hole. Standing on the other side of the door is my stepfather.

Grant, as always, looks perfectly put together. His suit is smart—designer, no doubt—his shirt undone at the collar, no tie, but it's not meant to be worn with one. He's wearing a thick black leather belt with a silver buckle, and a matching shade of leather shoes that are too shiny. His salt and pepper hair is swept back, but it's not quite as styled as usual. In fact, on closer inspection my stepfather looks a tad frazzled. There's a hint of tension just beneath the surface that suggests he's not quite as in control as usual. This puts me on edge. I'm used to Grant being entirely in command of everything he does.

"I'm just heading out, so whatever you want will have to wait," I lie, my heartbeat picking up its pace.

I don't care if my tone is abrupt either. I don't want to be left alone with him in the loft. Grant puts me on edge, unsurprisingly, given he slapped Mum and marked my arm when he grabbed me. He's always been so predictable in his behaviour, so this new unpredictability is unsettling.

He pushes inside without invitation. "I need a word."

"Hey! I told you I'm busy, and you can't just come in without asking!"

My voice is pitched far too high as I step back to avoid being trampled by him, but my fear kicks up a notch as he kicks the front door closed behind him. The last thing I need is to be shut inside with him. I move back a few more paces to give a little more distance between us, then cross my arms over my chest as I perfect a look of supreme irritation, even as my pulse races. This is not good.

"I'd like you to leave."

He ignores my request.

"I'm disappointed, Piper. Your behaviour lately hasn't been what I would expect."

His tone riles me. It's sweet, almost cloying, and irritating.

"I'm not one of your staff members, Grant. I don't have to do what you command, and as I told Mum, I'm done playing your games. I don't want to be a part of whatever schemes you're cooking up. It's over. You're both welcome to each other, but leave me out of it."

"My reputation means everything to me, Piper. You know this. I've told you time and time again over the years how important it is to me. No more so than during local election term. Yet you're running around with a biker gang."

"They're a club," I correct.

"What?" he sounds irritated by my interruption.

"They're a club, not a gang."

He waves this off. "They're a bunch of thugs."

"Says the man who thinks nothing about hitting women."

The look he fires at me has me shuffling back on my feet. I should probably mind my tongue, considering I'm in the loft alone with him and I have no idea when Cami is due back.

"I don't have to explain my actions to you, Piper, but I have explained them—several times."

"There's nothing you can say to justify it."

"You think you're so smart, don't you?" he moves into

the room, picking up a stack of mail on the end table near the door. It's mostly Cami's private correspondence, which makes his intrusion annoying.

"Do you mind?" I snap at him.

Casually, he tosses the envelopes back on to the table.

"You're not nearly as clever as you think."

"I'm cleverer than you. I was out of town for eight weeks before you even noticed I was gone, and you only noticed because somebody else told you." I don't hold back my vitriol. "I understand that I'm just a commodity to you, Grant, something to get out whenever you need a premade family to wheel out in front of the cameras, but I'm tired of playing the dutiful stepdaughter. I wasn't joking when I told Mum I'm done. I really am. So, unless there's a reason for this visit, you need to leave."

"Yes, Farrah told me that you threw down a ton of attitude and demanded to be left alone. I have to admit, I was very disappointed to hear you didn't heed my warning. I'm also disappointed that you didn't show either your mother or I more respect for the things we've done for you growing up."

I grunt at this. "Like controlling me? Forcing me to be your good little lapdog."

He lets out a fatigued sigh. "Good lord, the dramatics never end with you women. Hardly. You carry on as if you grew up in indentured servitude. Being asked to attend the occasional function or event or photo shoot is hardly a chore."

"No, but being paraded around like a prized mare for yours and Mum's gratification is. And what about being practically forced to marry Francis?" I hiss at him.

I finally get a response from him. He flushes a deep crimson. It's the first time he's ever shown any sign of embarrassment for his part in that shit show. Good, he should be ashamed, since him and Mum practically forced Francis on me, even though I had no interest in him and made my feelings on the matter absolutely crystal clear.

"He was a nice boy. You would have made a lovely couple."

"I didn't love him or want him."

"We were trying to do what was best for you. That's what parents do."

"No, Grant, parents love their children and nurture them. They don't treat them as photo ops. They certainly don't try to marry them off to men who will help further their fucking careers! You don't love me, Grant. You never have. I'm the selling point in your campaign trail—that's all. I make you sympathetic. You're the man raising a deadbeat dad's kid. That's all."

He stares at me a moment, before he says, "Yes, well, you always did see too much."

This confirmation, even though I suspected it, hurts. I keep my expression neutral even though pain lances through my chest.

"And this is why I want nothing to do with you and Mum."

"I can't say I don't find this response disappointing, Piper. Our arrangement benefits us all."

"It benefits you. I get nothing out of it."

"Wrong. You get plenty out of it—things you don't even know you get."

I have no idea what this means.

He leans back against the wall, his easy stance annoying. "Things are happening, Piper, things that are not in my control."

"Well, that's cryptic, and I really don't care. I wish you

all the best with your future endeavour to reach Westminster, Downing Street, or the moon, or wherever it is you're aiming to get to, but I will not be a part of it."

"I'm not talking about my political career." He scrubs a hand over his face and for a moment he looks worried. "I made a few bad business decisions—ones that may come back on me."

I wonder if this is what Mum and Grant were arguing about the day he hit her. They were fighting about something he'd got in deep with, but I never found out what. Frankly, I'm not sure I care—although, as much as I want to think this is true, I can't completely switch off from their plight. I'm not a monster and they are still my parents.

Even so, I'm not a doormat. Not anymore. "And why is this my problem?"

"It's not."

Grant's easy demeanour gets my back up.

"So, why are you telling me?"

"The people I'm dealing with are not the friendliest, nor the most forgiving. They're not exactly pleased with me, Piper."

"Again, why is this my problem?"

"They want to hurt me, and they may choose to hurt the people around me. I protect the people I care about. That would usually include you, but if you're not with me, helping me and doing the things I need you to, then I can't help you."

A cold shiver runs through me.

"Meaning what?"

"That if you won't scratch my back, then I won't protect yours."

What. A. Prick.

"So, you'd let these people hurt me because I'm not

willing to do a couple of photo shoots?" My blood runs cold then heats as fury boils. "You really are a complete bastard, aren't you? My God, what on earth does my mother see in you? How did I not see you for the complete shit you are all these years?"

He sniffs loudly. "I'm a shit? I took care of you, raised you, took you in as my own. I didn't have to take on another man's problem, but I did." My stomach twists at his words. "Your mother carried her shame. I took that stigma and gave you a family, legitimacy."

"Grant, no one gives a shit that Mum wasn't married or that I didn't have a dad. No one but you and her. You carry on as if I was some great stain on your unblemished record and like you did us both some huge favour by stepping in. Newsflash—we'd have been perfectly fine if we'd never met you. In fact, we'd probably have been better off. You ruined my mother. You turned her into a vapid, selfish bitch—"

His hand smashes against my cheek before I can step out of its trajectory. I stagger back and go down heavily, landing in a heap on the floor, the oak flooring biting as I hit it. My head rings with the force, my vision wobbling. I've never been hit before, not by a man. Not by anyone. My face burns, the skin tightening already over my cheekbone as fire stings across the area. He slapped me open palmed, but it felt worse.

"You always were an obnoxious brat who didn't know what was good for her. You haven't changed much as you've got older!" he spits the words.

I brace, not sure if he's going to attack me again, not sure if I need to move off the floor and prepare to defend myself, but he merely snarls at me, "You're on your own. I won't protect you when things get ugly, and they will get ugly, Piper, believe me. These men are dangerous and they will act. When they do, I won't step in for you. Not when you've decided you are no longer loyal to your family. If you want help, go and ask your precious fucking bikers. See how much of a shit they give. I'm sure your brother will walk away the moment he sees what a selfish, spoilt, troubled child you are."

He gives me one last glare, letting all his disappointment shine through that look and then turns on his heel and storms from the loft, leaving me staring after him in stunned shock.

CHAPTER TWENTY-THREE

Jem's late.

Usually, I wouldn't care. He's laid-back to the point of being horizontal, so being a little tardy here and there isn't that unusual for him, but he's over an hour and a half late. I'm feeling anxious about this. I hope something hasn't happened to him. He's a careful rider, but other drivers are not. Has he had an accident on the way here?

I chew nervously on my thumbnail, a habit left over from childhood that I've relapsed into in the last twenty minutes, as I stare at my phone screen. I've messaged him twice and phoned, but he's not replying or answering, which has my anxiety moving into critical levels. Logically, I know he's not going to be able to answer if he's on the bike, but the fact he's so late has me panicking.

"Still no word?" Cami asks as she moves towards me, handing me a coffee like a safety blanket.

I take it with a murmured thanks. "No. I'm getting worried, Cam. What if something has happened to him?"

Cami's been a rock for me over the past week. After she saw the mark on my face from where Grant slapped me, she was ready to murder him. I don't blame her. If the situation was reversed, I'd be spitting fire. She wanted me to go to the police, but I couldn't do it, and not because I feel any loyalty to Grant. What happened would go public, and my brother and boyfriend would end up in jail.

Luckily, my cheek barely bruised and by the mid-week —when Jem would usually visit—it was starting to fade. Some Club business kept him too busy to make the drive down mid-week, giving my face extra days to heal. It is practically back to normal now, but I still put on a healthy amount of concealer this morning, just in case.

"I'm sure it's nothing. He's probably got caught up in something. He'll be here soon."

I want to believe her reassurance, but a tendril of unease unfurls in my belly. I don't feel like this is a case of him being late. Something feels off, wrong. I'm considering calling him again when my phone buzzes in my hand.

"It's him?" Cami asks.

"Yes."

I swipe the message open.

JEM: Angel, shit's come up. I'm not going to make it to yours today. I'll call you later to explain.

I read the message again, then once more, looking for clues, answers in his words. I come up empty. There's nothing in this. I feel a hint of anger start to grow as I pass the phone to my best friend to read. Her eyes scan the message before widening a touch.

"Okay, well, at least he's safe, right?"

"Yes, clearly, but this tells me nothing. I'm sitting here worrying and that's all he gives me."

Cami frowns at the message again before handing me

the phone back. "At least give him the chance to explain before you tear his head off. There could be a perfectly reasonable explanation."

I try to let go of my ire, nodding. She's right. Jem has yet to let me down, and while I want to believe this is just the usual pattern for people in my life, I'm trying to be less negative, to see the good in things. Jem wouldn't risk everything—especially with Josh—just to toss me aside like this, so I have to believe there is a legitimate reason why he isn't here right now.

"Let's go into town, get some lunch. It'll take your mind off things," Cami suggests.

It's a good idea, so I agree.

The Northern Quarter of Manchester has some decent places to eat, so me and Cami have to flip a coin to decide where we're going for lunch. We decide on a place that does Mexican, which suits me perfectly because I'm in the mood for lots of cheese and spices.

I'm halfway through a rather divine tasting cocktail when I start to feel a little uncomfortable. I can't put my finger on it, but as Cam drones on about some event her and Spencer are attending next weekend, I can't stop from feeling like I want to grab her and leave.

It's such an intense sensation, I have to sit on my hands to stop from moving. I've never had such a primal reaction to anything in my life before.

I force my breathing to remain slow and steady as I let my gaze move around the restaurant, seeking what, I don't know, but I figure I'll know when I see it.

It's not overly busy inside, although there's a decent lunchtime crowd in, and there's a din of noise that is just louder than the pop song playing in the background. Waiting staff sweep between the tables, delivering drinks and dishes that smell mouth-wateringly good, giving the place a somewhat kinetic energy.

It's normal.

Everything is normal, but my senses are on hyper alert.

Even so, I want to leave, and the strength of the feeling to flee is so overwhelming, it scares me.

"P, are you all right? You've gone awfully pale."

I snap my gaze back to my best friend, who is staring at me with consternation. I force a smile, my hand going to the back of my neck, which is surprisingly clammy.

"Yes, I'm fine. Just hungry."

"Well, we ordered a while ago. The food should be here soon. I can ask about breadsticks if you're feeling lightheaded."

"I'm fine, Cam. Don't fuss."

"I'm your best friend. It's my job to fuss."

I laugh a little, even as my eyes start to roam around the room again.

And it's then I see him.

He's sitting at a table in the darkest part of the restaurant, obscured by a column holding up the roof. This is why I overlooked him the first time, but now I can see the guy, I don't know how I missed him. He's so out of place with this crowd of people. He's dressed in a brown, worn jacket with a dark shirt beneath, his head shaved, his hands tattooed, his neck too. He has a long scar running across one cheek, though it's old because it's faded to a silvery gouge, although it doesn't make it look any less severe.

And he's staring right at me.

I swallow, but my mouth seems to have stopped making any saliva, so it's a painful dry attempt. *What is he looking at?*

Cami glances over her shoulder, following my line of sight.

"Do you know him?"

I shake my head, unable to make words form.

"Darling, he's staring at you."

"I know," I manage to choke out. I'm completely freaked out.

"I mean, *really* staring at you."

"I know," I repeat, sounding a little stronger this time. "I have no idea who he is."

"Creepy bastard. I'm going to tell him to bugger off—"

She starts to stand, but I grab her wrist, pulling her down.

"Don't." Her confused expression has me explaining further, "Grant said he was mixed up with some bad people that he wouldn't protect me from."

Cami's eyes flare. "You think that's one of Grant's 'bad people'?"

"I don't know."

"Piper, if that's the case you need to tell someone—your brother, Jem, the police."

I glance back over at the guy and see he's gone. Scanning the restaurant, there's no sign of where he went either. Bugger. I sag back into my seat, my heart doing a staccato drumbeat beneath my sternum.

"I'm not telling either of them anything—the police neither."

"Um... why not?"

"Because likely we're both overreacting."

"I don't think so. That man was a first-rate creeper."

He was. I'm shaking, but I'm not admitting this. I take a sip of my cocktail to steady myself, the alcohol burning a path down my gullet. It doesn't help. Even so, I say, "Watching me doesn't make him guilty of anything."

"Are you serious?"

"He could have just been having a drink. Maybe he's not even linked to Grant, and I'm just being paranoid. I am a little bit stressed."

She leans over the table, her head close to me and hisses, "People who are just having drinks don't freakishly stare at random women, Piper."

"Maybe he was trying to flirt. Who knows? It doesn't automatically make him a thug. That's awfully judgemental of you to think that."

I have no idea why I'm defending this man. I felt all my instincts firing at me and telling me there was something wrong with that bloke. Cami clearly felt something was off too. Denial isn't going to change anything, but I don't want to believe my stepfather, who raised me from a little girl, would turn his back on me like this. I know he said it, but I didn't really believe it.

And that man... I don't like to judge people by how they look. I learnt my lesson with that the hard way. I judged the Lost Saxons and found they were not how I believed them to be from their appearances—Jem, in particular. But that man looks like a thug and he looks like he would hurt me.

"Sometimes books should be judged by their covers, because what you get inside does match the book jacket, and I get the feeling he's a 'what you see is what you get' kind of guy, P."

Me too.

"That still doesn't prove he's involved with Grant."

We're stopped from talking further by the arrival of our food. The waitress is all smiles and cheer as she puts our plates down. I stare at my meal, not sure I particularly fancy it now, even though it smells and looks delicious.

As soon as we're alone again, Cami leans over the table and says, "Grant's a dick, but your brother and your boyfriend are in a motorcycle club, Piper. If you're in trouble, they can protect you."

Hearing Jem referred to as my boyfriend is surreal and for a moment, I forget about the situation I'm in.

Boyfriend. I'm not even sure if that's where we're at yet. We're seeing how things go, but we've not labelled what we are. It seems like a woefully underwhelming word for what we're building, though. Jem is slowly becoming my everything, and that scares me to death. The only person I've ever let in that completely is the woman sitting opposite me right now. Cami knows all my darkness and all my light. She knows all my secrets, but I'm giving pieces of myself to others now—to Jem mostly, but also to Josh. It's terrifying, but it's liberating as well. The power Jem has over me, to destroy me if he chooses to, is frightening, I don't know if he realises it. Josh too for that matter. I worry that he'll walk away when he finds out about me and Jem, but I'm too far gone to give that silly man up now. He's mine. I don't know when I reached that conclusion, but I know it in my soul. Jem's mine and I'll do what I have to in order to keep him—even if it means fighting against my brother. If I handle it right, though, I'll get to have them both. I just have to be careful.

"Some bloke staring at me in a restaurant is hardly reason to call in the cavalry. Let's just eat."

"No, you being scared is a reason."

"I'm not scared."

"Liar."

I am a liar. Ever since Grant told me I was on my own,

I've been on edge, waiting, expecting. Nothing has happened—until today. But a feeling and a guy staring doesn't equal an incident. I'm just being paranoid. Likely Jem being late and his cryptic message has me on edge.

Cami and I eat, avoiding the conversation of Grant, mystery voyeurs, and head back to the loft, but I can't shake my unease. It stays with me all day. Jem doesn't call or message, and I hear nothing from my brother either. I hear nothing the day after and when I head to work on Monday morning, I'm starting to move from irritated to worried. What's going on?

After work, I'm debating getting on the train and heading up to Kingsley myself when Jem finally calls.

"I'm about a nanosecond from coming up there. What's going on?"

There's a long pause from him before he sighs and says, *"Angel, I can't... some shit went down in the Club. I can't talk about it. I'm sorry, but it's done with now. Wade was hurt—"*

"What? Oh my God—"

"Piper. He's fine, but shit got messy with a couple of brothers. Really messy. You're not supposed to know about this stuff, so you've got to keep quiet, unless you want to go public about us."

I close my eyes, my stomach churning. "What happened to Josh?"

"He's okay. He just got knocked about a bit. He's already back home with Paige."

Paige... the girl he's been pursuing. Clearly, things are going well there then.

"He's okay?"

"Yeah."

I take a shaky breath and release it. "Oh, God. I'll get on the first train."

"You can't. Piper, I'm not even supposed to have told anyone about this, and how in the fuck do I explain telling you?"

I open, then close my mouth. He can't, unless we come clean about us, and neither of us is ready for that.

"You're sure he's okay?"

"Yeah. Grouching, pissed off, but okay."

I bite my bottom lip and squeeze my eyes shut as I try to collect all my panic, all my stress into a box and shove it to the back of my brain. He needs me to be strong for him right now, not throwing a tantrum.

"Are you okay?"

There's a hint of humour in his voice when he says, *"I'm grouching too."*

"I've never known you to grouch about anything."

Other than when he first met me and thought I was being a bitch. Oh, and when I ran out on him at the hospital after he tried to kiss me. He was pretty grouchy then, but I keep that to myself. Usually, though, Jem is laid back, chilled.

"Yeah, well, it's been one of those fucking weeks." He huffs out a breath. *"I'm so sorry I stood you up. Worst feeling in my life knowing you were waiting for me and I couldn't contact you to let you know I wasn't able to get to you."*

I can envision him running his fingers through his hair so vividly. I wish he was here, with me.

"It's okay. I understand. I'm just glad you're okay—that everyone's okay."

My words surprise me. Months back, when I first arrived in Kingsley, knowing something like this had happened would have thrown me into a tailspin about the dangers of the Club. I would have freaked out and gone to town on Jem about how the Club should have protected Josh. Now, I know Jem and the others. I know it's not that simple. I also know those men would have done everything in their power to protect my brother. That they were not able to tells me it must have been serious—probably more serious than Jem is leading me to believe, and that scares me a little.

"Me too." He huffs. *"Things are going to be messy for a little while. I'll try to get up to you as soon as things have settled this end."*

"Just take your time. Get things sorted."

"I need to see you. I need you."

The desperation in his voice cuts through me. He sounds tired, and if I'm being honest, a little ravaged. What in the hell happened? I wish I knew Paige to ask her, or that I could message one of the girls, but that would raise flags— like who told me. For now, I'll just have to wait and see if Josh contacts me, or one of the girls.

"I'll be here. Whenever you're ready, just come to me."

"I needed to hear that so fucking much right now." There's a noise from behind Jem somewhere, voices talking to him, I think. *"Shit, I've got to go. I'll call you as soon as I can."*

"Bye, Jem."

He hangs up and I stare at the phone a moment before I toss it onto the coffee table.

CHAPTER TWENTY-FOUR

I'm going to kill Jem. When he said my brother was 'fine', that he just got 'knocked around a bit', what he failed to mention is that he had the top portion of his ear blown off after being shot nearly in the head.

Yes, shot.

In. The. Head.

It's two weeks after that phone call and my brother finally invited me up to Kingsley for Weed's birthday party. I'm not sure why I warranted an invitation, but it's been so long since I last saw him, I could hardly decline. Besides, I'm itching to meet his mystery woman, Paige. Jem's been filling me in about her, so I have details, but I want to see the girl who has ensnared my big brother so completely. Being around Jem and not able to touch him is going to be tough, though. I'm used to having him in my space and in my arms. I know we should just come clean already, but we're still figuring things out. The distance means in reality, we're still very early doors in our relationship. I'm not sure either of us are ready to reveal yet that we're together. I'm not sure we're ready to put a label on what we mean to each other yet even. I like him, he likes me. We have fun together, but is there something long-term here? I don't know. It would mean one of us moving—me, most likely. He's deeply rooted in Kingsley.

Could I live here full-time? Honestly? Give up restaurants and culture and fun for... whatever this is?

This party has to be one of the strangest events I've ever attended in my life, and I've been to my share of events over the years—galas, black-tie events, fundraisers. Josh's welcome home do after he was released from the hospital was tame in comparison, although I did find it a little odd. During that they presented him with his kutte like some sort of trophy and then tried to out drink each other while practically beating their chests like apes as if it was a challenge.

I could be tucked up on my sofa with a glass of Pinot watching *Sex and the City* re-runs with Cami, or snuggled up in bed with Jem having divine sexy time. Instead, I'm listening to Beth and Liv talk about 'tit tassles' and 'vajazzles'. I'm assured things are not usually so vulgar, a point that is immediately contradicted as a thong is fired across the room like a slingshot. I want to crawl under the nearest table and hide.

My brother's world and mine are poles apart—there's no denying it. This party is a classic example of where our lives dichotomize. My last birthday was a grand event, with ballgowns and tuxedos—although the only person I wanted there was Cami. The rest were invited by my parents. Josh's friend, Weed, is celebrating his coming of age in the Club's strip bar, Lace. At least it's not called Jugs or Bazookas, or something equally crass. This is also the bar Josh now manages with Paige, who is so sweet. I love her.

Despite the name there's not a hint of frills or dollies anywhere. It's more like a dungeon. Oddly, they've closed it down for the evening and decorated it as if it's a community hall with banners and balloons. There's even a buffet table with finger food, but that isn't the strangest part. It's the fact the women know they have to leave in a few hours, so their boyfriends can watch scantily-clad pole dancers put on a show for them.

And not one of them has kicked up a fuss about it.

I can't wrap my head around it. Despite the fact I'm not talking to him, I want to bodily drag Jem out of here, but that might raise some flags, so instead I'm gritting my teeth and drinking the bar dry.

This world is so different from mine, it might as well be Mars.

Then again, not one of these women seems remotely insecure about their relationship. Beth, Liv, Sammy and even Paige—who is practically my sister-in-law despite only being with my brother for a few months, (yes, really; somehow she's achieved more than Jem and I have in less time)—all seem confident their men would never cheat on them, so I suppose they don't have anything to worry about when it comes to leaving them alone with half-naked women. Personally, I'm a step from throwing the tizzy to end all tizzies, which Jem seems to find adorable, if the looks he keeps shooting my direction are anything to go by. This is not what I signed up for when I decided to get to know my big brother—or to date Jem. I thought there would be more walks around the park or days out at the beach, cocktails in bars. Maybe not the last one, given they are bikers, but certainly not parties at strip bars.

I take a sip of my wine and try to focus back in on the

conversation between Beth and Liv, but my attention wanders. Glancing around, seeing the men and the women interacting, the easy smiles and hugs and familiar touches, it's obvious to see—dare I say it—the love in the room. It's dysfunctional, so dysfunctional any psychologist would have a field day with it, but it is, in its own weird way, a family of sorts.

"I'm so glad you could make it this weekend," Beth says, pulling me back into the conversation.

"Oh, yes." I fiddle with the stem of my wine glass, not sure I'm so glad to be here at all. "Me too."

I take a long sip of wine, letting the taste explode on my tongue. My eyes scan the room, finding Jem. He's talking to Ghost, and he looks so divine tonight. Keeping my hands off him is going to be difficult. If it wasn't for the fact I'm currently not speaking to him, I'd march over to him, drag him somewhere quiet and kiss him senseless.

But I'm ignoring him.

Because he's an arse.

A lying arse.

I need more alcohol.

"I'm getting another drink," I declare. "Can I interest anyone else in another?"

Beth's lips quirk as she casts a glance at Liv. "Easy, girl. I have no objection to holding your hair while you puke, but Wade's giving you stink-eye. You may want to dial it back a notch before he comes over here and starts playing the big brother card."

I twist to glance over my shoulder and see that my brother is, in fact, standing over at the bar, and that he is glaring in my direction.

Well, bugger him.

He invited me here to his biker party. Did he expect me to sit in the corner quietly drinking lemonade?

Besides, I'm still pissed off at him. He was in the hospital—again—and didn't think to let me know. If it wasn't for Jem, I wouldn't have a clue. Josh told me he didn't want me to worry, but I don't need protecting. I just need honesty—I know, ironic, considering the stinking fat lies I'm telling everyone in my life, but I am still upset that Josh kept this from me.

So, I'm no longer talking to my brother for not telling me he was shot, or Jem, for failing to disclose how bad things were.

Shot in the head...

By Dylan...

What kind of life do these people live where this is considered normal?

And how many times does Josh need to be hospitalised before he realises this lifestyle is far too dangerous?

How many times do I need to nearly lose him?

I don't even know how I feel about this. I don't want to blame the Club, I don't, but I'm finding it hard not to put this firmly in the 'cons' column. I'm terrified this Club may be the death of my brother, and I'm terrified there's nothing I can do to stop it.

Paige (who is lovely, and I understand why my brother adores her) seems on edge about the whole situation, too, but she hasn't demanded he give up the Club—even though she would be well within her rights to. I'm not in a position to demand anything. I'm his estranged sister, and the last time I asked him to choose between me and the Club, I didn't win that battle.

So, all I can do is put up and shut up.

If I want to know my brother, I have to accept this part of his life, even if I don't like it or agree with it.

And now I have Jem to worry about as well.

I know he will never choose me over the Club. His entire family is deeply entrenched in the Lost Saxons—his brothers, sisters, mother. Can I deal with these things when they happen? If Jem was shot in the head, could I shrug it off? I'm so conflicted. On the one hand, I have my family in Manchester who wear suits and gowns, and are seen as respectable members of the community, but they're as crooked as the criminals they're fighting to keep off the streets. On the other, I have my brother and his family, who are upfront about their dealings, but the constant worry is a drain. Yet, for the first time in my life I feel like I belong somewhere with these people, and that is a heady feeling.

I force a smile at Beth, realising I haven't responded to her yet, and mutter, "I'm not scared of my brother."

This is almost true. Josh is intimidating and I don't really know him that well to know what he's capable of. He's never done anything to make me fear him but I don't doubt he could be violent if the situation called for it. I don't doubt that about any of the men in this room. They seem at ease now, laughing, joking, drinking, but I know that can flip on a dime.

"Besides," I continue, "this is a party, isn't it?"

"Piper's got a point," Liv mutters, rolling her wine glass filled with orange juice between her fingers. "I'd be drinking if I could." She glances down at her baby bump and smiles. "The first thing I'm doing as soon as I have this baby is drinking a full glass of wine."

Beth snorts. "That's what you've missed, wine?"

"That and being able to pee like a normal person."

I blink at this complete overshare, but Beth sniggers.

This is one thing I have learnt about these ladies in the short time I've known them; they have no concept of inappropriate. They tell each other everything, and I mean *everything*. I know more about their husbands and partners than I should. To the point where I'm not sure I can look some of them in the face without blushing.

"That does sound terrible," I say slowly. "I had no idea."

"Yeah, they don't tell you this crap," Liv says, her voice turning dark. "This kid isn't even that big, but it's sitting on my bladder all bloody day."

I've never really thought about children and if I want them. After my own upbringing, I don't think I should ever be responsible for another human being. The whole idea scares me half to death.

"Right." I smile. "You don't know what you're having?"

The last time I was here, Liv was barely three months along. She's far more rounded now, but she keeps referring to the baby as 'it'. She doesn't strike me as someone who is not emotionally attached to her child, so it seems bizarre to me, unless she doesn't know.

"Nope. At the scan the little bugger was hiding. We couldn't see if it was a boy or girl, so we're completely in the dark. It's killing me not knowing."

"Yes, I can imagine it would be."

"I hope you don't have a girl," Beth says.

This statement makes me frown.

"Why would you hope that?" I ask.

"Because Dean's going to cut the balls off any bloke who looks sideways at his daughter."

"Oh." I laugh. "That seems extreme."

Beth snorts, tossing her dark hair. "Have you spoken to any of these men? They're all about the extreme."

This is true, which makes me worry about what my

brother will do to Jem when he finds out about him and me...

If he finds out.

I haven't decided if I'm forgiving him yet for lying to me.

"I definitely need a drink," I mutter. "Same again?"

Beth grins at my blatant conversation change.

Liv shakes her head. "I don't think I can stand another orange. It's giving me heartburn."

"I'll have another wine," Beth says with a shrug. "Why not?"

As I head over to the bar, I notice Josh is no longer standing against it, guarding the alcohol like a dog. Thank God. I don't want to get into a discussion with him about how much I'm drinking, especially when I'm not even close to drunk. I'm barely even tipsy, but he takes the big brother act to the extreme at times. This is annoying, even though it's endearing. I don't need him controlling my life; I had enough of that growing up.

I slip behind the bar, which is laid out so we can all just help ourselves to whatever we want, and scan the rows of bottles and cans for the wine I've been drinking all evening.

"Raiding the bar while Wade's gone? Smart move."

I jolt at Jem's voice at my back, like a kid caught with its hand in the cookie jar, and snap my gaze up as he leans over the top of the bar, grinning at me. A shiver of pleasure rolls through me, and it takes everything I have to stop the moan from escaping from my mouth at having him in my space. I've missed him and I want to touch him. Hell, I want to devour his mouth, even though I'm annoyed at him.

Right, I'm still annoyed...

"I'm just getting a drink. My brother is not my keeper." I sound tetchy, because I am.

He moves around the end of the bar and ducks through the hatch, coming around the serving side. He moves in behind me, his hands coming to my hips and his nose goes to my neck for the briefest second, inhaling my scent before he pulls away. We're slightly concealed from the room, but not enough. It's risky, but also thrilling.

"What are you doing?" I hiss. "Are you crazy?"

"For you, angel? Absolutely."

"Josh is wandering around. If he sees you—"

He grins at me. "I don't care if he sees."

I give my attention to the rows of wine bottles. "Well, frankly, I don't care if he castrates you either right now, but once I've calmed down, I may do."

He moves in beside me, careful not to get too close, but his hand rests on my hip. "You're still pissed at me?"

I push his fingers off my side without pulling my gaze from the wine bottles. "Absolutely."

"I didn't want to freak you out. Telling you he took a bullet to the head would have done that, and he was okay."

"You still should have told me." I pick up a bottle of sparkling and examine the back, not really seeing it, but just needing to keep my hands busy.

"Piper, stop fucking looking at the wine and look at me."

He takes the bottle from me, and I turn to meet his gaze, my jaw tight, my gaze resolute. "You lied to me."

"I did."

The admission steals my thunder a little. "You shouldn't have."

"I know." He takes my hand, hidden by the bar, providing privacy from the rest of the room. I have to admit, I'm soothed by his thumb swiping back and forth over my hand. "I tried to protect you from being hurt. I'll always try to protect you. It's natural instinct. I'm sorry. I should have realised you're stronger than that."

I study his expression, seeing the sincerity in his face. Considering I'm lying to him about so many things, I don't have it in me to keep berating him about it. I squeeze his hand back.

"Just... don't lie to me about things that are important." I'm such a hypocrite, but I justify it by telling myself that my issues with my parents are not a big deal.

"I'm sorry."

"Well, you can make it up to me later," I mutter.

He gives me a look that has butterflies flapping around my stomach. "I wish we could get out of here right now, so I can make it up to you."

Tingles fire through my body and I swallow hard.

"Me too."

He glances at the wine bottle in my hand. "Are you really drinking that cheap prune-juice?"

I stare down at the wine bottle I'm clutching. I wasn't planning to drink it. I just grabbed it for something to busy my hands with, but his statement amuses me.

"What do you know about wine, Jem?"

"Well, you know what they say about books and covers and judging." He bends at the waist and stage-whispers, "Don't do it. Nothing good comes of assumptions, Pip."

He leans across me to grab another bottle, his warm body inches from mine. It shouldn't make my heart twitch, but it does. I swallow hard as I breathe in his aftershave and the faint tang of beer he's been imbibing before he pulls back, a different wine bottle in his hand. I don't recognise the name, but I know enough to know it's not some off-the-supermarket-shelf brand. Not that I care. My entire focus is on the man in front of me. This is a different kind of torture. I want to drag him somewhere and have him inside me.

I have to suck a breath in so I don't exhale loudly.

"Try this one."

I take it from him and note it is a decent brand. "Okay, I'm impressed. Where did you learn about wine?"

"I run a bar—not willingly, angel—but I do run one. I have to know about booze."

Of course. He's running Venom at the moment while Josh manages Lace. Although he spends such a lot of time at mine, I forget that he does. I know the bar has an assistant manager, who I think is getting the brunt of the workload in his absence. I wonder if his brothers have noticed his evening flits, or if they care.

"I need to fuck you, angel. I'm missing your pussy."

My face heats at his dirty words.

His hand moves to my thigh, my skirt suddenly seeming like a bad idea—or possibly a great idea—as he skims up towards the apex between my legs. I should push him off. Anyone could see if they round the bar, but I don't. I widen my stance and when he cups me, I bite my lip to keep from whimpering. He strokes over my underwear, drawing pulses from my core.

"I want to be inside you."

"I want that as well," I tell him, breathlessly.

"Come to me tonight?" He strokes back and forth over my thong, tracing a finger through the slit of my pussy. I quiver beneath his touch as he nears the bundle of nerves that are electrified with need. I want him to push the material aside, but he continues to torture me instead, making my underwear uncomfortably damp.

"Where?" I gasp out.

"My house. Can you get away?"

"Josh'll be busy with Paige, so probably." I don't even want to think about what he'll be busy doing.

He pulls his hand away and I moan at the loss of his touch.

"Come and find me later so I can see to you."

I watch as he lifts his fingers to his mouth and sucks them with a grin. Dirty bugger. Then he heads back over to his brothers to talk.

I spend the next hour mingling with the women and trying to avoid Jem for fear of humping him right here in the middle of the room. There's a strange atmosphere this evening that I can't quite put my finger on. Despite being a party, there doesn't seem to be a party atmosphere, at least not under the surface. I notice an altercation of sorts between Beth's father and two of the older men in the Club, which ends with Beth's father storming off. Beth tries to go after Jack, but is stopped by Logan.

Josh seems on edge, too. He only cheers up for a moment when he heads over to Paige and wraps himself around her like a vine. The love in his eyes when he looks at her steals my breath. It's a look that says the world could end and all he would care about is the woman in front of him. I wonder if Jem feels that way for me, or if he could ever feel that way. Would I want him to?

My head is so mixed up. Coming here tonight has things topsy turvy. I thought I could reconcile with this world, until Josh got shot again. Maybe this is the real reason Jem kept it quiet. Maybe he knew I would be freaked about it. Maybe he knew it would be a setback for me—for us. Getting shot again is a big thing. What I feel for Jem is intense and I think I do love him, but the danger... it's real and it's ever present. Can I ignore it? I don't know.

And the lies.

So many lies.

I can't talk to them about anything for fear of what they'll do. I can't tell my brother I'm dating his friend because I fear his reaction. I can't tell my brother what my stepfather is doing because I fear his reaction. These men turn me into a liar to protect them. Yes, I could just tell the truth and let them deal with the repercussions of their own actions, but I know Josh will murder Grant for hitting me. He grew up in a violent household. It's a trigger for him. Jem... I don't know. He's less predictable. Maybe I overestimate my worth to them both. Maybe they'll do nothing, I'm not willing to risk it, though. Josh already did time inside. He won't survive more, and he just found Paige. He's happy.

Needing fresh air, I head for the main doors and slip outside while no one is paying attention. It's early October so there is a nip in the air, and it's starting to drizzle, so I stay under the canopy provided by the door. The cool breeze washes over me and is welcome after the stuffiness of inside.

I take a long sip of my wine and tip my head back to stare up at the wooden overhang. How long can I keep juggling all my lies? I want to be able to come to these things and be with Jem, not sneaking off later. Jem and I need to get to a better position, though. We haven't even affirmed what we are to each other. We haven't even said the 'L' word yet. I'm not even sure I like him half the time. He drives me bonkers. Yet, I can't seem to give him up.

My thoughts scatter as a white van pulls into the car park, stopping outside the doors. Across the side of the panel is written in cursive letters 'Mim's Bakery' and there are little images of cakes.

A woman climbs out, her hair scraped back into a ponytail, flour on her cheeks.

"Are you with the party?"

"Uh..."

"I've got a cake. Can I leave it with you?"

Before I can protest, she's heading for the back of the van and opening the doors. I place my wine glass on the floor and wander to her. The cake box is cumbersome but I manage to manoeuvre back inside the building carrying it. I really should have got one of the women who was organising this. What if I drop it?

Carefully, I head towards the bar, seeing Josh and Paige emerging from the Staff Only door.

"Where do you want the cake, Josh? The lady from the bakery just dropped it off."

My brother moves to take it from me, but Jem steps in front of him and takes it from my hands. The weight lifts and I'm grateful for the reprieve because this thing is surprisingly heavy.

"I'll take that." His grin is lopsided and hints at mischief.

What's he up to?

I'm flustered for a moment before this melts into irritation. Does he think I'm that helpless, or that I need him to sweep in and do things for me? And why is he doing this so publicly? Everyone is watching.

"I don't need you to carry things for me."

His lips twitch. "Have it back then."

He tries to hand the box back to me.

What on earth...?

"Well, I don't need it back now, do I?"

His expression is bemused as he considers me, his head tilting to one side, and my mouth goes dry. He really is exceptionally good looking.

"So, you want me to keep hold of it?"

I open my mouth and then close it again. I have absolutely no idea what to say to him. He's tying me up in knots, and I'm aware of all the eyes watching this exchange take place. Is he seriously doing this in front of a room full of people? Including my bloody brother?

I'm sure my cheeks are flaming right now.

"Jem, quit tormenting her," Josh snaps at him, finally taking pity on me. Not that I need his pity either. I'm capable of kicking Jem in the bollocks myself.

Jem, as if sensing my thoughts, grins. "I'm just trying to be helpful."

"Yeah, well, be helpful by putting the cake on the buffet table," Beth tells him as she appears from behind Jem with Logan on her heels.

"Your old lady is a slave driver, Lo," Jem mutters, earning a glare from Beth and a snort from Logan.

"Did Mim leave an invoice?" she asks me.

Grateful for the distraction from Jem, who I may strangle later, I say, "Um, no, but you might just catch her if you hurry."

"When are we eating, B?" Jem yells after Beth as she heads for the doors.

"In an hour."

He glances up at the clock on the wall behind the bar. It's just after six-thirty.

"An hour? But I'm starving."

"You're always starving," she throws over her shoulder. "Eat a packet of nuts or something. I'm sure Wade can sort you out with some."

When he glances at my brother, Josh shakes his head. "Does this look like the type of place that stocks nuts?" At the grin spreading across Jem's face, Josh holds up a hand. "Don't fucking answer that."

He laughs and as always, the sound does funny things to me. I hate to admit it, but I'm completely and utterly smitten with this man. He has me firmly in his grasp, and boy, does that scare me. I don't know if Jem feels the same, I hope he does, but I don't know that I can let him walk away from me, which means I have big decisions in my future—first and foremost... where is my future? Secondly, can I get my head around the Club and the more dangerous elements that come with it? Thirdly... what do I do if my brother decides he's not keen on the idea of me dating Jem? He's continually made it clear he's not happy about me shacking up with any of his brothers.

"Everyone always thinks the worst of me."

Jem shoots me a wink and I roll my eyes, although I give him a smirk back, before I turn and follow after Beth.

As I walk away, I hear Josh say to Jem, "Leave my sister alone."

This makes my good mood dissipate. Josh is still warning his brothers away from me like I'm some teenager in need of protecting. It bothers me. I slow my pace, waiting to hear what Jem's response is.

"I would, but she's all kinds of adorable, Wade. It's really hard to leave her alone."

I can't help but grin behind my hand at that. Jem's an annoying shit when he wants to be, and he's clearly annoying my brother because Josh steps menacingly towards him.

Jem's not even remotely fazed because he laughs as he says, "I dig the big brother routine, though. It suits you."

"I mean it. Leave Piper alone."

The smile Jem gives him is genuine, but there's a hardness beneath it. "I don't make promises I can't keep."

I watch as my guy crosses the room, placing the cake

box on the table before he swipes a sausage roll off the buffet table, earning a smack to the arm from his sister, Sofia. He takes this with a grin before his eyes find mine. Then he gives me a cocky lip lift and I know everything, somehow, will be okay because I have him. And Josh is just going to have to get on board with it, because I don't think I can give Jem up.

CHAPTER TWENTY-FIVE

"Are you sure this is a good idea?" Cami demands, pulling my pillow against her as she sits cross-legged on my bed.

I gawk at her. "You're seriously asking me this? You? Queen of rebellion?"

One of her perfectly plucked eyebrows delicately arches. "I know. I can't even believe I'm asking it myself, but considering everything that's going on, it just seems like maybe it would be a good idea to let things settle."

I sigh as I pull my overnight bag off the bed and onto the floor. "Things are settled."

"Are they?"

"Cami, everything is fine. Josh wouldn't let me come if it wasn't, nor would Jem."

The look she shoots me is sceptical. "Your brother was shot in the head six weeks ago, and I didn't say a word about you going back there for that bloody party then. But honey, it's been six weeks and they still haven't caught that Dylan lunatic. The instructions your brother has sent you for when you arrive at the station in Kingsley, frankly, scare me.

They clearly think he is a threat. Maybe it would be safer to just stay home."

I drop my hands to my hips and stare at my duvet. We're standing in my bedroom after I just hastily packed up enough stuff for the weekend. I understand why Cami's concerned. Josh did send a laundry list of do's and don'ts for the weekend—most of which involve not going anywhere without a brother or escort. I have to admit, it does freak me out a little, but I don't want to miss Beth's hen do either. I also don't want to miss any chance to potentially see Jem. I'm not sure I'll have the opportunity, as he'll be off on Logan's stag weekend, but if I can see him, I'm there. I'm hopelessly addicted to him and I'll take whatever hits of him I can get—no matter how small.

"Like it's any better here. Grant's in trouble and he's not exactly playing nice either."

Her expression drops. "Has he threatened you again?"

I let out a long breath. "No, I haven't seen him or Mum in weeks."

The relief in her face is evident. "I can't deal with this level of drama. Maybe I should hire us some kind of bodyguard. Someone good looking to follow us around."

"And go against your 'living a normal life' mantra that you fought your father about for years?" Her eyes roll upwards, but I continue before she starts to think it might be a good idea. "Besides, how would I explain that to my boyfriend? You know the six-foot-three giant biker who is bound to be a tad miffed about some attractive beefcake following me around?"

She hugs the pillow closer. "You could always tell him the truth—that your stepfather is a piece of shit who is threatening your life."

I sink onto the edge of the bed with a sigh. "I don't know

that he is threatening me, Cam. I don't know anything. As far as I can tell, Grant is all talk."

"Darling, he didn't seem all talk when you came home with a bruised face or arm, or when that man was watching you when we were eating lunch." She shivers. "Grant scares me."

I frown at her, her words sending a slither of unease through me, mainly because I don't think she's joking. "Grant scares you?"

"He doesn't you? He's intimidating."

I consider her words. "It's all that power to rule over the local community. It's gone to his head. He thinks he's king."

"He's in local government. That's the same thing. This practically is his domain."

"Don't let him get into your head. He's a glorified paper pusher."

Cami snorts, pushing her red hair over her shoulder. "Dear God, don't let him hear you say that. Not unless you want a national emergency on our hands."

I laugh then sober. "I'm sorry you're being dragged into this. I don't want you involved at all. If he comes around while I'm gone call the police."

"You want me to call the police on your stepfather?"

"He's not my stepfather anymore."

She nods. "And what about this venture to Kingsley? I'm not happy about this either."

"So I gathered, but Josh won't let anything happen to me, nor will Jem."

"Right, Jem... who no one knows you're dating and have been for the best part of two, three months, now. P, every time you go up there you end up embroiled in some big Club event. I mean, last time it was the stripper birthday party, this time it's a hen do."

"Yeah, that is getting irritating. I would like to go for once and it just be me and Josh. I'm not sure why we need the leather-clad hot guy clan to tag along."

Her lips quirk. "Yeah, although, I do hate you for that. All those years I was kicking back against my parents, and your first rebellion you find a motorcycle club. Where did I go wrong?"

"I'm sure I can set you up with one of them. Biker Blind Date."

She waves a nonchalant hand.

"It's too late now. My parents no longer care what I do. Besides, I'm with Spencer."

This is only partially true, although her parents have given up trying to tame their wild daughter.

She launches the pillow at me. I catch it with ease and replace it on the bed.

"Are you going to tell Josh about the problems you're having with your parents?"

"Absolutely not."

"Why not? He's your brother. He'll want to know."

"Because he's my brother and he's a fuss pot who will want to fix it. He can't fix this. Besides, it's my problem. Not his."

"It won't kill you to let people in, you know?"

I freeze at her words, hating that she sees so much of me, glad that she's the only one who does. Cami is my oldest friend and has been with me for the good, the bad and the ugly, but that means she sees my worst and best faults.

"It's not about letting people in, Cam. He can't do anything to fix this, and I don't want him involved."

"And you and Jem? When does that become public knowledge?"

I chew on my bottom lip.

"After the wedding." We were going to go public with our relationship a month ago, but then Beth and Logan announced their snap wedding plans. Since neither Jem nor I want to cause an atmosphere at their nuptials, we decided it would be best to wait until after they tie the knot.

"Josh will kill him and probably never speak to him again for breaking the sacred bro-code. I'm fairly certain it's going to be the end of mine and Josh's relationship as well," I say, voicing my fears. "But it's time. Past time really. Sneaking around is getting old."

"P, he's not going to disown you for following your heart."

"You have no idea how set against me being with his brothers Josh is, and he's really not going to like that we've been lying. He just finished being lied to by Club brothers. He's going to lose it when he realises me and Jem have been lying as well. He'll see it as another betrayal."

"You haven't betrayed him. Honestly, this is all so theatrical. It's ridiculous."

"Yes, I know, but it's how he'll view it."

"Well, then your brother's an idiot."

I snort. "Quite possibly, but we're stupid for lying. We should have just come clean from the start and dealt with the fallout then."

Cami sighs. "Yeah, but you didn't, and Josh will have to be a grown up and deal with it. Now, get going or you'll miss your train."

The journey to Kingsley seems to take forever today, but eventually, I see the familiar landscape I associate as the entrance into the town. The rolling hills and greenery gives way to more industrialised urban sprawl before the factories and finally the skeletal remains of the old collieries come into view. As the train makes its way into the town centre and Kingsley's station, the tower blocks surround the carriages, once a claustrophobic sight, now a reassuring one.

I push up from my seat and grab my stuff, clamouring to get out of the carriage when it shudders to a stop.

When I step onto the platform, I see Josh leaning against the wall, his broad arms folded over his chest. He's wearing his kutte, as always, black jeans and his 'Ride or Die' hoodie. I thought Paige might have discretely removed that thing from his wardrobe, but alas, it still lingers on.

He gives me a lift of his lips that hints at a smile as he pushes up to greet me.

"Hey," I say as I approach.

He takes my bag from me before reaching for the handle of my pull-along suitcase, and gives me a chin lift. "Hey, Pipe. How was the journey?"

"Long. Boring. I managed to read an entire Cosmo from cover to cover."

He stares at me blankly for a moment before he says, "Paige is waiting in the car."

I can't help but grin at him. "Not a Cosmo fan? I thought Paige might have a subscription. It seems like it might be her thing."

At least that's the impression I got from meeting her at Weed's party. To be honest, I was surprised to learn she started off by stripping at Lace. I don't like to put people into boxes, but Paige struck me as someone who comes from money.

"Since I don't have a fucking clue what Cosmo is, I have no idea."

"It's a magazine, Josh. Cosmopolitan."

"Oh." We start to walk towards the gate that leads out to the car park. "She doesn't read that kind of thing."

This surprises me. "Really? I would have thought..." I frown. "She seems like a glossy magazine kind of girl."

He snorts as he pulls the gate open. It makes a screech that would wake the dead. "Paige loves TV. She's a TV junkie. I can't get her away from that thing. She'll watch any old shit, too. It drives me nuts. Reality shit, documentaries—although, I don't mind those so much—soaps, dramas... You name it, she'll watch it." He sounds annoyed, but the look in his eyes tells a different story. I'm guessing they watch these things together and Paige is curled around him when they do. It's probably not as terrible as he's making out.

"She's just full of surprises."

He beams, actually beams. I didn't think it was possible for my surly brother to crack such a big smile, but it's there, on his face, and it softens everything about his usually hard features. He looks so different, so carefree. It actually brings a lump to my throat. Clearly, Paige is good for him.

"You have no idea. She's the most amazing woman."

I swallow the enormous clogging feeling and trail after him as he starts towards the car. Paige waves frantically through the window at me, her smile wide. Considering I've only met her once before at Weed's birthday, her greeting takes me by surprise. I don't expect her to come at me like we're best friends. She opens the door and climbs out. I barely reach her before I'm pulled into her arms and swallowed in a hug that nearly crushes my ribs into my lungs.

"Breathing is a prerequisite for living, Paige," I grunt out.

She giggles and releases her grip on me. "Sorry. I got carried away. It's so good to see you again, girl. You look great."

This statement warms me in ways I didn't realise I could be warmed. The only person who has ever truly cared about me is Cami, but now, I have Josh, Paige, and Jem. Then there's the other women in the Club. It feels good to have this wider network and for the first time I understand why Josh is drawn to it.

"It's good to see you both."

"Okay, before this starts getting mushy, do you girls want to get in the car?"

Paige pushes Josh's bicep. "Don't ruin our moment, Wade."

He brushes his lips over hers. "I wouldn't dare."

A pang of jealousy goes through me as his hand goes to the back of her neck possessively, pulling her close. They haven't been together long, but already it's as if every breath he takes is for her. Their love is raw, deep and unapologetic desire.

It makes me miss Jem. I can't wait to see him, and I hope I'll have the chance over the weekend, although given he's going to be with his brother for his stag party, the chances may be few and far between.

I move to the back door of the car, and climb in while they finish plundering each other's mouths, and when Paige gets in, she turns in the front seat, wincing.

"Sorry. Your brother's an animal."

"It's fine. You don't have to apologise. I'm invading your personal space."

"Not at all. And you don't need to be subjected to a porno show every time you visit."

I snort at this description. I'm sure I'll have the opportunity to get some revenge once Jem and I go public.

"Thank you for that image."

She laughs. "Anyway, you don't have to worry about him and me." She says this as the driver's door opens and

Josh climbs in. "We'll be mostly with the girls all weekend, so it'll be a man-free zone."

Josh reaches for his seatbelt, his eyes seeking mine in the rear-view mirror. His huge frame seems to suck all the space out of the vehicle and I understand why he prefers his bike. He seems so ill-fitted to a car—or cage, as he calls them. It is a good description, because it seems to strangle him.

"Yeah, apparently we're banned from Lace while you girls are having the hen do."

"You're out on Logan's stag do anyway," Paige says. "Why would you want to be at Lace?"

Josh scowls. "There better be no strippers."

"Will *you* be having strippers?"

He doesn't answer.

"That's what I thought. So, you boys don't get to tell us we can't have strippers if you're having them."

"I didn't say we were."

"Your silence said it for you, handsome."

"I'm not going to watch them."

She snorts a laugh. "You're not going to watch? Well, neither am I."

Josh growls. "Fucking hell. Whose idea was this fucking shit?"

Paige leans over the middle console and squeezes his thigh. "Wade, I love you."

This seems to soothe my brother and his anger seeps out of him. Hmm, interesting. Paige might be a good person to get onside when it comes to spilling the beans about me and Jem.

"I love you too, sweetheart."

"So, what've you been up to, Piper?" Paige catches me off guard by suddenly turning in her seat and addressing me.

Bugger.

Mostly, I've been shagging Jem.

"You know, working, the pub, going to the gym..."

The last is a lie. I don't think I've ever set foot in the gym. I'm using Cami's life to round out my own here.

"I need to join the gym." I can barely see her around the passenger seat, but her hand goes to her stomach. "I'm getting flabby since I came off the poles and started working behind a desk."

My brother's gaze snaps in her direction. "The fuck you are."

"Handsome, my bum has its own postcode."

He growls a curse. "You're fucking perfect. Don't talk that shit."

The vehemence in his tone is both a little scary, but also warming. Hearing my brother reject Paige's insecurities so intensely is unique. I can't imagine Grant doing that for Mum.

She waves him off. "You're biased. You don't have a vote. I could just lose a little off my hips."

"I fucking like your hips as they are, Paige."

"Yeah, well, I don't, and since they're my hips, I get the final say."

Josh lets out a frustrated breath. "Fuck my life, woman."

"It's easy for you, Wade, you're sitting there looking like... well, a sex god. I don't want to be on your arm looking flabby."

He turns the steering wheel a little sharp to the left and I have to hang on to the handle above the door to keep from sliding across the back seat. I see her point, though. Josh does have a good physique. I also wish I was anywhere but in the back of this car right now. I'm really wondering if they've forgotten they have a passenger.

"Number one, you're not flabby. Number two, I don't give a shit if you weigh a hundred pounds or six hundred pounds, you'll always be beautiful to me. Number three, I'm not exactly perfect either, sweetheart, so you don't get to look at me and ignore my imperfections and highlight what you perceive to be your own."

"Wade... you don't have imperfections," she says quietly.

"Sweetheart, I'm missing half my fucking ear. My nose is crooked as fuck and I have a scar under my lip. We all have our battle wounds."

I swallow hard and glance out the window. We all have our battle wounds. It's true. Some are visible, some are not. Externally, I look okay, internally is a different matter. The scars inside me are ugly and irreparable. Does Jem see my imperfections? Does he look past them? Are we still in that phase were everything is shiny and the bad things are not noticeable?

I watch as Paige reaches across the central console of the car and grabs my brother's hand.

"I love you, handsome," she says quietly. "Just as you are."

He squeezes her hand. "I love you, too, Paige."

The bachelorette party is exactly how I imagine it. There are penis-related things everywhere—the cake is the main attraction and there are tiny metallic cut out penises scattered over the top of the table. The rest of the room is decorated with banners and balloons. I feel both part of the group, but also slightly on the peripheral. I'm not quite an outsider, but I'm not yet in the inner circle either. The girls are rowdy, but there's a reassurance about their banter. I can tell they are worried about this situation with Dylan.

I wish Cami was here. She'd like them.

I'm struggling to keep up with their chatter when Sofia, Jem's youngest sister, suddenly chirps up, "Kenzie said you were visited by a P.I."

Beth freezes, her eyes sliding around the table.

A P.I.

It takes my brain a moment to realise what it means—a private investigator.

The other women are all looking at the brunette woman, with a mixture of intrigue and concern. I'm wondering why in the heck a P.I. would be talking to her in the first place.

Mackenzie, Jem's other sister, lifts her hands and signs something. I have no idea what, but I need to learn British Sign Language if I'm going to be in her brother's life—and probably stat. I know his sister is unable to speak, but can hear, but I'm not sure what caused her inability to vocalise. I should talk to Jem, find out more about his family.

Jamie snags a chip, digging it into the dip, saying, "What the hell did a P.I. want?"

"Can we not do this now?" Beth says, her eyes skittering towards Liv, who simply responds with, "He's looking for Simon."

"What?" Clara demands at the same time Sammy asks, "Your nutty ex?"

Jem's mother, Mary, who I'm not going to lie, scares me half to death, decides to step in at this point. "Girls, I'm not sure we should be talking about this at Beth's hen do."

No one pays her the slightest bit of attention, and I don't blame them. I also want to know more, even though I have no idea what any of this is about.

"He accosted me outside the supermarket this afternoon," Liv admits. I don't miss the way her hand goes to rest on the top of her baby bump, a protective move, almost.

Beth sits back in her seat, her face rippling with guilt and a hint of panic. I don't blame her for this. Liv isn't small height wise, she's taller than Beth, probably just a little shorter than me, but she is pregnant.

"Fuck, does Dean know?"

I watch as Liv bites her lip. I'm guessing from that look, she hasn't told him. I don't know Dean well, but I would hazard a guess that it is not going to go down well.

"He'd lock me in the house if he knew," Liv mutters, trying to justify her reasons for holding back. "I didn't want to miss tonight," she adds, then says quietly. "I'll tell him, though. I don't like to keep things from him."

"Why were you alone in the first place?" Sofia asks.

"I nipped out for five minutes to grab some milk. It seemed crazy to bother a prospect or a brother to come over for that. I know it was stupid, but things have been quiet lately. I thought it would be okay. I didn't expect to get accosted."

"Why'd Brosen come to you?" Beth asks after a moment. "You weren't the last person to see Wilson. I was."

"The P.I. is working for Simon's parents." She winces, colour staining her cheeks pink. "I don't think he's interested in me. I filed for divorce months ago and had to disclose my address on the paperwork. He's just looking for Simon. Reading between the lines, the police investigation has stuttered. He's poking around for any information he can find."

"Did he hurt you?"

She shakes her head. "I was in a public place."

"What a piece of shit," Sofia mutters. "It's not enough you had to go through all that crap with your ex, now you have this arsehole harassing you."

I have no idea what to make of this, other than trouble

seems to follow the Club like a lost puppy, only this puppy has teeth. Not that my life back home is any less trouble free. I still have no idea what misfortune Grant has brought to my doorstep—if at all. Maybe it was just posturing, designed to scare me into submission. Although he hasn't tried to push me into doing what he wants since he wiped his hands clean of me, and that was weeks ago.

Mary reaches over and takes Liv's hand, squeezing it gently.

"You need to tell the boys. They need to be able to look after you, sweetheart."

"I will," Liv promises. "Believe me, I'm not taking any chances. The man wasn't aggressive anyway, just forceful. I don't really know what I can tell him. The last time I saw Simon was weeks before everything happened in the colliery."

"We all just need to be vigilant," Beth says, dragging her gaze from her to address the others. "This guy is like a dog with a bone and he's not scared of the Club. Logan practically smashed his teeth in, and he barely batted an eyelid."

Paige glances around the table, "Okay, someone is going to have to fill me in on all of this."

"Liv's ex is a nut who went on a two-week rampage that concluded with him beating the shit out of Liv before shooting up the clubhouse, injuring Logan, then abducting Beth and Dean and putting a bullet in your man," Sammy explains like she's talking about the weather. "That's the short version."

Paige's brows arch before she whispers, "Holy shit."

"That about sums it up."

"Tap and Dylan used that situation to create chaos to further their own agenda to destabilise the Club, but you know about that part, since you were involved in that bit," Sofia adds.

Sammy reaches for a chip, dipping it in the salsa. "You know, just another day in the life of the Lost Saxons."

"Well, at least it's never boring," Jamie leans back in her chair with a wiggle of her brows.

"I'm fine with boring." Beth says. "In fact, roll on boring."

"You'd die with boring."

"I would not."

"Girl, ten minutes of boring and you'd be throwing yourself into the trajectory of something dramatic. You can't even walk ten paces without something happening to you."

Beth's eyes roll. "I don't go looking for drama. It just... happens."

"Yeah, yeah. At least you have Mr Tall, Dark and Brooding to save you from the drama," Jamie says. "Me? I'm out there alone facing it. Shark food, that's what I am. While you're being stalked around town by the hotness that is Logan Harlow, I'm being followed by Rabbit or Charlie. Hell, yesterday, I had Lucas on my arse all day. He's a little weasel. I couldn't get Jem or Weed or even King. Fucking Lucas. The guy is a miserable bastard with the personality of a damp sock. Jem on the other hand—close your ears Harlows—is sex on legs."

I'm fairly certain my entire body goes wired at her words. I've never felt possessive before, but hearing her talking about Jem like that does something, unlocks something. I don't like hearing him being discussed like this and the need to stake my claim on him is overwhelming. I have to bite my tongue to keep the words behind my teeth. I had no idea she even liked him.

Does she like him?

Does he like her?

Insecurity washes over me as I peer at her. She's pretty. Very pretty. She has soft red hair that bounces around her shoulders and freckles that sweep over her nose. She's confident, brash, not afraid to take what she wants, fun. I'm none of these things. She's more like Jem than I am.

Would he be better with her?

"Oh my God," Mary mutters looking like she would like the ground to swallow her whole.

"Is it time to cut the cake yet?" Sofia demands briskly, getting to her feet, glaring at Jamie.

"Absolutely," Mary replies, following just as fast.

"Can we not discuss my future brother-in-law like that?" Beth chastises.

Kenzie's hands flash.

"What? You have hot brothers, Kenz," Jamie replies to whatever she signs. "I can't help that. Jem is like a walking sex god. All that blond hair and muscles. And Adam..."

Oh my God...

I need to lay claim to Jem as soon as this wedding is done. I get some cake and settle in the corner, sliding the cake back on the table. Then I pull out my phone.

ME: Do you think Jamie is attractive?

I don't expect a response back, but to my surprise it pings back almost immediately.

JEM: Angel, how many wines have you had?
ME: Not nearly enough. There are penis shaped things everywhere that I can't unsee.
JEM: As long as none of them are the real deal.

ME: You haven't answered my question.

JEM: Piper, why are you asking this?

ME: She fancies you.

JEM: Well, she is only human.

ME: Everyone fancies you.

JEM: I don't care about everyone else. I only want you.

ME: Smooth talker.

JEM: Absolutely. I don't know what is going on in that head of yours right now, but hear me when I say I don't give a shit about anybody else. When are you going to understand this? Angel, you're mine. I don't give a shit about Jamie or any other women. I've only got eyes for you.

Yes, I'm his. Completely and irrevocably. He's under my skin, buried deep in my soul and embedded in my heart.

But that makes you mine too, Jem Harlow, and Jamie and everyone else can keep their mitts off.

CHAPTER TWENTY-SIX

I TAKE the Wednesday off after the hen do, so I can actually spend some time with Jem. He comes up to Manchester to see me, and we spend the day in the city centre, doing nothing but wandering around, window shopping and chatting. It's cold, and the last week in November, so although the official Christmas markets are not yet set up, there are lots of Christmas gifts around. I mentally pick out things I can buy for Jem as we walk, wondering whether he likes everyday things or if he's more about the outrageous gift. In the time I've got to know him, we haven't delved that deeply into each other's likes and dislikes, so I'm not sure what would pass as the perfect present for him, but I'm getting antsy, the nearer the holiday is getting.

I push out thoughts of presents as we manoeuvre around the mid-week shopping crowd. Walking around Manchester with Jem feels so normal, so pedestrian, I can't help but relax. He isn't wearing his kutte, opting for just his leather jacket and shirt below. There's another Club that operates in the city—the Devil's Dogs—and while Jem told me the Lost Saxons and Devils are allies, he doesn't wear his colours while we're out in town. I haven't asked why, but I suspect it's a respect thing. Frankly, it's nice to be civilians for a little while. Walking hand in hand, we look like any normal couple. There's no Club, no Grant and no expectations. There's just him and me. It's wonderful.

We walk through the city centre, looking at the shops, but not really paying attention, just happy to be in each other's company. Even without his kutte, Jem draws attention because of his size and his appearance. The man is intimidating and attractive to boot. He also oozes a confidence that naturally draws attention. He keeps his hand locked in mine, though, and his focus completely on me, which reassures me.

"Have I told you how beautiful you look today?" he says out of the blue.

Considering I'm wearing a dark plum skirt and cream sweater with boots, I don't think I'm particularly dressed to impress, but I still flush pleasantly at the compliment.

"Flattery will get you everywhere."

"I'm not flattering you. I'm telling you the truth. You're beautiful."

I duck my head slightly, letting my hair curtain my face. "You're crazy."

"For you, yes." He lifts our joined hands, kissing mine. "Once my brother's wedding is done, we're telling Wade about us. I can't keep this secret anymore, Pip. I want you and not in private. I want you in my life, in my bed, in my world."

His words aren't new; he's been saying these to me for weeks now, but they still hit me squarely in the chest, as they do every time. Mainly because the wedding is in just a few days' time and I'm not sure I'm ready to go public yet. It's a mixed feeling—one of elation followed by fear. I'm happy he wants this because I want it too, but I'm terrified of letting him in as well, of allowing my walls down completely.

But I want to be happy, and I think I can have that with him, if I allow myself the chance. I just have to overcome one big obstacle first—Josh, and keeping him from murdering the only man I've ever cared about. The only man I'm certain I've ever loved.

"You're sure about this, Jem? Doing this is going to open up a lot of wounds. Josh is going to flip."

"With the greatest respect, I don't give a shit about Wade. He's not my concern. You're my concern."

"I love my brother. I care about him, and you should too. God, this isn't just something we can do without hurting him."

He stops walking, tugging me to a stop with him, and a group of pedestrians have to sidestep around us. They mutter angrily under their breath, but Jem doesn't notice or care. He places his hands on my shoulders before bringing them up to cup my face.

"Babe, I've said it before—I care about Wade, but I won't sacrifice my happiness nor yours for him throwing a fit over us being together. He doesn't get a say. You're his sister, not his kid. And even if you were his kid, he still wouldn't get a say. I want to be with you. You want to be with me. That's what matters. Wade's going to have to suck it up. I've only been so patient out of respect for you."

He draws my face to his and brings his mouth down over mine. His kiss is warm, wet and filled with promise. I cling to his jacket, needing to ground myself as the world disappears around us and all that exists is him and me and this kiss.

He's right. Josh will have to suck it up. I love my

brother, I do. But I'm coming to love Jem as well and I need him in my life more. I won't let him walk away.

I don't know who breaks it—him or me—but when we part, we barely move an inch apart. Jem's breath is warm against my face as it rips out of him in little pants.

"Why not just tell him now then?" I say.

"Because your brother's an arse and I don't want him to ruin Lo and Beth's big day. They've waited a decade to reconcile. They deserve to have the bells and whistles shit."

While I'm not exactly happy he's calling Josh an arse, I'm not sure I can disagree. Josh will lose his shit.

"Okay, after the wedding," I agree.

He kisses me again.

"Thank you, angel."

"What happens then?" I ask.

"What do you mean?"

"Well, short term travelling back and forth is fine, but long-term it's not ideal. I mean, do we have a plan here, Jem? I don't want to presume things but—"

"I'd prefer to stay in Kingsley, given my whole family's there and the Club, but if you're set on staying in Manchester, we'll make it work somehow."

Considering I have no roots in Manchester at all, other than Cami, it would make sense for me to move to him—and I can't believe I'm even considering this, given how short a time we've been together.

"I wouldn't ask you to leave your family, Jem."

He squeezes my neck, the gesture reassuring. "I know you wouldn't, but I wouldn't ask you to give up your life either."

He is asking, though. He has far more ties to where he lives than I do. I have my job and Cami. That's it. I'm done with my parents and the toxicity they bring into my life. But Jem... He has the Club and his family, which is huge.

And it's not like I don't have ties to Kingsley as well. There's Josh, Paige, and I have friends there now. At least I think so. I like Beth and Liv, even his sisters and Jamie.

I blow out a breath. "It's a big change. What if we don't work out?"

"Then move back to Manchester and pretend I never existed."

"I doubt I could ever pretend that. You'd never allow it."

He smirks. "No probably not. But angel, what if we don't try? What if we don't give it our all and we spend the next forty years wondering if we could have done better? Life is too short for regrets and speculating."

His words unlock something in me. "You're kind of poetic when you want to be."

"I'm just misunderstood."

I draw my brows together.

"Moving's a big thing. A scary thing. What if you get bored of me after a week?"

He frowns at me. "Pip, I'm not sure you're understanding me when I'm saying I'm in this for the long haul. Those words aren't empty, angel. I mean it. You're mine."

What...

My brain must short circuit because words and thoughts disappear.

"Piper, say something."

"I'm... I'm yours?"

"Babe..." he scratches at his head, one eye closing as if he has a tension headache coming. "This isn't a game for me."

"It's not for me either."

"So, let's throw caution to the wind, go nuts, live on the

edge." He presses his lips to my forehead. "Don't let fear hold you back now. Be brave with me."

"Let's just get telling Josh out of the way first. He's already going to have a fit when we drop this bomb on him. Let's give him time to deal with this before we start moving in with each other, okay?"

Jem sighs dramatically. "You're such a spoilsport."

I laugh.

"Come on, let's go find somewhere to eat. I'm starving."

"You're always hungry," I point out.

He releases me from his arms and I move back to his side to take his hand. As I do, something catches my eye. Watching me from further up the street is the man from the restaurant—the same man who was watching me with Cami. It could be coincidence, except Manchester isn't that small a city and the guy has been in two places I've been now. Plus, he's staring right at me.

I must stiffen, because Jem stops and glances down at me.

"You okay?"

"What?"

"Angel... are you okay?"

Tell him. I should tell him, but that would mean divulging everything and honestly, I don't even know if I'm being ridiculous. Grant is probably just trying to scare me into doing what he wants, which is to be his lapdog, and I won't do that. I won't. I'm tired of playing his and Mum's games, of going to his photo shoots and acting the dutiful daughter, of being grateful for his input into my life, as if he's some saint for what he's done. I know this is just an attempt to manipulate me again and I'm not falling for it.

So, I smile at his dumb lackey and then turn my attention to Jem.

"I'm perfect. Let's feed you before you waste away."

I take Jem to a small American style diner in Spinningfields and get some sustenance into him, but I do decide I need to be at least semi-honest with him about my parents. If we're going to be in a relationship, he's going to want to meet them at some point and I need him to know why that can't happen.

"I'm not speaking to my parents," I tell him as he's finishing off his dessert.

He glances up, mid spoonful.

"Why not?"

"Grant hit my mother."

He blinks slowly, then puts his spoon back in the bowl, his jaw tightening. I watch in fascination as his knuckles whiten as he curls his hands into fists on top of the table before he seems to get control of himself enough to speak.

"Do we need to go in and get her out?"

My heart warms at this. No questions asked, just do we need to rescue her.

"No, Jem. My mother's perfectly content where she is."

I watch the confusion play across his handsome face as he tries and fails to make sense of my words. I don't blame him. My words are confusing.

"You're going to have to give me a little more to go on here, Pip."

"Farrah likes the lifestyle she has. Even living with a man who hits her isn't enough to give that up."

I watch as he works through this in his head. "You had to go home for a family crisis when you were staying with Wade. Was that to do with your mum being hurt?"

I glance down at the table and my hands folded on top of it. Shit. He remembers that? Then again why wouldn't he? He came barging over to Josh's flat that night like a bear with a sore head, ranting about me missing the Club's monthly family party. He thought I was still slighting the Saxons. In reality, I'd been lured home under false pretences and got between my parents' spat. Grant hurt me that day, too, but I'm not telling Jem that.

"It doesn't matter, Jem. She's made it clear where she stands, and not because she's scared to leave him. She'll never leave him because she likes what she has."

Jem stares at me and his entire face darkens in a way I've never seen before as his voice drops low. "Has he ever touched you?"

Oh, bugger.

I should have pre-empted this question. I should have, and yet, I didn't.

"Jem—"

"Has he? And no lies, Piper. I want the truth. Has he ever laid a finger on you?"

"It's done with."

His entire face contorts as an ugly rage rolls through him. I'm both disturbed and fascinated by it as I watch him get angry on my behalf. I've never had anyone but Cami defend me before, so having someone in my corner feels righteous even though it scares me to see his reaction, because he's unravelling in front of my eyes. It's like watching a volcano readying to erupt—beautiful in its natural ferocity but terrifying in its power.

"I'm going to kill him," he growls out.

"You're not going to do anything," I tell him. "It happened twice and it wasn't even that bad, Jem."

"Twice is too much. Once is too much." He grinds his jaw. "When?"

"What does it matter?"

"Was this while we've been together? Before? When?"

I freeze.

"When, Piper?"

"While we've been together," I admit on a hushed groan. "Really, it's not that big a deal. As soon as it happened, I cut contact with him—"

"What did he do?"

"Jem, honestly, what does it matter?"

"Just answer the question."

"The first time he grabbed my arm, the second time he slapped my face."

He stares at me in stunned silence. "A man puts his hands on you, and you don't think this matters?"

I feel all the fight leave me at the fury radiating from him. I've seen him annoyed before, but this is something else.

"No, I don't. I handled it. It's over with. I didn't want to cause trouble."

Jem leans over the table towards me. "The only trouble would have been the trouble visiting him."

"Exactly," I hiss at him. "Between you and Josh, things would have got messy and I didn't want to spend the next decade visiting you both in jail. I handled it. I'm not completely useless. I can take care of my own business, Jem. God knows, I've been doing it for years."

"Yeah, well, you don't have to take care of shit on your own now because you're not on your own. You've got family, and I know that's a foreign concept to you. I'm starting to understand a lot more about why that's hard for you to grasp, now I'm getting an insight into the pieces of shit who raised you, but you've got real family who care about you."

I glance down at my empty plate and let out a breath.

"Jem, let's get real here. The moment we tell Josh we've

been sneaking around together for pretty much the past three and a half, nearly four months, my family disappears. He's going to drop me faster than a rock. And you can sit there and say he won't, but he's going to. He's going to lose his mind when he realises I've lied to him, especially in the light of recent events."

He nearly died at the hands of two people he trusted—two people who lied to him, and the Club, for months. At least that is what I understand from what I've heard through the grapevine from the girls and Jem. I don't get a lot of news in Manchester, but I get bits and pieces.

"What Tap and Dylan did isn't even comparable."

"They betrayed him, just as we have, and that's all Josh will see—betrayal. It's coming at him from all directions and he's not going to care whether it's on a sliding scale of how bad."

Jem stares at me. "You're doing your brother a disservice by thinking he would be that way with you."

"Maybe, but I've been here before with Josh. I've had him walk away from me. I know what's on the horizon." I steel myself for what I'm about to say next. "And you'll have to make a choice too, Jem. Your brother—your Club—or me." I laugh a little, but there's no humour in my voice. "Either way, I lose in this scenario."

"I'm not picking sides."

"You say this now, but that's how it works. Josh'll be angry and push me out. You'll have no choice but to choose."

"You're talking about shit that hasn't even happened."

"No, but it will. Maybe we should just head it off before it does."

"No fucking way. I get you're scared, I do, but I'm not giving you up. Josh doesn't like us being together, he can suck it. I'm happy. For the first time in my fucking life, angel, I'm actually fucking happy. And I think you're happy too. You are happy, right? I mean, I know I'm a delight to be around."

I giggle. I can't help it. "Yes, Jem. I'm happy and you're definitely a delight to be around."

"Thank fuck for that. I was getting worried." He signals to me. "Come sit over here. You're too fucking far away over there."

Considering we're in a restaurant, I'm not sure it's entirely appropriate, but I scoot my chair around the side of the table, so I'm sitting adjacent to him, rather than opposite. His hand instantly collars the back of my neck.

"I'm not choosing anyone over you, you hear me? There's no choice. You're it for me."

"Jem—"

"No, Piper. Stop talking, and listen. Wade's going to spit his dummy and he's going to have a tantrum. That's going to happen, but he'll calm down and when he does, shit will be fine. He loves you. Beneath all that gruff ridiculousness, he loves you."

"I thought he loved me last time too, but it didn't stop him leaving then."

"Well, I can't say what was going through his head last time, angel, but I will say Wade was screwed up when he first joined the Club. His head was a mess, he was reckless, spiralling. It took us a while to straighten him out. I'm not saying him doing what he did was right, but I'm just saying he was dealing with stuff after getting out of jail and residual shit from his past. I don't think he had it in him to consider anyone."

I let out a breath. I have some inclination of what Curtis did to him from the police reports Cami managed to dig up.

They did not make for pleasant reading. I do know the broken nose and scar to his lip are souvenirs left behind from his days with our father.

"Look, don't worry about Wade. We'll get Lo and Beth married. Then we'll sit down with your brother at the end of the weekend and talk to him about us, okay?"

I nod slowly. "Okay."

He pulls me in for a kiss. "It'll be all right, angel. I promise. You just have to be strong for a little longer."

Be strong.

I can do that.

CHAPTER TWENTY-SEVEN

"Oh my God, pastries solve everything," Cami moans, licking the stray piece of flaky filo pastry from the corner of her mouth as she tries to shovel in, rather indelicately, the cake she's devouring.

"Do you need a napkin?" I ask her, tightening my hold on my coffee as I chuckle at her.

It's early, barely even seven. I have to catch a train in about thirty minutes. I'm heading to Kingsley for the weekend. It's Beth and Logan's wedding, which I'm looking forward to. I get to see Jem in his finery—although he's told me he's not wearing a suit as you would expect at a 'civvy' wedding, but a shirt with his kutte. I don't care. He's going to look bloody fine either way. Too bad I won't be able to ravish him on the dance floor, since we're not telling my brother about us until after the wedding. We'll probably do it Sunday, possibly at Josh's flat away from prying eyes. I'm terrified, which is why Cami took me for breakfast this morning. It was meant as a sort of send-off. Dutch courage, if you will, minus the booze.

Unlike my best friend, I wasn't able to stuff breakfast

pastries down my throat. I did manage to throw back a latte, though. Caffeine is all that is keeping me sane right now. Cami bought a second pastry to eat at lunch, but since she's licking the last of the crumbs from her fingers right now, I think that plan is out the window.

I don't blame her for needing a sugar overload. It's been a crazy week. I feel like I've barely stopped. With the hen do on Sunday and then seeing Jem on Wednesday, now I'm up early and getting on a train back to Kingsley in—I glance at my watch—shit, I need to leave... now.

I pick up my pace, rushing towards the front door of the loft. Why the heck is the hallway so bloody long?

"I hate to eat and dash, Cam, but I'm going to have to duck in, grab my bags and head over to the station—or I'll miss my train. We're meeting at Beth's this morning to help her with hair and makeup. I said I'd meet Paige there."

Cami leans against the wall by the front door as I dig in my bag for the keys, wiping the last of the crumbs from her mouth.

"The new sister-in-law seems to be a hit."

"She may be my only ally against Josh when I tell him I've been shagging his Club brother for months behind his back. I'm keeping her sweet."

I push the key into the lock and shove the door open with my shoulder. I step inside, Cami on my heels. She barely shuts the door behind us when they appear from around the corner of the kitchen. Men. There's two of them, burly blokes in jeans and dark brown leather jackets. Not like Jem or the boys wear in the Club. One of them is the man that was watching me.

I reach blindly behind me for Cami and push her towards the door.

"Run," I murmur and shove her as I latch onto something solid.

We both turn and make towards the door but as we do, another man is standing behind us, blocking the exit. He must have been waiting in the small utility room next to the front door. Fuck. My heart starts to race as I realise the man from the restaurant is sitting on the sofa.

Cami moves close to my back, and I grab her clammy hand in my equally sweaty one. I don't think I've ever been this scared in my entire life. She suddenly shrieks and she's torn from me. I spin to see her dragged back by the guy behind us, his arm banded around her waist.

What the—

I grapple for her, trying to grab her, but she yells at me, even as she fights against her attacker's hold, "Piper, run!"

I don't want to, but the only chance we have of getting out of this is for one of us to get help, so I rush for the door. My fingers hit the latch and pull it down. Then my head slams against the wood. I see stars for a moment before pain explodes through my skull. A fist ploughs into my back, stealing the air from my body.

God, ow.

I try to draw air past the weight in my chest and fail. I try again and manage to get something through.

Then I forget about breathing. Fingers curl into my hair impossibly tight, pulling at my scalp, and I'm dragged back from the door, from our one chance of escape. Cami screams and she's cut off by what I'm sure is a hit to the face, from the sound of flesh being struck. I want to go to her, to help her, but I'm being pulled by my hair into the main part of the loft. All I can do is go where I'm being directed and when the guy holding me finally releases me with a shove that sends me sprawling onto the floor, it's actually a relief to slam into the wood. At least the pressure on my scalp is gone now.

Blinking through the haziness in my vision—blood, I realise belatedly—I try to locate my best friend, but as my sluggish gaze starts to move around the room, a blow to the head regains my attention.

"That's enough, Perkins. Take the photo and send it."

I sway on my knees, one hand pressing into the wood beneath me. I feel sick and my head is spinning. I can hear Cami trying to say something, but what I don't know, because my ears are ringing.

"What now?" the one called Perkins asks after he lowers his phone—presumably having shot this beautiful moment of me trying to keep my stomach controlled, trying to keep upright.

"We take her with us."

"The other?"

"Don't need her. Get rid of her."

"No..." I whimper, but my voice is weak, pitiful. I hurt everywhere.

I try to fight, but I'm tugged up to my feet by men who easily overpower me. It's hopeless. I'm no match for them, and even if I was, my head is spinning and my vision is swimming. I can barely keep my feet under me as they all but drag me to the door.

Cami fights like a wild cat. I can see her through the cascade of blood running into my eyes. I wish she wouldn't. They hurt her. Hit her, slap her, but she fights them to get to me. The last thing I see as I disappear through the door is one of the men slap her so hard she goes to the floor. Bile rises in my throat at this. She should just let me go.

I think someone will stop them from taking me. I live in

a big building. There are sixteen flats in it. Okay, it's early in the morning, but surely someone will be around, right?

Wrong.

They get me outside without hindrance and I'm put in the back of a van without being stopped. It's dirty inside, the floor metal and covered in dust and debris. One of the men sits on the back of my thighs as he pulls my hands behind my back and roughly binds them with thick ropes. I try to kick out, but my legs are held firm under him and I can't move my top half either. So, all I can do is squeeze my eyes shut and wait for the inevitable.

I twist my head to the side, my thoughts racing as the van doors are shut behind us, the dawn light disappearing with it. Material is pulled over my eyes and my sight is taken from me, heightening my fear further.

With only four of my senses to rely on, I feel hyper alert, even through the haze of dizziness, and when the guy behind me tugs the ropes to check them, I jolt.

You're okay, Piper. Just relax. Keep breathing. If they wanted you dead, you'd be dead already...

"Get up front, fucker," another voice barks from somewhere overhead. It's hard to tell.

Then the weight lifts off and I'm aware I'm alone in the back of the van—at least I think I am. I can't sense anyone, anyway.

I'm in trouble. Maybe the most trouble I've ever been in. No one knows where I am, where I'm going, because I never told anyone what was going on with Grant—no one but Cami, who could very well be in trouble herself. My stupidity, my arrogance may have very well got my best friend killed.

At least, I assume this is because of Grant. The man on the sofa was the same man in the restaurant and the man I saw earlier in the week. I assume this is all to do with my stepfather, but in reality, it could be linked to my brother and his Club dealings too. It could be linked to anything.

Face down in the back of this dirty, smelly van, all I can do is lie here and wonder what the hell is going on. Fear grips me. When I don't turn up for the wedding, Jem will know something is wrong. He'll come for me, right?

Oh God... will he think I got cold feet about telling Josh about us?

The van rolls as it moves and I jiggle about. I wish I could see. I'm terrified. I don't know where I'm going or why, but the fear clutching my heart has the power to stop it in my chest. I try to calm myself because I need to be level-headed, but I'm so dizzy I'm struggling to maintain even a loose grip on anything right now.

By the time the van stops, I'm barely clinging to consciousness and when the doors open, I don't even have the strength to fight when I'm pulled out.

I can't see anything through the blindfold and the two men holding me up set a ruthless pace as they march us forward.

I try to make sense of my surroundings, but it's next to impossible. I know we move from outside to in by the change of acoustics and the lighting I can make out through the blindfold. Plus, the temperature drop. It's cooler inside. The men talk about some football match last night, like they haven't just abducted me and beaten my friend. It's so surreal. I can hardly believe this is happening.

Finally, they stop walking and I hear the scraping of a lock and the whine of hinges as a door is opened. Then I'm pushed inside what I assume is a room. One of the men drags me in and pushes me down. I hit something softer than expected—a mattress I realise. A cot, of some sort.

"Hope you enjoy your accommodation, Miss Hollander. You're gonna be here for a while."

I don't correct him on the name. It doesn't seem like the right time to be throwing my weight around about being an Ellis and not a Hollander or Ellis-Hollander or whatever the heck Grant wanted me to be. He's also confirmed my suspicions that this is because of my stepfather, which means I really am in trouble because my brother and boyfriend have no idea I'm in deep shit, and the only inkling they're going to have that there's a problem is when I fail to turn up for the wedding—a wedding that neither of them are going to be able to leave to come looking for me.

I hear the squeak of the hinges again and then the scrape of the lock being re-engaged. And I realise I must be in a cell. He's locked me in a cell.

I'm totally fucked.

CHAPTER TWENTY-EIGHT

I'M FROZEN, so frozen I can barely breathe. I wish I'd worn jeans, because my bare legs are like ice, but like an idiot, I put on Jem's favourite skirt when I left the house, thinking it would drive my guy a little crazy when I got to Kingsley. I'm regretting that now.

My coat was taken from me some time ago, as was my sweater, leaving me only in the thin white top I wore beneath to layer up from the cold. I was also divested of my boots, so my bare feet ache fiercely as the frosty air licks up my soles. I've never liked having cold feet, but this is a different level of frigid, one that is embedded so deeply in my bones I don't think I will ever be warm again. Every inhalation I take is like breathing in tiny shards of ice.

I keep my head tucked down towards my chest, tipped into the smelly, dirty mattress I'm lying on, and take shallow breaths, hoping it will provide some protection from the elements. So far, it has not, but it's all I can do until my situation changes.

Even though I'm certain I'm locked in a cell with no chance of escape, they have kept my arms tied behind my back, and my blindfold still in place. Considering I've seen their faces, I can only assume they keep my eyes hidden to keep me afraid, and it is working because I am terrified. When they first placed me in the cell, I tried to free my hands from the ropes. I worked them until my skin felt raw and I could feel the blood pooling behind them, but they haven't moved. Whoever tied them did a good job with the knots. I tried to escape, believe me, I haven't been a passive abductee, sitting quietly on my bed, waiting. I've screamed, shouted, cried, pleaded—done all the things expected. They let me, for a while. Then they came back into the room, hit me, hurt me, and threatened to rape and kill me if I didn't shut up.

I should have fought more, but I was scared, so I shut up. I'm also in so much pain, the thought of being hit again is enough to silence me. Besides, I need my energy because if I'm going to escape, I'm only getting one shot at it, and I will take it.

That was the plan hours ago.

Now, I'm too cold, too exhausted to try anything.

For a while, the terror sitting in my gut gnawed at me like a constant ache, but it's settled to a dull pain now that I'm mostly able to ignore—unless the door opens. Then it returns with full fury.

I don't know how long I've been here for, or if anyone knows I'm missing yet, but I've been brought nothing except water some time ago. I didn't drink it. I was scared to, in case it was laced with something. One of them held my face and tried to force it into my mouth, but it spilt down me, soaking my top. They seemed to find this funny, but this was a new form of torture. The cold of the water added a whole new level of pain.

If they're going to kill me, I wish they'd just get it over

with. I can't stand the waiting, the not knowing. Lying here, trying to make myself as small as possible to stay warm, I think about Cami. Did she get out okay? As much as I want to believe she did, I doubt it. The last time I saw my best friend, she was being beaten by a bunch of thugs because of me. Because of my arrogance.

If I had moisture left in my body, I would cry at this, I don't have the ability to make tears. Even my mouth is an arid desert. I should have talked to Josh, to Jem. They could have protected us. But God, I didn't think Grant was serious. My stepfather plays the big man in town. How was I supposed to know he was actually not playing the big man for once? And these men he's pissed off seem like bad news. I have no idea where I am, but this doesn't seem like it was planned spare of the moment.

I need to think. I need to find a way to get myself out of this mess, because I'm not dying here.

No.

I just found good in my life.

Jem.

He's an idiot, but he's my idiot, and I haven't even told him that. I haven't even told him that I'm falling hard for him, and that I see a future for us—a future that involves him and me growing old together. I haven't told him that as well as being an idiot, he's a good man, a man that I'm head-over-heels in love with.

Yes, I'm in love with him.

I have no idea when it happened. Maybe from that first meeting five months ago in the hospital when I walked right into him and he tried to flirt with me. I bit his head off then and he still wasn't deterred. Maybe it was when I thought the flat had been broken into and he refused to let me stay on my own. Maybe it was when he tried to kiss me in the lift that night and I ran off.

I don't know what the turning point was. All I know is I don't want to be without him.

I was so scared of upsetting Josh that I didn't stop to look at what I had in front of me.

And Jem's right.

Josh is going to have to get on board if he wants to be in *my* life, because Jem's it for me. My world stills with him in it. Everything is chaotic without him. Jem slows things down. Things make sense when he's around.

Trying to shift on the mattress brings a fresh wave of agony lancing through my back. I don't know what they did to me, but I'm really hurting there. Every time I move something feels off, wrong. I try to keep still, but my body needs the movement to give reprieve to my aching shoulders.

The door latch squeals and I freeze. I didn't even hear their approach this time. I need to be more vigilant. I need to be ready for them. I try to rouse myself, but outwardly make it look like I'm out of it. I want their guard down. I need to get out of here. I won't die in some dank, dark, dingy hole.

"Hmm, rise and shine princess."

Hands grab my bicep and I'm dragged up. The move from lying to sitting makes my stomach roil and I have to swallow hard to stop bile from spilling out of my mouth. I'm really dizzy and my head is splitting. The blindfold covering my eyes is tugged down and I wince against the dull light filling the room.

"Time to eat." The voice belongs to the guy called Perkins, the one who slammed my head into the front door—the arsehole responsible for my blinding headache.

He's not a bad looking guy, tall with dirty blond hair

and a hint of a tan. He doesn't look like a thug, even with the scar running down the side of his neck.

"I'm not hungry," I deny, even as my stomach growls.

I glance down at the sandwich on the plate on the edge of the mattress. It looks edible, not tampered with. Not mouldy. Not gross. I'm still not eating it. I have no idea how long I've been here for, but the gnaw of hunger in my belly is getting hard to ignore, even through the churn of nausea.

"Eat it."

"How can I eat? I'm trussed up like a bloody turkey." I shouldn't snark at him, but I can't help myself.

Perkins scowls. "You're a fucking pain in the arse."

He holds the sandwich out to me, so I can bite it. I don't. He throws it back on the plate. "Suit yourself. You can just starve."

I watch as he gets up, grabbing the plate.

"Wait, why am I here?"

"You don't know?"

I shake my head.

"Your dad pissed off my boss. My boss doesn't take too kindly to that."

He must be talking about Grant, since I've never met Curtis. I don't correct him on the fact that Grant isn't my father. What would be the point?

"And who exactly is your boss?"

I don't expect him to tell me, but he surprises me by saying, "Trevor Merrick."

My blood runs cold. I've heard of him. Christ, everyone in Manchester knows that name. He runs a gang out of the north-west part of the city. I know from reading the papers, there's been a few clashes between him and the Devil's Dogs—the motorcycle club that has a base in the city centre, not too far from where the loft is, actually.

"Well, I'm sorry Grant annoyed him. He has a habit of being fairly annoying full stop, but if you'd bothered to do your research, you'd realise that he and I aren't even talking."

He stares at me a beat. "You better hope that ain't the case, darlin', because the only hope you've got of getting out of this shit in one piece is if your daddy plays the game."

He heads for the door and slams it shut behind him. I jolt at the sound. Bugger. Bollocks.

I want to cry, but I don't let the tears fall. I need to be strong. I need to find a way out of this. Perkins made a mistake. He left the blindfold off. And if he screwed that up, it's only a matter of time before more mistakes are made. One of those mistakes might enable me to get out of here.

With my eyes unhindered, I take a moment to glance around my prison. It's a small room. Dirty, damp, exactly what I expected it to look like. The walls are a dark green. I think at one point they were papered with a lighter peach colour, but it's peeled off to reveal this horrible tone beneath. There's a window, but it's boarded up. At least I assume it's a window. There are slits of light coming in around the edge of the wood board.

Sitting on the bed, I bring my bound hands under my bottom and feed my legs through, so my wrists are now tied in front and not behind. Then, carefully, I push up off the grubby mattress and cross the floor.

It's some kind of concrete beneath my soles. It's freezing, but I'm so numb I barely notice as I move over to the wooden board covering the window. With my fingers, I feel along the edge of it. It's nailed down, as I expect, and it doesn't move.

Peering through the slit, I can't see much but a shaft of light. This doesn't give much indication of how long I've been here, nor the time of day, but I feel a weird sense of hope seeing the outside.

Glancing around the room, I try to find something that I can use to pry the board off the window, but my accommodation is sparse. Other than the bed, there is a bucket in the corner, which I've used for the toilet a few times (with help—not my finest moment), the bed and that's it.

I move back over to the bed. There has to be something.

I lift the mattress and see there are metal slats on the base of the frame. Carefully, I wiggle one. Nothing happens. I wiggle the next one. Nothing. I go through them all until one halfway down moves.

Oh, God. I wiggle it and it moves. I give it a fucking good shove and it moves out of the grooves either side of the bed frame. I nearly drop it onto the concrete below, but manage to catch it before it clatters.

Holding the piece of metal in my hand like it's the Holy Grail, I stare at it a beat. Then my brain remembers I'm being held captive and time is of the essence.

I rush back over to the window. Can I pry the board off...? It's going to make a hell of a noise. Maybe I can be careful.

I place the metal through the slither between the board and the frame of the window near to the screw and try to get some leverage. Careful not to push too hard, but to exert enough pressure, I lever the metal. The wood creaks and cracks. It sounds loud to my ears, although it's not, I'm sure. I lessen the pressure to reduce the noise and work the screw.

The wood splits with a crack and I fall backwards, hitting the floor heavily. Light spills into the room from the hole I've created.

Shocked, I blink up and then I'm moving. The noise

was loud—loud enough to bring my captors? I'm not sure. I scrabble to my feet, a challenge with my hands tied, and quickly glance through the hole. When I look outside, my stomach drops.

The building is an old factory and it's in the middle of nowhere. There are fields for as far as the eyes can see. I can't see any houses on the horizon. I can't see anything on the horizon, in fact. My screaming was pointless. I could have screamed until I was blue in the face, no one would have come.

Where in the hell am I?

I hear noises coming from the bowels of the building behind me. They must have heard the wood breaking.

I quickly lever the metal against the wood and try to break it more. My only option now is to go out of the window, if I can. I barely manage to get a second piece off before the door opens behind me.

Voices roar in anger and surprise, and then hands are on me, dragging me back. I swipe with my weapon at them. I think I connect with flesh, I'm not sure.

And then the last thing I see is a fist come straight towards my face before I black out.

CHAPTER TWENTY-NINE

When my brain reboots, it does it with a blinding headache. My skull feels like it's going to shatter from the pressure. I whimper. I can't help it. The pain is unbelievable. I try to curl into myself to stop the agony, but I can't move my body.

I'm tethered, I realise. I force my eyes open and I'm met with a shaft of light from the window. They didn't repair it or put my blindfold back on. I squint against the brightness, blinking rapidly to clear the spots dancing in my vision and the stabbing in the back of my retinas. It settles after a moment enough for me to try to move.

I can't.

I glance up over my head and see ropes tethering my wrists to the head of the bed's metal frame. Dipping my gaze down, my feet are similarly tied to the base of the bed. Panic crawls up my throat as I take stock of my new situation. This is not good, not good at all. My white top is no longer white, but stained with blood and grime, ripped at the shoulder to reveal more bra than is decent, and my skirt is rucked up practically to my hips, revealing hints of the lacy underwear I'm wearing beneath. I don't feel sore down there, and everything feels as it should, so I think they've left me alone.

I breathe a sigh of relief.

At least no one has violated me.

Yet...

The word fires through my brain and I shut it down.

No one is going to touch me like that full stop. I'll die before I let them.

Not that I'll have any choice. I'm spread out like a sacrifice for them. Fear spreads like acid through my veins. I have no idea how long I've been here or what they plan on doing to me. All I know is Grant pissed this Merrick bloke off and I'm collateral for whatever is going on between them.

As I come around a little more, my aches and pains start to make themselves known. I'm hurting everywhere. The old hurts are joined by new. My face feels swollen, the skin tight across my cheeks. I'm sure I must look a fright. My left eye is barely open more than a slit, although the right is less puffy, so I can see better through this. The temperature in the room is so frigid, my breath steams in front of my face with every exhalation I take and the air burns as it hits my trachea with every inhalation I make. I don't think I'll ever be warm again.

The sound of the lock makes me freeze and my eyes shift towards the door as it opens. Perkins and another man I recognise from the attack in the loft step inside.

"Boss wants to see you," Perkins mutters.

I stiffen. I have no interest in seeing Merrick at all.

"I'm fine here, thank you."

The other man laughs. "Listen to this fucking princess."

Perkins says nothing, but his lips pull into a line. He

pulls a knife from his pocket and I barely contain my scream.

"Are you going to be difficult?" he demands.

"It's not really in my interest to be an easy prisoner for you," I manage to blurt out, even though my voice wobbles. I'm proud that I say it, that I'm fighting back.

"If you want to keep breathin'," the other man grins, "it is."

I swallow hard and watch as Perkins cuts through the ropes at my feet.

"Make yourself fucking useful, dickhead. Grab her ankles."

The other man moves to do as commanded and seizes my ankles. His touch on me makes my stomach twist, but I keep still. I don't think I can take another beating. I'm hurting too much as it is. I need to keep my strength in case the chance to escape presents, because I'm not staying here. The first opportunity to get gone, I'm going. I realise from the window this place is in the middle of nowhere, but I'll risk it. I want to believe rescue will come, I truly do, but it may not. I can't rely on it. I can't hope Jem and my brother know I'm missing, that they've worked out where I am and are coming to find me. I can't. This isn't a movie. The girl doesn't get rescued by the dashing hero. This is real life, where the girl gets violated and dumped in a shallow grave to rot for eternity.

Well, not *this* girl. I'm living.

And I'm going to save my bloody self.

Even if I have to die trying.

Perkins moves to the head of the bed and slices through the ropes, freeing my arms from the headboard. Pain fizzes through my shoulders and biceps as he drags them down by my sides and pulls me into a sitting position on the edge of the mattress. He doesn't give me time to let the feeling return to the limbs. He tugs my arms behind my back and ties them at the base of my spine.

"The hospitality here could really use some work," I complain.

The other man guffaws. "We've got a comedian on our hands."

I shoot him a dirty glare. "I wasn't trying to be funny."

Although it's good that he thinks this. If I can get him to let his guard down a little, it might make my escape plan easier. Not that I have a plan. At the moment, my only idea is to find a chink in the armour and seize it. It's a terrible strategy. I'll probably get caught and beaten again, but it's better than sitting here waiting to die. My flight response is in overdrive and the primal need to survive is driving all my decisions.

Perkins slips a meaty hand around my arm and tugs me up. My legs nearly buckle, but he keeps me on my feet. On second thoughts, running might not be on the cards. I'm as weak as a spindled-legged foal. Good God. My legs are jellied. I can barely walk without his help.

It's not just my legs either. I'm dizzy, nauseous, and every step sends pain lancing through my entire body. Escape might be a challenge.

Perkins walks—or rather drags—me through the door of my cell. I try to focus beyond my pain and staying upright on everything that lies beyond it. This information could save my life.

He leads me into a narrow hallway with multiple doors off it. There's an industrial feel to the building, which is unsurprising, considering I'm sure from what I saw of the outside this was once some kind of factory. As we move deeper into the bowels of the building, it opens up more and

I see more mechanical remnants of the factory's former glory days.

The other man talks nonsense at Perkins, but he barely responds. He's a man of few words, it seems. In fact, if I am to guess, I'd say the man annoys Perkins.

Eventually I'm pushed into a large room, a former office I think, but there's plastic tarpaulin on the floor and a chair in the middle of the plastic. This doesn't seem like a good thing. It looks like some kind of kill room, which has my heart skipping frantically in my chest.

Perkins steers me to the chair and pushes me into it. I want to fight him, but with so many people here, there's little point.

My eyes go to the man leaning against the edge of the desk on the far side of the room. He doesn't look that large, but there's a formidable air about him. His dark hair is styled in a messy just-got-out-of-bed look that seems to fit with the trendy jacket and dark jeans he's wearing. He looks like he should be in a bar, not in a dingy factory holding women prisoners.

I shift on the chair, the ropes digging into my wrists as I glance around the room. My chest heaves as my brain races.

"Miss Ellis-Hollander. I'm so glad you could join us."

"I wasn't exactly given much choice."

"Yes, I am sorry you've been dragged into this unpleasantness."

Not sorry enough to avoid it, though.

I bite my tongue to keep the words from slipping out.

"You're Mr Merrick, I assume?"

He throws his head back and laughs. The other men join in.

"Mr Merrick... the only people who call me 'Mr' are my

doctor, my solicitor and the plod. Since you're none of those, sweetheart, I think you can just call me Merrick."

"Well, *Merrick*, I want to go home."

"I'm sure you do, and as soon as I get my business straightened out with your stepfather, that will happen—providing he does as I demand."

The finality in his tone makes my throat constrict. "And if he doesn't do as you demand?"

Merrick shrugs. "I'll have to make some unpleasant decisions."

Perkins takes a call, moving to the back of the room to answer it. I watch him for a moment before I slide my eyes back to Merrick.

"I'm not involved in his business."

"It doesn't matter. Grant Hollander crossed a line. He threatened things that are precious to me, so now I'm threatening things that are precious to him."

I drop my chin to my chest and laugh. It's probably not the best response, but I can't help it. A mix of nerves and hysteria are getting the best of me.

"Oh, God. The only person Grant Hollander thinks is precious is Grant Hollander. You'd have been better taking him." I raise my gaze to meet Merrick's eyes. "You think he'll care if you hurt me? He'll care more about protecting his stupid reputation, about making sure the press doesn't get wind of his dealings with you, about spinning a story about how his family got caught up in mob warfare and his stepdaughter paid the price for him trying to clean up the city. Nothing sticks to him. This won't either. He'll come out smelling of roses. You'll go to prison for whatever you do to me. It's how it always works."

"Yeah, well not this time. Your stepfather pissed off the wrong people."

He lifts his phone and snaps a photograph of me sitting in the chair, bound, beaten, cowed. I'm sure he's sending it to Grant, and I'm sure my stepfather will not give two shits.

Perkins moves to Merrick and says something in his ear. I watch the man stiffen then his eyes come to me.

"Chat's over. If your stepfather does as he's told, you'll go home and everything will be fine."

He juts his chin over my head and I'm seized by two men behind me and dragged up. They take me back to my cell. I try to catalogue everything I pass on the way, but it's a fruitless exercise because the moment I'm back in the room they let me pee, then wrestle me onto the bed and tie my hands and feet to the frame. The bigger man cops a feel of my breasts as he does, but they leave me otherwise unscathed.

I fight the restraints for a while, but they hold fast. I don't know where those bastards learnt to tie knots, but I can't shift them at all and all I manage to do is shred the skin on my wrists even more. Bleeding, I lie on the smelly lumpy mattress, exhausted, my bladder bursting again, until the sun starts to set through the hole in the wood board covering the window. It's darkening in the room, the solitary bulb that usually is on to keep light in here not yet lit, so shadows dance along the walls where the setting sun doesn't reach.

When I can stand it no longer, I yell for assistance. It's disturbing how relieved I am to hear the latch slide back. I'm not relieved to see it's not Perkins that enters the room, but Mr Handsy—the arse who copped a feel while re-tying me. I think his name is Smythe, but that could have been the other guy he was with. It's hard to keep track.

He smirks at me, his arms crossing over his chest.

"You yelled?"

"I need to pee."

Humility washes over me.

He grins. "All right then."

I hate how much he enjoys this, but I notice he doesn't lock the door behind him when he comes to the bed. He's too focused on me. Hope surges in me. A mistake. Can I use this to my advantage?

I keep my expression neutral as he unties me, his fingers lingering too long in places they shouldn't. He pulls me none-too-gently up to my feet and stands in front of me while I stand over the bucket.

"Well, turn around then," I snap at him.

He doesn't move.

"Are you honestly going to stand there and watch me pee?"

He still doesn't move. Dirty bastard. With a scowl, I pull down my underwear, trying to cover as much of myself as I can, and I squat over the bucket. Mortification fills me as I pee into it, but also blessed relief as I empty my screaming bladder. I glare at Smythe as I urinate.

"You're tapped in the head, do you know that?"

He shrugs.

I quickly finish up, recovering myself. This guy creeps me out. He's just about to reach for me, when I hear a noise. It sounds like a 'pop'. Smythe stops too, his attention going straight to the door.

It's out of place, wrong.

A wail of agony suddenly rends the air. It doesn't sound human, but I know it is. Claws dig around my heart and clutch it as fear stalks into the hallway, shrouding me in cold more frigid than the icy temperature.

What the hell was that?

It's also perfect cover to act.

I don't know what possesses me to do it, but some

primal instinct urges me to act. I grab the bucket by the handle and as hard as I can, I clobber him around the head with it—urine and all. Disgusting, I know.

He goes down to his knees, coughing and spluttering. I don't give him time to recover. I reach into his belt, snag his knife, and before I even contemplate what I'm about to do, I jab it towards his exposed neck.

I don't reach my target. He grabs my wrist, my ravaged, bloodied, raw, rope burnt wrist and squeezes until I feel like the bones are going to shatter. My whimper turns into a scream of agony. I let go of the knife. It falls to the floor with a clank, but he doesn't let go of me. He uses his superior strength to force me backwards and onto the mattress. He comes down on top of me, his weight pinning me to the bed, crushing me.

My chest tries to heave in terrified breaths, but fear clogs my throat as I thrash beneath his huge body, trying to unseat him. The unmistakable cacophony of gunfire punches through the air. Screams follow. I can't even think about what is happening beyond the door of my cell, because I'm in the fight of my life. If he takes this from me, there's no going back.

So, I fight him, I fight him because what choice is there? I'm not going to die like this, but God, he's strong and I'm hurt. I can't win this. His knee goes between my legs, and I yell my frustration and my fear and everything pours out of me. I see stars as his hand wraps around my throat and my air supply is cut off. My lungs can't draw in a breath and panic sets in. I'm going to die and there's nothing I can do about it. I'm never going to see Jem or my brother or Cami again.

Darkness doesn't creep into the edges of my vision, it

slams. I'm shutting down fast. I'm blacking out. I can feel my eyes going.

Then his weight is gone and he's no longer on top of me. I suck in a breath and another. Oxygen floods my cells and I feel shaky as my body starts to reboot piece by piece. Bonelessly, I lie on the mattress, trying to regain my strength. I want to move, to see what's going on, but I can't.

All I can do is listen.

I hear the sound of flesh meeting flesh. It seems to go on and on, and the gargle of choking before silence.

I hold my breath as the heavy footfalls of boots move back towards me.

"Piper." My name is said softly but with desperation.

I blink and when my vision clears, I see him.

Blond hair dripping down like a curtain, his brow drawn into an angry furrow, but an underlying fear in his eyes.

And blood.

There's blood splattered all over the left side of his face.

But it's him.

It's my Jem.

He staring down at me like an angel. Funny because he always calls me that, but right now he's my angel, my avenging angel. He sinks onto the mattress next to me, his Adam's apple bobbing as his hands skim over my body, close but not touching—as if he's afraid to.

"Fuck... Piper, can you hear me?"

I reach up with trembling fingers and rub over the scruff on his jaw. It scratches the tips but there's a softness to the hair.

"You're real..." I sound disbelieving.

He snags my hand and brings it to his mouth, kissing it. "Yeah, angel, I'm real."

His voice is raw, like silk tearing over glass. He's studying me as if he doesn't know if he should touch me or leave me be. I take that decision for him. I struggle up onto my elbows, wincing at the pain and burrow into his chest, ignoring how much it hurts my body to do this. I need to feel him, I need to be touched by someone familiar. His arms immediately come around me and I seek his warmth.

"You came for me." I cling to him like he's my saviour because he is. He saved me from a fate I can't even imagine. I don't want to imagine.

"I'll always come for you, angel, always," he says into my hair. "There's no me without you. I'm sorry I got here too late to stop that piece of shit."

I shake my head against his chest. "No, Jem, you got here just in time."

CHAPTER THIRTY

JEM REMOVES his kutte and jacket, tugs off his sweater and carefully pulls it over my head. It doesn't cover as much of my body as I would like, but it covers enough. The sleeves pass my hands and I fist them up inside, relishing the warmth and loving being surrounded by his smell.

He redresses himself then lifts me carefully into his arms. I offer to walk, but he won't entertain the idea. I don't look at Smythe's body as Jem carries me out of the room bride-style, my face burrowed against his neck. I'm exhausted, hurting and my adrenaline is crashing. I let myself relax into Jem's hold, certain he'll protect me.

"Angel, I'm so fucking sorry this happened to you."

"It's not your fault," I whisper into his neck.

"I should have protected you. You're mine."

My heart skips a beat. Even after all this he still wants me?

"I'm yours?"

"Always, Pip, always." I hear voices ahead and tense. "It's okay. It's just Weed and Adam."

Sure enough, I hear Weed mutter, "Jesus, what did they fucking do to her?" as Adam says, "Shit."

I must look as terrible as I feel.

Jem doesn't answer Weed's question. Instead, he asks, "The building's clear?"

Clear?

What does that mean? Jem killed a man for me. Did the others kill Merrick's men too?

Did they... kill everyone?

I should care, I should, but I don't. They dragged me out of my home, hurt Cami, hurt me...

"Cami?"

"She's fine," Jem assures me. "She's at the clubhouse. Clara patched her up."

Relief fills me, overwhelming relief. It rolls through me like a tidal wave and I clutch him tightly as I let it flow over me, just grateful my best friend is alive and safe. "Thank God."

Jem kisses my hair. "We need to get you home."

"Fuck!"

I pull my head out of Jem's neck and peer up to see Josh. My brother's jaw is working, his Adam's apple bouncing as he takes me in. The rage in his eyes is like nothing I've ever seen before. Josh is usually fairly emotionless. He doesn't wear anything outwardly, but right now, he looks homicidal.

In my overwrought, confused state, I think it's because I'm gripping Jem like a limpet. I don't consider the fact I look like I went ten rounds with a cement truck and lost. All I can think is that hanging off his Club brother's neck like he's my saviour is probably not the best way to come clean about our relationship, so I unfurl my fingers from Jem's neck and try to pull away. I have no idea why, because I don't think I can walk if I try. Jem isn't going to let me go anyway. If anything, his hold on me tightens.

"He knows about us," is all he says.

My stomach drops. This is not how I wanted Josh to find out. I wanted to sit him down, explain things. I didn't expect to be covered in blood, battered, telling him about me and Jem after leaving a string of dead bodies in our wake.

"Oh."

I glance back over to my brother and look for censure there, hate, anger—any reaction. I see disappointment beneath the concern. I take a shaky breath and glance away as my chest aches with a pain that has nothing to do with the beatings I've taken.

"Piper?" Josh's voice draws my gaze and I swallow before I meet his eyes. He takes me in, his mouth pulled down, then he crosses the room, stopping in front of me and Jem. I feel Jem tense and I have the feeling my brother better choose his next words carefully, otherwise he might find Jem's fist in his face. I prepare for whatever might happen next.

Josh's hand scrubs over his face as he catalogues every bruise on my face. "Jesus, fuck. Look what they did to you."

"I'm okay," I tell him, grabbing his hand and squeezing it.

"Kid, you're not okay. You're not even in the same postcode as okay. They beat you black and blue, Pipe. You're a mess." Josh seems to lose his composure for a moment and it takes him a second to regain it. "They paid for what they did, know that."

Ice fills my belly at the hardness of his voice. I've never heard my brother sound so detached before.

"We need to get Pip to a doctor," Jem says quietly.

Josh snaps his eyes to him and I see the anger blaze. I tense without meaning to, and I feel Jem squeeze me, reassuring me maybe, that he'll keep me safe. Not that I need protecting from my brother, right?

Josh looks over his shoulder to the other brothers. "We good to go?"

"Yeah, Foz and Ax are just doing a final sweep before the clean-up crew get here, but I think we're good."

Who the heck are Foz and Ax?

Jem kisses the side of my head. "We need to get you home."

Josh growls under his breath, whether at Jem kissing me or at him saying we need to go home, I don't know, but he mutters, "I'm going to get the car," and takes off.

Jem watches him go before he glances down at me. "Come on, sweetheart, let's get you out of here."

He carries me outside and the cold air hits me like a freight train. Mixed with my adrenaline crashing, I can't stop shaking as he gets me into the back of the car. Josh is sitting up front with Weed. Adam, and the other two men, who I assume are 'Foz' and 'Ax' mount their bikes. The latter two wear kuttes that have the Devil's Dogs arced over the back, Manchester on the bottom. Jem climbs in the back with me and pulls me against him. A blanket is tucked around me and I start to feel heat seep back into my bones.

I snuggle into Jem, ignoring all my aches and pains, ignoring everything but the feel of my man's thighs beneath my head and his fingers as they stroke over my neck.

Safe. I'm finally safe.

"Turn the heat up," Jem orders Josh as the car starts up. "She's freezing."

Josh leans forward and turns the dials on the dashboard. He glances over his shoulder at me, his brow heavy as he takes in Jem holding me, but he doesn't say anything. He just turns back to the windscreen.

Lulled by the engine and the movement of the car, I doze against Jem. I don't know how long I'm in and out for, but Jem murmurs in my ear after a while, "Angel, I need you to wake up for me."

I force my eyes open, seeing the orange glow of streetlights streaming through the windows of the car and the outline of buildings surrounding us. "Where are we?"

"The Devils' clubhouse. Their doc's going to take a look at you before we head back to Kingsley."

I'm surprised we're still in Manchester. I thought we were miles from the city, considering the lack of civilisation when I looked out the window of the factory. The back door of the four-by-four opens and Josh ducks down to look in.

"Leech is here already. He's waiting inside."

Jem nods. "Okay." He glances down at me. "You need to sit up, Pip, so I can help you out of the car."

Right. Slowly, I manoeuvre up, with both Josh and Jem helping me. It's just as well, because scrunched up on the back seat for however long I was out for has not been kind to my ribs, and I'm stiff as hell. I can't stop the moan of pain that escapes my mouth.

Josh growls under his breath. "Fucking shit heads."

Gently, he and Jem help me out of the car. I wobble a little once I'm on solid ground, Josh steadying me while Jem climbs out of the vehicle and comes around the back to us.

The Devils' clubhouse sits behind a large set of gates just off the main road. It's deep in the centre of Manchester's Northern Quarter, a stone's throw from mine and Cami's place. In fact, if it wasn't for the high-rises surrounding us, I'd be able to see the building from here.

The clubhouse is different from the Lost Saxons,

though. It's an old three storey building, detached, with land on either side, but it's surrounded by other properties. Behind the gates, it's actually surprisingly screened from prying eyes.

There are rows of motorcycles parked up on a scrap of land at the side of the building and I can smell marijuana heavy in the air. I can also see a guy with his jeans down to his thighs, ploughing into a blonde woman against the wall in a darkened corner of the compound, his pale backside catching the security lights as he moves.

I snap my gaze back to my brother, not wanting to be caught gawking. I'm also not sure if I should say something to clear the huge elephant in the room—the fact I'm with Jem and we lied about it. Josh hasn't broached the subject at all, not that I expect he would. There hasn't really been a great time to bring it up between murdering people and running away from the scene of the crime.

"Josh?" I say his name quietly and he glances down at me. "I'm sorry."

His jaw tightens then relaxes a little. "You've been through hell, Piper. I can't even fathom what shit you've been through in the past three days, so I'm not going to get into this with you while you're standing in front of me still bleeding, bruised, hurting."

"But—"

"You need to go inside and let Leech look at your injuries," he cuts me off before looking to Jem. "I'm going to call Prez and check in."

Jem nods and watches as Josh takes off, heading for the clubhouse. Tears clog my throat and I feel Jem's hand on the back of my neck. He rubs soothingly at my nape.

"He hates me."

"He doesn't hate you."

"He's only not disowning me because he feels sorry for me."

"Angel, he's pissed, but he'll calm down. Come on," Jem says quietly. "Inside, now."

I glance around the compound, shivers running up my spine. "Are we safe here?"

"I wouldn't bring you somewhere you weren't, angel. The Devils are good people. They're friends of the Club. Axel and Fozzie helped us recover you, and Leech—that's the Devils' doc—he's going to take a look at your injuries before we hit the road back to Kingsley."

Jem picks me up again, despite my protests I can walk, and carries me inside the building. This time, the blanket from the back of the car is wrapped around my lower half, maintaining some of my dignity.

Inside the clubhouse is more similar to the Saxons clubhouse, although it's dirtier and there's a lot more women wearing very little wandering around. Jem takes me to a room at the back of the clubhouse and when we enter there's a large man with a shaved head, covered in tattoos, waiting inside for us.

The room is set up like a doctor's clinic, with a bed, medical supplies and a chair in one corner. His kutte is draped over the back of the chair, the Devil's Dog emblem staring back out at us.

"I've got everything ready," he says to Jem, then addresses me. "I'm Leech. I'll be your doctor for this evening." He grins at me and I can't help but smile back at him. The movement pulls on the split in my lip and I wince, my fingers moving to brush over the injury. He watches the movement, his eyes hard.

"I'm guessing you took care of the fuckers who did this?" Leech asks Jem, who just snorts.

"What do you think, Leechy?"

He makes a noise of approval in his throat. "Can you get on the bed, darlin'? We'll have you patched up in no time."

After a thorough examination, he concludes I have a couple of cracked ribs, a sprained wrist and a lot of bruising. He stitches up the wound to my head, which hurts so bad, but I grit my teeth the entire time, because I don't want to cry in front of two burly bikers. When he asks me if I was sexually assaulted, Jem lets out a string of curses that make my ears heat. I squeeze his hand as I tell Leech I wasn't.

Leech, it turns out, becomes my new best friend. He might be a biker doctor, but he also has access to some fantastic pharmaceuticals. I know I shouldn't take drugs from strangers, especially not ones called 'Leech', but he's a medical professional. So, I chug back those pills like they're candy. Within ten minutes, I'm flying high.

Leech leaves me and Jem to it, and I doze for a bit, riding the wave. I'm not entirely sure what planet I'm on when I hear raised voices.

Confused, I glance around for Jem, but he's no longer sitting at my bedside. Where'd he go?

"...keys to the front door as well?"

Josh.

His voice sounds clear on the other side of the door, and he clearly sounds pissed, considering how much sarcasm is dripping from his tone.

Oh boy...

"I don't need a front door key," Jem responds. "I'm never there when she's not."

"Are you looking to get matching bruises?" Josh fires back.

Matching bruises?

Jem did have a bruise on his face... I assumed he got that in the fray. Did my brother do that to him?

Oh my God, did Josh hit him because of me?

I want to get out of bed, open the door and tell them to knock it off, but the drugs are making my motor functions a little sluggish.

"No, but I want you to stop being a prick to Piper. She's been through hell. She doesn't need you to add to that."

"I haven't said shit to her."

"Exactly, Wade. She was abducted, held for nearly three days by a bunch of psychopaths in that room. They beat her, hurt her, humiliated her. And you want to give her shit about a relationship with me? Really?"

"You lied to me! For months!" I can hear the pain in my brother's voice and it makes my stomach ache. I want to go to him, to apologise. "If this hadn't happened, if she hadn't been taken, were you both just going to keep fucking lying to me?"

"We would have told you eventually, when we thought it was any of your fucking business to know."

He doesn't mention that we were planning on coming clean after the wedding. Jem's purposely needling Josh, and I don't like that he is.

"I just unravelled months of lies and deceit, dickhead. Months of it! Now I find out that my fucking sister and another brother—someone I thought was closer than blood to me—have been feeding me a line of shit."

"I'm not sure why you're so interested in my love life, Wade."

Jem's tone is that exasperating one, the one that says 'I'm really bored of this conversation'. It riles almost everyone up—me included. I'm sure it's annoying Josh. I want to smack him for being purposely irritating when he should be apologetic.

"Don't be so obtuse. If you were shagging some random woman, I wouldn't give a shit, Jem, but she's my fucking sister. I told you she was off limits. I told you—all of you—to leave her alone, and you just couldn't help yourself, could you?"

This is getting out of hand. I can tell by the volume increase in their voices and by the words being tossed around. I throw back the blankets and swing my legs out of the bed. Leech, as well as being my saviour, also found me clean clothes to wear, so I'm in snuggly joggers and a tee with thick socks.

I stagger across the room, the drugs making me wobbly.

"Yeah, maybe if you hadn't been such an unapproachable bastard, she wouldn't have felt the need to shut down and hide the truth—"

I open the door just in time to see Jem's kutte fisted in Josh's meaty paws, his face dragged close to his. My brother has a couple of inches on Jem and he's heavier than him, but Jem doesn't look like he's planning on backing down. He shoves Josh firmly in the chest and then both men erupt into a full-blown brawl. I stand, stunned, as Jem takes a hit to his left side before landing a punch to Josh's gut.

What the...

"Stop..." I murmur, gripping the door frame as my body wavers. I'm still dizzy and the drugs are not helping either. "Stop, both of you."

Jem takes a punch to the head and I lose it.

"Stop!"

Then Weed and Adam are suddenly there, between them, pulling them apart. Tears well in my eyes and I let them fall. I can't do this. I can't have them fighting about me.

"You want to know why she lied, you dumb bastard?" Jem growls, wiping blood from his face with the back of his hand, his breath ripping out in pants. Adam stands between him and Josh, but Jem doesn't attempt to restart the fight. "Because she was scared of telling you about me and her."

"Jem, don't," I whisper.

Josh wipes blood from a cut above his eye and I watch some of the anger bleed from his face as his eyes skitter to me before moving back to Jem. "Why in the fuck would she be scared of telling me?"

"Because she thought you'd walk away from her. Again."

I see the confusion for a moment before his expression steels. "Why?"

"You really have to ask that? You practically threatened every one of us to leave her alone. You made her unattainable. You made her feel like she wasn't good enough, that going there with a brother would be a fucking huge deal to you. You scared her into thinking that you'd turn your back on her, like you did before." I watch my brother's face pale a little before his shutters come down. I wish Jem would stop talking, but he's not done, not yet. I also wish we didn't have an audience.

"Look, this thing between me and Piper, we didn't know where it was going. We didn't want to put it out there 'til we knew what we had because we knew you'd flip about it."

Josh shakes off Weed. The brother lets him go, but stays close, a watchdog, ready to leap into action.

"You said she's yours, Jem. That implies you know exactly where it's going."

Despite the situation, this makes me feel warm.

"Yeah, well, I knew I wanted her from the start, but your sister's got hurt in the past so I had to tread carefully." Jem scrubs a hand over his jaw. "When Cami told me she'd been abducted it was like my whole fucking world was gone, Wade."

My heart soars at this and I have no idea what to think. His gaze comes to me as he says it. "You're my world, Piper. Angel, without you life doesn't make sense. You're mine."

I swallow and then I nod, accepting, knowing, because it's the same for me.

I watch the anger drain from Josh's face. "You both could have told me at any point you were starting shit. I thought there was something going on at Weed's birthday, but Paige told me nothing was happening, made me think I was being paranoid."

"Paige was wrong," Jem says.

"Before that?"

"Yeah."

"How long before?"

"Officially... not until she went back to Manchester, but really, it started while you were in the hospital."

He scrubs a hand over his face. "Fuck."

"I love him," I say, speaking for the first time. "I love Jem with everything I have. He says I'm his, but he's mine too. And I'm sorry I lied, Josh. I'm more sorry than you can know, but I was terrified of losing you, of losing Jem, too. And I hope I haven't lost you now because I love you as well. You're my big brother, and I know we don't have the easiest relationship, but I only have one big brother. I'm just starting to get to know you, and I like having you in my life. I don't think I want to have a life without you in it."

I pause, taking a shaky breath, readjusting my grip on

the door frame before I continue, "I don't have a lot of people in my world that care about me. My own stepfather threw me to the wolves. My mother would rather let a man hurt me to keep her position in society. My father... well, you know all about him, Josh, and the kind of man he is. I need my brother in my life. I want my brother in my life." My words choke me and I have to swallow to regain control. "Please don't leave me again, Josh. You promised me you wouldn't walk away again no matter what happened. Don't break that promise."

He scrubs a hand over his face, then says, "Fuck. I'm not going anywhere."

Only he does go somewhere. He closes the space between us, and he pulls me into his arms and my brother hugs the crap out of me.

"Fucking hell," Weed mutters. "This is way too chick-flick for me. I'm going to get a beer."

When I pull back, everyone has disappeared, even Jem, although he's only gone as far as the end of the corridor, giving me and Josh space to talk, but staying close enough in case I need him.

"I'm pissed you lied," Josh says. "No lies between us, Piper. You tell me the truth, even if it's hard to tell."

"I'm sorry."

Josh sighs and glances up the corridor to where Jem is standing, waiting for us. He gives my brother a daft grin and I have to bite my lip to stop from laughing at him. Josh doesn't seem amused.

"As much as I hate the idea of you with a brother, at least I know you're taken care of. When Jem found out you'd been taken, nothing was stopping him from getting you back. He'll always fight for you. I can't see any civilian guy doing that."

"I do love him."

"Yeah, I can see that, although, I think you're fucking crazy." His lips lift a little.

"I think I'm probably crazy too. He drives me insane."

My brother scans my face, his brow drawn down. "I'm so fucking glad you're okay, Pipe."

I'm glad I'm okay too, and I'm starting to think things might actually work out.

CHAPTER THIRTY-ONE

The drive back to Kingsley seems to take forever. The Devils lend us a trailer so Jem can get his bike back. Jem drives the car, while the others ride in formation behind the vehicle, protecting us, I think. I alternate between watching Josh, Adam and Weed out of the windows and lying across the back seat when the pull of exhaustion gets too much.

Jem talks to me as he drives, his eyes flicking between the rear-view mirror and the road. He tells me jokes, keeps things light, and I love him for it. Everything has been so serious, but I do need to know something before we get back to Kingsley. Things are happening so fast, and this might be the last time for a little while before we get a chance to talk alone.

"Jem?"

His eyes flick to the mirror. "Yeah, angel?"

"What happened to Merrick?"

His gaze goes back to the road, but I don't miss the flash of fury in them. "You don't need to worry about him."

I struggle to sit up, wincing at the pull on my bandaged ribs. Leech did a good job patching me up and sending me off with a baggie of medicines, but I'm still hurting and will likely hurt for a while yet. Once we get to Kingsley, Jem seems to think Clara can get me actual medical care at the hospital without raising any flags with the authorities. How she does this, I don't know, but I'm not going to argue. It would be prudent to have X-rays done, considering how much of a beating I took.

"That's not an acceptable answer."

His eyes come back to the mirror and meet mine. He huffs out a breath. "He was dealt with."

"Meaning what?"

"He's no longer a problem."

My throat constricts and air locks behind the blockage. I know the Club isn't exactly law abiding, it's one of the reasons I was so against my brother being a part of it, but hearing Jem say this so blatantly makes me feel off kilter.

"You killed him," I surmise.

I heard the gunfire, the screams. What else could've been happening?

He doesn't speak for a long moment. "Merrick took something that belongs to me."

I'm not overly thrilled with this 'belonging' thing, but I'm not surprised either. The other women talk often about claiming and ownership.

"So, he is dead."

Jem's eyes close for a moment. "Yeah, Piper, I fucking killed the bastard, and I'd do it again. He abducted you in broad fucking daylight, kept you captive for days, beat you, sent photographic evidence of what he was doing to you. I called Merrick, told him who you were, that you were my old lady, Wade's sister, that you were tied into the Club—Lost Saxons property. He had chance to give you back without bloodshed. He refused."

I remember Perkins taking a call when I was in with Merrick. Neither of them seemed happy. Was that them learning who I was? Maybe. Then again, men like Merrick probably piss off many people.

"He was never going to give you back whole, Piper. Merrick was making a point to Hollander about crossing lines. Your stepfather fucked up, and you would have paid the price. Merrick couldn't back down. If he handed you over to the Club, he would have looked weak, so he had to play the game through. I wasn't playing, though. Not with your life. So, yeah, I shot that cunt. I killed him and his men. And I don't regret it for a second. They would have killed you without remorse to make a point."

I let his words sink in and I swallow back the vomit crawling up my throat. I have no idea what to do with what he's telling me, how to handle it, but I do know he is right. If Jem hadn't come when he did, that man would have done irreparable damage to me—damage I could never have come back from. And I have no doubt Merrick would have put a bullet in my head without a hint of remorse.

"I'm sorry you have to hear the ugly truth here, baby, I am, but if it comes down to a choice between them or you, I'm always picking you."

"I know. I'm glad you picked me too."

And I mean it. Merrick and his men did horrible things to me, and Cami as well. I'm sure they've done worse to other women, other families.

"Will this blow back on the Club?"

Jem taps his fingers against the steering wheel. "Don't you worry about that."

"Jem..."

He sighs. "Merrick's a medium sized player in town, but he's also playing in a patch the Devils want. They were more than happy to get involved in taking him down and we were more than happy to let them keep Merrick's territory after all was said and done."

It all sounds very complicated and surprisingly political. "Oh."

He pushes his hair out of his face. "You don't need to worry, angel, it's handled, okay?"

I nod. "You guys don't mess around."

"Not when it comes to women and kids, no. You let those fuckers think it's okay to touch either and things get ugly. Suddenly, old ladies are getting attacked taking the kids to school or getting groceries. It can't happen. A message needed to be sent, Piper. Merrick and his crew got that message loud and clear, and so did any other fuckers who even think about touching our families again. They want to come at us, fine. But you touch our women, our babies, we'll destroy you."

The fierceness in his voice is alarming, but also understandable. When I think about Beth, Liv, his sisters... all the women in Kingsley. Any one of them getting hurt like I was would be unthinkable.

It's strange to see this side of him. I'm used to Jem being laid back. Don't get me wrong, I've seen him annoyed, and I'm not naïve—I know he's deep into the criminal world, it's one of the reasons I was so reluctant to go there with him— but seeing it so clearly, so blatantly is surreal. I'm not sure what the heck to do with any of this. He saved me, of that I have no doubt, but he also killed people—and he doesn't have even an inkling of guilt about it.

Should he have?

I don't know.

I hate those men for what they did to me, to Cami.

But Jem played judge, jury and executioner...

I stare at his broad back, at the man who risked everything for me. He threw himself into the fire to protect me. I've never had anyone willing to go that distance before. Jem would have laid down his life to protect mine. I see that clearly.

Why?

Because he loves me.

He loves me.

And not because he wants something from me or because he needs me, but just because he loves me.

It's a startling revelation and it makes my entire body physically jolt.

I stare at him. This man would risk everything for me, and I would do the same for him.

"Jem?"

"Yeah?"

"Thank you."

His brow furrows in the mirror. "I've got to say, Piper, I wasn't expecting a thank you here."

"I've never had anyone in my life willing to stand up for me before."

"Well, get used to it. I'm always going to stand up for you."

When we get to Kingsley, it's strange, but it feels like coming home. Driving into the clubhouse compound is a relief, even. Jem gets out and comes to the back door of the car. He opens it and helps me out. Just as well because I'm still not steady on my feet. I wrap my arms around him as soon as I'm on the ground and hug him tightly. His fingers go to my neck, as they always do.

"I'm sorry," I tell him.

"For what?"

"Everything."

He pulls me back. "You've got nothing to be sorry for, Pip. None of this shit was your fault."

"I should have told you what was going on with Grant and Mum."

Brushing my hair back from my face, he says, "Yeah, that's your fault." He grins. "No more secrets."

"No more secrets," I agree.

"Piper!"

I pull back from him at the sound of my name and see my best friend half-running, half-staggering towards me.

And my heart contracts.

They really did a number on her. She's battered. Her face is a swollen mess, bruised black in places and her collarbone, visible beneath the line of her sweater, is mottled purple.

My hands fly to my face as tears threaten to fall. Not that I look much better, I'm sure. I took a heck of a beating myself.

"Don't you dare cry," Cami warns me, looking on the verge of tears herself.

"I'm not going to," I lie.

She pulls me into her arms and clings to me. "I thought you were a goner, P."

"I thought you were too," I tell her.

"It'll take more than some gangster wannabes to get rid of me."

She steps out of the hug and roves an eye over me—or tries to. They're swollen. I suddenly wish Jem killed those men more painfully. My beautiful, kind, funny best friend didn't deserve this.

"I'm so sorry, Cam."

"Don't. Don't you even go there. This isn't on you. This..." She points to her face. "This is all Grant's fault."

"If I'd told someone—"

"The what ifs will drive you insane, darling. It's not a game worth playing. What's happened has happened. And you and me... we're strong. We'll come out the other side singing." She squeezes my hand. "Although, don't take this the wrong way, but I'm selling the loft. I don't think I can go back there."

I don't blame her. I don't think I can either.

"I'm sorry it took me so long to get you help, P. They tied me to the radiator in the utility room and gagged me so I couldn't scream for help. It took me a while to get free."

Her wrists, I notice, are bandaged heavily like mine. She must have rubbed them raw to escape.

"Don't apologise. We're both here, whole, breathing. That's all that matters."

She glances up at Jem. "You kept your promise."

He squeezes my hip. "I didn't need to promise it, Cami. I wasn't coming back without her."

Cami glances at me. "I like this one. You can keep him."

I tut at her. "Thank you for your endorsement. I'll take it under advisement."

"I'll have you know, I'm a catch," Jem says. "I have my own place, I cook a mean carbonara, and I can tie cherry stems with my tongue."

Cami stares at him a beat before saying to me, "Definitely a keeper."

We head inside and we're greeted by brothers and old ladies alike. Logan steps in front of us in the foyer, his eyes scanning over his little brother, checking every inch of his face.

"You okay?" he asks finally.

"I am now."

Logan seems to understand this and nods.

"Any problems while we were gone?" Jem asks.

"No, but we kept the whole Club on lockdown. I wasn't risking anyone being out there. Some of the Devils who were still here from the wedding stayed behind and helped with security, which was a blessing."

"Is Beth pissed you missed your honeymoon?"

Guilt rolls through me.

"You missed your honeymoon because of me?"

Logan's gaze shifts to me. "Darlin', you can wipe that look off your face right now. Family comes first. You were in trouble and we took care of it."

I swallow hard. Family. Is that what I am? Josh has been telling me since I first arrived in Kingsley that I'm family. I didn't believe him, but hearing Logan say it... it makes something unlock in my chest.

With a sigh, Logan adds, "If I'm being honest, I think Beth was kind of relieved."

"Relieved? You're going to have to explain that one to me, bro." Jem rubs a hand over his jaw.

"Jimmy's barely out of the hospital, Jack's only just back in the country after his impromptu flit, Dylan's fuck knows where and there's still the small matter of this Brosen dickhead. Now, you're on Wade's hit list for boning his sister," he winces, "—sorry, Piper. Things are still really unsettled in the Club. I think she would have been worried about leaving."

I can understand why she would be worried, but missing her honeymoon...

"You guys should still find time to go," I tell him.

Logan smiles at me and when he does, I understand why Beth is smitten. He's *very* attractive—all three brothers are.

"We will. I'll take her somewhere special. Don't you worry." He turns to Jem. "Adam okay?"

"Our little brother is fine. He's outside with Weed."

I watch as the eldest Harlow brother scans an eye over my man.

"So, you and Piper..."

"Me and Piper." Jem repeats it lightly, but there is a hint of steel in his voice, a hint of challenge.

I move closer to Jem, my hand slipping into his. The last thing I need is the Harlow brothers throwing down, but Jem's shoulders seem to relax.

Logan's lips kick up at the corners. "Wade called me and asked if I'd bury him if he kicked the shit out of you."

Jem snorts.

"He did what?" I demand, mortified and a little disturbed.

Logan shrugs his huge shoulders. "I told him as long as he left you breathing it was fine."

I expect Jem to yell at his brother, but he just grins. "I knew I could rely on you to have my back."

"What did you expect me to say, Jem? You lied to Wade. That's a shit thing you did."

"I know, but I didn't risk Wade's wrath for shits and giggles, Lo."

Logan runs a hand through hair that is as dark as Jem's is fair. Looking at them, it's hard to see they're brothers—at least until you examine their mannerisms. Jem and Logan are a lot alike in that respect. Although both men do not share personality traits. Logan is as serious as a heart attack. Jem takes very little serious—until I got abducted.

"At least that's something because I've got to say, Jem, if you'd gone there just to get your dick wet, I'd let Wade beat your scrawny arse bloody."

I blush at his choice of words, while Jem lets out a growl.

"A little respect, Lo. I will smack you if you talk about my woman like that."

"Your woman?" Logan's brows raise. "You love her?"

My heart stops.

Jem grunts under his breath. "Jesus fucking Christ. Are you done with this inquisition? Are we going to braid each other's hair in a second? Start talking about how to win over our girl in thirty days?"

"Shut up, you daft prick. Just answer the fucking question."

I don't breathe. I also don't think Jem will answer with me standing right next to him. He doesn't seem to care about this.

"Yeah, Lo, I fucking love her. She's mine, I'm claiming her, putting my patch on her back, my ring on her finger, my babies in her belly. Whatever the fuck else you want to say."

My body freezes at his declaration, but also soars. He wants all that with me? I fight back the panic that tries to spark to life and drop my hands to my hips.

"As declarations of love go that was terrible, Jem Harlow."

He turns to me and grabs the back of my neck drawing me in for a kiss. "You want hearts and flowers, angel, I'll give you hearts and flowers."

I roll my eyes at him. "Can you even do romance?"

"I'm offended. I'm the king of romance."

"That's my cue to leave," Logan mutters.

Jem's mouth comes down on mine. He doesn't plunder, he's soft, gentle—he has to be, my face is a swollen mess and my lips are split from being hit. He's mindful of this fact as he tastes me.

"I want you in my bed, on my bike, in my life, Piper. I'll give you anything you desire."

"I want you too." I touch my forehead to his. "I love you."

"I love you too."

EPILOGUE

TWO WEEKS LATER

"It looks like Santa threw up in here."

I glance around the room and scowl. I might have gone a tad overboard with the decorations. Okay, I've gone completely over the top. Jem's living room is like a grotto. Aside from the tree, there's tinsel covering every available space, lights twinkling over the fireplace, and even a full-sized nutcracker standing near the hearth. He's going to have an apoplexy when he gets home.

I turn to Cami, pulling my bottom lip between my teeth. "Do you think he'll be mad?"

Her brow arches. "Darling, I think you could put a giant inflatable reindeer dick in here and he wouldn't bat an eye, as long as you're smiling. The man is smitten."

I wrinkle my nose at her and consider the room, wondering what I can remove to tone it down, but it looks so good.

Maybe I can lose the mini North Pole scene...

"I had a buyer put in an offer on the loft this morning."

I snap my gaze towards her. "That's brilliant."

"Yeah." She sounds glum.

"It's not brilliant?"

She sighs and drops onto the sofa. "I don't know, P. I don't know what to do. Staying in Manchester without you seems pointless."

I pause, clutching a fake reindeer statue in my hand. It's two weeks until Christmas. Cami's been staying since the attack and abduction, mainly because she can't go home looking like she went ten rounds with a heavyweight boxer. Her bruising is fading, as is mine, but neither of us look back to normal yet, despite the fact it's been a fortnight since Merrick's men snatched us from the loft.

A shiver runs through me as memories flash across my mind of that terrible event. Jem's been good at keeping me level since. I've moved in with him, staying in his terraced house in Kingsley, since he more or less claimed me the moment we got back into town, but I wonder who is keeping Cami level. She hasn't mentioned Spencer, her tumultuous relationship. I surmise they may be in an 'off-period' of their on-and-off relationship.

"Why don't you just move here, Cam?"

She glances at me. "I can't just follow you around forever like a stray dog."

"Why not? I've followed you around for years."

"I don't know. Isn't it kind of needy and pathetic?"

I roll my eyes at her. "Just move to Kingsley. If you need help finding a place, Jem'll help. He has contacts." I lift my fingers and do air quotes on contacts. "Or so he's told me a hundred times in the last fortnight."

Every time I need something doing, he'll tell me he'll get a contact to sort it. I need my things moving from Manchester to Kingsley... he's got a contact. I need to quit my job... contact. I need to get a Christmas tree... well, you get the point.

The man thinks he's a Don.

"I don't know. I don't want to step on your toes."

"Nonsense. I'd love to have you here. These people are crazy. I need an ally."

I hear keys in the front door and my stomach fills with butterflies. Jem's home.

"I like that look on your face," Cami tells me, her voice soft.

"What look?" I ask as I fix my skirt and top.

"The happy one. It's been a long time."

A warm glow goes through me. "He's a little bit good for me, but don't you dare tell him I said that. He already thinks he's God's gift to the universe."

I snap my mouth shut as he steps into the living room looking absolutely delectable. He's wearing his kutte, as always, his jacket beneath and a pair of thick gloves. He's got a beanie hat on his head, which he's in the process of tugging off as he takes in the room with a frown.

"Fuck me," he mutters. "Angel—"

"Do you want me to take it down?" I cut him off.

He meets my eyes and whatever he sees in my face has him shaking his head. "No. Fuck no. You like it, it stays."

He pulls me into his arms and presses a kiss to my forehead before taking my mouth.

"Okay, I'm going to head into Kingsley and do some Christmas shopping," Cami says. "Jamie said she'd meet me."

I love that she's making friends. It will make it easier for her to move up here, but I wish she'd pick better friends from the group. Jamie is a bad influence. Even so, I say, "Be careful and stay out of trouble."

"Always." She turns to Jem. "Be good to my girl."

"You know I will."

As soon as the front door shuts behind her, Jem turns back to me, his hand skimming over my hip. "I had no idea you liked Christmas so much, Pip."

"I don't."

"So, what's with all the decorations?"

"I have no idea. I just wanted to make it special, I guess. It's our first Christmas together."

He captures my mouth, his tongue licking inside mine. I open up, giving him access, nipping at his lip as he does. "It'll be special," he says between kisses, "because you're here and we're not sneaking around anymore."

"Hmm." He works down my neck and I pant as he hits a sensitive spot. "I must admit, I do miss our clandestine meetings. There was something very sexy about you dragging me into shadowy hideaways to fuck me."

His hand skims up my thigh and under my skirt to cup my pussy. I tense, gasping as he touches me, everything pulsing between my legs.

"If you want me to keep doing that, Pip, all you have to do is say."

He pushes my underwear aside and his fingers slide through my wetness before pushing inside me. I grip his shoulders as he tunnels into me, widening my stance to give him better access. It feels good, too good.

"Jem..."

"Shush, angel. Take what I'm giving you."

I do take it. I take it all. He pushes his fingers deeper inside me even as he nibbles along my neck, up to my ear, licking and kissing the shell, driving me crazy as he gets to the spot just behind it that sends me wild. I'm practically sagging onto him as he finger-fucks me into oblivion and when I come around his fingers, I yell garbled nonsense into his ear.

"Are you okay to do this?" he asks.

Am I still hurting is what he's really asking.

I am recovering, am still bruised, still aching, but he's barely touched me like this in a fortnight, and I'm hungry for him. I need him.

"If you stop now, I'm going to kill you."

Chuckling, he hooks his arms around me and lifts me carefully up his body. Then he carries me over to the dining table and lies me back on it. Baubles go flying, and I start to protest, but he silences me with a finger to my lips.

He pulls his jeans down. His boxer briefs disappear next and he's standing in front of me completely naked. I take a moment to appreciate his body. And it is a body worth appreciating. His ink is amazing and covers most of his torso, a good proportion of his arms and he has a little on his legs too. He's sexy as hell.

"What are you waiting for?" I demand.

"Well, angel, you're wearing far too many clothes. I'm feeling a little exposed here."

"Get over here and rectify it then."

He doesn't need telling twice. He does just that. My skirt is first to go, pulled down my legs and pooled in a heap on the floor. My top follows next. He pauses for a moment, taking stock of the bruises along my ribs.

"Piper..."

I grab his hand. "I'm okay," I tell him, and I mean it. I am.

"It takes weeks for cracked ribs to heal. Maybe we shouldn't do this."

I take his hand and place it on my aching breast. "Just go slow and don't do any gymnastics and we'll be fine."

He squeezes my tit. "You need to stop, you say, okay? I don't want to hurt you."

"Jem, I plan on just lying here and letting you do all the work. I don't plan on hurting at all."

He laughs. "You're a nut."

"I must be to love you."

"Angel, you're the one who turned our living room into the North Pole. That shit cuts both ways."

He runs the tip of his cock through my folds then enters me. I whimper, widening my thighs and gripping the edge of the dining table as he pushes deeper inside me. The burn of his intrusion settles into something else, something more pleasurable as my body takes him. Then he drags his cock back and pushes back into me. He makes love to me slow and steady, his eyes locked on mine as he does. His fingers work down my arms and find mine, tangling together as he brings our joined hands over my head.

"You're mine," he tells me as he circles his hips, driving his cock deeper inside me. "Say it."

"I'm yours," I agree.

He leans down and kisses me, and it's a kiss that says more than words can. It's a kiss that tells me what I am to him.

"Love you, angel."

"I love you, Jem."

The clubhouse is busy when we get there. I'm surprised, given it's only a couple of weeks until Christmas and I know everyone is busy getting ready for the holidays—well, the girls are anyway. I don't think the boys have even noticed.

Slade and Clara are sitting together by the bar, but they appear to be having an argument. Clara looks mighty annoyed, while Slade looks like he's about to throw a hissy fit. Eventually, he storms off. I wonder if one of us should go and say something to her, but she leaves herself.

I kiss Jem's cheek and head over to the girls. Jamie passes me a gin and tonic as soon as I sit. Liv, who is at least eight months pregnant now, shifts uncomfortably.

"This not drinking over Christmas malarkey is going to suck," she complains.

"Just have a wine. It won't kill you," Jamie says.

"No, but Dean might kill you for suggesting it," Beth tells her brightly.

Jamie puts her straw between her pink glossy lips and sucks back a huge amount of drink before saying, "Good point." Then right out of the blue she says, "So, you and Jem."

I nearly choke on the sip of gin I'm taking. "What about me and Jem?"

"You know if I'd known you were secretly screwing him, I would never have said all those things I said about him at Liv-Liv's baby shower, right?"

I stare at her. "Come again?"

Jamie leans across the table and stage-whispers. "You know, about how hot he is and how much I want to get in his trousers." Her eyes roll slightly. "Well, I mean, I might have said it. The man still is hot, even if he's hooking up with a sister, but there's a code. You don't cross it with a girl's guy, you know?"

I'm not sure I do know.

"I think," Sofia says, "what my esteemed friend is trying to say, and doing badly, is she wouldn't have been a slutty potty mouth about my brother if she'd known you were boning him at the time."

Jamie mulls this over then nods vehemently. "That

about sums it up." She grabs my hand. "I'm really sorry. I love Jem... like a brother. A really sexy, hot brother who I crush on frequently, but I would never break the sisterhood. Hoes before bros. Always."

I smile at her. "I have no idea what anything you just said means, but okay."

"Great." She beams then frowns. "I'm just checking Adam is still okay to drool over, right?" When no one says anything, she glances to the ceiling and mutters a, "Thank God," before adding, "I'm going to get another drink, and see if I can find Weed and a couple of the prospects. They're usually up for a game of strip poker and it's so easy to get Weed naked. He's really bad at poker, although he thinks he's not."

Cami's eyes light up. "That sounds intriguing."

I stare at my best friend like she's grown two heads.

"What? I've never seen a biker naked." She leans towards me and whispers, "You don't get to have all the bloody fun, P."

I watch them go off, shaking my head.

"So, how *are* things going with you and Jem?" Beth asks and I shift a little uncomfortably. Mainly because Sofia is sitting at the table. Thankfully, Mackenzie is at the bar with my brother and Paige, so I don't have to deal with both Harlow sisters giving me the third degree.

"It's going fine."

Beth arches a brow. "It's going fine?"

"Better than fine," I amend. "Things are wonderful."

Sofia snorts. "Jem's an overgrown child. You can say it."

"He's irritating beyond belief at times," I admit, my eyes gravitating across the room to where he's standing talking with Logan and Derek, the Club's president, "but that also makes him endearing."

"Annoying is the word you're looking for. But someone had to put up with his shit. Rather you than me."

My phone buzzes and I glance down at it, still shaking my head at Jem's sister's words. I know she loves him really —at least I hope she does.

As I swipe the screen, cold clenches around my heart. It's a message from my mother. Both her and Grant have tried to contact me a few times since Jem saved me. I'd like to say they were concerned about my safety, but I think they were mostly worried I might go to the media with my story.

When I open the message, I expect it to be the same sort of thing as before. It's not.

MUM: I'm outside the gates of the clubhouse... place. If you don't meet with me, I'm coming in.

What. The. Heck?

I stand abruptly and the girls have to steady the table as it wobbles with my movement.

"Piper? Is everything okay?" Beth demands.

"No. No, it's not."

She can't be here. Why would she come? I know she can't get inside. Logically, I know this. There's security, but my heart is pounding. Surprisingly, my first instinct isn't to fix this myself. In the past, it would have been. No, my first instinct is to find Jem.

I push around the table, mindful not to knock the table into Liv as I pass her, and I push through the crowd until I reach Jem who is laughing at something his brother is saying.

I grab his arm and his eyes come to me. The warmth fades as he catches my gaze and his smile dies.

"What's wrong?"

"My mother's here."

His whole face turns to granite. "Here, where?"

"At the gate. She messaged."

Jem scrubs a hand over his chin. "I'll handle it."

I grab his bicep before he can take off. "No, I don't want you to handle it." At his questioning look, I add, "I want you to come with me while I handle it, please."

He stares at me a beat and then nods, "Okay."

He hands his pint glass to Logan, who says, "Do you need me to come with?"

"I think we've got this."

Jem slips his hand into mine and we walk outside together. I feel a little anxious but with him at my side, I'm less scared.

"She says anything nasty, I'm just going to say, Pip, I might kill her with my bare hands."

"She's probably going to be very nasty," I warn him. "Just ignore her."

We head to the gate at the front of the clubhouse, passing the security booth. King pops his head out, confusion playing across his face, but Jem gives him a chin lift, which has him stepping back inside.

There's no sign of her at the gate and I glance at Jem, unsure. But after a second I hear the sound of a car door further up the road and see her and Grant coming towards us. Jem growls low in his throat, and I place a hand on his chest.

"Try to stay calm, honey."

"I'm not sure I can promise that, Pip. Your stepfather's a piece of shit."

This we both agree on, but I still say, "He's nothing to me anymore, Jem."

We watch as they approach, wary, and I think Grant's grateful for the gate between us.

"You're fucking brave coming here, Hollander," Jem growls.

"I didn't think you'd bring your watchdog out with you," Grant says to me, but I feel a hint of satisfaction at how nervous he looks.

"He's not my watchdog. He's my boyfriend."

Mum looks disgusted. "You're sleeping with them now. Dear God, is this how low you've stooped?"

"Well, I thought since we've tried kidnapping and nearly being killed, I'd have a go walking on the wild side a little more thoroughly." Grant blanches and Mum flinches. I hit a nerve. "What do you want?"

"You need to come home," Mum says. "It's insanity hanging around here with these bunch of hooligans."

"This bunch of hooligans," Jem snaps, "didn't get your daughter abducted and beaten. That was your husband. You both need to go. It didn't end so well for the last person who upset my woman."

"If it gets out that you're hooking up with criminals—" Grant starts.

"I'd be more concerned about what it'll do to your reputation if it gets out that you're dealing with gangsters," I fire back at him. "How about you and Mum worry about your own lives and leave me to mine. I don't want anything to do with either of you. We're done."

Mum gasps, her hand covering her mouth. "You can't mean that."

How is she this deluded?

"I nearly died, Mum. Cami too. They kept me locked in a room for three days. I had to piss in front of them. They beat me and threatened to rape me if I didn't do what they wanted. All because Grant wanted power or whatever the fuck it was. So, yes, mother. I'm done with both of you. You can both get fucked. I never want to see either of you again."

I turn and walk away from the gate.

"Toodles," I hear Jem say before he follows after me. Toodles? Jesus, Jem.

His arm wraps around my shoulder and he kisses my head. "You're amazing."

"I feel terrible."

"You shouldn't."

As we approach the main doors, Josh is standing in the doorway, Paige at his side. His eyes move from where we left my parents to me. He gestures for me to come to him. I do and he wraps me in his arms, pulling me against his chest.

"Love you, Pipe," he mutters against my hair.

My chest aches at his words. "Love you too, Josh."

"You make sure those fuckers stay gone," he says over my head.

"Yeah, I will," Jem replies. "Hollander covets his position in government. A few well-placed threats to expose him and his dealings with crooks will be enough to keep him and mumzilla away, I think."

Josh lets me go and says, "Come on, Pipe, your family's waiting for you inside."

Family. Who would have thought all those months ago that these people would become my family? But this is what they are. These are the people who took care of me when I needed it the most, the people who love me as I am, without question or judgment. My parents only want me for what they can use me for. I thought my brother's lifestyle was the criminal one, but Grant's is just as crooked—if not worse because he pretends it's not. I'm not naïve. I know Jem's life is dangerous and I know my life will never be normal with him, but to be with him, I'll make sacrifices. He's worth it.

"Okay, we'll be in in a second."

He takes Paige's hand and they head inside. Jem gives me a questioning look. "You don't want to go inside?"

"I do, but I seem to recall you promising more sneaking around."

He grins and grabs my hand. Then he tugs me down the side of the clubhouse to a secluded spot. Within a matter of seconds, he has my skirt up around my hips and his cock in me.

And I couldn't be happier.

Did you love reading about the Lost Saxons Motorcycle Club? The story continues in book six with Weed and Chloe in Flawed Rider...

To find out more about The Lost Saxons series and to subscribe to my newsletter, visit my website
www.jessicaamesauthor.com

ALSO BY JESSICA AMES

LOST SAXONS

Snared Rider

Safe Rider

Secret Rider

Claimed Rider (A Lost Saxons Short Story)

Renewed Rider

Forbidden Rider

STANDALONES

Match Me Perfect

ABOUT THE AUTHOR

Jessica Ames lives in a small market town in the Midlands, England. She lives with her dog and when she's not writing, she's playing with crochet hooks.

For more updates join her readers group on Facebook:
www.facebook.com/groups/JessicaAmesClubhouse

Subscribe to her newsletter:
www.jessicaamesauthor.com

- facebook.com/JessicaAmesAuthor
- twitter.com/JessicaAmesAuth
- instagram.com/jessicaamesauthor
- goodreads.com/JessicaAmesAuthor
- bookbub.com/profile/jessica-ames